Our Lady of the Overlook

R.L. Carpentier

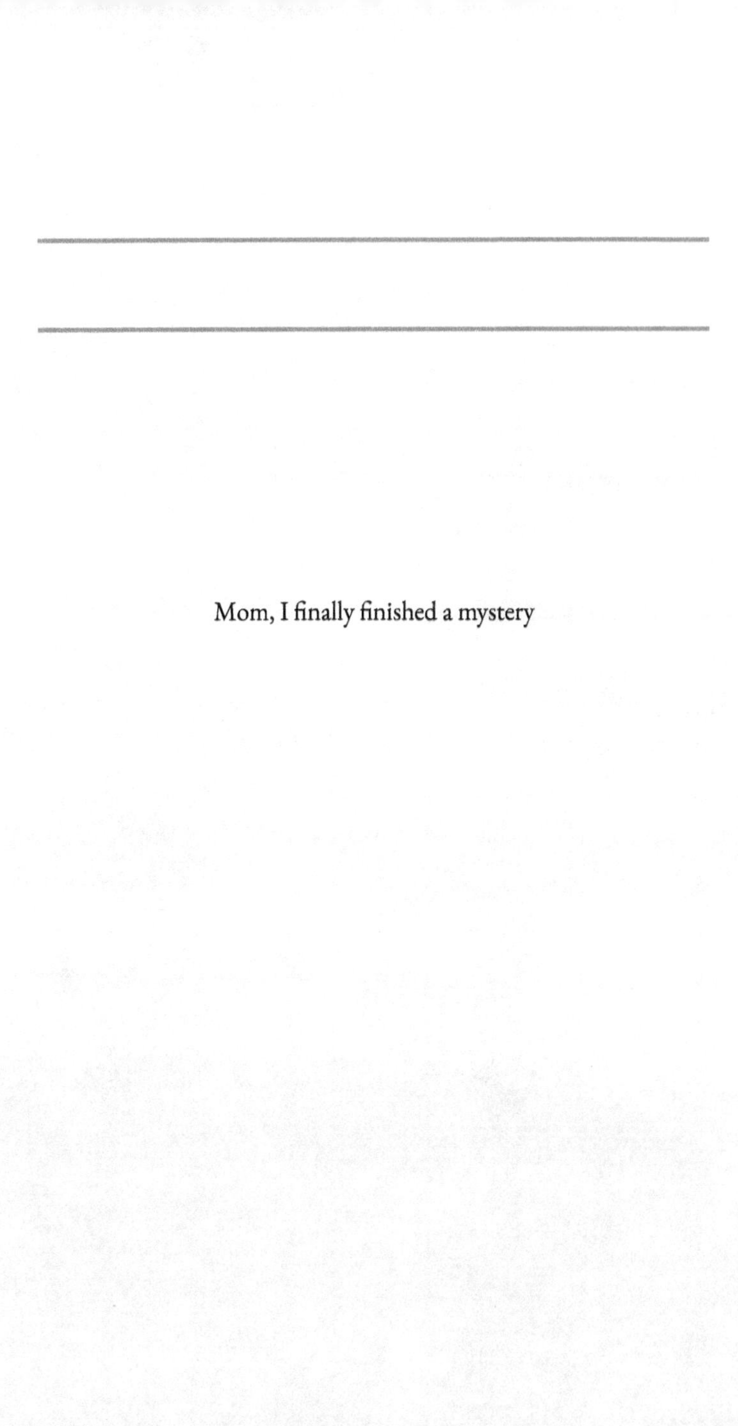

Mom, I finally finished a mystery

A NOTE FROM THE AUTHOR

From where I sit right now, most would consider me a villain in this story I'm about to tell. I cannot blame the public for feeling the way that they do, but here you are my dear reader, drawn into what I have to say. In the beginning, I sought only to shine a light and bring forward an injustice. I wanted peace for Jane Doe. I wanted to share her story. Little did I know the long path I would end up on.

I will not delve into specifics here and now, for why would you continue if I laid it all out? But like the map posted at the trailhead, I will at least set some expectations of the twists and turns, the ascents and descents that await you. The hope is that you will finish this journey satisfied and proud of the accomplishment.

Therefore, everything that follows in this story is true. The major points all happened, and they happened to the people that are portrayed. But most did not happen to me. I heard of them second and sometimes, third hand, I confess. For story synchronicity purposes, however, I present them as if the reader was there first hand. I characterize each person as I see them, but sometimes put myself in the avatar of another real person who was present. All of this is done to put some cohesion to the narrative and just make it a good story to read.

So, you think to yourself, this man is controlling the narrative. He has an agenda. Of course, I have an agenda and don't forget it. The purpose of this book is to, as I said, provide justice for Jane Doe. But so many others have been affected in the process, not the least of which is me. I began writing this in the law library, in my orange jumpsuit, not knowing where the next hours or days would take me. But also, for my good friend Mike Ellis, who journeyed an immense distance within himself, sacrificing so much for me. Let me not forget Maggie Farley, who lost so much but gained the world in the end, showing bravery throughout.

I don't know how many parts this will turn out to be, but trilogies were the staple of my growing up, so let's maybe start there. I don't think that I have enough for an entire universe, but I won't sell myself short. Dear reader, thank you for choosing this book, thank you for believing in me. Now, let's get on with our story:

Allow me to begin with Bradley Salazar. He was driving his turquoise blue Ford 350 dual-wheeled pickup truck well above the posted speed limit, winding through the curved mountain roads with precision, deftly managing the downward, plunging contours of roadway and growling the truck up the sudden inclines so common in the Catskills. Inside the cab, Bradley maintained rhythm on the steering wheel with the aggressive hard rock blaring from the speakers. He did not sing along but grooved his dark head and thick neck with the relentless bass, his eyes squinting behind a pair of Oakley sunglasses. The evening summer sun hung precariously behind him in deep reds, dousing the whole world in a cruel glow.

Bradley's truck came off an incline and leveled out with the road as he passed the first of two speed limit signs indicating that he had entered the town and village of Hunter. Bradley took no notice, and the vehicle maintained its speed. It took nearly a mile for him to notice the emergency lights in his rear-view mirror, and almost another half mile for him to slow down and stop as the police car behind him began spitting its siren noises and goose honks. He took one furtive glance toward the back of the cab, swallowed hard, and turned his head forward. He slid the Oakleys from his eyes, laying them across the dashboard. Then, cutting the radio off mid-song, he rolled down both windows and placed his hands on the steering wheel. He waited, staring straight ahead.

Moving just his eyes, Bradley picked up the cop in the rear-view mirror exiting a Dodge Durango. The cop placed a Stetson on his head, taking a moment to straighten it. Bradley watched as the officer then considered his approach before he retreated behind the Durango, coming up the passenger side. Bradley's eyes shifted to catch the image of the officer in the passenger side mirror. The cop moved ungainly with big steps in baggy pants and the outer carrier Kevlar vest was like a hula-hoop around his chest. As the cop came closer, Bradley could even see that the Stetson sat on his head like a bucket. Finally, the officer arrived at the door of the truck.

"Good afternoon, Officer Ellis, town police," the cop's voice said from the passenger window.

Bradley could see in his periphery that the cop was tactically positioned behind the B-pillar. A sharp grin cut through Bradley's lips, his eyes dancing in their sockets. Maintaining his body position, Bradley swiveled his head toward the window. The smile melted from his face as his eyes connected with the cop. Officer Ellis had pudgy, youthful cheeks and wide, staring eyes. He stood straight at attention and Bradley thought he might have been holding his breath.

"I observed your vehicle going over the posted speed limit," Officer Ellis said. "May I see your license and registration, please?" The words were deliberate and rhythmic; well-rehearsed.

Bradley smiled innocently. "My wallet is in my right rear pocket; can I reach for it?"

"Yes, you can." Officer Ellis drew himself closer, his head peeking inside the cab as much as it was able.

Bradley's eyes grew larger as he studied the young cop. He was trying to decide whether Officer Ellis suspected anything. The guilty part of Bradley's conscience, however slight, fought to remain locked on the cop and not on the backseat. After a moment, Bradley leaned to the left and slowly moved his right hand so that he could dig his wallet from his rear pocket. He opened it and retrieved his license and a second plastic card. Holding the second card between his fingers, he noticed the fading image, especially around the edges. He flipped it over and noticed the ink signature on the back was smudged, but legible. His smile dissolved as he passed both to the cop. Officer Ellis accepted the documents and considered them.

"And your registration card?" he asked, looking back up.

"That's in the center here," Bradley said and pointed at the console next to him. "Can I open it?"

This time the cop nodded, his eyes growing even wider, his focus training on Bradley's hand as it hovered above the latch. Bradley grinned as he opened the lid and dug through the space. After a moment, he produced the orange-colored slip of paper. He handed that over, too. Officer Ellis looked at the registration along with the license and the other plastic card. He took hold of the microphone positioned in the center of his chest.

"Greene 911, Hunter seven-zero." He waited for a response. "Separate CID." He read the numbers from Bradley Salazar's license. "Check for validity."

Bradley relaxed in his seat and looked the cop over some more. His face was soft, and razor burnt with bulbous eyes and dry, chapped lips. As he waited for the response to his inquiry, the cop kept his eyes on Bradley and Bradley heard the cop's deep, rushed breaths. Bradley turned himself all the way around in his seat, looking out the back window of the truck, looking for another officer, but he did not see anyone. He stole a telling glance toward the back seat—to the mound of plastic under the bench. Bradley returned to his original position and noticed the cop looking down again at the three items in his hand.

"Hunter seven-zero, that CID returns to a Bradley Salazar subject, date of birth June 6, 1996. Both he and the vehicle are valid, negative wants," a disembodied voice said through the microphone. Officer Ellis acknowledged the transmission.

The cop looked up. "Who's Veronica to you?" he asked.

"My mother," Bradley said.

"How long has she been a trooper?"

"She did like thirty-something years. She's retired."

Officer Ellis shuffled the cards in his hands for a moment and said, "My dad was a cop, too. But he never gave me a courtesy card."

"Sounds like a mean son of a bitch," Bradley said.

"I don't know," the cop said. His face dropped into a frown.

"Where'd he work?"

"For the town. He was the Police Chief."

"Then I guess you wouldn't really need a card around here then."

"Wasn't around here. But I couldn't get into much trouble where I was."

"Convent?" Bradley asked. He chuckled with some good nature.

The cop did a double take. He was examining the contents of his hand, weighing some choice in his mind. Bradley saw the indecision gathering behind Officer Ellis' whittled brow. Bradley's expression became grim and expectant.

"I'm sure any cop would done him a favor if you needed it," Bradley said.

Officer Ellis did not respond immediately. After a pregnant pause, he said, "He wasn't big on giving favors. He wouldn't have wanted one on my behalf."

Bradley cracked a half smile. "Would he have wanted one for me?"

Officer Ellis responded quickly, "Probably not."

Bradley pouted briefly before a smile again crawled up his face. "Listen, Officer Ellis, I haven't ever been a cop. But I grew up with one in my house. You look new, right? You want to fit in with your buddies, eh? Well, I've been stopped here many times and never got a ticket. My mom used to work up here, and they all know her. You don't want to be the guy who opens a can of worms. Over me? I don't think so. There are plenty of other people to stop and give tickets to. Some of them might even have some bad shit in the car. I can tell you; this isn't the one you want. So maybe don't think of it as you are doing me a favor, think of it as me doing you a favor. I can make this decision very easy for you."

Officer Ellis regarded the words for a long time with his eyes fixed on Bradley. He glanced down at the license, the registration, and the courtesy card in his hand. Finally, he presented Bradley with his paperwork. Bradley reached across the cab and took all three documents back. His smile faded as the cop began to back away from the truck, moving toward the Durango. Bradley shook his head and made a derisive snort. He looked at his backseat again, the plastic stuffed beneath the bench. Bradley exhaled a long breath.

"Fucking new jacks," he said. He turned the music back on and rolled the windows up. Collecting his sunglasses, he settled them back over his eyes. Bradley made another sly glance backward. He laughed out loud as he pulled away, his tires squealing defiantly as he stared at the cop in his rearview.

###

All right, on second thought, perhaps I should begin with Carolina Velez. She moved around the diner with grace, her comfortable white sneakers gliding on the faded tile flooring, a trim body maneuvering between tables with ease. Carolina disappeared into the kitchen just as the door opened and the bell affixed to the frame announced the entrance of a customer. She dropped the ticket and turned like a ballerina to exit the kitchen.

Coming through the doorway, Carolina greeted a face she'd never seen before. She was accustomed to strange faces, as many people came through from their mountain adventures, but the face she met sat upon a body encompassed in a blue uniform and bulky police equipment. Both the uniform and the equipment looked impeccably new. A metal badge was pinned over the left breast of the turtle shell-like vest and a name tag beneath the badge read: *ELLIS*. Carolina looked at the cop's face, which was pleasant, dull, and fleshy. After giving him a thorough once over, she glanced toward the rear of the diner where she had seated the other cop.

"Are you with him?" she asked.

Officer Ellis turned his head at the same time and they both saw the other man in uniform looking back at them. They looked back at one another and their eyes met. He smiled bleakly at her and nodded.

"Go on back, then. I'll bring you a menu."

She watched Officer Ellis walk away, ambling with all the equipment affixed to his belt. His gait was awkward as he moved past some of the tables, trying to avoid knocking into them. Carolina allowed him to arrive at the faraway table before she scooped up a menu and followed him. She overheard the conversation as she approached.

"So, I wrote a couple of movers earlier. Do you want to set up and take some speeders after dinner? Maybe we can get a DWI," Officer Ellis said.

The other cop, one that Carolina was familiar with, lounged in the booth and stared ahead. He was much older with worn creases on his face and a spark of silver beneath his dark hair. The grays were also slowly invading his thin, manicured mustache. He looked up and met Carolina's gaze. "Oh hey, Carol."

"Good evening, Officer Bell." And then, handing the menu to the younger cop, she added. "Here you go."

"How many times do I have to tell you?" the older officer said.

Carolina sighed and gave him a warm smile. "Yes, I'm sorry. How are you, Hugh?"

"Thank you, my dad was Officer Bell. This, my dear, is Mike Ellis."

Mike looked up at Carolina, and their eyes met for the second time. He looked at her differently than he had a few moments earlier. His eyes wandered from her face to her neck, then back up.

"I'm Carolina," she said. "What can I get you to drink?"

"I'll have coffee," Hugh said.

Mike looked back to the menu. Carolina saw his eyes frantically pour over the page. He mumbled to himself and looked back at her. "A Coke?"

She nodded and turned precisely on her heel. As she moved away, she heard Hugh say, "She's a nice girl." The words made her smile. She collected the beverages and returned directly.

"If you don't, I'll ask her out myself," she heard Hugh say. He looked up and saw Carolina approaching. "You are too quick!"

Carolina's whole face reddened. Hugh's mustache curled up with his smile. The whole of his big, round face beamed. Moving closer to him as she placed the coffee on the table, he was as tall as she was standing. Hugh scooped the coffee closer with his large hand and then reached for the big canister of sugar lined up with the Heinz bottle and the salt and pepper shakers.

Carolina put the plastic cup filled with ice and Coke in front of Mike. She slid a straw from her apron and set it next to the cup. Mike reached for it as she let go, their hands brushed ever so close together. He pulled his hand back as if he had touched a hot stove, leaving the straw where it was. Carolina's hand hovered in place for a second, her mind dissecting the reaction.

"So, what's for dinner?" she asked.

Mike dove his face back into the menu. Hugh stared at him with exaggerated contempt.

"It's a diner menu. They have whatever you want," Hugh said. He looked up at Carolina and smiled.

She made her eyes wide and rolled them away, a toothy grin sliding across her mouth. Mike remained invested in the menu, so Carolina focused on Hugh.

"And what are you going to have?"

"Well," Hugh said. "It's Thursday so I'll have…"

"The meatloaf?" she said with a laugh.

"How did you know?" Hugh mimed shock.

"You always get the meatloaf." Carolina made a show of writing the order on her notepad.

Mike looked up at Hugh, and then at Carolina. She now looked over at Mike and rolled her eyes.

"He gets the meatloaf every time," she said.

"It's not every time; just on Thursdays. Sometimes Tuesdays, too. It's a pretty okay meatloaf."

Mike's face scrunched into puzzled bemusement, and then he went back to the menu.

"I think I'll have…" he said. "I think I'll have a happy waitress."

"Wouldn't we all," Hugh said. "I'd like two." He laughed heartily.

Carolina smiled broadly. She brought her notepad up and scribbled Mike's selection. She looked at Hugh. He winked at her and smiled. She collected both menus and glanced at Mike, who was blankly gazing at her. He seemed to be staring at her chest. Carolina's smile faded into a placid, stone contentment as she pivoted and marched off to the kitchen.

"Well done, my boy," Hugh said. She could hear him although he was whispering. "If you were any tighter, you might have ripped in half."

She did not hear Mike's response. She passed into the kitchen and dropped the ticket for the cook before returning to the counter. From this distance, she could not hear the two cops chattering away, but as she looked on, Carolina could see the animation in Hugh's gestures and the low cock of Mike's head. She frowned toward them, her thoughts turning to anger at the odd younger cop. The obvious way he had been staring at her breasts and how awkward he had been with her in general. She decided she did not like him. The older cop, Hugh, flirted in an overt, comical way. He was a character, she decided. Mike, the younger cop, was a creep.

The bell rang inside the kitchen, and she slid in the door and slipped out quickly carrying two plates. As she moved closer, she was able to pick up the exchange between the two men.

"I'm not really concerned about getting together with a girl right now," Mike said. "I need to be good at this job."

"Quite the opposite," Hugh said. "If you go after a girl, you won't take this job so seriously. Take things as they come. Life will throw so much at you, but you have to choose what to go after. If you don't, they just pass you by. Then you just look back on the things that were. Your old man grabbed onto everything he could. He had a great life and a great career."

Hugh saw Carolina approach, and as his eyes migrated up, a smile popped onto his face. Mike turned around suddenly and looked at her face as she dispersed the meals.

"Do you have a moment to sit?" Hugh asked her.

Carolina shifted her weight, looked at Mike, and then at the entrance to the diner. Uncomfortably, she turned back. "I have some side work to do."

Hugh grabbed an unoccupied chair from a nearby table, his long arms reaching with little effort, and pulled it up.

"Come on, you probably haven't had a break in hours. I'll watch the door for you. If someone comes in, I'll tell them to go away."

Carolina shook her head but found herself lowering into the chair. She sat, her posture ramrod straight. She whispered out loud to herself, "Sure."

"So, I've been coming to this diner for more than twenty years. You've only been here for the last month or so. Tell me about yourself."

Carolina looked at Hugh genially. "My parents moved up here a couple years ago. They always had a wild dream to run a farm."

"Which farm?" Mike asked.

She glanced at him. "Never really came together for them. At least not the way they thought it would. Who can ever explain the dreams people have?"

"And you?" Hugh asked.

"I was in school when they made this decision. I spent a little time at college but followed them up here a couple months ago. I put school behind me for a while."

"What did you study?" Mike said.

"Hospitality mostly."

"So, this is your graduate seminar?" Hugh asked. He opened his big arms toward the whole diner.

Carolina laughed with some unease. "You could say that. I like it up here in the Catskills. It's slow. Peaceful."

"Not like the Big City?" Hugh said. He mimed air quotes for her.

"A lot different. I feel safe here."

"Well, you have us around," Hugh said. "I've been on these mean streets for eighteen years, and my old man was a cop before that."

Carolina warmed her smile. "You're sort of a legacy."

"Well, my partner here, his daddy, was the chief. He's the real legacy. My pops worked with his pops."

Carolina turned her attention to Mike, fighting the apprehension in her mind. "Did you want to be a cop because of your father?"

Mike shifted in his seat, and his eyes avoided her, looking up past her. Then he looked down at the table. "I guess you could say it was something I fell back into."

Carolina twisted her nose and squinted her eyes in reaction to Mike's body language and his words. She began to shake her right leg, then fidgeted around in her chair as she looked at her watch.

"I'm sorry. I've got to go," she said. Standing up, she smoothed her khaki pants. She retrieved her notepad from her apron and tore the check out, setting it on the table. She walked away, deciding not to hear what was said after she left.

Carolina busied herself with monotonous side work. She never saw the younger cop, Mike leave the diner. Hugh approached with the check in his hand.

"I'm sorry about that," he said.

"About what?" Carolina said. She thought she sounded innocent.

"I'm trying to open the kid up. Thought it'd be nice for him to have some human contact. The truth is, I don't know a lot about him. He just showed up about nine months ago, and the department hired him."

"I thought his father was the chief?"

"Chief Charlie died more than seven years ago. Mike was away at some private school or something. The last time I saw him was at the funeral."

"Oh, that's terrible."

"It was sudden, and I think it really affected Mike that he wasn't here. Chief Charlie was a good man. I think Mike just wants to prove himself as a police officer. It's the only thing in his mind."

"Was his father very demanding?"

"Chief Charlie was all business, a cop's cop. I don't know if Mike ever saw that."

"So, what does he have to prove? That he's worthy?"

"For some reason, I think he wants to show that he's not the same. But the truth is, he's so much like his father. He just doesn't want to admit it."

2

The crash of the sixteen-pound ball smacking grouped pins echoed through the large converted warehouse. It was Friday night, and two-thirds of the lanes were occupied by organized league bowling league in the midst of a summer season. The last three or four lanes had a smattering of men that I deduced to be cops and firemen. On one lane were five men all dressed similarly in jeans and black T-shirts. One shirt read in checklist format: *Grumpy, Old, Cop.* Another shirt declared: *Not A Cop, Ask My Sergeant.* A third had the image of a thin blue line flag and the statement: *Sometimes it's Justice, Sometimes it's Just Us.* One of the men wore a shirt that was blank on the front but had the same thin blue line flag stretched across the back. The last one spelled out the words *Stupid Rooky* in a cute kindergartner script.

I would learn their identities later and in order. The first man was Hugh Bell, lining himself up on the approach, eyeing a lone ten-pin. The second and third were Dennis Jones and Kevin Haverthy, standing together at the ball return, glancing over their shoulders occasionally and chuckling. The fourth man was Paul Hunter, coming from the bar with a fresh pitcher of beer. The final man was Mike Ellis; the person I was there to see. He sat back in a molded plastic seat with a plastic cup full of beer. I had been lying in wait and observing him all night.

Hugh made his spare and joined Mike. "See, that's how you do that." His voice was happy and sloshy.

Mike smiled, looking uncomfortable. He shifted in the chair and drew his arms tight to his sides. Paul tapped his shoulder and offered to top off his beer. Mike frowned and shook his head. It was pointless as the beverage was down only a quarter inch from the top. Paul shrugged and looked up at the lane's display screen. He set the pitcher on the table behind Mike and hurried to the ball return to collect his ball.

"You've only had one sip," Hugh said. "I've really gotta teach you how to drink." The big man stood up and helped himself to a refill from the pitcher.

"Sorry, I'm not a big drinker," Mike said. He tasted the beer and gave a halfhearted smile. It was the first time I heard Mike speak. His voice was mature, tenor-tinged, and direct.

Paul threw a strike, returning quickly, and it was now Mike's turn. He got up slowly, accepted a high five from Paul, and took small steps toward the ball return. Kevin and Dennis were still posted there, and I could see their eyes scan him up and down. Hugh shouted some encouragement in a backhanded way as Mike picked up his ball. It looked like an alley ball, scuffed and generic. Mike held it in his right arm, close to his body. He made his way to the dots on the approach and stood in the center. He took a deep breath and began what I deemed to be an interpretation of a bowling motion. The flutter of his arm retreating behind his back and coming out in an underhand maneuver as the three fingers on his right hand let the ball fly. However, Mike hit his leg as he brought the ball forward, and the ball did not so much as fly out but deflected onto the lane. Both he and the ball limped away in opposite directions. Three pins were struck and knocked down.

Retreating to the ball return, he looked sheepishly at Kevin and Dennis, who were both laughing, poorly pretending to hide their amusement.

"Should give you an extra pin," Dennis said.

"Yeah, for hitting your leg," Kevin added.

Mike did not respond. He retrieved his ball as it rolled onto the return. He mounted the approach and lined himself again. He repeated his tried-and-true method, somehow missed his leg the second time, and hit five pins with the shot. As he came back off the approach, he looked at Kevin and Dennis. They turned away, toward where I was sitting, hiding smiles in their hands. Paul held his fist out, which Mike obliged with a weak tap. He sat again next to Hugh.

"See what you did was, well, you sucked," Hugh said.

"Thanks for the expert dissection. You know I didn't want to come." Mike sounded sincere. He lifted his plastic cup and took a long swallow.

"That's the spirit," Hugh said. "Listen, the drunker you are, the more bowling doesn't suck. You will still suck, but bowling won't. Same story with golf. I'll show you sometime."

"You should write a book, Hugh," Paul said. "A book of Hugh-isms."

Hugh did not react and kept his attention on Mike. "What I'm saying, little brother, is that you have to lighten up. Forget about those assholes, drink some beer, and stop sucking."

Mike nursed another sip of his beer as the line of their lane went around. He threw some more lame and then less lame shots. Hugh continued to grow more drunk as he continued to coach Mike, his advice becoming less practical and philosophical, and more pointed and pungent. Later, in the late part of the third game, Mike finished his second cup of beer and started toward the approach. He walked differently now, with more swagger, maybe alcohol-induced confidence. He passed Paul coming off the approach. Paul had just thrown a strike, and Mike held up his hand for a high five as he came up to the ball return. Kevin leaned across as Mike retrieved his adopted ball.

"Listen, Ellis," Kevin said. "It's one of the golden laws of bowling that if you don't follow a line of strikes, you have to buy a round."

Dennis motioned toward the LED screen above the ball return. Mike looked up and verified that, indeed, each of his compatriots had just thrown a strike.

"I'm thinking of something top shelf," Dennis said.

"Yeah, Denny, I think I'll get some shots of Crown."

Mike looked helplessly back at Hugh and Paul.

"It's actually like Supreme Court starey decisions," Hugh said. The words slurred.

"It's how I've always lived," Paul said. His voice stilted a bit.

Mike groaned and heaved the ball into the crook of his arm. He lined up again in the center of the dots, and his concentration appeared to be more focused. I will say that I was rooting for the guy. Mike began his motion, and it looked from my perspective to be loose, nearly smooth. His arm retreated like a pendulum and as it came forward, he missed his leg, setting the ball in motion down the center of the lane. I watched with bated anticipation as Mike's shot rolled with speed toward the headpin. The ball struck dead center, and the sharp crack as it met each pin became a cacophony as one by one, they fell.

The catcalls, laughs, and groans of the four men watching Mike rose like a thunderstorm. I am sure I made some desperate shriek of horror, as the entire building turned their attention toward us. Mike stood aghast as the seven-ten split grinned back at him like a toothless smile. He hung his head and retreated to the ball return to set up for the next shot. Kevin and Dennis cackled hard and pointed at him. Hugh laughed incredulously and shook his head. Paul had a toothy smile spread on his face, but he applauded sincerely.

"It was the best ball you've thrown all night," he said.

"He needs more damned beer," Hugh enjoined.

Mike collected his ball as it rolled up into the return, went up onto the approach, and took his shot. The ball ambled down the lane and wound up going right through the middle of the sentinel bowling pins. When he turned around, Paul and Hugh each had their arms raised to signal a field goal. Kevin and Dennis continued their enjoyment at Mike's expense, bent over and snickering. Mike took a deep breath and came back toward the ball return. He reached into his back pocket and took out his wallet.

"So, what's everyone drinking?" he asked.

The men cheered, and even Kevin and Dennis joined in, slapping the kid on his back.

I followed Mike over to the bar, casually, and with some distance. He stood near the center of the bar with his wallet in his hand. It was crowded, and I had to force my way to get near him. Mike looked down the far end of the bar at a male bartender who was taking an order when someone touched his shoulder.

"What can I get you?" It was a low and sweet female voice.

Mike turned his head before his whole body pivoted to meet the soft brown face of the female bartender. I caught her face at about the same time as Mike. This was the first time that I laid my eyes on Carolina Velez. Of course, she and Mike should have recognized one another at this point. As I gazed upon her, though, my breath was taken away. Her skin was a smooth caramel accented by the dark midnight of her hair and eyebrows. She had vibrant, dancing golden eyes that sent a pulse of electricity when she looked at you.

"Oh, it's you," Carolina said. She downcast her eyes for a moment, then brought them back to meet Mike's gaze. "You probably don't recognize me 'cause I'm not in uniform."

Mike stared at her dumbfounded, taking a moment to look her over also. Her hair was done up, and she wore a lot of make-up. Not to mention the halter top and hip-hugging jeans accenting her feminine qualities. I thought for a moment he was going to say he didn't know her.

"Of course, I, uh, recognize you..." he said. "I wasn't expecting you to be here."

"Yeah, I just started doing this to supplement the big bucks I get at the diner. Tips are better here. So, what can I get for you?" She smiled, and her top lip parted slightly so she could show off her teeth.

Mike recited the order, trying to remember all the obscure names of top-shelf liquors he had been assigned.

"Missed a strike, eh?" Carolina said. "You'd be surprised how often this rule gets invoked." She set to work mixing and manufacturing his drink order.

"Yeah, I thought the guys were messing with me," Mike said. "This isn't really my game." He laughed uneasily.

"What is your game?" Carolina asked. She said it with a challenge in her voice. She returned to the bar with two liquor bottles.

Mike's answer was automatic. "I don't really like games."

"Not even tag? Or hide and seek?" She turned away, returning the bottles and retrieving another. "How about red rover?"

I watched her intently. She was graceful and comfortable in her body. After the initial disdain she had shown toward Mike, she allowed that to melt away, and she adopted a familiar tone with him. She built an instant connection that was genuine. Mike kept his eye on her too, and I could only imagine the thoughts in his head. He was awkward, but certainly not blind or stupid. The confidence of her movement drew him in. He leaned across the bar, his shoulders square and his hands apart and open toward her.

"I've never been one to chase after anything."

Carolina came back, and it seemed as if she hadn't heard him. "How about getting chased?"

"No one's ever pursued me," he said.

"That means you haven't found the right one then."

Mike thought for a moment. "Maybe I'm just elusive."

"What are you good at then?" Carolina asked. Her interest seemed to wane.

Mike was not so automatic with his response. He took a breath and let his thoughts collect. "I guess I'm pretty good at puzzles. You know, like word problems or riddles."

"So, you like games, just games you do by yourself. No chance to lose." She turned to put the liquor bottle away, and when she returned, she said, "I think maybe some healthy competition is what you need."

Carolina's coyness laid out like a red carpet. Her subtle jabs were sincere, and maybe there was something that she liked about Mike. I watched Mike as he considered his next move, the next statement.

"Do you like puzzles?" he asked, the words stuttering out.

He had waited too long, and she never heard him, as Carolina was reaching for another bottle. The words went out into the noise of the bar and became mist. The last concoction was made, and she arranged the drinks on the bar. She was going to get away, and I looked on to see if Mike would chase.

"Here you go, Mike," she said. "That'll be ridiculously expensive." Her laugh was easy and melodic. She went over the price list taped next to the cooler and tapped the order into a tablet on the bar. She announced her calculation, and Mike handed over cash. "Well, better luck on the next one."

Two of her fingers grazed the palm of his hand as she set a few coins in it followed by a stack of bills. He seemed to have taken a shock, and he looked up into her eyes. His face was dumbstruck as she smiled and walked away to another customer. Mike looked as though he wanted to reach out to keep her there. But the moment was gone.

He and I were both startled when another tap came to his shoulder, this one violent, like bear mauling. I felt myself ripped from the unfolding human drama. Mike appeared to rebound back into his thoughts immediately.

"Oh boy, oh boy," Hugh said. A gleeful lilt in his deep voice. He grabbed two of the glasses and retreated toward their lane.

Mike set the stack of bills back on the bar without counting and put an empty glass on top of them. He grabbed the remaining glasses and followed Hugh. I turned to watch them cutting through the crowd. I was startled a bit when someone tapped my shoulder, and when I shot around quickly, I found myself eye-to-eye with Carolina.

"Can I get you something?" she asked.

I hesitated, but I played it off coolly. I smiled a wolfish smile, knowing my proclivity for words. She looked back unimpressed and more impatient. I decided that I'd be manageable in my drink order.

"Well, dear, can I have a dry Martini? With gin, of course."

She nodded and turned to pull the liquor bottles from the shelf behind her. I stared at her body, and when she faced me again, I averted my gaze as quickly as I could. When my sightline wandered back toward her, she wore a scowl. She mixed the Martini, shook it, and poured.

Accepting the triangle stemmed glass from her, I thought to ask, "You live around here?"

Carolina, taken aback by the cliché, batted her eyes at me and frowned. She looked me over, obviously not impressed, and countered with "That's twelve."

I looked at the beverage, considering in my head its intrinsic value. I set the Martini glass down, so I could retrieve my wallet. I pulled a twenty dollar bill out, then extended it toward Carolina.

"I ask because I want to know about the young man that was just up here. You know, 'Stupid Rookie'"

"What do you want to know?" she asked. She reached for the bill. I pulled it back with a swift bend of my wrist. Her frown grew deeper.

"How well do you know him?"

"Seen him around. Don't know him at all."

"I'm a reporter here to do a story about him. Sure would appreciate anything you had."

I flicked my wrist and sent the twenty back into the void between us. Carolina looked at the bill but did not move a muscle. Her eyes set deep into mine, weary and cold. But still beautiful and encompassing.

As we stood locked in our stalemate, someone bumped into me from behind causing me to break eye contact and to rock some of the precious alcohol from my glass. I glanced over my shoulder and met the face of Mike Ellis. He made a sheepish, apologetic grin at me before he lifted his eyes to catch Carolina's gaze.

"I need a whole round of the same stuff," he said.

I sighed, barely audible in the din of the bar. I brought my attention back to Carolina, who waited with one hand on her hip, the other resting palm up on the bar. I nodded and placed the twenty in her hand.

"Keep the change," I said.

###

My next tactic was to ingratiate myself with Mike's more social allies, as he was currently retrieving a round of reinforcements. I began with Paul Hunter, discussing my limited military career and building a connection to his four years of service. Leaning on our difference in age, I compared my youthful days in the early 1990s to his late 2000s. Hugh Bell heard our laughter and decided that he wanted to join in the fun. I poked and prodded quickly to discover his sports proclivity. I guessed correctly and chose the right New York baseball team, analyzing the Yankees' teams of the late '90s. With sobriety as my superpower, I infiltrated the inner circle and wound up slapping backs with Kevin Haverthy and Dennis Jones. Then, I laid my cards down.

"Actually, fellas, I'm sort of a journalist," I said.

The slack-jawed reactions were priceless.

"And I'm here to talk to your friend, Mike Ellis."

"What do you want to talk to that jackass for?" asked Dennis.

"Yeah, that little shit doesn't know anything," Kevin said.

"I want to talk to him about his father. And some town history."

"You talking about Chief Charlie?" Hugh said.

"Yeah, Charles Ellis. That's Mike's dad, right?"

"I don't know if you'll get much," Paul said.

"Why do you say that?" I asked.

Hugh shook his head. I looked at each of the four men. Kevin and Dennis faded off, the topic of either Mike or his father did not interest them. I saw Mike starting to return from the bar, and Kevin and Dennis met up with him to collect their drinks. I saw Kevin gesture toward me.

Looking back at the faces of Paul and Hugh, I asked, "Mike doesn't talk about him?"

"Not in the way you'd think. Their father-son thing wasn't so good."

"Why is that?"

"Well, here he is. Maybe he'll tell you," Paul said. He looked at me as if he had a mouthful of sauerkraut.

I glanced over my shoulder to where Paul was looking. I made eye contact with Mike and gave him a thin smile. I placed the empty Martini glass on the table, and I turned to extend a greeting hand.

"Hi, my name is Tim Figueora," I said.

Mike slowly put his right hand out to meet mine. As we shook, I took a deep breath and took charge of my energy. Mike stole glances at Hugh and Paul before settling back on me. His eyebrows rose. I smiled. It was time for my pitch.

"You're Mike? Mike Ellis, Charlie's son?"

"Yes, I am," he said.

"Awesome, so nice to meet you."

My voice was high-pitched, the cadence of my words rapid. Mike did not say anything else to me. He gave me a sideways look, trying to size me up. I mirrored him and looked at myself. I wore a simple button-down shirt, light blue in color. The sleeves were rolled up to my elbows. The shirt sat untucked over khakis which I personally had ironed flat, and the cuffs of the pants rested upon brown loafers. Namely, I looked out of place.

"Wanted to know if I could have a word with you, Mike," I said.

"About what?" Mike asked. He looked over my shoulder now, and I imagined either Hugh or Paul giving him a curious look. I could feel their eyes on my back.

"If you don't mind some privacy, we can sit down and sort that out."

I led him away from his friends, and Mike tentatively followed. I brought him to a table in an actual quiet corner of the bar. We were out of earshot but within eyesight of where Hugh and Paul were sitting. Mike chose his seat and ensured that he could at least see his allies. I sat next to him, leaving little space between us. Deftly, I produced my Olympus voice recorder and activated it. I set it between us carefully. Mike eyed the device and gave me a narrow-eyed stare.

"Only the best for me," I said.

"Who are you?" he asked.

"So, Mike, my name is Timothy Figueroa. I know I said that before, but I want it to sink in."

I gave him a moment to see if my second introduction jogged any recognition. He looked at me with skeptical eyes and a thin, emotionless look on his round face.

"I run a popular and ever-growing, highly rated and reviewed true crime podcast. I call it: 'Figure it Out With Figgy.'"

Those words now hung in the air. I gave him another beat to see what his reaction was going to be, but I did not let him speak. I kept going, leaning ever so slightly toward Mike.

"I have been doing the show for about three years, and I've found a bit of a niche profiling some of the most obscure, under-reported, yet fascinating criminals and unsolved crimes. I don't bother with the mainstream. Everyone's done Dahmer, they all got Gacy, and Manson's memory has been molested."

Another pause and Mike's expression remained blank, betraying little of his inner thoughts. There was surprise underpinned in his eyes and confusion in the furrow of his brow, but nothing indicating that he had any inkling where I was going to go with the conversation.

"I search for small-town crimes, the Mayberry Mysteries, so to speak. I go in-depth to the bottom layer and seek to scrounge up every plot line and possible lead, trying to paint an exhaustive picture for the audience. The motive? Well, to bring attention, open the hearts and minds of the listeners, and make them care about these cases. Also, to aid law enforcement by stirring up renewed interest, new information, or adding different spins to existing investigations."

Mike leaned in. My inner brain smiled.

"So," I continued, "what am I doing here? Why Hunter? Why am I bothering you now? And thank you for your time, if I haven't done so already. Well, Mike, you are the son of Charlie Ellis, which we also established. And do you know why that's significant?"

Wide-eyed, Mike looked back with incredulity. He looked like he was about to answer.

"It's significant," I said, "because your father found Jane Doe of the Overlook. That's my name for her: Jane Doe of the Overlook. It's sort of catchy, and it'll look good on a book someday, depending on how much you can help me."

"I don't have any idea what you're talking about," Mike said.

"I knew you'd say that. Jesus, she was killed almost two decades before you were born."

"Who is she?"

"A poor, unfortunate young woman, still unidentified to this day, who was murdered, and the bastard who did it left her displayed out on the Overlook. No one has any clue who she was and even less ideas about who could have killed her. And your father was the first cop on the scene. My bet is he never, ever spoke to you about it."

"No, he never did," Mike said, interjecting into the discourse. He looked past me now toward his friends.

Unfazed, I said, "But why didn't he? That's what I want to know. Why doesn't anybody in this town talk about Jane Doe? Why hasn't there been any progress made in forty years? Maybe something lies in your family's secrets?"

"We don't have any secrets."

"Then they wouldn't be secret then, would they? I'd love to interview you some more. This isn't the right place or time. But I wanted to at least introduce myself. Get your gears turning a little."

"What are you looking for?" Mike asked.

"That's the thing. I don't know. Maybe if you think about it, you can tell me how he was at home. What he'd say that stands out now after all these years."

"Well, I... I don't think I can help you. My father and I weren't close." He leaned away now. He folded his arms.

"Hey, look, I ambushed you here. Again, I appreciate your time, but let's give this a chance to percolate—a chance to breathe. I don't even have my notes with me."

Mike unfolded his arms. I leaned over and retrieved my card case from my front pocket. Its gold trimming gleamed in the fluorescent lights. I pulled a card from the stack and offered it to him.

"Here's my card. You give me a call. Your terms. I'll be here for the next week or so doing my research."

Mike kept his eyes on mine for the moment. Then they tracked down my arm, to my hand, to the fingers, and finally to the card. He reached out and accepted it. He pulled it toward him and read it.

"So, you call me, and we'll sit down?"

He lifted his face to me. "I can help you with one thing, something to consider."

I tilted my head, my hands opening before him.

"I scarcely saw or spoke to my father for the last four years of his life. I wasn't even in town. So, that may affect my ability to help you."

"Just think about it. You give me a call."

I ended the recording and slipped the recorder into my pocket in a swift and discreet motion as I stood up smoothly. I made my exit before he could try to talk himself out of it. I left him at the table, probably confused. But I hoped I had built some intrigue.

3

The next morning, Carolina was at the trailhead early, sneaking from her parent's home even before her father was up to tend to chores around the farm. She drove to the parking area at the bottom of the mountain and parked her old, dinged-up Ford Focus in the lower lot. With a small pack slung over her shoulders, she set out to the Overlook. Her nimble legs were quick up the sharp, immediate incline. She liked having a good quick pace, knowing her destination was worth the journey. Being so early in the day, she was completely alone in the natural world. The sun was just crowning, and her eyes began to pick up the forms of the tree shapes. Things were becoming clearer to hear as she ascended.

Once she reached the escarpment, the trail leveled out. The effort to get to this point drew a light panting breath and perspiration moistened her brow. The trail meandered around to different scenic viewpoints. The sun finally came up over the crest of the nearby Highpoint and spilled out into the trees nearby. The birds began to sing. Carolina slowed her pace. She closed her eyes as she took in a deep breath, slowly letting it out in a satisfied murmur.

But still, Carolina moved, and the undulating path was no match for her athleticism and youth. She reached the fork in the path, where she would lose some of the elevation she had gained in order to reach the Overlook. Without so much as a hesitant thought, she turned and followed the descending trail, finally reaching her destination. The sun continued up past her and illuminated the entire valley that stretched out before her, all the way to the Hudson. It was clear, which delighted her. The humidity sometimes caused haze and dampened the brilliance of the view. She looked at her watch and noted the elapsed hour it had taken her to climb up.

After admiring the view, Carolina found a spot to rest and reflect. She considered the stone chair that had been assembled sometime in the last hundred years, but she knew that snakes frequented the flat fieldstone stack. Carolina instead chose a place with height advantage that also had a clear line of sight to the broadest part of the valley and nearby Highpoint. She scrambled up a boulder and lay back, using her pack as a pillow. Her eyes closed. The very distant sounds crept past her ears on the refreshing summer wind. Sounds of chainsaws, fire whistles, birdsongs and snapping branches. She must have fallen asleep.

When she stirred from her nap a few minutes later, she realized that she was no longer alone. There was someone poking around below her; she could hear heavy panting and the scuffling of boots. She looked but saw no one initially. Then, she caught sight of him. He approached the edge of the escarpment, standing where she had been before to admire the view. He cast his view about, she assumed looking for somewhere to sit. His eye caught the stone chair. He slung his pack off and placed it in the chair before settling back into the seat. Carolina watched him wipe his brow and take a long swallow of water from his

Camelbak. It was then that she recognized him. It was the young cop from the diner, Mike.

Mike appeared differently now. In his uniform, he looked clumsy and uncomfortable in the getup. At the bar the night before, in his non-uniform uniform, he was tight and awkward. Now, unencumbered, stripped of armor and tools, as well as any pretense, Mike looked more mature in natural movement. His body was soft. His legs were short, and in general, he had a stocky build. His waist was not trim, and she figured there wasn't a six-pack hidden beneath the sweat-wicking T-shirt he wore, but he also didn't have a belly protruding over his pants. Mike was like a lump of clay, she figured. He needed some molding.

After he caught his breath and took in the view as well as some more water, Mike rose to his feet and began looking around. He was apparently searching the area for something. He carefully moved out to the edge of the Overlook, tentatively looking down at the dark mass of trees. He turned back from the precipice, his head scanning back and forth. Carolina moved silently to keep her eyes on Mike when he began to leave her line of sight. He stopped and seemed to have discovered something. Carolina watched as he disappeared, moving completely out of her view. Knowing the area as well as she did, she believed that he located the lower part of the Overlook. It was typically overgrown in the summer and obscured from the general hiker. It was a ten-foot drop to a roughly fifteen-square-foot area. The face of the rock had some foot and hand holds for the scramble down and back up. Carolina became concerned.

She got up and collected her pack. Gracefully, she dismounted the boulder and approached the drop off to the lower overlook. Mike was on the outcrop. He was not visible, but he was moving around and making plenty of noise. The snaps of twigs and rustle of old, dead leaves gave Carolina a good idea of Mike's movement. She was lost in the swishing sounds before she realized that he was climbing back up. She backed away just as his hand reached over the top and took hold of the ground. Mike hoisted himself up. Seeing Carolina, he did a double take.

"Good morning," he said. He stood up and wiped his hands on his hiking pants, not looking directly at her.

"Hi there," she said.

"I didn't know anyone else was here."

"Well, I wasn't expecting anyone either."

Mike began moving back toward the edge of the Overlook, his head moving all around. With an exasperated look, Carolina watched him walk away. Then she followed behind him, her focus dead set on him. He always acted so serious.

"Are you looking for something?" Carolina asked.

Mike did not allow his concentration to break. From the edge of the Overlook, he began looking toward the boulder Carolina had been on a few minutes before. He made his way toward it and climbed up. Once settled and balanced on top, Mike looked down over the entire area. His eyes seemed to look right through her.

"I come up here a lot. Maybe I could help you," Carolina called up to him.

Mike surveyed the ground below him. He finally stopped, dissatisfied. His whole body sagged into itself.

"Okay," he said. "Let me come back down."

He ambled off the boulder, sliding down the last part on his backside. Back on the same level with Carolina again, he wiped dust from his pants and approached her. As he came up to her, she stood next to him for the first time without anything between them. He was taller than she expected, and she actually had to look up at him. Up close now, the boyish face was taut with the hint of stubble spread across his fat cheeks.

"I'm sorry," he said. "I was trying to get up here before anyone else today. I wanted some time alone."

"Me too," Carolina said. She laughed softly.

Mike stared at her as his eyes brightened with the thought in his head. "I didn't think about that."

Carolina smiled at him. "It's okay. No one owns the Overlook. We're both here, and that's just fine."

Mike nodded. He maintained his eye contact with her, his expression warming.

"So, are you looking for something?" she asked.

Mike's face now twisted, and he looked as if he were searching for what to say. "Yes, I am. But I don't know what it is."

"Intriguing." Carolina brought her hand to her chin, her thumb and forefinger stroking the soft, fleshy skin.

"I shouldn't even have come up here, you know. I'm chasing a ghost that I don't really care about." He crossed his arms loosely.

"Ghosts? That's interesting. What do you mean?" Carolina dropped her hand from her face to her hip.

Mike exhaled gruffly. "Okay, I guess I'll tell you what I know. So, there was a murder forty years ago. The woman's body was left up here. Somewhere."

"Oh, wow," Carolina said. "I've never heard that story before."

"No one has, apparently. It's some sort of local secret."

Carolina did not immediately respond as both she and Mike glanced around the space of the Overlook.

"Why are you looking around?" she asked finally.

"I guess I wanted to see if I could tell where the body was found. I assumed it would be simple."

"Like a sign that pointed it out?" She forced a chuckle, cracked a smile.

"Or a forty-year-old chalk outline." He chortled a little and his eyes sparked to life. Carolina smiled more broadly.

"Why the sudden interest? Especially if it's some big secret?" she asked.

Mike's arms opened, his hands feathered out toward her. "So, this podcast host told me about this the other night at the bowling alley."

"Older, creepy-looking guy? Blue shirt?" Carolina said. She curled her nose at some foul odor in her mind.

"Yeah, that was him," Mike said. He laughed out loud now.

"He told me he was some reporter and he asked me about you."

Carolina dropped her eyes, gazing blindly at the ice carved rock face beneath her feet. When she looked up, she found Mike looking directly at her. His eyes were big as if he were waiting for the Jack in the Box to pop out.

"What did you tell him?" he asked. His voice cracked on the inflection of inquiry.

Carolina shook her head. She forced herself to be reassuring when she said: "Nothing. I don't know you."

Mike considered this statement, his face reddening as the moment dragged out. He sucked in a breath and he held out his hand. "Mike Ellis."

"Carolina Velez." She held out her hand, and they shook.

"It's nice to meet you," Mike said. Their hands fell away from one another. "Listen, I think I owe you an apology from the other night."

"What do you mean?"

"I think you caught me, uh, looking at your chest."

Carolina thought back for a second, recalling her flash of anger at the diner. She frowned in the shallow dip of her mouth. "Yeah, I thought you were a little obvious."

"The truth is that I was admiring your medal. The one you were wearing that night."

Carolina cocked her head to the side. Her eyes searched him for sincerity. Then she reached behind her neck with her left hand and pulled up a thick rope chain from beneath her shirt. As the chain came up from her chest, a shiny, reflective medal came up. She took hold of the jewelry in her right thumb and forefinger.

"This medal?" she asked.

Mike nodded. "I was trying to read it when you caught me staring. I was too embarrassed to tell you the truth at the time. Thought it would sound fake."

"You're probably right. It's a medal of... " "Saint Mariana of Jesus de Paredes. The Lily of Quito."

Carolina stood with her mouth open. Mike gave her a sheepish smile, acknowledging the small chance that anyone else would know the specific image on her medal. Carolina's mouth closed slowly and turned up into a gracious smile.

"How'd you know that?"

Mike's sheepishness gave way to a confident grin. "I've been around. Talked to some people."

"You've been to Ecuador?"

"Not quite, but I met some people from there. Studied Saint Mariana a little, in my other life."

Carolina shook her head, confusion languishing in her face. "But anyway, why the interest in this murder? Despite some creepy guy telling you about it."

"Because my father was the first responding officer back then."

"Now you're inexplicably tied?"

"I don't know."

"Your father was a big deal?"

"I guess so. He was always at work. Even at home, he was at work. He could never put it away and just be a dad. He was alive for seventeen years of my life, and I never really knew him."

"And now here you are," Carolina said. She gestured to the area of the Overlook.

"Chasing ghosts." Mike nodded, looking around again.

"Who was this woman? The dead one."

"No one knows. That's the tragic part, I guess. She was killed and left up here, and no one even knows who she was, let alone who killed her."

"Makes this place pretty eerie." Carolina shivered as she cast her eyes around.

"Some people I think would find it interesting. In a morbid sense."

Carolina shrugged her shoulders. She looked at her watch, the digital numbers indicating it was nearly seven o'clock.

She sighed and looked back at Mike apologetically. "I have to get going."

"I think I'm gonna keep looking around for a little bit," Mike said.

Carolina smirked. "That's fine. I'm a woman of the millennium. I got up here all by myself. I can get back down."

Mike finally smiled. "I'll see you around."

Carolina started up the path. She called back over her shoulder, "Have fun with your ghosts."

###

George Hunter saw Mike enter the library just after the automatic locks on the front door opened at nine. The young man was dirty, dressed in hiking pants, and a sweaty wicking T-shirt. He walked past where George stood guard at the reference and check-out desk. George watched him with relaxed curiosity, perched upon his swiveling stool. He spun around to keep tabs on the filthy kid, watching him mill about aimlessly. Mike looked sideways at a few of the professional librarians but kept moving deeper into the building. George lost sight of Mike as the stacks swallowed the interesting youngster up. George decided that he had had enough excitement and faced toward the checkout counter where his newspaper was spread out.

George gazed through his bifocal lenses and moved one of his calloused and scarred index fingers carefully across the words in the article that had been titled: "New Face and an Old Name." The opposite arthritic, swollen, and wrinkled hand held the thin paper down flat to guard against the air conditioning positioned just above the desk. George wore his typical library uniform of tan Dickies slacks and a long sleeve collared green and gold Tartan pattern flannel shirt. The buttons were fastened all the way to his neck. Then, over his shoulders was a red cardigan, the empty sleeves hanging loose in the artificial breeze. His name tag was affixed to the outside layer. He did not hear Mike approach his desk.

"Hi," Mike said. "Where can I find old newspapers?"

George, not startled, took the time to finish the sentence he was reading and pointed his damaged digit at the end to make it stick in his mind. He looked up, his eyes finding the appropriate part of the lens to look at the boy. His mind clicked with some familiarity, and he took a beat to study the kid's face.

"Well, we have a digital archive now," George said. "Thanks to some state grants. How far back are you looking?"

"Forty years or so."

"A lot of interest in the time period lately."

George's voice was wizened and wise, nasally and no nonsense. His expression read like a weary old clock face, worn and slow. He shook his head. He reached one stiff hand up to his jowls and stroked his chin. He stood, slipped the cardigan from his shoulders, and placed it on the back of his swiveling stool.

George moved in quick, shuffling steps, coming around the checkout counter, and he beckoned Mike to follow him with short motions of his elbow. He moved swiftly as though his feet were not on the ground. He looked over his shoulder at Mike, expecting the younger man to follow. As Mike took a few steps after George, George stopped altogether, waiting for the kid to catch up. The gap increased again, and George pushed himself into the periodical lab alone, the door sliding silently closed behind him. It was a cubby-hole-sized room, cramped with three sleek Hewlett-Packard computers lined up in a row. The door behind George opened, a burst of air following before he heard it woosh closed. He could feel the presence of the kid next to him, as well as the stench of perspiration and dirt.

"The grant paid for the computers and the digitation. Not the space," George said.

He looked humbly around the room and then at Mike. Being up close next to the kid now, George was convinced he recognized the face, at least the contours of the chubby cheeks with the round chin. With those grayish-green eyes and the sandy blond hair that, despite its short length, was tousled in a mop atop the kid's head. But George's mind did not connect to anything specific, and after a moment of consideration and study, he let the thought go.

"What date are you looking for?" George asked.

He tapped the mouse at the middle computer and signed himself into the system. The screen booted to the home screen with a search bar in the center. George looked over his shoulder and met a blank stare. Mike's face betrayed him that he was not prepared for that question. He stammered that he was looking for something from forty years ago.

"You said that before. You'll need to be a little more specific," George said. "This thing can get broad. Despite what you think, a lot of stuff happens around here from quilting fairs to graduations, angry locals and wide-eyed visitors, facts, opinions, and straight-out lies. It's amazing what you'll find in a local newspaper."

"Okay, well I'm interested in crime. A specific crime."

"Forty years ago? A crime?"

"Yeah," Mike said.

His voice sounded particularly vague to George. George turned all the way around now and looked Mike in the eye. The younger man turned his eyes away, casting them down toward the floor.

"I've been in the mountains my whole life, son. There's only one crime that crosses my mind. And it happened just about forty years ago."

Mike looked up and swallowed a lump in his throat. George gave him a stern expression. He wasn't angry, in fact, but concerned. He gave Mike an opportunity to speak, but after a solid minute of silence, it didn't look like he was going to.

"You can say it, son," George said. His tone was soothing now, his face softening.

Mike cleared his throat. "Sir," he began. "I am interested in reading about the woman who was killed and left out on the Overlook."

George nodded. He smiled. "That's a little more specific, isn't it."

He turned back to the computer and typed in a specific date: *January 3, 1982*. The search engine returned instantaneously with blue hyperlinks. George scrolled the page, counting the links.

"Here's five stories. The system is pretty good, so if you click on one of these stories, related stories will populate."

George shifted out of the way, his arm extended offering Mike a chance to explore. Mike tightened his face into an uncertain grimace. He moved up to the computer, his right hand grabbing control of the mouse.

"Happy hunting," George said.

He moved out of the room, leaving Mike alone to perform his research. He glided out into the main stacks, past the librarians, and back to his post at the checkout desk. He pulled the cardigan from the stool and settled it across his shoulders, adjusting the name tag so that it could be read by the next patron. The newspaper was still spread out over the counter, although the air conditioner had flipped a couple pages in his absence. George lifted the whole paper, looking closely through the bottom part of his bifocal at the page number. He pulled the thin newsprint together and pulled it apart again, back to the page he had been on. Then he carefully scanned and found the article titled: "New Face and an Old Name." Then he used his calloused, scarred pointer finger to again process the words till he found the place he had left off.

"The new police officer," George read in a low, audible whisper. "Just completed his field training and is on solo patrol. Chief Bernard Justin said that Officer Ellis has been well prepared by the police academy and thinks he will be an asset to the department going forward."

George stopped reading. His brain worked the sentences from the article around like a piece of bubble gum. He grunted an answer to himself and refocused himself on the article.

"Ellis is the son of Chief Charles Ellis who served the town police for thirty-seven years before his untimely death in 2015," George continued, this time in a soft voice instead of a whisper.

The sound of boots crossing the hardwood floor perked his ears, and the transition of the sound onto the carpeted floor around the checkout desk made him look up without taking the time to point out his spot in the article. He saw Mike coming across the space directly toward him. Mike's face looked like it was weighing a decision of whether to accost the clerk again. After a couple hesitant steps, Mike picked his momentum up toward George.

"There wasn't really anything in those articles. One was only a blurb," Mike said.

"Yeah, I know," George said. He folded his newspaper closed, then in half and set it aside.

"How do you know?"

"I told you, son, I've lived up here my whole life."

"So, no one wrote anything about finding a dead body? A murder?"

"I didn't say that. But you're not the only customer to ask about her in the last week."

Mike's face brightened with some thought in his head. "So he came in for the same information?"

"I would assume so. He wasn't disappointed."

"Well, I am," Mike said.

Mike smacked the counter lightly with his fist. His eyes shot up toward the ceiling like he was looking for something else to say.

"This other fella had a lot of questions. Some were good; some were bad. He actually spent a few hours in the lab. Left here with what he said was a full notebook and a grateful smile."

"Sorry I wasted your time," Mike said. He smacked his fist on the counter again, this time with some more force. His eyes shifted down to look at George, and Mike's face melted into a sincere look of dejection. He turned and slowly walked off.

"Come back sometime," George said after him.

4

Paul Hunter sat on the bench in the locker room polishing his boots. His reflection was already peering back from the toe, but Paul added just another small coat of wax, melted it with a Zippo lighter, and massaged the polish into the boot. Once the mirror image returned, he frowned and shrugged his shoulders. Paul placed the boot next to its mate on the floor and stood up. He considered each individually, then together. Frowning again, he shook his head. He mumbled under his breath.

"Just put the damn things on," Hugh Bell said. He stood at the other end of the bench already dressed in his uniform and was in the process of slinging his equipment belt around his waist, trying to keep his belly above the leather.

Paul did not respond. He turned toward the locker to grab his uniform shirt, then hung it on the door of the locker. Then Paul retrieved his lint roller, taking the tool to the shirt in long rolling strokes.

"Oh, Jesus, man," Hugh said.

"Don't take the Lord's name," Paul said, not looking at Hugh. "I don't worry about your process, Hugh. Don't worry about mine."

Paul completed his lint roll and held the roller up for Hugh to see.

"You and your OCD," Hugh said with a grunt.

Paul finally picked the shirt from the hanger and slid his arms into the shirt. The cuffs of the sleeves were tapered, and they wrapped around the definition of his bicep muscles. The globe and anchor tattoo on his right arm stopped just short of the edge. He repeated the process of rolling his trousers also, ignoring the disapproving stare from Hugh. As he finished putting on his uniform, he heard Hugh sigh.

"Trying to get some phone numbers tonight, little brother?" Hugh asked.

Paul looked up and saw that Hugh had walked to the opposite side of the wall of lockers. Paul tied his laces and put his garrison belt on. He grabbed his equipment belt, and closed his locker. He went around the end of the lockers to see Hugh towering over Mike Ellis near the sinks and the full-size mirror that hung over them. Mike was flattening his collar and smoothing his uniform shirt.

"No," Mike was saying. "I'm just trying to avoid scrutiny." He rubbed his cheeks and neck, feeling his shave before running his hand up to the stubby hairs near his close-cropped scalp.

"You're the newest guy and son of the most renowned cop to ever work in this town," Paul said. "There will be scrutiny." He pulled his equipment belt on and began placing his keepers.

"Renowned?" Hugh said. "I am too old for this conversation."

Paul walked up to the mirror, smoothing his shirt across his trim build. In the reflection, Paul saw Mike poke at his pudgy midsection. Paul looked at his own image. His face was sharp, angular, and mature, skin smooth with just the slightest onset of wrinkles. He looked back at Mike's large, round head and his neck broken out in razor-rash.

"It's a word that means well known," Mike said. "What I don't want to be."

"It's just something you gotta deal with," Paul said.

They kept looking at one another in the mirror. Paul smiled, and Mike frowned.

"We'd better get going," Hugh said.

Mike and Paul now both looked over to him. Hugh motioned over his shoulder at the analog clock that was inching toward three. Each man collected his patrol bag, a medium-sized duffle bag containing extra equipment and tools. Hugh held the door for Paul and Mike, and three men filed into the hallway. When they exited the locker room, they were at the midpoint of the hallway. They turned to the right which led them down toward the sergeant's office which was opposite the public entrance vestibule. At the end of the hallway was the chief's office.

As they began moving down the hallway the sound of a door opening and natural light spilling down the passage caught their attention. All three stopped and turned, looking at the far end of the hallway to the door opening out to the parking lot. Kevin Haverthy and Dennis Jones were coming in, chattering away with one another before they noticed Hugh, Paul, and Mike. They stopped dead about a third of the way down the hallway, directly in front of the booking room to one side and the break room to the other.

"Oh, hey, it's our cover model," Kevin said. He laughed heartily.

"Oh, it's Chief Charlie's pride and joy," Dennis said.

"You ever get an article about you, Denny?"

Dennis feigned modesty. "Oh no, Kev, never. Especially after a hot second on the job."

They laughed as they started coming closer to the locker room. Paul rolled his eyes and looked over toward Mike, who was in the process of turning away. Paul opened his mouth, but no words came out. He watched Mike move away slowly.

"Shut the fuck up," Hugh said. Paul turned back and looked up at him.

"You assholes want to go bowling again next week?" Kevin asked.

Dennis laughed and said, "Yeah, maybe the kid can buy another few rounds."

Mike stopped in his tracks. Paul's face brightened with anticipation that Mike was about to say something.

"Maybe next time we can get him laid," Kevin said. He snickered now, a deviant and maniacal noise.

"Yeah, you saw the way he was talking up that Spanish chick at the bar," Dennis said.

"He's gotta pop that cherry," Kevin said. "From what I heard, he's still got it."

The laughter from the two older cops grew from a tiny giggle to a full belly-fed roar. Dennis' gut vibrated as he leaned back into his enjoyment while Kevin doubled over and faced the floor. Hugh looked down at Paul. Paul's face softened into a helpless puddle, and he looked over to Mike, who was still standing with his back to the group. Without turning, Mike walked down toward the sergeant's office.

"Well, Kevin, at least he won't be competing with you," Hugh said. "Can't imagine he's looking at chicks over two bills."

Dennis paused his laughter, pulling himself together to look at Hugh before looking at Kevin. Then he started laughing all over again. Kevin straightened, his smile fading.

"At least it still works," he said.

"We gotta go," Paul said. He looked back up at Hugh's snarling face.

The big man nodded with an insincere smile and turned. "Don't want to be late."

Paul and Hugh walked away and turned into the sergeant's office. Mike was standing off in the corner chewing on his fingernails. Sergeant Grant sat behind the large gun-metal gray desk, nearly hidden behind a giant computer drive and a tube TV-sized monitor. The Sergeant sipped a cup of coffee through his bushy mustache. His cheater glasses were perched on the middle part of his nose as he read over the computer monitor. He was old in an aged cigar sort of way—preserved and stately with an odor of aura and vintage. The Sergeant looked up at Paul and then at Hugh. He seemed to have forgotten Mike as he stood up and addressed them.

"So, there's nothing new," he said. His voice was a crisp tenor, soothing in its melody. "Still have a lot of activity over at the campground. Will be that way till after Labor Day at least. We've seen an increase in overdose calls, mostly fentanyl. Fortunately, EMS has responded in time to administer Narcan. Make sure you have your supply with you. You never know when you're going to need it. As for assignments, Hugh, why don't you take post one? Ellis?" Sergeant Grant looked up, took stock again of Hugh and Paul, then scanned the room.

Paul glanced to the corner as Mike moved a little closer into the Sergeant's peripheral. He looked at Paul with a sheepish grin, and Paul snapped his attention back forward, catching the long look that Sergeant Grant aimed at Mike. The cheaters had crept to the tip of his nose, making him an interesting caricature with the red mass of hair beneath a gin blossom nose and the small reflective lenses.

"Ah, yes. Officer Ellis, you will have post two. Hunter, you can be the floater tonight."

Sergeant Grant looked around the piles on his desk, carefully searching. He found something and deliberately picked up the piece of paper. The Sergeant adjusted his spectacles and examined the words.

"I wanted to congratulate Officer Ellis on his first DWI arrest. It was a nice stop. I just have a few things in your report I want to go over. Let's talk about it later."

"Sure thing, Sarge," Mike said.

Paul saw the nearly paternal look on the old Sergeant's face. The hard, blustery expression had eased, and a beam of pride exuded from the blue eyes. Paul stole a quick glance at Mike. He had pulled himself up a little straighter, a little taller in his posture. Mike's eyes were locked on the Sergeant.

"That's all. Any questions?"

All three of the officers shrugged, shook their heads, and looked between themselves. Sergeant Grant dismissed them to patrol, and they all left the office, turning left and heading toward the door that led outside. Hugh led the way with Paul and then Mike bringing up the rear. The locker room door opened as they approached and Kevin and Dennis exited, each dressed in jeans and a T-shirt. Kevin's eyes caught Mike as he came closer.

"What do you say, kid?" Kevin asked.

Paul heard Mike gulp before he said, "About what?"

"We hit the lanes on Friday nights. Especially when the wheel goes around, and we're all off. We can get you hooked up. I meant that. Little charity from old Uncle Kev."

Paul held his breath to know Mike's answer.

"I'll let you know," Mike said. He said it in a sharp comeback, never breaking stride as he walked.

Paul stopped at the locker room door along with Hugh. Mike continued up the hall and out the door.

"Seems very approachable," Dennis said.

"Well, you guys are assholes," Paul replied.

"It's true," said Kevin. He elbowed Dennis in the ribs.

The four of them traded a few more insults before Hugh and Paul made their way to the back door and into the parking lot. The hazy mid-summer humidity adhered to Paul's skin right away. The sun beat down without mercy, bleaching the outside world as his eyes adjusted. Paul pulled his sunglasses from his patrol bag. He saw Mike settling into a Dodge Charger, looking over his mobile data terminal as it booted up.

"Don't let those guys get to you," Paul said. He stopped by Mike's open door.

Mike kept his eyes on the computer screen. "Don't worry about it. I'll sort it out."

Hugh opened the driver's door of the Durango parked on the other side of Mike's car. He looked over the Charger's roof at Paul. Paul gave him a look that translated as: *We should say something*. Hugh shrugged in response. He knelt and rapped his bear-paw hand on the passenger side window of Mike's car. Mike looked up, acknowledged Hugh, and turned his attention back to the computer. Paul reached down to the open door and hit the button for the window.

"Hey, little bro, you want to hit them hard and meet up at the diner around seven?" Hugh asked.

Mike breathed out heavily. "Yeah, okay." His voice was low and monotone.

"Listen, I'll even buy tonight. I think I'm up anyway. You can try that meatloaf."

Mike looked up and gave Hugh a polite nod.

"Alright, I'm not going to make this an after school special. Fuck those B line scumbags," Hugh said. He straightened his long frame and stretched his back, making eye contact with Paul again.

"You got it, Hugh," Mike said. His attention was again locked into the interior of the car.

Paul looked on helplessly. Mike looked up at him with a look that said, *Do you mind?* Paul moved out of the way, and Mike closed the car door. Paul took a step back, and Mike pulled forward and made his way out of the parking lot.

"That boy ain't right," Hugh said. His voice drawled through the words.

"Is it wrong for us to want to open him up?"

"Hell, no. Listen, I'll take care of him. I'll see you later."

Paul nodded and walked across the lot to his car, an older Chevy Blazer. He busied himself setting the vehicle up, turning on the computer, and putting his patrol bag just the way he liked it. In his peripheral vision, he saw the rear door of the police station open. A man in a starched white shirt stood holding the door, surveying the parking lot. The man was Chief Bernard Justin. Paul easily recognized him. He was a short, demure man. The Chief caught sight of Hugh and said something that Paul was unable to hear. Hugh reacted, made a half-hearted salute, and answered the chief's question. The Chief then motioned for Hugh to come back inside the building. Paul read the reluctance in Hugh's body language, but he followed the chief back inside.

###

To this point, I've presented Mike Ellis through the eyes of others, but for what follows, there is no other perspective to give other than Mike himself. He told me the following events personally more than a half dozen times in the years after I really got to know him. It was something that never left his memories, and he described every bit of it as if it were in slow motion. But allow me the standard leeway in setting up.

Mike was conducting stationary patrol, sitting alone in the driveway of the County Paramedics substation with radar up and ready.

But there was no traffic. The afternoon hustle and bustle had subsided, and it was as if Mike were the only person in the entire Town of Hunter. He yawned and fought the drowsy droop in his eyes. He cracked his neck slowly, feeling the stretch of the cartilage. He had not slept after his climb to the Overlook and his visit to the library. He had rolled from the library to his house for a shower and shave before he went to work. And all that was after being out late at the bowling alley the night before when he had first met me. He was ready for bed. The crackle of the radio drew him from his tired haze.

"Greene 911 to an available Town of Hunter patrol," the distant female voice said.

Mike hesitated before he scooped up the microphone. "Hunter seven-zero."

"Seven-zero, check the welfare. Passerby noted a vehicle sitting at the Overlook trailhead with open doors. No one was near the vehicle."

"You can show me en route," Mike said.

"Received, twenty-two eighteen hours."

Mike stared into the microphone as the words crawled through his brain. He replaced the mic and put his Charger into gear. The V8 kicked gravel and the car gathered some speed as it left the first village. The emergency lights were not on. There was no one to move out of the way. The Charger found a groove at about seventy miles per hour. As it approached the second village, the deserted shops and restaurants stood witness as Mike tore through.

At the wheel, Mike breathed in and out purposefully as his eyes scanned for obstructions. There was nothing around, no people, no cars, and, thankfully, no deer. He guided the Charger past the police department and then the diner, sitting dark and abandoned. Exiting the second village, he entered the third, and his foot sank a little more into the accelerator and the Charger increased speed toward eighty.

Between scans of the road, he looked at the clock on the car's stereo. It glowed back indicating 10:21 p.m.

The Charger reached the steep decline in the road that wound down the mountain. It maneuvered gracefully around the switchbacks before reaching the Falls, where the car came to a halting stop as it negotiated a flat, sharp turn to the right before it dropped like a rollercoaster down the next hill. The Charger continued to twist with the roadway, reaching the floor of the valley.

Reaching the Overlook trailhead, Mike slowed his patrol vehicle and turned into the parking area without coming to a complete stop. The headlights of the Charger spilled out into the darkness, spreading over the gravel lot.

"Greene 911, Hunter seven-zero is out," he said into the microphone.

"Received. Twenty-two twenty-four."

Mike squinted his eyes, looking into what the light illuminated. There was nothing to see. He pulled further in and swung the Charger around to see if anything reflected. Still nothing. Reaching for his patrol bag, he grabbed a D-cell Maglite and exited the car. He closed the door silently and walked out toward the pool of luster, keeping himself outside the beams of the headlights.

Mike turned the flashlight on and scanned the tree line bordering the parking area. Having been there myself, the lot is approximately five hundred feet by a thousand feet. Trees bordered the one side, and someone's backyard bordered the opposite side. Although the house was an acre away. Straight ahead the parking lot's entrance was a wide and steep trail that inclined at a thirty-degree angle. Above this area was a wide, flat space with a picnic table and the divergence of two trails. One went up to the Overlook, the other traversed a long pathway to the other side of town. Mike determined through his search that there were no vehicles in the parking area.

"Greene 911, Hunter seven-zero," he said into the microphone at his chest. "I am not showing anything. Possibly G-O-A. Do you have a callback?"

There was silence, and Mike continued to survey the area. He explored the wide, steep path that led up to the plateau. Where the gravel parking lot ended, dirt and grass began. Embedded in the soil were tire marks. Mike thought they looked fresh.

"Hunter seven-zero. No answer on call back."

"Received. I'm going up the trail a little. Is there another unit available?""Hunter six-nine is en route," Hugh's voice said from the microphone.

Mike proceeded to walk up the trail, following the tire tracks. He panted a little and adjusted his Kevlar vest as he tramped up the side of the path. His flashlight was off, and the rhodopsin building in his eyes allowed him to see clearly in the dark. After a minute, he reached the small plateau, and that was when he saw the car. It was a red Ford Focus, four-door, probably about ten years old. The driver side door was wide open, and Mike could hear the faint key-in-ignition alarm sounding.

"Greene 911, I've located a vehicle." Mike read the plate out into the microphone.

He approached the Focus slowly. Some automatic sense made his right hand move toward the firearm in his holster and flip the retention bar down. The dome light in the Focus was on, and Mike saw that there was no one sitting in the car.

"Hello," he called. "Town police. Is there anyone in the vehicle?" His voice trembled a little, but the volume smoothed the delivery.

No answer. Mike continued his slow progress, making a wide sweep toward the Focus. Now, whatever instinct had prompted him to lower the retention made him remove the Glock from the holster. He kept it low as he made the final approach to the driver's side door.

Empty. Well at least no person. There were plenty of other items that were cataloged later when the car was inventoried and searched. However, as Mike was satisfied no one was in the Focus, he holstered his weapon. He turned the flashlight on and spread the light on the ground in search of more information.

"Greene 911, anything back on the plate?" he asked, keying the mic with his open hand.

"Hunter seven-zero you should have a 2012 Ford Focus color red registered to a Jorge Velez subject with an address in Brooklyn."

"Received," he said in a soft voice, keying the radio mic.

Mike backed away from the Focus. He put the light up the trail to the Overlook. The trail he had been on earlier that day. The sharp beam of light moved around, up the trail, back down, and then side to side. Mike turned toward the other path, and light played over it. Finally, some luminescence reflected from the side of the path as it ran down from Mike's position. The shining was about a hundred yards away.

"Six-nine to seven-zero," Hugh's disembodied voice said from the microphone.

"Go ahead," Mike said. He began moving toward the spot.

"I'm about zero three out. You secure?"

"Ten-four."

"I'll come right up to you."

Mike's steps were soft, and his left hand manipulated the flashlight, so its beam danced on whatever was reflecting it. Mike described to me later that this was when everything slowed down for him. Details became sharp. The hoot of an owl and the breeze coming from the east that soothed the sweat on his brow. The stench of humidity mixed with dirt. The way that the woman's body lay, and the ornament on her neck that caught the shaft of light, sending it back to Mike as a beacon.

"Hugh," Mike said, keying the radio. "Leave the car at the bottom. Repeat, do not drive up here."

"Copy."

Mike froze after making the transmission to Hugh. The silence became deep as everything in his focus sharpened to a point. He felt the nausea in his belly and a well sting of tears formed in his eyes. The light from the D-cell mag illuminated the entirety of the body. The metal of the necklace's ornament glinted at her chest, and the narrow bruising around her neck was obvious, the pattern of chain links rising in welts.

She was face up, arms over her head, legs straight and pinched together. She wore jeans and a light blue T-shirt. The outstretched arms pointed away from her car. A hoodie was balled up and placed on her face. She was young and petite.

Mike became aware of the heavy breathing coming from behind him. He did not turn away, his eyes taking in all that they observed.

"Mike," Hugh said. It sounded like he was at the Focus.

"Stay wide if you come over here," Mike said. He pointed toward the far side of the path with his right hand.

At the fringe of his vision, Mike saw Hugh coming up far to his right, forming a tactical L shape. Mike looked over to him.

"Jesus Christ," Hugh said. A mutter of disbelief and derision. He leaned into his shoulder mic. "Hunter six-nine to Green 911. I need a boss, a coroner, and crime scene. We have a DOA."

Mike remained transfixed, his gaze left Hugh and returned to the body of the woman. The ornament on the chain around her neck radiated in the flashlight's beam. He told me later that it came to him all at once.

"Hugh," Mike said. He choked on the next words. "It's Carolina."

5

Ann leaned in to listen at her son's door as she rapped at the wood.

"Michael, it's nearly eleven, dear," she said. "Why don't you get yourself up?"

Ann's voice was sickly sweet, a sing-song bird melody with maternal force behind it. She leaned closer to the door. She knocked again in quarter note percussion for four measures. Before she had time for another verse, she picked up the faint groan inside the bedroom.

"Okay, Ma." Mike's voice was distant and indistinct. "You know I was at work till two."

"What?" Ann asked.

There was motion in the room. A creak of the bed as weight left it. The ruffling sound of clothing being tossed. A few light footsteps moving toward the door. The rattle of the doorknob. The door opened, and the odor of a young man escaped. It was full of sweat and cologne, hair gel, and Barbasol. Ann looked up a little to the face of her son.

"I said I was out till two. I..." Mike said, his voice catching. "I, uh, arrested another guy for a DWI."

"Well, that's good for you. Your father never slept this late. Even if he did work till two."

"And that's why he had a heart attack at fifty-seven."

"He had a heart attack because he ate like shit. Plus, the damn cigarettes he thought I knew nothing about. And he was all work. No play."

"I play, Ma. I was out the other night with some of the guys from work."

"Yeah, I just bet. Well, anyway, you want some breakfast?"

"Sure. I gotta be back in at three."

"Put some clothes on then."

Ann turned and walked back up the short hallway to the kitchen. I was in this house once or twice. It was a robust country mountain home, well-appointed with knickknacks and heirlooms. It was clean, but everything had a coating of age. Items were settled in their places and had not moved in some time. It was a two-story A-frame. The kitchen was adjacent to Mike's bedroom on the first level, so Ann's trip was only about a dozen feet or so. She had already set out all the supplies for breakfast: eggs, bacon, and a pot of coffee. The table was set. All that was missing was Mike.

Ann waited in the center of the room as she watched Mike enter. He looked unkempt, haggard, and tentative. She motioned toward the small table with two chairs sitting opposite one another. He sat, and she set to work. She removed three eggs from the carton and broke them into an already positioned bowl. She added some milk and whisked the components into a mixture.

"So, tell me about this DUI or whatever," she said. She tried to sound interested.

"It's a DWI in New York."

"Didn't need the legal lesson. Tell me about what you did."

"There's not much to tell," he said. His voice trailed off like he didn't want to say anything else.

Ann turned around, still whisking, and stared at her son. She fixed motherly scorn on her face. She set the bowl next to the stove and kicked on the gas burner beneath the cast iron pan. She placed the bacon in the pan as it warmed.

"So," Mike said with some hesitation. "So, I stopped a guy coming out of the state campground. Yeah. He was weaving and going a little fast."

The sizzle from the bacon coming to temperature permeated the room. The aroma encompassed the whole space. Ann turned again to look at Mike, who seemed lost mid-sentence.

"A little fast?" Ann asked to prompt him.

"Yeah, like forty in a thirty-five. So, I stopped him, and when I got to the door, I could smell the beer. He was in a little pickup truck. I looked in the cab and could see a whole six-pack of empty bottles on the floor." Mike's words gathered momentum as he let the story build.

"Guess that's why you smelled beer."

Ann turned the bacon over in the pan using a set of tongs. She had to raise her voice over the growing volume of sizzle.

"Yeah, so I got a little excited. I pulled him out right away and brought him to the back of the truck, and I asked him 'So, you had anything to drink tonight?' and the guy goes, 'Nope.'"

Ann laughed. She returned the bacon to its original side. "So he just lied to you?"

"I said, 'What about the bottles in the car?' He says to me, 'Bringing them to the grocery store for returns.' Of course, he's slurring every word." Mike repeated the man's excuse, emphasizing the slur in his voice.

The bacon was to Mike's normal liking, so Ann pulled the strips from the pan, placing them on a waiting plate. She transferred the whisked egg concoction to the cast iron pan and scrambled it in the bacon's grease.

"Oh, man, and then Hugh showed up. You remember Hugh Bell, right? He worked for my father."

Ann twisted around at the words "my father" and looked at Mike disapprovingly. She frowned as her mind worked. Instead of admonishment, she said, "Oh yes. Big fella?"

"That's Hugh. He's huge. So, he shows up and starts making a big deal. 'You know what time it is?' But then he saw this guy, and he shrugged it off saying, 'Guess you had no choice.'"

The eggs were scrambled at this point, and Ann scooped them out onto the plate with the bacon. She turned toward the table.

Mike continued his tale. "So, I got into SFSTs. Man, this guy's eyes were bouncing around like ping pong balls. Fail."

"What? I can never get these acronyms."

"Standardized Field Sobriety Tests. It's how you show that someone is intoxicated."

Ann put the plate before Mike, making an agreeable noise, trying to show she understood. She came around the table to the other chair, listening as Mike began shoveling food into his mouth. She turned and looked at him again with soft contempt. Mike caught the glare and slowed his pace.

"Then I showed him the walk and turn. He almost fell over in the starting position. The one leg stand was a joke. We collared him right then and there. He wound up blowing a two-four. Three times the legal limit."

Ann smiled, nodding along with Mike's story. He dug into his eggs and bacon again, her eyes rolled. She let him eat, sitting quietly and reflective. She made up her mind not to say anything else. Mike slowly finished the meal and set his fork down. Ann watched him recline back in his seat and look at her. She thought that he had something to say, his look became like a thousand-yard stare. It was as if he were trying to forget something.

After a few silent moments, she asked, "Do they still talk about him?"

"My father?" Mike asked. He saw her look. "About Dad? Hell, they have a plaque dedicated to him in the public vestibule."

"He'd tell me stories like that all the time, too."

"I didn't get to the best part."

"What's that?"

"We get him back to the station, and he's already got two pending DWI arrests. His license is suspended for it. So, bang, felony aggravated unlicensed operation."

"Sounds serious. Did he go to jail?"

Mike made a derisive sound. "No, we released him to his girlfriend around two. Boy, she was pissed." Ann focused an appalled look at Mike, and he caught it. "I mean angry."

"I bet." She released her expression, letting the slang go. She got up and cleared Mike's plate, bringing it to the oversized farm sink. She looked out the window at the yard and tree line behind the A-frame.

"Hugh keeps busting my balls about my living situation," Mike said.

Ann turned sharply with a renewed wide-eyed and scathing look on her face. Her lips curled and her teeth chewed at the skin as she held back words. Mike held up his hands and Ann again let her features relax.

"Well, your father was a full-time police officer and married at twenty-three. You're already past that point and no girl to speak of. Just a cop."

"I told him you're my roommate."

"Roommates share rent, dear."

"I'll let him know that you agree with him. He was trying to set me up with this waitress from the diner."

Ann saw Mike become wistful, his expression blank without warning. He looked again like he just remembered something that he was trying to forget. She moved back toward the table.

"How's that going?"

"She doesn't know I exist." His response trailed off.

Ann studied her son deeply. He swallowed a lump in his throat before he looked over at her with a straining look. She closed the distance to the table with small steps caught between whether she should comfort him.

"What was life with Dad like? Early on, I mean."

Ann felt her approach change. She returned to her chair and sat. Her hands folded neatly on the table.

"Kind of like this. Quiet and simple. I'd cook meals, and he'd tell me about his day. It was the best time of our lives."

"What about me?"

"You were a different kind of special. When you're young and newly married you are learning constantly. It's hard to be comfortable because you want to please the other person so much. And your father was learning his job, which was so new and exciting for him."

"What changed?"

"What do you mean?"

"That's not the man I remember. He didn't tell me stories. He hardly acknowledged me. Then, he sent me away to school. It was like he didn't want to be around me."

"Police work changes a man, Michael. I guess you'll see that. Your father became more serious as the work became more serious. There were things he just couldn't tell me after a while. And by the time we were blessed with you, he was an older man, an older cop."

Mike fiddled with a napkin without saying anything. Ann watched his face as he dropped his look away from her. He seemed to be searching for certain words to say, a thought that could break the ice wall forming between them.

"Why are you asking?" she asked.

"Do you know anything about the dead woman he found?"

Ann's face furrowed, and her mood darkened. "Where did you hear about that?"

"Just something I heard about."

"What did you tell him, Michael?"

Mike's head shot up, and his eyes found Ann's fierce stare.

"I didn't tell him anything. I don't know anything."

"This man, Figueroa, is nothing but trouble. He's digging around, and he's eventually going to find the right place. You will not be in that place."

"He's just looking for some perspective. What does that matter?"

"That woman's memory weighed heavily on him for decades. I hope that he found peace when he died. Stirring the thing back up again will only lead to misery. For me, for you, and for the memory of your dad."

"But why? What aren't you telling me? You've never kept anything from me."

"And I'm not keeping anything from you now. I'm warning you that Tim Figueroa is no good. You will steer clear of him."

Ann's anger spat venom with each word. She found herself standing now, her entire body weight leaning onto her hands which were affixed to the table.

"Is there something else I should know?"

Ann heard the emotion that crept into Mike's voice. Her fingers gripped at the plastic tablecloth. Her heart pounded in her ears.

"Your father, if you want it your way, was a very private man. I'm sure he had his secrets. At a certain point, the work stories trailed off and your father became a dark and brooding man. It was gradual and began well after him finding that poor woman."

"Did you ever want to know what those secrets were?"

"No, Michael, I didn't. I accepted whatever he told me and then let it go."

"Do you think he'd ever lie to you?"

Ann's fingers relaxed, she released the weight on her hands and arms. She lowered herself back into her chair. She sighed heavily.

"Why do you think that?" she said.

"He never let me know him. He never showed me anything, never taught me a life lesson. I didn't trust him. Then he died before I ever got the chance to call him out on all that. All I have of him are the stories the other guys tell me. I wonder if any of them are lies."

"He didn't want to burden us. I honestly couldn't think of a worse thing than him knowing that you became a cop."

Mike's eyes softened. His face trembled.

"You were the joy in his life. He wanted so much more for you. But the only thing he could do was try to shield you from whatever demons were inside his head."

"Why wouldn't he want me to be a cop?"

"Because he was afraid that those demons would find you."

Mike nodded to himself. Whatever thought was in his head caused him to stare off again, somewhere past Ann.

"What should I do about Tim Figueroa?"

"Tell him that you're not going to help him. He's going to have to do whatever he wants to do without us."

"It's funny that you asked me if they still talk about him. And I told you that we had a plaque."

"Yeah?"

"That plaque was the only sign of him until I started there. Now I'm his reincarnation."

I was not surprised that Mike called. It took about the amount of time that I expected after my ambush at the bowling alley. I had first contacted him on Friday night, and at about noon on Sunday, he had given me a ring. I was cool in my outward reaction, although my heart skipped in my chest when he said he wanted to meet. I agreed to meet him at the diner before his afternoon shift.

Sunday mornings at any diner in the country are a loud, boisterous affair, but Sunday afternoons are like hospital waiting rooms. I walked in just before two o'clock and asked for a booth in the quietest section. The waitress, a heavyset older woman, smiled sardonically and gestured to the vacant restaurant.

"Your choice, sweetie," she said.

I thanked her with a gentle nod. I wandered into the space, lifting my head high to scope the place out. I found the perfect booth along the back wall. I pointed to where I wanted to sit, and the waitress handed me a menu. I requested a cup of coffee, then I made my way to my hand selected spot and slid inside the booth. The coffee came just as Mike strolled in through the front door.

"He's with me," I told the waitress as she set the cup and saucer of steaming black liquid in front of me.

She smiled and started toward the front. "Back here, young man," she said. She waved toward Mike and gestured her thumb toward where I was sitting.

Mike acknowledged her with an inaudible greeting, moving past the waitress and coming right for me. He was dressed in jeans and a black T-shirt, a discreet bulge in his waistband which to the average onlooker would have been unnoticed, but a billboard if you knew how to look. I tried reading his body language as he approached. His arms swung in a relaxed motion. His gait was unhurried. His face was set like stone, very serious and devoid of specific emotion. Mike reached the booth and stood over me.

"Please, Mike, have a seat. You want something to drink?"

Mike considered the open booth seat. Then, he considered me. He sat and pushed himself along the cushioned seat until he sat across from me. Immediately, his arms crossed high near his shoulders, his chin tucked, and his eyes slipped around me directly to the table.

"You look upset, Mike. What's going on?"

"Mr. Figueroa... " he said.

"Whoa, it's Tim. Remember, you're Mike, and I'm Tim. This is a friendly exchange, and let's keep it that way."

"Okay, Tim. I just don't know what kind of help I can be."

His eyes remained averted. Up close, I could see the tiredness and tension in his face. He looked as though he had aged a decade in the thirty-six hours since I had first met him. I looked over to my friend, the waitress. I held up my coffee and then pointed at Mike. She nodded her understanding. I waited for her to arrive with the caffeinated beverage before I spoke again.

"Don't be so hard on yourself, Mike. I know most of the facts. I'm trying to understand the people. And your dad is the most important and, unfortunately, completely out of reach."

Mike looked up at that statement. I chagrined a little. He took hold of the coffee cup, lifting it toward his face. He sniffed it.

"Not too big on coffee," he said. But he took a sip of the hot liquid anyway. He winced and shook his head, a shock running through his body. Once it passed, he took a larger swallow. He set the cup on the table.

"That's a boy," I said. "It's true, though. The only person with more to say about it is poor old Jane herself."

"Like you said the other night, this happened twenty years before I was born. What do I have to offer?"

"That's true, but you knew Charles Ellis for seventeen years. That's more time than I will ever have. And you were in the same home. Under the same roof."

"That's not true. I was away at school from about fourteen on. And he never said anything. I only heard about this murder the other night when you told me about it. I almost didn't believe it. I didn't want to believe it. If it weren't for my mom sort of confirming it and the four newspaper articles, I wouldn't have believed it."

"I'm sure you know then that I tried to talk to your mother, and she told me to pound salt."

Mike sat up but kept those arms protecting him. "She was vague, but yeah, she mentioned that she knew of you."

"She's a tough woman. The best women are tough like she is. Bet she's a great mom, brought you up right. She doesn't like me, and she probably shouldn't. I'm no good. I'm a tomb raider. Howard Carter at the entrance to King Tut's tomb. But I'm also here to shine the light of truth, expose the secrets, and let the whole world see what lies in the depth of the darkness."

"There was a curse associated with King Tut, wasn't there?" Mike asked. His arms fell slack, crossing near his abdomen.

"Curses are in the eye of the beholder. Let me ask you a question. What did you think of your dad?"

Mike bit his lip. He pulled the coffee cup back up to his face and took another gulp. He returned the cup to the saucer. His eyes flashed with a thought, but some filter or check system slowed the response. He was careful and slow in what he wanted to say.

"He was very serious about his work. He didn't spend a lot of time at home or with me."

"What's a good memory you have of him?"

Now Mike rolled his gaze up to search for an answer. He was no longer hesitating. He simply did not have anything.

"Never mind that," I said. "What comes to your mind when you think of your dad?"

Mike tried to be quick with his answer. "The memorial plaque they have dedicated to him at the station."

I nodded. I had seen it, read it. "He was the cop's cop."

"That's what they say. He wasn't much of a father's father. Have you talked to any of the guys he worked with?"

"I have my methods. Right now, I'm focused on you and your relationship with your father."

Mike's arms grew taught again and rose back to the level of his chest. He began to fiddle around in his chair. He looked down at the coffee cup. The waitress came over, interrupting my next approach in discourse.

"You want anything to eat?" she asked.

Mike looked up at her and shook his head. I picked up the menu but didn't read it. I handed it to her and said, "Grilled cheese and soup. What do you have today?"

"Chicken noodle and clam chowder."

"Chicken noodle, please," I said. "And a warmup for me and my partner."

My waitress friend accepted the menu from my hands. She wandered off with a limp.

"Look, Tim," Mike said. When I moved my attention back to him, he was looking at his watch. "I've got to be in to work at three."

I looked at my own watch, nearly two-thirty. In the distance, I saw the waitress coming over, a plate and bowl in her hands. Mike began to shift himself out of the booth. I chewed the inside of my lip for a split second. I had to do something.

"Listen," I said. I snapped my fingers to draw his attention back to me. "I have deadlines. I run a show, and I need to pay the bills."

The kid looked at me, eyes wide. My tone had changed. He knew it was different. The waitress came up and left food in front of me. Neither Mike or I moved. She glanced between us and left absent-mindedly.

"I've had plenty of conversations about Charlie Ellis. I know what he was like as a cop. Both young and old. I know that he had secrets, and if you and your momma want to hoard them, that's your choice."

I was done being nice. You developed tactics as a journalist and an interviewer, but also you built intolerance to bullshit. And that was what I was smelling here.

"Tim, I don't know what you're looking for."

"This, Mike, this is the last chance you have to exercise any control over the image of your father I put out to the public. Maybe I believe you, and maybe I don't. Your mother knows. You know you could help me."

"I already spoke to her, and she told me to stay away from you."

"Okay, well it seems like you've decided. Millions of listeners around the world will know only what I tell them about Charlie Ellis. The Ellis family will not cooperate."

Mike hung his head, something in him telling him to be ashamed. I held onto my anger and cold indignation. Of course, millions of listeners were a stretch. And what I really had on Charlie was shallow. Hence my need to strong arm and emotionally manipulate this young man. Mike's arms opened fully, and his shoulders sagged. His face turned up with his eyes wide and his face pouting. I really thought that I had him.

"No, Mr. Figueroa, we won't," he said.

6

Sergeant Grant entered the office, a travel mug of coffee in his left hand. He stopped a few steps in so he could drink in some of the piping hot liquid. Once satisfied, he shuffled further into the office and settled into his high back office chair behind his gunboat of a desk. Small piles of manilla folders formed a topographical map along the right side of the desk. Sergeant Grant set the travel mug down after another sip and then glanced at the computer monitor. He pushed the cheater glass up his nose as he focused on the electronic information.

The sound of catcalls down the hall did not register in his ears as he carefully considered the bright glass of the monitor. The voices in the hallway walked closer, and Sergeant Grant peeked at the digital clock on the desk. His left hand rose up to support his chin; the fingers curling up to meet the ends of his mustache. A deep sigh escaped his chest, sputtering beneath the mass of hair above his mouth. The squeak of boots on linoleum told him that the men had finally reached the office. He looked up with only his eyes.

Paul Hunter was the first through the door, followed by Hugh Bell. Sergeant Grant scanned them from head to toe. Each man was properly attired, mostly clean, and early. He ignored them and shifted his focus back to the screen. In the distance, his ears picked up the closing of a door and shuffling steps growing closer. Another stolen look at the digital clock. His left hand retreated from his chin and blindly found the travel mug of coffee. He took a long draw, nearly emptying the contents. Then the quick movement of another uniform passing through the doorway grabbed Sergeant Grant's attention.

"Glad you could join us, Officer Ellis."

The travel mug lowered from Sergeant Grant's face, and he turned in his chair to face the full complement of his shift. Mike stood in line next to Paul. The Sergeant's eyes examined him carefully. Mike appeared neat, certainly presentable. His face was shaved, recently from the burn along his neck and in-grown hair pimples along his chin. Hair still close-cropped. Sergeant Grant thought that Mike looked different, though. He stood up and grabbed his clipboard.

The lineup was conducted. Assignments were delivered. A few bulletins reviewed. Target areas discussed. The three officers stood intently. He dismissed them.

"Oh, and Ellis, get yourself set up and come back in here."

Mike nodded and followed Hugh and Paul out of the office. Sergeant Grant returned to his seat. He finished the remainder of the coffee in the travel mug. On his screen, he moved the mouse cursor around looking to print the document he had been reviewing. The sound of the printer starting up caught his attention. He nodded to himself. Grabbing the mug, Sergeant Grant crossed the office to the pot of coffee on a shelf. Its contents filled the mug about halfway. A knock made him turn around suddenly. Mike stood in the doorway to the office, leaning in slightly. His right hand retreated from where he had knocked at the jamb.

"You wanted to see me?" Mike asked.

Sergeant Grant looked at his coffee. "Yeah, we have to do an evaluation."

He gulped the coffee down in a one long swallow. Then, he moved to the furthest end of the office and grabbed the document from the printer. He shuffled through the sheets of paper as he made his way to his desk. He placed the travel mug on the ring of an old coffee stain.

Finally, he looked at Mike. "Anyone else in the building?"

"I didn't see anyone."

"The day shift guys are gone?"

"Yes, sir. I saw them leave. Hugh and Paul were pulling out when I came back in."

"Alright, let's go down to the break room."

Sergeant Grant pushed Mike down the hallway, past the locker room, and into the break room. It was a humble space. Two vending machines stood along the outside wall. One was for drinks, the other snacks. The inside wall to the right had a countertop with a sink and a basin. A drying rack sat with a few loose dishes and plastic containers in it. There was a small circular table with three mismatched chairs placed haphazardly in the middle of the room.

"Have a seat," Sergeant Grant said.

Mike sat. The Sergeant waited for him to settle before selecting another chair. As he sat, he pulled his chair close to Mike's, piling the sheets of paper between them. Mike looked at the stack, his eyes steady and calm. Sergeant Grant slid the top page off, holding it in his left hand, peering at it through the cheaters.

"I'm tasked to do quarterly reviews of your performance. This one happens to be whether I think you should get off probation."

He looked up over the top of the frame of the glasses directly at Mike. The corners of the Sergeant's mustache lifted. Mike nodded. His face was flat.

"Maybe I'll keep you in suspense," Sergeant Grant said. He placed the sheet of paper down on top of the pile and moved the whole stack to the side. His smile receded. "Truly, you are competent as a police officer. Your attitude is good. Your work ethic is strong. You've progressed nicely and have started to handle many calls on your own."

"Thank you, sir," Mike responded. His face remained flat.

Neither man moved. Mike mirrored the Sergeant, discerning that the conversation was not over that quickly. Grant felt a little uneasy as he sought to choose his words with care.

"I want to talk to you about last night," he said.

"What do you want to talk about?"

"How you feel. Shit, you gotta get this off your chest. You're like a robot."

Mike shifted his head to the side as if he were thinking. His eyes remained fixed on Sergeant Grant, unblinking.

"It's part of the job, Sarge. Sometimes, you save a cat from a tree, and sometimes, you find a dead body."

"Yeah, that's true. But there's something else, isn't there?"

"What do you mean, sir?""Well, your old man was my boss for over twenty years. I knew him as well as anyone. I still remember when you were born. It was the same month he made chief. And you know, he never talked about you. It was like one day you were born, and the next, I was interviewing you for a job. My wife has taught in the school district for thirty years, and when I asked about the kind of student you were, she said she'd never heard of you. Where have you been for twenty-four years?"

Mike watched him closely and said, "I grew up. I went away to high school. My father died. I did some soul searching and decided to become a cop. Pretty straight forward."

The Sergeant's face drooped with disappointment at Mike's response; his frown accented by the fiery red mustache. Mike continued to look back at him blankly.

"Well, maybe you're just like your dad. He was a cop's cop. You think you want to follow in his footsteps?"

Mike thought for a moment. "No, sir, it's not my intention."

Sergeant Grant leaned forward, removing his glasses. "No?"

"I'd really like to do something different. I just don't know what that is yet."

"This is a small department. There's not exactly a lot to do here."

"Might not stay." Mike nodded, leaning into Sergeant Grant. Mike's expression had grown defiant, but the Sergeant stood his ground.

"There are worse things you could be than like your dad."

"Maybe."

"He did a lot of great things for this town. The community is grateful for his service."

"I know they are. I've read the plaque. But, Sarge, I don't want to be him."

"You're wearing his first shield, lad. It's a little bit of a dichotomy between thoughts and actions."

"Well, I seem to have his luck. He found the dead body his first year."

Sergeant Grant sat back, some shock to his face. "You know about that? Not many people do. Unless you were there at the time, no one knows about that."

"It's the best secret in town. Or it was. It's about to be broadcast to the whole world. There's going to be a podcast all about her and my father."

The Sergeant had no response. He sat with a confounded look. Mike began to crack a small smile, but he didn't change his posture.

"Well," Sergeant Grant said, "I guess this is kismet. I have an opportunity to lay out for you. I told you, you handled yourself as well as anyone could last night. And then, you came in today. That takes guts. It's something to be proud of. The state police are taking over the investigation, but they requested a local resource to assist them. Act as sort of a liaison and know where the good coffee spots are, where to get a good deli sandwich. That sort of thing. It could be a great opportunity for you, and now that you're officially off probation, it's being offered to you."

Mike didn't budge. The Sergeant watched him with gentle eyes. The young officer's arms began to fold, high up on his chest, but as they cinched, Mike became aware and untucked his position. Sergeant Grant could tell there were a million thoughts in the kid's head.

"Sarge, is that really appropriate?" Mike asked. His tone was serious.

"Well, we haven't had a detective here in almost a decade. So, you're as prepared as anyone else. None of the rest of these guys wants a task like this. Half of them double tin with the Sheriff or in Windham. And you've got skin in the game."

"It was the same offer my father had forty years ago."

"Well, yeah, it is."

"You said before about the dichotomy of thoughts and actions. Maybe I'm walking the same path as my father, to the same crossroads. But I think I will choose differently."

"I believe you can do this," Sergeant Grant said. He paused for a moment, looking straight into Mike's eyes. "But you should think about it. I'm not putting a gun to your head."

###

The call disconnected, and Chief Bernie Justin guided the phone receiver back to the dock. He was a small man but hard to miss. Hard to miss the way that you were always avoiding him. I had met him a few days earlier when I had first rolled into town. His nasally monotone drilled through my inner ear. He had a sharp intonation to his voice and a razor precise wit that could rip you to pieces. My meeting with him was short, sweet, and to the point. Chief Justin was very cooperative, to a point. He provided me, after the necessary forms were completed, with as many reports from the Overlook murder that still existed. It wasn't his fault that there were very few written records that were maintained for the last forty years. But he provided enough. I asked him about Charlie Ellis, and that was when the floodgates opened.

But that was not where we were in the story. It was seven o'clock in the evening, and Chief Justin sat behind his desk in his white uniform shirt, two stars pinned to each of his collars. His desk sat on a six-inch platform so that despite his demure size, he could look down on his prey as they sat before him. He shuffled through papers on his desk, blue folders marked confidential, invoices for procured items, and a stapled document with a cover page that read: *Police Officer Michael Ellis Probationary Evaluation.* A keen eye remained on the hall and the open doorway. He brought his attention to the stapled mass of paper and thumbed through it unconsciously, not really reading the words, but catching the overall theme.

The faraway sound of a door closing drew his attention, and he saw the distant silhouette form in the hallway approaching the sergeant's office. The figure came closer step by step until finally, Mike's form appeared in the light.

"Officer Ellis," Bernie Justin said. "Please come in. Take a seat. Close the door."

Mike moved into the room, swinging the door behind him, and it slammed closed. Mike shuddered. He sat in the only other chair in the room, which sat on the floor directly in front of the chief. The chair had narrow arms which made sitting in it with a belt full of equipment difficult and very uncomfortable. Mike looked up at the chief as he tried to fit himself into an agreeable position.

Chief Justin looked down at Mike with a degree of admiration. He saw right away the physical features he shared with his father: the fat face and the bright eyes. Mike's hair was more straw colored, making it a lighter shade than Charlie's chestnut brown. He studied Mike, and the kid kept trying to reposition himself in the chair, not keeping his attention on the chief.

"Well, Ellis, you and I haven't really had too many interactions."

"No, sir," Mike said. He stopped squirming in the seat, setting his eyes on Chief Justin's face.

"Well, you know that I worked with your father. I took over when he died."

Mike nodded along, following the chief's animated hand movements. He shifted here and there but had mostly relaxed into the seat well enough. He had a complacent, passive look to him. Chief Justin smiled, showing his teeth.

"It was me and Grant on the list, and bang, one day your old man just didn't wake up. Next thing I know, I'm the chief. It's nice how things work out sometimes."

A pallor dropped over Mike's face. He began moving around again, shifting his hips and twisting his shoulders.

"I thought I owed it to the old man to pick you up. I had a spot. He made this all possible for me, so I thought I'd give you a chance," Chief Justin said. He spun his hands in circles and moved them like a magician performing a sleight of hand. Then he added, "But don't think that we liked each other."

Mike remained awkwardly positioned in his chair. He was silent, and Chief watched his face for some tell. Mike shifted uncomfortably but drew himself closer to the words coming from Chief Justin.

"Truth be told," the Chief said, leaning back into his overstuffed chair. "Your dad hated me with a passion. He thought I was lazy. He thought that I was a politician. I'll give him that. He didn't mince words. You knew where you stood with him. And while everyone else was loved by him and in turn they loved him back, I loathed him."

The Chief noticed Mike's reaction at this point just as he was bringing his domed fingers together beneath his chin. He closed his eyes, intentionally adding to the drama. When he opened them again, Mike was as close to the edge of his seat as possible considering the encumbrances.

"He was such a ball buster that I stopped trying to please him early on. He was the detective when I started, which was sort of like an unofficial position of power. He'd deride my work till I just quit doing any. Then he became a sergeant. All he wanted was numbers, and all he did was find reasons to send reports back. He made me hate this place."

Mike had his mouth open, and an obvious itch in his face like he wanted to say something. As Chief Justin made another purposeful pause, he took the chance.

"Sir, I just wanted to say that I didn't get along with him either. He didn't criticize me though. He just ignored me."

The Chief snorted. "I wish I had that luxury. He became Chief, and I thought that I was going to be insulated. Sergeant Grant was the other sergeant, and back then, I thought he could protect me. Little did I know that I was going to be up next to get promoted. And you know what? That motherfucker promoted me. He stood at the town meeting and told them all what an asset I was. Pinned his old shield on me. The gall."

Mike sat back again as best he could just as Chief Justin rocked forward in his seat and placed both of his hands on the desk.

"Of course, the standards went up once I got my stripes. He'd run me ragged. The bar was at the top rung."

The Chief paused again. He waited now to see if Mike was going to say something. The silence rose up like a fog. Satisfied that there was nothing to be said, the Chief continued.

"Why am I telling you all this? When he passed seven years ago, I thought I'd be rid of Charlie Ellis for good, other than walking by that damn memorial every day. But then your name appeared on our eligible list. And I had an opening. The town supervisor was on the phone to me in a heartbeat, telling me 'Bernie you gotta hire the kid.' And Grant told me how well you interviewed. So, I was stuck with you."

Chief Justin laughed at his own expense.

"But you're doing well, apparently. I just read this," he said. He held up the evaluation Sergeant Grant had submitted. "Your reports are solid, and your numbers are good. Ironically, your old man may have approved. You outshine most of the other guys in this department."

Mike lifted his chin at the positive words and the praise coming from the chief. Bernie Justin knowingly narrowed his eyes at the kid and let out a genial laugh.

"I'm sure you get all the comparisons to your father. And that business last night, so eerily similar. Do you believe in coincidence, Ellis? I don't, usually, but Jesus, it's like some movie reboot. I know you spoke to Sergeant Grant. You signed the evaluation. But did he tell you what we're thinking?"

Mike nodded slowly.

"So, it looks like you're going to get a chance to walk in your old man's shoes. You get to play detective."

"I don't know if I want it, sir," Mike said. His voice was emotionless.

"Of course you do. There've been exactly two honest-to-God murders in this town in the last forty years, and each time, a cop named Ellis finds the damn body. I'm sure you know there's some guy running around town trying to dig up information about the original Overlook case."

"Yes, Chief, I've had a couple run-ins with him."

"And now we have this brand new investigation. What I'm asking you is a request from the town board. Jesus, Ellis, I have nose hairs older than you are. My bootlaces have more time on the job. You're as green as it gets." He took a breath. "But it'll play nice in the papers. Politics always plays, my boy. So, just go down to Sergeant Grant and tell him you're in. You'll get to wear Dockers and a polo for a few weeks. Maybe a nice suit. Do you have a nice suit?"

Mike did not answer. Chief Justin did not expect him to and kept on talking.

"Then the state police will find this asshole, and you'll get your picture in the paper. And that'll put a bow on the whole thing. Then you're back in the bag, running radar and writing tickets. Seems like a win-win to me."

Mike pulled himself from the chair in fits and starts, haphazardly moving all of his equipment to avoid getting caught in the chair's arms. He stood and adjusted his uniform and his belt. He looked at the chief with a sallow, apologetic look.

"No, thank you, sir," he said.

7

As Bradley Salazar came through the first village, his foot came up from the accelerator. He looked tentatively at the Greene Paramedics substation and saw nothing. His cousin, Laura, gave him a sideways glance from the passenger seat. Her face was moist with tears.

"Looking for a friend," he said.

Laura wore a long cotton dress of a shadowy shade of black , accented with pearl colored lace trim. Her hands clutched at a handkerchief, and she stared forward blankly. Bradley reached over to rub her shoulder. He too was dressed in dark clothes, black slacks with a gray button down, collared shirt. He did not have a tie on, but there was one sitting on the dashboard of the truck. A suit jacket hung from the coat hook in the rear of the cab.

The massive Ford pickup kept moving, its speed a little over the prescribed limit, but at this part of the evening, the pedestrian traffic happened to be light. The sun hung like a great basketball in Bradley's rearview mirror as he reached the village line. He gunned the truck forward with the increase in speed limit. His passenger was thrown back in her seat, and she shot an annoyed look in his direction. The distance between the two villages was only seven or eight miles, and Bradley decided he was going to limit the time to a minute or two.

As they reached the second village, Bradley's foot again pulled off the gas. He looked with some guilt into the rearview and saw the emergency lights. He whispered a curse under his breath, which caught Laura's attention. She glanced at her side mirror and made a loud noise in disgust, directing it toward Bradley.

"It'll be alright," he said.

He looked in his side mirror and saw a familiar sight. The young cop, Ellis, he thought, with his oversized vest and ambling approach. But Bradley caught the determined march to his step, which was different from their previous encounter just two days ago. Officer Ellis skipped the passenger side approach and came right to Bradley's window.

"Good afternoon, town police. I observed your truck traveling at seventy-two miles an hour, in excess of the speed limit," Officer Ellis said.

Bradley's driver side window was barely down. The kid was serious, the automatic cadence of his speech was rushed and direct.

"Well, I'm sure sorry, Officer," Bradley said. He let the words drip slowly in a drawl.

"May I see your license and registration?"

"Not sure where that is." Bradley feigned searching his pockets and tapping his upper body.

From the passenger seat Laura said, "It's in your wallet, dingus. Don't play around. Give the officer what he needs. We don't need this shit. We have places to be."

Bradley turned from Mike and gave Laura a mocking look. He leaned left and reached into his right rear pants pocket, coming up with his wallet. He opened it, still looking away from the cop and thumbed through the cards blindly. Bradley retrieved the license. He sneered at Laura and turned back toward Officer Ellis.

"Here you go," Bradley said. He handed the document over, then sat back in his seat. He could see in the fringe of his sight that the cop was looking at it, studying it.

"Bradley Salazar," Ellis said. "Any issues with your license? Any unpaid tickets?""Never gotten one." He then pulled the second card out of his wallet and handed it over.

Officer Ellis looked at this card. "Veronica Salazar," he said with some familiarity in his tone.

"That's my mom, bro. She was an investigator and retired a couple years ago. We've played this game before."

Ellis considered the courtesy card and then excused himself. He returned to his Dodge Charger, stepping backward till he reached the tailgate of the truck, then turning around to get in behind the steering wheel of his car. Bradley could not see what was happening.

"This guy is going to write you a ticket," Laura said. She teased him lethargically.

Bradley looked over at her confidently. Her jest had calmed her tears for the moment. He batted his eyes at her. "There's no way in hell."

"If he does, just take the damn ticket and let's go."

"Fuck that," Bradley said. The longer the cop was in his car, the more his cool boiled off and the uncertainty of the situation made his anger more intense. "I've talked to this new jack before. We have an understanding."

Bradley kept a vigil in his mirror waiting for Officer Ellis to return. After five minutes, he saw activity. Officer Ellis exited the Charger carefully, placing his Stetson on his head. Then he made a beeline for the open driver's side window.

"Mr. Salazar, here is your license and your courtesy card," the cop said. After a momentary pause, he added, "I am sorry, but I did write you a ticket for speed, seventy-two in a fifty-five. You have two weeks to plead guilty or not guilty and return it to the town court. The address is on the ticket." He presented Bradley with a thin computer paper print out.

Bradley's face scrunched up and became a deep red. "This is bull-shit. What's your name, you little asshole?" He felt Laura's hand on his shoulder, but he shrugged her off.

"Officer Ellis, shield two-eleven. We've met before."

"Wait till my mother hears about this. She'll have your fucking badge," Bradley said, a deliberate sneer crawled across his face.

"I ask that you slow down and drive safely. Have a nice day."

There was a finality to the word, and the cop began to back away. Bradley came outside of his body to watch what happened next. It was an automatic response to open the door and lean out on the running board of the truck.

"Hey, asshole, I'm not done with you."

Ellis ignored him, continuing his slow backing steps toward the Charger. He kept a sharp eye to maintain visual observation. Bradley exited the truck and saw the surprise on the cop's face.

"Get back in your vehicle, sir," the cop said. He moved his hand toward his firearm.

"I'm not done with you," Bradley said, punctuating each word. He had nothing in his hands and pointed his right index finger as he began his approach.

"Stop where you are and return to your vehicle," Officer Ellis said a second time.

Bradley disregarded his order and, in his haste, his steps rapidly closed between him and the cop. Officer Ellis quickly reached across his body and pulled his Taser. Bradley was just shy of six feet from the cop and not about to stop. Ellis took a few steps backward in a shuffling motion. Bradley saw the Taser but continued going forward.

"Stop, or you'll be tased."

But it was already too late for Bradley. The next thing he knew he was on the ground. The pain coursing through his muscles was endless. The electric circuit crossed from his upper abdomen to a spot on his right quad, running across his midsection. The five seconds of the initial burst ended.

"Stop resisting, lay out with your hands at your side."

Bradley lay on the ground in a daze. He considered moving, but the recency of what had just happened made him think for an extra second.

"Seven-zero, Taser deployed. Requesting EMS and a supervisor."

The disembodied voice of a dispatcher began chirping, her voice echoing distantly. Something else automatic in Bradley caused him to try to struggle to his knees.

"Stay on the ground."

Bradley did not listen, and he then felt a second shock blast through him, disabling his movement.

"Stay where you are. Put your hands out to the side."

Bradley could now hear sirens in the distance. He decided not to challenge Officer Ellis again. He lay on the ground, extending his arms out to the side. It occurred to him to look up, and he saw feet near the bumper of the truck. The sirens grew closer.

"Stay. Where. You..." Ellis said. His voice trailed and dropped off.

Bradley looked up and saw that Laura had exited the vehicle. From the ground, Bradley could just see her putting her hands up.

"I'm not getting involved. I just want to check on my cousin."

"Stay right there," Office Ellis said. His voice strained, but Bradley could not see him from where he lay.

"You alright, lad?" a voice said.

The sirens had arrived and then stopped suddenly. Bradley could tell there was a crowd of uniforms around him. He remained very still. There were orders barked at him, and with clarity of the two shocks, he complied implicitly. Once he was on his feet again, his hands cuffed behind him with the two Taser barbs still stuck in his body. He looked at Officer Ellis again. All the color had drained from his face and beads of sweat were limping down his cheeks. The cop's eyes were wide and staring, not at Bradley but passed him. Two uniformed officers, one giant of a man and one a little more Bradley's size, held each of his arms as they divided his body to search him. But Ellis' face kept Bradley transfixed.

It's not possible. Bradley read Ellis' lips as he repeated the inaudible phrase again and again.

Bradley followed Officer Ellis' gaze over to the rear of his pickup. His cousin, Laura; a pretty, petite brown skinned woman, was talking to an older cop with stripes on his shoulder and a bright red mustache on his face. The cops with his arms began guiding him toward the collection of patrol cars that he became aware of as he saw them, all their emergency lights ablaze.

"Laura. Laura, tell them to call my mom. Tell them about your sister. Tell them who you are. Laura, tell them what happened."

Paul Hunter sat on the bench in the locker room silently changing into his street clothes. He was alone amongst the lockers, wearing only his jeans. As he pulled his T-shirt on he heard the door to the locker room open and light footsteps moving along the row of lockers opposite him. The tinny sound of a locker opening echoed. Paul slid the white socks on his feet and tied his sneakers. He got up and went around the other side of the lockers.

He saw Mike standing before his locker. Mike's outer carrier for his Kevlar vest sat drooping against the back wall. Mike unholstered his duty weapon and placed it on the top shelf of his locker. He took off his equipment belt, then he pulled his shirt off, dropping it to the floor. He shivered a little. Mike sat down and worked the laces of his boots, removing the black footwear before he stood up and dropped his pants. He kicked them into a pile with his shirt. Fully out of his armor, he slumped down on the bench in the locker room and buried his head in his hands.

"You alright?" Paul asked.

Mike turned his head slowly. He looked at Paul with drowsy, heavy eyes.

"The last few hours have been so long," Mike said. "First with getting that guy checked out by EMS and dealing with him back here."

"What did you charge him with?"

"OGA and resisting. Hugh brought him back for me, but Sarge wanted me to do the process."

"Was he still an asshole?"

"No, his demeanor changed. He wasn't happy, but he went along with everything."

"Wonder what changed him."

"Maybe something happened before I got back. Sergeant Grant was in the booking room when I arrived."

"I'm sure he gave him the old, 'Listen, lad, this is gonna happen' speech."

Mike nodded. "I bet.""Everything else good?"

Mike had not moved, sitting in his undershirt and boxers, staring back at Paul. He slumped with a startled look on his face. Mike heaved a sigh and stood up, turning to face Paul.

"Are you thinking 'what if?'" Paul asked.

Mike shook his head. "No. It's not that."

"When I was in Afghanistan, I used to get that way."

"I feel fine about the use of force. It was the girl in the truck."

"What girl?"

"He had a passenger. I couldn't see her during the stop, but I heard her voice. It was so familiar."

"Someone you know?"

"Well, after he came at me, she got out of the truck. I saw her at the tailgate just as I deployed the Taser. I thought she was a ghost. I was looking at Carolina Velez."

"That's impossible." Yeah, the logical part of my brain said the same thing, but I was in the process of tasing

someone and there she was, screaming at us."

"Then what happened?"

"You guys all showed up. I got wrapped up in talking to ten different people and whoever she was, she disappeared."

"Maybe she was a ghost."

"Salazar just kept yelling for her, calling her Laura."

"Evil twin then?"

There was a buzz from inside Mike's locker. He looked inside and retrieved his cell phone.

"I've been ignoring texts all night," Mike said. "Hugh's calling. Hello?"

"Oh shit, the electrician finally answers," Hugh said through the speaker.

Paul could hear the wistful catcall in Hugh's voice.

"Where'd you run off to?" Paul asked. "You abandoned the kid with this monster."

"Old Sarge put the fear of God in him. Then he told me to beat it. I just clocked out a little early. Had a hot date with a cold brew," Hugh said. He chuckled sloppily. "I've been texting you for four hours, little brother. What took you so long to finish booking that dude? How do you feel, Megavolt?"

"Lucky, I guess."

"Yeah, that guy would've ripped your head off and shit down your neck."

"Just might have. But I'm okay, and he's okay."

"All's well that ends well. Well, I've had a couple and can't drive. You want to roll by the house and have a beer? Might ease those nerves."

Mike thought about it for a second. "No, thanks. I'm gonna head home and relax. The Chief and Sarge both beat me up over this assignment."

"What assignment?" Paul asked.

"That's right. You never come to dinner," Hugh said. "The bosses want Mike to help the troopers investigate the murder. Mike doesn't want to."

"Why?" Paul asked.

"'Cause he's a pussy and worries what Jonesy and Haverthy will think."

"Really?" Paul asked Mike.

Mike shook his head. "Look, I'm already failing at not calling attention to myself. The last thing I need is some special assignment and my picture in the paper."

"So, you're going to turn it down?" Paul asked.

"I did already. Twice."

"Fucking nerd," Hugh said. "Well, if you're not coming over, I'm gonna call someone else to hang out. When you get home, try to rub one out for me."

The call ended. Mike set the phone back in his locker, retrieved his shorts, and slid his legs in.

"If you don't want to see Hugh or have a drink, you're welcome to come sit at my place for a bit. Jessica and the boys wouldn't mind."

Mike retrieved his off-duty weapon, a baby Glock, and slid it into the holster in his shorts. He grabbed his phone and wallet, then slammed the locker shut.

"No thanks, Paul. I appreciate it. But I think I just want to be alone for a little bit."

Paul nodded and moved out of Mike's way. Once Mike left the locker room, Paul returned to his locker and collected his off-duty weapon and yanked a button down shirt over his head. He took stock of his uniform and equipment, adjusting some of its placement before he closed the door to his locker.

When he stepped into the hallway, Paul heard voices coming from the public vestibule. He recognized one of the voices as Mike's, and he walked up the hallway. The corridor was dark, and no one else seemed to be around. As he got closer, he could clearly hear Mike's voice and the mature, heavy voice of a woman.

"Did you know he was my boy?" the female voice said.

"Ma'am, I didn't know who you were."

"Well, you do now, don't you?"

Paul reached the plexiglass window covered with horizontal blinds. He could see into the vestibule, but his view was obstructed. He decided that he could not be seen by any of the three people standing in the tiny space. Mike stood with his back to the window. There were two women in front of him that Paul could only see parts of. One woman was older, her face creased with some wrinkles and wisps of silver darting through her tightly pulled back hair. She was dressed in a black pantsuit with a white blouse. With her heels, she was taller than Mike. The second woman was younger, although Paul could not see her face. She was petite and also dressed in black: a long dress with white trim around the neck and sleeves.

"Mrs. Salazar, I am sorry. I had no idea," Mike said.

"Aunt Roni, Bradley never told him where we were going," the younger woman said.

"I bet you never asked," Veronica said. She spit anger, and Paul saw the stains of mascara on her face.

"I didn't," Mike said. "I've run into him before. He speeds around everywhere, and I thought he needed the ticket."

"He was very professional," the second woman said.

"But now Bradley's been charged, and he missed the entire service. You almost missed the service." The older woman turned toward the younger.

"But I didn't," the younger woman said.

Mike hung his shoulders loose.

"Mrs. Salazar, I know this was the last thing your family needed. And I'm sorry. I was there when Carolina was found," Mike said.

Veronica turned toward Mike again. "You were there?"

Mike nodded. "I was," he cleared his throat. "The first one there, unfortunately. I am very sorry for your loss."

The younger woman let loose her emotion now with muffled sobs and tiny shrieks. Veronica's face moistened with a fresh run of dark mascara. She looked past Mike now. Paul thought that she could see him, but she merely was looking off into an indeterminate distance.

"What's your name, young man?" Veronica asked. She still stared off a thousand miles away.

"Officer Ellis," Mike answered.

"I worked with a man named Ellis once."

"Maybe you mean my father?" Mike asked.

"Mikey?" Veronica said. She wiped her eyes, clearing her vision. She studied his face, and something clicked for her as familiar.

"Yes, Michael Ellis," Mike said.

"Oh my God," Veronica said. She turned toward the younger woman. "Laura, do you know who this is? He's the one Felix was talking about." She turned toward Mike now. "I heard you're going to help with the investigation."

Mike held up his hand and was about to say something when Laura, the younger woman, moved toward Mike, and Paul could see her clearly now. She was nearly identical to Carolina, as Paul remembered her, and he felt something in his chest drop.

"Officer Ellis, will you help find my sister's killer?"

8

When I first met Felix Acosta, I was impressed with his size, especially because he was a New York State Trooper. He stood eyes up to my chest, and those of you that know me, know that I am the most average height as a man can be. Although small in stature, he was solid as a rock. His taught dark brown skin stretched over his barren scalp and wrinkled over the furrow of his brow. Felix had a mean scowl permanently ensconced upon his face, giving the impression that he did not like you. And, truth be told, he probably didn't.

He stood in the parking lot of the Hunter Town Police Department staring as Mike Ellis came into his view. Felix was poured into a tailored three-piece suit of a cerulean sheen. He wore wraparound Ray-Bans that hid his sharp foxlike eyes. Those eyes dissected Mike as the young man ambled toward Felix. Mike was not in uniform, rather he wore a pair of ill-fitting brown khakis and a pacific blue polo shirt with the little alligator over his left breast. He wore his department-issued Glock 22 in a paddle holster with his big police shield carelessly affixed to his belt. Felix looked down at his own hip with the Glock 27 positioned discreetly next to the stop sign-shaped shield. He raised his head again and shook it slowly.

"Should've just worn your uniform," Felix said.

Mike was still out of earshot. Felix didn't say anything else, but he began walking toward Mike. Mike increased his pace, and the two men met at the center of the parking lot. Mike held his hand out. Felix considered it before grabbing hold. Mike's hand slid in strongly but went limp as Felix's grip tightened.

"Investigator Felix Acosta."

"Police Officer Michael Ellis."

Their hands disengaged. Mike's hand swung back to his hip. Felix kept his chest high.

"First day in plain clothes?" Felix asked.

Mike scrutinized himself. He made a serious face as he looked back at Felix.

"I didn't have a lot of notice."

Felix pursed his lips and clucked them. "It's okay. Let's go down to the crime scene."

Mike dumped himself in the passenger seat of Felix's unmarked Charger as Felix removed his suit jacket and put it on a hanger in the rear of the car. They rode in silence from the police department to the Overlook parking area. Police tape still blocked the entrance to the lot and a marked troop car was stationed adjacent to the yellow markings. A female trooper exited the car when she saw the Charger pull up. Felix rolled the window down and identified himself. The trooper allowed them access.

"Acosta," he said. "Adam-Charles-Ocean-Sam-Tom-Adam. And Ellis. Edward-Lincoln-Lincoln-Ida-Sam. He's with the town PD."

The trooper recorded their names in her notebook, looked up, and smiled sincerely. "Thank you," she said. Her face and tone were grim.

Felix pulled the car up next to the marked Troop car. He shut the Charger off and exited the vehicle. He ditched the suit jacket and came around the back of the car to meet Mike at the trunk.

"After you," he said. He motioned for Mike to lead the way.

Felix followed behind Mike as he quietly ascended the trail. Upon reaching the plateau area, Felix took stock of the space. He had been here in the dark two nights before when he got the call out. But he had not been here since crime scene technicians took over. They had set up two pop-up canopies in specific areas of the space.

"That's where the car was," Mike said. He pointed to the nearest canopy. There was no car there now.

"And that's where the body was." Felix pointed toward the further canopy.

Mike did not respond. The body was gone now, too. Felix kept walking toward the canopies, and after a few steps, he realized that Mike was not following him. He glanced over his shoulder.

"Come here and show me something."

Felix observed Mike take a deep breath before taking a step forward. They walked together to the first canopy. An outline of the Ford Focus was painted on the ground in red.

"Take me through it."

Mike explained his observations and detailed his movements. Felix held his hands on his hips and looked around as he listened. He let Mike talk. But he took in every word.

"So, the car was clear. Then I looked up."

Felix let the statement hang out there. Mike did not continue speaking. Felix began to walk around the outline of the vehicle, looking down at the ground. He came around to a position across from Mike before adjusting his gaze back on the kid. Mike's eyes looked past him.

"So, the techs went through the car. Pulled a bunch of prints, most were the victims, but a couple were unknown. We have elimination prints from most of her family and friends. Still doing the comparisons on those," Felix reported. "You didn't touch anything, did you?"

Mike shook his head absentmindedly.

"Good boy. Anything else you noticed about the car?"

"No more than what I already said. It was off. The driver's door was open."

"So, you saw the body next?"

Mike nodded. He explained how his flashlight caught the medal around the victim's neck, alerting him to investigate further.

"Are you up for going over there?" Felix said. His tone was bathed in disdain.

Mike nodded again, slowly. Mike retraced his approach to the body as Felix followed behind. Arriving under the canopy, another painted outline of the body's position lay at their feet. Mike described what he had seen, and Felix proceeded to explore the ground as he had at the first canopy.

"Cause of death was strangulation. The ligature was most likely her chain. It was just thick enough and her throat was just fragile enough. She had a superficial bruise on her head. So, the guy popped her and then choked her. Again, we did prints, collected fibers."

Mike stared at the spot on the ground. Felix watched him casually, measuring Mike's worth. A thought came into his head.

"No, I didn't touch her," Mike said. "That's what you're going to ask now, right?"

Felix was unimpressed. He pursed his lips, clucked, and began walking around the body outline for the second time. Without looking at Mike, he asked, "So what's your opinion?"

"What do you mean?" Mike said.

Felix looked at Mike, seeing that he was looking away from the body outline.

"You were the first guy here. You must have made some conclusion in your own mind."

"I haven't really thought about it."

"This happened a few days ago?"

"Almost three."

"And you haven't thought about it?"

Mike shook his head. Felix rolled his eyes, pursed his lips, and clucked. He motioned for Mike to follow him. They moved away from the canopies toward the Overlook trail, stopping at the trailhead.

"Where does this trail go?" Felix asked.

"Up to the Overlook."

Felix looked up the incline with his fists resting on his hips. He glanced at Mike, who looked back at him.

"The Overlook," Felix said. There was resignation in the words. He turned on the ball of his foot to face Mike directly. "Anything else you want to tell me about that night?"

Mike shook his head.

"You're a local, right?"

"Not exactly, but my family has roots here."

"Ellis? Wasn't there a cop named Ellis here before?"

"My father."

Felix nodded. "Yeah, I met him a few times. How is he?"

"Dead. Almost seven years."

"Sorry. So how are you not a local?"

"I was away for high school and college. I've been gone for ten years."

"Did you know the girl?'

"I had met her a couple times. She was a waitress at the diner and a bartender at the bowling alley."

"What do you know about her?"

Mike took a moment to think. Felix watched him closely, his fox eyes rolling back and forth beneath his Ray-Bans.

"Only that she came up from the city a few years ago with her parents. She dropped out of college."

Felix shook his head, and his face tightened. "Was she hot?"

Mike cocked his head to the left. "What's that have to do with anything?"

"Did you find her attractive? Was she hot?"

"She was good-looking."

"Did you want to fuck her?"

Mike bristled, and the color of his face turned tomato red. He looked away from Felix.

"Come on, bro," Felix said. "This is called victimology. You're a young guy. You got a dick. Right? Did you consider hooking up with her? That's what you kids say now."

The color of Mike's face drained, and a pale sweat came over him. His fat cheeks puffed out a little, and he looked like he was holding back vomit. Felix relaxed his face a little. He gave Mike a long once over. He changed his approach.

"Was she involved with anyone that you know of?"

Mike looked up. This question was more palatable. "No, I never saw her with anyone. Never mentioned anyone either."

"You said something about her family?"

"They own a farm. Not sure where it is. Somewhere in the mountains though."

Felix nodded along, smiling. "That's my next stop. Are you feeling up for it?"

Mike's eyes narrowed to a glare as Felix passed him, heading back toward the car. Felix's smile faded away as he walked, his face setting into sober stoicism.

9

George Hunter puzzled over what he had been observing for the better part of ten minutes. It was the strangest first date he'd ever seen: two young people. One was a terrific-looking young woman with caramel skin, straight dark hair, and dressed smartly casual in slacks, a three-button camisole topped with a jean jacket. The other was an awkward young man in jeans and a T-shirt with a zip-up sweatshirt over top. The young man looked familiar, but George could not place him from this distance. His assessment that it was their first date came down to the body language he gathered from afar.

They were at a worktable in the open public space of the library. This was a place for group study, typically, so conversations were common. She sat upright, her hands clasped before her with the knuckles facing toward the young fella. She was wearing makeup, but not in a way to impress but rather to express. There was a stern look on her face that was softened by her eyes. Eyes that were swollen from what was evidently crying. The boy, on the other hand, leaned toward her obliquely, his arms wide apart to provide a base for his upper body.

His forearm and hands moved like a conductor. His motivation was to provoke, entice, and illicit.

At last, George made the connection in his mind. This was the young man who had come in three days prior to look up newspaper articles. He lifted his head toward his newspaper, folded and banished to the garbage can beneath the counter of the check-out desk. George fished the crinkled newsprint out of the bin. He laid it on the counter, still folded. The picture above the fold was a picture of the young man sitting at the table. It was set beneath a headline that read "Local Police Aid State Investigation." The text of the article framed an inset photo of the poor young lady who had been killed. George made a double-take and saw the near-identical resemblance between the young woman at the table and the murder victim in the paper. His whetted curiosity got the best of him, and he hopped off his swivel stool, shouldering his cardigan off. He crossed the floor, heading over toward the table with the young folks, thinking of some pretense he could invent. As he approached, he could hear their conversation.

"So, after that, we went to interview her parents," Mike said.

"You mean my parents?" the woman said.

"Yeah, that's what I meant. I'm sorry."

"What did they have to say about me?"

"Honestly, you didn't come up."

"You didn't ask them about me?"

"You told me to leave you out of it."

"So, what did they say?"

Mike's eyes wandered to George, who was organizing books on a nearby shelf. George grabbed a small handful of books, inspecting the spines before shuffling a couple titles and replacing them. Something forced him to glance up at Mike, and they made eye contact for a brief second. George broke the connection, keeping himself busy.

"What did you talk about?" the woman asked again. Her tone was more insistent.

Mike refocused his attention. "Really, just her typical daily schedule. When she left, when she came home. The last time they saw her."

"Her meaning Carolina?"

"Yeah, of course, Carolina."

"And what were their answers to those questions?"

"Laura, you do realize the position you're putting me in?" Mike said.

Laura let a beat go between them. "I do."

"What are you trying to avoid?"

"You heard what Aunt Roni said about Acosta. He's looking to hang this on the first person that makes sense."

"How do you 'make sense?' You haven't even been around."

Laura didn't respond. George stole a quick peek over his shoulder. He could see the young woman chewing on the inside of her bottom lip. She had her hands reached out across the table toward Mike now.

"I'm just not ready to dive into this whole thing with some real cop."

Mike recoiled, closing his arms around him and looking away.

"I mean someone who's not on my side. Someone looking to pin the murder on anyone. You agreed to be my advocate. Aunt Roni was a cop. She knows this guy, and she doesn't trust him. She trusts you."

Mike turned his head up at Laura.

"I want to trust you. And it's not forever. I just want to know the direction everything is going before I get interrogated."

"I don't know why I agreed to this," Mike said. He sighed and his posture collapsed.

"Because like Aunt Roni said, this guy Acosta will find the most accessible person to hang this on."

"And the estranged sister who just happens to be in town just before the murder is more than suitable."

She retracted her hand, her face aghast. George moved to the adjacent table, collecting pieces of an incomplete puzzle. He kept his eyes averted until their conversation started up again.

"Acosta knows your family well enough. We may not have talked about you with your parents, but he knew them—so that means he knows about you. It's only a matter of time till he calls you in."

"But Aunt Roni is going to head him off."

"She really doesn't trust this guy?" he said.

"Bad blood," she replied.

George was behind Mike now, his covert eavesdropping becoming less hidden as time wore on. Laura's eyes found him and she stared at him nervously as he hovered.

"What aren't you telling me?" Mike asked.

The question drew Laura's attention away from George, who eagerly wanted to hear the answer.

"Nothing," she said. Her hands went up, palms out, in an innocent gesture.

"How do I know you didn't do it?"

"Because I told you. Listen, Mike, you're doing the right thing. Aunt Roni knows what she's doing."

"I feel like a puppet. I'm the mole in the investigation. And I think Acosta sees right through me."

Mike adjusted himself in his seat before slouching back, draping himself in the chair. George completed his task of collecting puzzle pieces. When he looked over at the couple, Laura was again staring back at him. She and George made momentary eye contact. George broke it off but reestablished it once again. Laura seemed very concerned with the old man spying on their secret rendezvous. Mike, with his back to George, didn't appear to notice Laura's apprehensive eyeline. He kept talking.

"It was hard talking to your parents. They are devastated. And I know you are out here, but I couldn't mention you. I didn't even see a picture of you anywhere in the house. Well, the living room at least. Have you tried talking to them?"

Laura blinked her eyes back to Mike. "It's complicated. Believe me, they don't want to hear from me, especially now that Carolina's gone. They probably blame me for her death even if I had nothing to do with it."

"Why?"

"I told you it's complicated. Don't you start being a cop on me."

"It's hard. And I don't know if it's me being a cop. I used to talk to people a lot, and they'd tell me what was on their minds."

"So what else did you guys do?" Laura said. It was a quick turn of the subject.

George meandered around behind Laura now. The puzzle box was in his hands. He tottered around, moving toward a shelf that contained a stack of similar puzzle boxes. George wondered if he could still hear them.

"We went to the crime scene and walked it. He asked me a bunch of questions. We had lunch. He talked on his phone while pacing around for about an hour in the parking lot. I sat in the car. We went to talk to your parents. Then he dropped me back off at the station."

"And you don't know what the plan is for today?"

"No, he didn't say anything other than that we were doing a one-to-nine."

There was a low buzzing sound that cut into the conversation. Mike reached into the pocket of his sweatshirt to retrieve his cell phone. He showed the screen to Laura, and even from his distant vantage point,

George could see the name *ACOSTA* spelled out on the display. Mike answered the phone.

"Hello? Yeah, I'm in town. No, I'm not going in till one, like you said. You are? Yes, I can be there. What are we doing? No reason, just trying to plan my day. Yes, I have a shirt and tie today. Okay, see you in a few."

Mike ended the call and looked first at George before adjusting his gaze to Laura.

"So?" she asked.

George left his puzzle box on the shelf and hurriedly shuffled closer.

"Apparently, I'm late. He made some sort of appointment to meet a witness, and he's been at the station for like fifteen minutes wondering where I am. Finally thought of picking up the phone, I guess."

"What's the plan?""He didn't say who we're meeting."

Laura made a frustrated noise. "Okay."

"I'll meet up with you later. If that's alright?" His tone had optimism in it.

"Yeah, I'll call you," she said.

Laura got up, and as she turned, she saw George again. He looked away. She said her goodbyes and left the library, going downstairs to use the basement exit. Mike stayed behind, and George felt the kid's eyes on him. He swiveled gingerly to face Mike.

"You've been here before," George said.

"Yeah, you helped me look up some old newspaper articles."

"Now, you're in the paper. It's funny how things turn out."

Mike curled his smile uncomfortably. "Yeah, I guess so."

"Do you remember that they wrote the same thing about your father? When I showed you how to look up about the Overlook? They wrote the same thing about him."

"I must've glossed over it. Read too quickly."

"Or ignored it because you saw his name."

Mike flat-out frowned at the words from George. The buzzing sound came again from Mike's sweatshirt pocket. Mike glanced at it.

"I know you want to go. But you should come back sometime," George said.

Mike looked back up and met the older man's eyes. The buzzing insisted, and Mike excused himself with a gesture of his hand. He answered the phone as he walked away, going toward the main entrance.

"Yeah, give me two minutes," he said as he walked.

George stood firm and watched through the window as Mike left the building, walking to an older model Honda Civic. He was still on the phone. George shook his head before he was startled by someone tapping on his shoulder. He turned in a drastic motion and met Laura's angry, accusing face. She apparently had not used the basement exit.

"You'll give this old heart an attack," he said. He placed both of his hands over his chest, feigning concern.

"Hi, I'm Laura. Laura Velez," she said.

"George. George Hunter." He extended a hand.

Laura ignored the token and said, "I know you were listening to us."

"It's rare," George said, "for such cloak-and-dagger activities to occur in a library. I was curious. And in my defense, you two were awfully indiscreet. Thought maybe you were on a date at first, something romantic, but I said to myself, no one today is going to court in a library. I don't think anyone courted in a library when I was younger, either. But then I saw both of your faces on the front page of my newspaper. Well, not your face. I'm guessing your sister's face. Guess you can take the detective out of the job, but not the job out of the detective."

Laura's face flushed, and her eyes fell.

"I'm not going to say anything to anyone," he said. "You kids can stick to your plan. But I think I just might be able to help you both. You should tell him to come back around sometime."

Laura lifted her eyes. "Can you help?"

George nodded. "I think so. Tell Mike Ellis to come see George Hunter."

10

Felix Acosta pulled into the parking lot of the diner. He slid the column gear shift into Park and looked over at Mike sitting in the passenger seat. Behind the Ray-Bans, Felix glowered impatiently. He had waited for Mike to make himself presentable, changing from old jeans and a T-shirt into a blue dress shirt and a sporty red necktie inlaid with pearl-colored diamond with dark blue slacks ironed with a razor-sharp pleat. Over the outfit, Mike wore a plaid sport jacket, which Felix thought was warm and inviting. Felix smiled genuinely. Mike stared back wide-eyed.

"This is a much better look for you," Felix said.

"Thank you..." Mike said. He let the words trail off.

Felix shut the engine off and grabbed at the handle of the door. Mike looked straight ahead but did not move his body. Felix pulled his hand back. He studied the kid and thought he should say something.

"You said that you used to see the victim here?"

"Yeah, she was a waitress. But this isn't my first time being back here since..."

"Since she died. Okay. Then what's on your mind?"

"Nothing," Mike said. He looked over to Felix now. His whole face was puckered tightly, his eyes fighting to connect with Felix.

"No, really, what is it? You seem nervous?"

"You're being very cagey. Yesterday, you were open about what we were doing. Whatever this is going to be, you've been avoiding telling me."

"Okay, you're right. Haven't been a good partner on this. Well, I set up a meeting with an old colleague of mine. She has some inside noise on the Velez family. She's related. But I need your help. She and I don't get along so well."

"Bad blood," Mike said.

"What?"

"Nothing," Mike said. "What's her name?"

"Veronica Salazar. She retired a few years ago, but we worked together in the backroom in Catskill for a while."

Mike shrugged. Behind the Ray-Bans, Felix's eyes searched the kid a little more. He nodded and opened the door to the Charger. Mike reciprocated this time, opening his door and climbing out into the unseasonably cool air. Felix pulled the rear door free, grabbing the jacket that matched his cream-colored suit as well as a compact leather briefcase. He slammed the door and charged across the parking lot. Mike struggled to keep up with Felix's double time march. They went through the door and were greeted by an older, plain-looking waitress, short and plump.

"We're meeting someone," Felix said.

He took a moment to survey the entire restaurant. It was the height of lunch, and most of the tables were occupied by couples or groups of four. After a while, he identified who he was searching for.

"And there she is."

Felix made his way toward the back part of the diner. He looked askance over his shoulder. Mike was still near the entrance. He seemed paralyzed, hesitating in place as he stared at the woman Felix had found.

"You alright, kid?"

Mike nodded slowly. "It's still weird being here."

"Yeah, sure. She was employed here. We should talk to some of the staff afterward. Just more work. Come on."

Felix waited a moment for Mike to move before continuing. He arrived at the table well ahead of Mike and greeted Veronica. Felix slid into a chair across from her, then made another long look over his shoulder to see where Mike was.

"New kid," Felix said to Veronica.

Mike finally arrived, and Felix made a show of offering introductions. Felix offered the seat next to himself for Mike to sit. The kid balked for a second before pulling the chair out and settling in, making eye contact with Veronica. Felix looked between them.

"Everything alright?" he asked. "I brought you along to be the neutral party."

"Well," Veronica said. "Officer Ellis used force against my son."

"*Your* son," Felix said. "Oh, shit. Did you?"

Mike just nodded, keeping his eyes on Veronica.

"It's all in the past now," she said. Her voice was reassuring. "But just understand that we're not strangers, and I'm not all that friendly."

"Well, that gives us something in common," Felix said.

A different waitress, a younger woman, came over. Felix quickly dismissed her to retrieve coffee. He pulled a yellow legal pad from his briefcase and produced a click pen from a pocket in his vest.

"Now, Roni, when was the last time you spoke to Carolina?"

Veronica thought about the question before she answered. "She was at my home two days before her death. My son, Bradley, and she had been hiking, and she came over for dinner."

"*Your son,*" Felix said, pushing the words. "That's your friend, Mike?" He began to draw the letters in a precise manner, recording both the question and the answer. "He's the only son I have," Veronica said. She was curt.

"Sorry, please continue." Felix finished his recording and looked at Veronica intently.

"She came for dinner. We ate. Bradley gave her a ride back to her car. It was that simple."

"Her car? That's the 2012 Ford Focus?" Felix wrote some more on the page.

"Yeah, I think so."

"Okay. And where was the car? That your son had to give her a ride?"

Veronica was thoughtful again. "Back to whatever trail they were hiking, I guess."

"Where did they hike?" Mike asked.

Both Felix and Veronica swung their focus on him. The waitress arrived with a carafe of coffee for the table along with three cups and saucers. She glanced around, looking to see if anything was needed. Their impermeable silence was answer enough, and she plodded away.

"Devil's Path," Veronica said finally. "Well, at least half of it."

"Which side?" Mike asked.

"Hunter to West Kill."

"Two car drop then?" Mike said.

"What?" Felix said. He leaned into the table, his palms slapping the top.

Mike turned his head and clarified, "They left a car on each side of the trail. So they didn't backtrack."

Felix lounged back with an impressed smile on his face. He caught Veronica's hard stare across the table. It was classic Roni: not liking to be challenged, not liking being unprepared.

"Yeah, I guess. They probably came from West Kill directly back to the house. So Bradley had to bring her back to Hunter, which was closer to her house."

"What did you talk about at dinner?" Felix asked.

Veronica gritted her teeth and changed her focus. "Normal, every-day things. I asked about my brother, her father. Asked how the farm was holding up. She said she was working a couple different jobs. Here at the diner and tending bar. She and my son talked about their hike."

"When was the last time you spoke to your brother?" Felix asked.

"It's been a while," Veronica said.

"Why's that?" Felix began to write again, not taking his eyes off her.

Veronica pinched her whole face into a tight scowl. She aimed her dagger eyes equally between Felix and Mike. Felix's smug smile receded into a straight, serious line. He fought the urge to look over at Mike.

"Some people just aren't in your life the way you or they want to be," Veronica said.

"Okay," Felix said. "When we spoke to your brother and his wife, they said Carolina wasn't seeing anyone. Is that true?"

"As far as I know. She didn't talk to me about any romantic inter-ests."

"You said you saw her two days before her death. How often was she around?"

"Couple times a week. Pretty regularly."

"But she wasn't telling her parents about it?" Felix asked.

"I don't know what she was telling them."

Felix took some time to write on his legal pad. He had filled one page and gingerly flipped it over to continue his notes on the next page. He finished, then set his pen down. Felix poured coffee from the carafe into his cup and cracked two individual half-and-half buckets to add them to the steaming black liquid. Deliberately, he unwrapped the silverware from its napkin and retrieved the spoon so he could stir the mixture of cream and coffee. Once it was to his liking of consistency, he set the spoon down and ingested a gulp.

"Okay," he said. "So, when are you going to let me talk to her sister?"

Veronica's pinched face relaxed. She looked as though she was finally hearing something she was expecting.

"I know she's staying with you. Her family wants nothing to do with her. When did she show up?" Felix asked. He gestured the mug toward Veronica, sloshing the coffee around, drops falling to the table.

Veronica glanced at the spill, then lifting her eyes, she set her face like stone. Felix's smile returned as he watched her struggle. He knew as much as she anticipated the question, she wasn't ready with an answer.

"No, he didn't give up anything, Roni. Jesus, how long have you known me? How long have I known you? The sister turned up out of nowhere just around the time Carolina was killed. Seems a little bit suspicious. I'm trying to give you the benefit of the doubt, Roni. You were a trooper. A trooper and an investigator that I respected."

"You didn't respect anyone, and you still don't. You never will," Veronica said. "And damn right, I know you, Felix. I know how much you love your case closure rate. You're looking for the easiest suspect to sink your teeth into. And why not the estranged sister?"

Felix's smile grew wider. Next to him, he felt Mike tense up.

"Why not, indeed? But you're going out of your way to keep her from me. Again, if you weren't a trooper and a friend, I'd be concerned."

"We're not friends," Veronica said. Her voice was low, almost silent.

Felix lifted his pen again and took some more careful notes. Setting the pen down, he looked over to Mike.

"And you, if you're not going to help me, I don't really need you. You seem to have sided against me."

"I'm not on any side, other than finding Carolina's killer," Mike said. His hands were folded into a tight ball. The muscles in his neck were thick and taut.

"Yet, you actively hinder my investigation."

"Leave him alone, Felix," Veronica said.

Felix turned toward Veronica, giving her a half grin. "I'm just following the same course you did. Drag a local along with me to shield me from the criticism."

"I didn't drag anyone along, I was the one who was pulled in."

"Did you tell Mike who you really are?"

Veronica bit her lip and stole a glance at Mike.

"Go ahead," Felix said.

"I worked with your dad almost twenty years ago. He was still involved in the Overlook murder, and I caught it as a cold case."

"You worked with my father?" Mike asked.

"Yes. He was a sergeant at that point but still had all the information for me when I came around asking questions."

"He just had no answers," Felix said.

"You haven't found anything in the ten years you've had the case, have you?" Veronica said. Her tone was biting.

Mike shifted his eyes to Felix. "What does she mean?"

Felix pursed his lips and clucked. His smug smile lingered, dripping like rabid saliva.

"I've had that Overlook case for a while now. There haven't been any leads in twenty years, let alone the last ten."

"Did you work with my father?"

"No, I didn't see the point. He was the chief, and when I took over, he had been failing at it for thirty years."

"You never spoke to Charlie?" Veronica asked. Her face held genuine surprise.

"He was already long in the tooth. Besides, no one ever thinks about her anymore. Except for this wacko podcast guy."

"Tim Figueroa," Mike said, his voice resigned.

"Yeah, that guy. But anyway, when can I talk to the sister? It's Laura, right? Laura Velez?"

"I will talk to her and have her reach out. She didn't do anything, Felix, so get that out of your head."

"I'm just working victimology, Roni."

Felix lifted his coffee mug and took a long swallow before bringing the empty cup onto the table. He looked at Mike and Veronica.

"I'm done with you, kid." He turned his attention to Veronica. "Can you give him a lift back to the police station? I've got to head back to Catskill."

###

Entering through the public entrance of the police station, Bernie Justin paused to look at the prominently displayed plaque in the vestibule. The dull, reflective bronze, actual bronze, had very simple words embossed in it. *Chief of Police Charles P. Ellis 38 Years of Service 1978-2015 With the Light Always On*. There were two busts of Charlie Ellis flanking the inscription. One was an image from the 1980s based on the hair and the uniform. The second was from the mid-2000s, as Charlie's receded hairline and the stars on his bronzed collar were visible. Bernie pulled a handkerchief from his pocket and shined the cheeks of the bust, then ran his fingers over the words *With the Light Always On*. To the left of the plaque was a green light that was perpetually lit.

"You son of a bitch," the Chief said, his voice low.

He fished the key from his other pocket so that he could access the interior of the police station. As he came in, he heard voices coming from down the hall. Bernie surmised that the sound was coming from the break room. He raised his eyebrows and began to walk down the hallway. He glanced into the sergeant's office as he moved past, seeing no one in the room. The voices started becoming clearer.

"You're going to get burned," said one voice, deep and serious.

"But Hugh, I gave them my word."

"Go along to get along, little brother. This could be a good thing for you. But if you are just going to fuck the guy over, he's gonna drop you."

Mike's voice replied, "He's already done that. It's a game he's playing."

"That might be true, but this Salazar lady, she's playing you too. And so is the sister. Just a hot piece of ass to distract you."

"It's not working. At least not like you think."

Bernie Justin slumped against the wall outside the break room. He had a sinister, mischievous smile spread across his face as he continued to listen.

"You're a sucker no matter what. You gotta play the side that is going to get you ahead and figure out who killed Carolina," Hugh said.

"You guys always want me to stand up for myself, right? 'Mike, you gotta assert yourself' and 'Stop letting them walk all over you.' Well,

I'm not letting Acosta get the better of me. And, so you know, neither is Veronica or Laura."

"Oh, you're the big detective now? You got your method after a day and a half? You've already been kicked to the curb. And that advice is for shitheads like Haverthy and Jones. Acosta can take you somewhere. This bitch Salazar is no good for you."

"Both of those things may be true," Mike said with resignation in his voice. "But I made a promise to Laura. I can't fulfill that if I just sit back and let either Acosta or Veronica run the whole thing."

A door closed behind Bernie, and he whipped around. Sergeant Grant stepped out of the locker room dressed in his uniform. Grant looked in the opposite direction first, down toward the sergeant's office. Bernie thought that he would just turn and go straight down the hall. But, to his disappointment, Grant swiveled his torso around toward the break room and started walking down to him.

"Hey boss," Sergeant Grant said in his normal, blustery tone.

Bernie looked away from the approaching sergeant and scowled. The conversation in the break room stopped. Bernie held in his despondency and cleared his throat before turning toward Grant. He took a few deep breaths and smoothed the light flannel shirt he was wearing.

"Hey, Jimmy," Bernie said. He began walking up the hallway.

Sergeant Grant adjusted his gaze beyond the chief, and Bernie spun around. He saw Hugh Bell's head poke out of the break room, then slowly retreat in. The scowl returned to Bernie Justin's face. Sergeant Grant closed the distance, and the two men stood together.

"What's that?" the Sergeant asked.

Bernie screwed his face up inquisitively. "Oh, I just heard someone talking. Was about to stop in and say hello. That's all."

Sergeant Grant's narrow eyes told Bernie he was skeptical, and when the Sergeant's meaty hand moved automatically to his mustache, the chief realized he wasn't convincing. Bernie tried to maintain his eye contact with Grant, but he could not control the movements up and to the left. He decided to take a different tact.

"Sergeant, do you know why Officer Ellis is here and not out in the field? He's started his new assignment, correct?"

"Yes, sir. I know he started yesterday. I didn't check on him for his schedule today."

"Well, he seems to be here. After your lineup, send him in to see me."

"Certainly. Is everything okay?"

"I don't know. I'll talk to you about it later."

"Yes, sir," Sergeant Grant said. He turned slowly, shoulders first followed by his torso, then hips, and finally legs. His head, oddly, was the last thing to move. Then, the Sergeant began his flight toward his office.

Bernie Justin remained in the hallway. He strained to hear if the conversation between Bell and Ellis had recommenced, but it hadn't. Shaking his head, he began to walk back up the hall to his office. As he passed the sergeant's office, he felt a vibration in his breast pocket. He pulled out the cell phone and made a curious noise as he recognized the number.

"Investigator Acosta, how are you?"

He listened as he got to the door of his office, unlocked it, and entered. He listened some more as he stepped onto the platform and circled behind his desk. He sat and then listened some more.

"I see," he said. But that was all he was able to say.

Felix Acosta was upset. He complained about the lack of cooperation. He thought that the rookie officer assigned to assist was ill-equipped. He claimed that a former colleague was interfering with the investigation, with complicity from the poorly prepared cop. Something about a niece or sister. Then, he said the name Charlie Ellis. At about this time, Bernie cut him off.

"Investigator Acosta, I hear you. I want you to know that my options were limited and again, Officer Ellis was the first one on the scene. But I know the family. If he's anything like his father, he'll be an issue. I understand. But if I pull him out, I don't have another body to spare. I know you could work it without our support, but I'm getting political pressure to keep my department involved. Let me talk with Ellis, and I will set him straight."

There was no immediate response from Felix Acosta on the other end of the line. In uncomfortable silence, Bernie Justin reclined in his chair and swung his feet up on his desk. His face lightened as he heard the words of doubtful acceptance.

"Excellent. You'll have Officer Ellis back tomorrow then. Yes, I will talk with him and set him straight."

Bernie ended the call and placed the cell phone on his desk. He retracted his legs and hopped up. He unbuttoned the button down shirt and removed it as he approached the armoire he kept in the office. He changed into his white uniform shirt and blue slacks and was just completing his transformation when there was a knock at the door.

"Enter," Chief Justin said.

He settled himself behind his desk as the door opened. Officer Mike Ellis came in through the opening. He was dressed in his uniform. The Chief motioned toward the chair. Mike worked himself into the narrow seat.

"So, not going out with Investigator Acosta today?"

Mike turned his head sideways. "He told me not to bother anymore. I thought he would've told you."

"Haven't spoken to him, but I'm sure that by tomorrow you should hear something different. Go ahead and patrol tonight."

"Okay, sir."

"How's it going so far?"

Mike straightened his look before speaking. "We've been working on victimology, trying to understand Carolina."

"That's the girl's name?"

Mike nodded.

"Any suspects?"

"Acosta thinks it may have been her sister."

"Spoken to her yet?"

Mike did not answer right away. He swallowed hard, his eyes averting direct contact with the chief. "Yes, sir, I have."

"You? Only you? Is she a good suspect?"

Mike shook his head.

"Maybe let the experienced detective get a crack at her? If she's not any good, we can move on. I don't want a week to go by without any leads."

Mike nodded. It seemed as though he had no more words to speak.

"Get back with Acosta tomorrow, bring the sister to him, and eliminate her as a suspect."

Mike sat still with a blank stare back up at Chief Justin. The Chief glared back, pushing all his authority through his eyes.

"That's all," Chief Justin concluded. He sat up tall in his chair, rolling his shoulders back. "Tell you what, on second thought, take a little admin time on me tonight. You haven't taken any time since this whole thing happened. Let Sergeant Grant know."

Mike stood and gave a halfhearted salute. "Yes, sir."

He sulked heavily out of the office. The Chief could hear his boots all the way to the far end of the hallway, then the opening and closing of the back door. Bernie retrieved his cell phone off the desk and redialed the last caller.

"Yeah, it's Bernie. Take the kid back tomorrow. Do it as a favor for me. Call it a little vendetta. But I'm sure he'll lead you to the sister."

Bernie listened to the objections—the asserted theory regarding the sister and the hemming and hawing about Mike's obstruction. Then Felix began in about reciprocity for the indulgence.

"You take Ellis back and have a little patience, I am sure we will both make out in the end. I've never steered you wrong before, have I, Felix?"

The quiet on the other side of the phone endured. Chief Justin again assumed his reclined, relaxed position. He yawned a little and glanced at his watch. Finally, the acquiescence slid from Felix Acosta's voice. The matter was settled. "Oh, and I gave the kid the rest of the night off. I don't know what his plans are, but maybe he'll make some now that he's free."

Felix thanked him. The call ended. Bernie Justin smiled with smug satisfaction. Maintaining his tilted-back attitude, he reached his stubby arms out to open the top left hand drawer of his desk. Without looking, his chubby little hands pulled out a file folder. Chief Justin held the faded brown file, reading almost aloud the big block letters labeling the top tab. *OVERLOOK DOE, JANE.* He thumbed through it, absently counting the two dozen or so pages. Then he grabbed his phone again, scrolling through his recent calls till he found the one he wanted. Bernie selected the number, and the call was sent. After just one ring, there was an answer.

"Hi, Tim? This is Chief Bernard Justin calling. Do you have a minute to talk? Yeah, it's about Charlie Ellis. I think I have some information you might want to add."

11

Laura Velez sat in the waiting area of the Rock Mill Restaurant, her left leg vibrating and the thumb on her right hand up to her lips, teeth nibbling away at the cuticle. She glanced around, looking at the patrons as they entered or exited. Laura smiled at the hostess when the older lady looked over at her from her podium. She felt the woman's eyes look her over, silently judging the long red skirt with starched white blouse and red tartan sweater vest. Laura felt confused as she felt the outfit was conservative, complete with the tight bun she had built for her hair and the demurred crucifix she wore around her neck. But still, Laura thought the old woman's eyes were seeing right through her. She pulled the nibbled thumb away from her mouth and crossed her hands on her lap. The front door of the restaurant opened, and Laura looked over expectantly. She was relieved to finally see a familiar face. Her eyes lit up, her spasming left leg subsided. Laura got up in a hurry.

Mike came through the door, dressed in blue slacks and a crisp blue button-down dress shirt. The outfit looked new as Mike moved stiffly in the clothing as he approached her. She smiled with her whole face—her mouth full of teeth, eyes wide and bright, her nostrils flared. Mike blinked and gave her a second look.

"You're glad to see me," he said.

Laura blushed. "Just happy to see a kind face."

"You won't know anyone here. I thought moving towns would give us a chance to talk more openly."

"Yeah, with no one spying," she said.

"What do you mean?"

Laura waved off her comment. "I've been here before, a long time ago."

Mike looked over at the hostess. "I'll get us a table."

Laura waited as Mike arranged the table. She followed as the older lady led them to a corner of the dining room. Mike pulled a chair out for her and helped her to sit. She smiled at him as he came around the table to his own chair.

"Good?" he asked.

She nodded. Her left leg began to quiver again, so she moved her left hand on top of her knee, applying pressure to soothe the vibration. She closed her eyes and whispered to herself. When she opened her eyes again, she saw Mike staring back at her, his head sideways. A waiter came over and asked about drinks. Mike excused himself as he looked at the menu, stealing glances at Laura to see what she was going to have.

"I'll just have Diet Coke, please," she said.

Mike looked over the menu desperately, scanning his choices. Laura watched him quizzically, before glancing up at the waiter with an odd look.

"He'll have the same," she said.

Mike stopped his search, realization in his soft face. He looked at Laura before he also peeked up at the waiter sheepishly. "Yes, the same. Of course."

Alone together, they each finally relaxed.

"So, this is our...third date?" she asked. Her laugh was short and pointed.

Mike looked back at her very seriously. Then he seemed to get the joke and chuckled.

"So, you're back on the case? You sounded dismal earlier this afternoon."

"Yeah, it looked bleak for a few hours. Acosta drew me and your aunt into an ambush. He knew that we met before but didn't let on. And he knows that we're both protecting you. When our meeting ended, he told me I was finished."

"Then what changed so quickly?"

"I don't know. My Chief called me into the office and told me to go back with Acosta tomorrow."

"He pulled some strings?" Laura asked. She watched Mike intently.

"I guess. But I don't know why. None of this makes sense to me."

"Well, it's lucky for us. Stick with him and keep feeding me and Aunt Roni the developments."

The waiter returned with the soft drinks. He inquired about food. Laura took the lead and ordered an appetizer of calamari. Mike breathed a sigh of relief as the waiter took the order, offering to give them a little more time to decide on entrees.

"Let's decide on our meals before that guy comes back," she said.

"Okay. I sometimes have difficulty with decisions. Especially under pressure," he admitted.

They each reviewed the menu, but instantly, Laura announced that she was going to have the chicken parmesan. Mike took a few more long minutes, then decided that the chicken parmesan seemed like a good choice. Laura laughed at him. Mike nodded knowingly. The waiter returned with the appetizer, and they placed their order. The waiter appeared pleased that Mike was prepared as he smiled broadly when he wrote the selections on his pad.

"So, you have no further leads since this morning?" Laura asked.

Mike sipped his diet cola through a straw. He shook his head. "No, we talked to Veronica and then he left. I have no idea what he's been up to."

"Shit," she said. "We don't know what else he's thinking."

"He's rather dead set on you at the moment," Mike said. "That's all he could talk about. He also made it sound like Veronica was holding something back."

"Like what?" Her face sank into concern, eyes darting around the table.

"He didn't say. He also made a connection between your aunt and me. Well, a connection to my father."

Laura's head lifted to listen. She brought both of her hands onto the table.

"You see, there was another murder at the Overlook forty years ago. On top of the mountain, not at the trailhead. My father was the first officer on the scene, and he investigated it for years. It's never been solved."

"Okay," Laura said.

"And your Aunt Veronica worked with him on it for a period. She never mentioned that. She just said she knew my father. Not that she had worked a murder case with him."

"She worked a lot of cases. She used to tell us, Carolina and me, stories when she visited," Laura said. She kept her tone as flat as she could, waiting to see where the conversation as heading.

"And it just so happens that Acosta has the cold case in his workload right now."

"And you are trying to catch my sister's killer. I don't get it."

Laura looked across the table intently. She studied Mike's face as it furrowed with irritation.

Mike said finally, "Acosta is trying to get me to not rust Veronica, I think. He wants me on his side."

"Well, that's not working," Laura said. She added a hopeful inflection.

Mike became very sober as he said, "I think it's time you spoke to Acosta."

The words fell into her sharply, and she winced. "I'm worried about how that will go. Don't you think it's dangerous?"

"I'm not your lawyer. I'm a cop. I'm not supposed to be on your side," he said. He looked away from her now, his eyes cutting to the ground.

She reached across the table, gathering up Mike's hands. "No, no, Mike you're not my enemy. You're my protector."

He glanced back at their intertwined hands. Gently he raised his head and his eyes back to her. "I don't know how long I can protect you from this. Acosta knows you're around. He thinks you've been here for a while. He knows your aunt is running interference for you, playing on her professional courtesy. He also knows that we've been meeting. He is, for some reason, patiently waiting for you to go to him."

"Because he knows if he draws me in, he's got me."

"What does he have on you? Veronica makes him seem like this big, bad spider waiting to catch flies. But what's the web he's going to trap you in?" Laura bit her lip. She withdrew her hands from Mike, the left hand retreating beneath the table to control the jitters in her left leg.

She looked away as Mike leaned in, his hands now reaching across for hers.

"What are you hiding?" he asked. His voice was soft, the question innocent.

Laura could not bring herself to look at Mike. "Nothing," she said. It was a mere whisper.

"You have to trust me," Mike said. His hands touched her right hand now, encapsulating it.

She looked at his hands, not Mike's face. The waiter returned with two plates of chicken parmesan, his presence breaking the tension. With their meals before them, Laura and Mike fell into silence as they began to eat. They each cut the meat deliberately, politely, and with attention to their chewing. After a period of silence, Laura took a new tact.

"Tell me something about yourself," she said. "Trust me."

Mike stopped eating, setting his fork and knife on the plate before wiping his mouth with the cloth napkin.

"What do you want to know?"

"I don't care. Give me something, anything."

"Okay," he said. He thought for a moment. "I went to Catholic school for eight years, graduated, and then started preparing for the seminary."

Laura nodded her head along with the words. "So, you've never been on a date?"

Mike shrugged his shoulders. "I wouldn't say that."

"But how did you end up a cop?"

"Long story. How about you? Tell me something about you."

Laura closed her mouth tightly, her teeth clicking as she did. She set her own utensils down. She threw her eyes askance as she thought of what to say.

"You asked me earlier today about my family. You said there were no pictures of me in the house. That's because my parents have completely disowned me. I am not welcome in their home."

"How did that happen?"

"Now that's a long story. So, we're even."

"Is that what Acosta knows? The long story?" Mike asked. The question was pointed.

Laura felt the quiver in her leg again. "I don't know."

She looked up at Mike, but Mike's eyes were looking past her. He pulled the napkin from his lap. His face began to twist with multiple emotions—hurt and confusion, but not anger. It seemed almost like betrayal. Laura's leg began to jackhammer the floor as Mike stood up. She felt the air change as a shadow dropped over her.

"Ms. Laura Velez?" asked an unfamiliar voice over her shoulder.

She turned and came eye-to-eye with Felix Acosta. He was, as always, dressed sharply. His round, bald head gleamed in the artificial light. Despite his short stature, his presence held a power in just his look. Laura was paralyzed.

"Ms. Velez, I've been trying to contact you. I certainly don't want to make a scene and embarrass you. Please, don't embarrass me."

Laura took a deep breath and considered her options. She looked away from Felix and back at Mike. He had slumped back in his seat, his head in his hands.

"Mr. Acosta, I will go with you," Laura said.

"That's a good girl," Felix said.

Her resigned face looked between Felix and Mike again, suspicion rising in her brain. She tried to remember the phone call Mike had made some two hours earlier. His idea to meet out of town and the safety it provided.

"Good job, Officer Ellis," Felix said as he placed a hand along Laura's arm to lead her away. "Worked out just like you said it would."

Mike's head popped up, and his eyes met somewhere just behind her, probably on Acosta. Laura glared at him, the warmth of anger flowing from her heart to her head and back down. Mike's stare caught hers now.

"I think he told you that you shouldn't trust him," Felix said. "Now, let's get up like we're old friends."

"He can stay here," Laura said. She maintained her eye lock with Mike and did not move.

"That's fine. I have a female investigator in the car. It's not Tia Veronica, I promise you. Officer Ellis can finish dinner. I'm sure he has no problem paying."

Laura finally broke off her scrutinous stare, looking at Felix Acosta. She got up slowly, and Felix allowed her to go ahead of him. She never looked back.

12

Just like that, it was Friday night again. And again, I found myself back in the bowling alley. I was covertly observing Mike Ellis amongst his colleagues. Paul Hunter and Hugh Bell were there as well as Kevin Haverthy and Dennis Jones. The majority wore similar cliché cop T-shirts still, except for Mike. As he picked up his ball, I saw that he wore a greenish-blue T-shirt advertising the band Collective Soul. He took his shot which had a fresh self-assurance behind it. Same results as the previous time, but he had some swagger in his motion.

The group was unexpectedly joined by an older man with a billowy red-haired mustache wearing an obnoxious Hawaiian floral pattern button-down shirt and khaki shorts. This, of course, was Sergeant Jimmy Grant, who I desperately wanted to interview about Charlie Ellis.

"See, now you suck less," Hugh said. He was blustery and intoxicated.

Mike looked back up at the flat-screen monitor with the scoreboard displayed. I could not see the score, but Mike seemed pleased with what he read. He stepped off the approach and moved toward where Paul stood near the pitcher of beer.

"You seem pretty loose," Paul said.

Mike nodded and poured some beer into a cup. "Been a busy the last few days."

"How is it going?" Paul asked.

"Well after a little hiccup and then a complete disaster, it's evened out the last two days."

"Yeah, detective," Kevin said, his voice loud. "How's your big murder investigation going?"

Mike shrunk a little as he directed himself toward Kevin. "I'm just helping out."

"You gonna solve it? Get your picture in the paper?" Dennis asked, sarcasm and snark oozing with each word.

Mike's body recoiled even more. "We hope to." He paused. "We hope to solve the case."

"And then the big articles."

"And interviews."

Paul moved his body between Mike and the other two. "I think you're doing the right thing."

"He's doing better now that he dropped those two bitches like a bad habit," Hugh said. He concentrated very much on the words, and they came out clear, if not a bit stilted.

"What bitches?" Paul asked.

"That Salazar woman and the sister. What's her name?"

"Laura?" Paul asked.

"That's it. They had my little brother all twisted up and couldn't understand what he was doing. Then he did the right thing. Got the little sister to talk and neither one of them has butted in since. Mike can just focus, you know?"

Paul looked at Mike and then Hugh, and then back to Mike, each movement at length. I couldn't see the expression on his face, but the hands on his hips told me that he was displeased.

"I thought you were going to help Laura?" Paul said.

Mike looked up at him with an admonished face. "I was. I am. I mean, I want to. Acosta snaked me good."

"But you rebuilt trust with the state police investigator, that's what's important," Hugh said.

"What have you been doing?" Paul asked.

"Well, since he got a chance to talk to Laura, Acosta seems content with exploring other options. But he won't tell me what he learned. He's just moved on. So, I think that's good. Maybe it helped Laura in the long run—even if she doesn't trust me."

"Learn anything?"

"We've talked to the family twice now. Carolina's parents, that is. Then her co-workers at the diner and some of the people here. No one has a bad thing to say, but no one has anything helpful either. She was just a sweet young girl doing her best."

"And didn't deserve to get killed," Hugh summed up.

"Hey," Kevin said, bumping past Paul. "Whatever happened to that asshole you tased? I heard his mommy came to the station and was gonna kick your ass."

Mike did something that I didn't expect. He straightened his posture, standing as erect as he could, and looked Kevin Haverthy in the eyes. "His mother is a retired state police investigator and Carolina Velez's aunt. That 'asshole' was on his way to his cousin's memorial service when I tased him."

Kevin shut his mouth and looked up at the scoreboard. Hugh made an indiscreet appearance of amazement, and Paul turned away toward me, inadvertently showing me the smile on his face. Sergeant Grant pulled his limbs together and rolled himself out of the chair. Once standing, he approached Mike. Whatever he said was inaudible to my ears, but the Sergeant placed his right hand on the kid's shoulder at the end. He excused himself before crossing the building toward the restroom.

I continued to observe secretly as the final game wound down. Mike kept to himself, occasionally joining in on a joke, but primarily just rolling his shots before retreating to the table just above the lanes. Kevin and Dennis stood vigil at the ball return, their focus directed at Mike, whether he was sitting, bowling, or just standing around waiting for his ball. Intermittently, they catcalled at Hugh as he stumbled down the approach or whistled at Paul when he bent o throw the ball. Even Sergeant Grant, upon his return, was ribbed about his aged bladder and his novel way of throwing a bowling ball. But Mike was offered deference from his tormentors. In fact, after Mike threw his last shot, leaving a ten-pin standing, Kevin and Dennis had already packed up and were ready to leave.

"You had a decent night," Paul said. He worked at removing his bowling shoes.

"I guess Hugh is right. The less you care, the less you suck," Mike said. He whispered loudly and looked sideways toward Hugh as he did.

Hugh shot his head up. "My philosophy is tried and true, young padawan. If only you'd listen to me more."

"Maybe I just want to give you credit," Mike said.

"Told you to take that chance with the murder investigation."

Mike nodded. He sat in his socks looking at both Paul and Hugh.

"How is the guy you're working with?" Paul asked.

"He's intense. I feel like he's always interrogating everyone. Including me."

"What's his name?"

"Felix Acosta."

"Never heard of her," Hugh said. He chuckled although Mike and Paul did not.

"I feel like I've heard that name before," Paul said. "I just can't think of where it was."

Sergeant Grant cleared his throat from where he still sat, behind the group, but in front of me. Mike, Hugh, and Paul each directed their attention to him.

"Felix Acosta is a glory-seeking, stature compensating, little prick," Sergeant Grant said. "I knew him as a trooper. He'd pull anything over. He'd write Mother Theresa a ticket. Little scruples in his discretion. Plus, he'd steal any case he could, trying to make a name for himself. The lazy shits like Haverthy and Jones would gladly turn over everything to him. Can't fault him for ambition though. He was thirsty."

Mike had an expression on his face like he wanted to say and ask so many questions. But something made him hold his tongue. They all waited to see if the Sergeant was going to continue, but Grant had apparently nothing more to say.

"What's the next step?" Paul asked Mike.

"Don't know, really. Acosta makes all the plans. I just try to keep up."

"Keep up with him, little brother," Hugh said. "But don't get caught up like Chief Charlie."

"What do you mean?"

"Bro, you know about the Overlook lady. That shit haunted Chief Charlie his whole career. Took it to his grave. You don't want that. Am I right, Sarge?"

Sergeant Grant again drew their attention. "Yeah, I saw it, lad. Charlie never let that one go. But he just could never figure it out. Nothing to tie things together."

The Sergeant rocked back up to his feet and steadied himself. He shook each man's hand in what looked like a firm grip, then meandered his way toward the exit.

"I don't care what kind of guy this Acosta is, you keep up with him. Learn some shit because he's gotta be one of their best." Hugh had become sober and serious out of nowhere.

Mike tied his shoes, and when he looked up, he saw that Paul and Hugh were already standing, waiting for him. He stood up and collected his belongings. The three men headed to the exit. I made my move then.

"Mike," I called after them.

When he turned, he frowned at me. He glanced at his companions and made a motion for them to go on without him. He doubled back to me.

"Yes, Mr. Figueroa," Mike said. "What can I do for you?"

"Man, I am glad to see you. How's your big case? It's all over the place. So strange, ain't it? So tragic, of course. Breaks my heart as I'm sure it does yours."

"Certainly," Mike said. "What do you want?"

"I don't want anything, Mike. I just wanted to tell you that I've finished the Jane Doe of the Overlook episode, and it's due to drop imminently. I'm sure the attention focused on the town and the Overlook will be mutually beneficial. My podcast will draw extra witnesses out for you, and your investigation will send people to my podcast."

"I'm glad it all works out for you," he said. It was a sardonic statement.

"Works out for us, Mike. Listen, I know you don't like me. You don't trust me. But I could be your best friend if you just give me a chance. Yeah, I recorded my podcast and what's on tape is on tape, but it's not over for you just yet. Keep thinking it over. You still have my card, right?"

He automatically reached for his wallet, as if touching the back pocket would tell him he still possessed the item. "What else can I do for you, Mr. Figueroa?"

"Jesus, call me Tim. I'm talking about friendship, a partnership here. We can still help each other. Did you ever think that maybe these cases are connected somehow? Some way? It burns me up inside. But I don't have any power over that."

I took a long pause, my eyes shifting, trying to catch him thinking, trying to guide his thoughts.

"But maybe you do," I concluded.

"Alright, whatever," he said. "Is that all you want?"

"I want you to know that I'm around."

"Fine. I'll look you up if I need you then," he said.

I nodded. He kept staring at me, trying to discern whether he was down with me or not. He wearily turned away, moving toward the exit.

"Check out the podcast. It's on all the outlets," I said.

13

Veronica poured whiskey from the nearly empty bottle over a single ice cube in the small rock's glass. Her thin, almond-hued hands rattled the cube around in the glass, attempting to cool and dilute every ounce of alcohol. Conscious of the racket she was making, Veronica excused herself to her son, Bradley. Bradley was busy watching baseball on the large television in the oversized living room. She knew she was barely heard over the sounds of the announcers, but she repeated herself anyway.

"I'll be in my office. Please don't disturb me."

Bradley was sprawled out on the leather sofa and raised an arm in acknowledgment. Satisfied, Veronica turned down the long hallway along with the drink. She paused briefly about halfway down and tapped lightly on the door. A quiet voice called her in. Veronica cracked the door open a little and caught sight of Laura laying on the guest bed, above the covers. She moped dejectedly as she had done for the last two days, hanging her head upside down off the bed. An agitated female voice echoed in a low volume from a song playing on Laura's phone. The music was acoustic but hard-edged. She looked both hurt and heartbroken. She informed Laura that she was going to be in her office and was looking for some time to herself. Laura nodded complacently and closed her eyes, letting the music take her someplace else.

Veronica shut the door carefully and continued to the end of the hall. She entered her office, a converted bedroom, and came around the small wooden desk and sat. It was a well-organized and neat work-space. A laptop computer sat centered before the supremely comfort-able captain's chair. Veronica settled herself, the glass of whiskey going onto the slate coaster on the right side of the desk. She woke the laptop from its slumber and opened an internet browser. She typed: *Figure it out with Figgy* into the search bar and allowed the results to return. Finding the link she desired, Veronica clicked the hyperlink and waited for the website to load.

The website—my website—was a sleek design of soft greens and blues with a professional headshot of yours truly at the top. I love that picture of me. I'm in an open-collared shirt, the sepia tone of the photo not hiding the grays in my goatee or the chest hair. There's a slung heavy woolen suit coat over my left shoulder, dangling by the index and middle finger of my left hand. The capper is an Indiana Jones-style hat sitting slightly askew on my head. I can only imagine the face Veronica made in reaction to the image of this handsome devil. I bet she reached over for a taste of the whiskey.

She scrolled down the page, then back up. There were links across the top for the biography page, a merchandise page, and the link she was searching for- the episodes page. After clicking that link, she waited for that page to load, again taking a belt from the whiskey glass. The episodes page had a list of URL links, but at the top was the most recent recording. The one she was seeking: "Jane Doe of the Overlook." She took a deep breath and clicked the episode link. It took a moment, but the embedded audio player started. The episode then took another long half-minute to buffer and begin. Veronica sat back with her rocks glass in hand, closed her eyes, and listened.

"Hey! I said, 'Hey!' Wait, is this thing on? Well, there you are, I'm Timothy Figueroa and this is *Figure It Out With Figgy.*"

The introduction music played—a playful major key rendition of a mysterious and creepy mash-up of television themes that were all thirty years old. I looked far and wide for the music, mind you. Veronica opened her eyes to look at the timeline crawl, shaking her head. After the theme ended, my voice took over again. Every show starts the same. I thank all the listeners and let them know that they are the real heroes for taking their time, etcetera, etcetera. Then I got down to brass tacks.

"Tonight's case was one of the most obscure, most difficult cases that I have yet had in my podcasting career. I will take you to upstate New York, to a small mountain town with a deep, dark secret and a forty-year-old unsolved homicide that no one seems to want answers for."

Veronica rolled her eyes at the drama I was trying to sell in my voice. I call it my conspiracy rasp, because as you reach the word "secret," you naturally lower the tone of your voice and rattle your tonsils. She was not interested in this part of the story but with another swallow of whiskey, she allowed it to press on.

Next up was the exposition dump. It was 1980. Some hikers were out for a winter's hike just after the new year and just so happened to find the body of a young woman dressed only in a nightgown. As advertised, this all occurred at the Overlook. I told the audience how I had been there, walked the trails, and stood at the same Overlook. I was there in the summer, of course, and I explained that somehow, I didn't think I could brave the ice and snow. Back in 1980, two of the four hikers who discovered the body decided to hike out to find a phone. I reminded anyone born in the last twenty-five years—a strong demographic for me actually—that there were no cell phones at the time. When the two hikers reached the bottom of the trail, to their surprise and their indeterminable luck, there was a police car sitting in the parking area. Inside was Patrolman Charles Ellis and the pounding on his window startled him. Little did he know that his whole life was about to change.

It was at this point that Veronica turned the volume up, leaning into the words I was about to use.

"Now Patrolman Ellis was a young, inexperienced, and scared kid on his way to the biggest event to ever occur in the Town of Hunter. He radioed for assistance, left one hiker at his Dodge pickup and followed the second hiker back up to the Overlook. The weather was crisp and clear. A few inches of snow had fallen overnight, and the only tracks were those of the hiking party. Patrolman Ellis reached the crime scene at about 12:30 p.m., finding the remaining two hikers relieved to see the police. They reported that no one else had been through the area. They told Ellis that they had approached the body initially but had not touched her. From Patrolman Ellis' own report, he stated, 'Witness reports body of female propped up in the stone chair. I approached from the east side, following two sets of prints reported to be those of two witnesses left to guard the area. Observed frozen corpse of female, aged seventeen to twenty-five years sitting upright in stone chair. Approximately one inch of snow on her.' Using his notepad and a pencil, Ellis made a crude sketch of the crime scene, marking out footprints and other small disturbances in the snow. The written narrative and the pencil sketch are the only remaining records maintained by the town police.

"At approximately 1:30 p.m., two state troopers and a state forest ranger arrived. Ellis, the rookie, directed them to canvass the trail and the surrounding area for other evidence. He remained with the body. A town detective, the police chief, as well as two state police investigators, arrived at 2:30 p.m. After a short briefing, the state police took control of the crime scene, and the case was turned over to them."

Those were the simple facts. Well-documented, not disputed. They came from written reports and corroborated statements, all things Veronica herself had personally seen and held in her hand. She reached for the whiskey glass, took a small sip, and replaced it on the coaster. She sighed, growing bored with the developments of the podcast so far. But I was patient in this episode, waiting to unveil the twisted underbelly.

Veronica attended to the audio description of the victim's body, comparing it to her memory of the photographs taken by the original investigators and the coroner. Jane Doe, as she became designated after a week of no identification, was a mixed-race African American woman of Hispanic descent between the ages of eighteen and twenty-five. At the time of her discovery, she was dressed only in a light blue nightgown with no undergarments. The autopsy determined that her cause of death was manual strangulation based on bruising around her neck and petechial hemorrhaging in her eyes. She had no defensive wound or other marks made either ante or postmortem. There was recent trauma to her vagina which had begun to heal, but the coroner would not say that she had been sexually assaulted. Her stomach contents were a mix of meat, vegetables, and beer. Toxicology showed that Jane had a blood alcohol content of .07, but no other drugs in her system.

The next part, after the gory details, was always the theories and in the case of Jane Doe of the Overlook diverged into who she was and who killed her. Veronica sat back and took in these myths, some of which she had personally followed up and debunked. There was the serial killer angle. The idea that poor Jane had killed herself, somehow, manually strangling herself. The ever-favorite mob or cartel whack job. I always threw in the aliens bit because you gotta play the hits. As for her identity, no solid theories had ever emerged to provide a name. She was most likely some drifter who ran into the wrong person. Her image, both photographic and artist rendering, were broadcast throughout the country with a total of zero possible identifications. No one who wasn't directly involved in the case attended her funeral at the local cemetery. Some enterprising investigators had the services surveilled and photographed in secret. I saw these images in the official cold case folder that I was able to examine. There are about fifteen people present—all law enforcement or emergency workers except for the town supervisor and a woman identified on a list as "press."

"Jane Doe was interred without a headstone. The costs of the funeral were covered by a donation drive. I stood at the marker of her grave. She lies in an open field surrounded by what I imagine are complete strangers. I can't say how frequently she is visited, if at all. She has been completely forgotten; a legend lost to time."

The last article even mentioning Jane Doe was around the time of the twentieth anniversary of the crime. The local reporter interviewed newly promoted Chief Charles Ellis, who said that the case still haunted him after all those years. He said that he was still seeking answers, even though the investigation had long been out of his hands. Following his initial involvement, Charles Ellis was lent out to the short-lived task force assembled to collect information and interview potential witnesses. He spent eighteen months in a part-time capacity with the state police and rose to the rank of detective for the experience. He remained a local liaison as the case moved from active, to inactive, to the cold case bin, around the time Ellis became a sergeant in 1990. It was around this time that he relinquished his role in the investigation.

However, his former colleagues, supervisors, and subordinates said that he never let the case go. Chief Ellis was known to frequent the Overlook parking area and occasionally the Overlook itself in search of long-lost answers to all the questions he had in his head. Charles Ellis died in 2015, taking some of the last memories of Jane Doe with him.

"And while Jane Doe lies beneath the ground shrouded in mystery, Charlie Ellis was laid to rest as a revered hero. His nearly four-decade career is ensconced in the annals of the police department with busts of the deceased chief and a plaque commemorating his long career. The men who worked for him have nothing but great things to say. But no one has a voice for Jane Doe of the Overlook until now. My hope is that the attention brought to this case can help bring the first leads in forty years. I implore all of my listeners that may have an old family story, a mysterious gap in their family history, or flat-out new information to please contact New York State Police Investigator Felix Acosta." I give the number to the backroom in the Catskill barracks.

Veronica rolled her eyes but did not reach for her drink. She saw that the cube had dissolved completely, removing whatever burn was left in the alcohol. It was a shame because she thought it was over. But I saved the best for last. The conspiratorial rasp crept back into my voice. Something in Veronica's brain made her listen with extra clarity.

"But stay tuned dear listeners because some more recent events have blown things wide open. Not only has there been a new death at the Overlook which is currently being investigated, but I also secured an exclusive interview with a secret source who has inspired my theory brain to cook up a wild theory. So, the next installment will feature my assertion that Charlie Ellis himself was involved in the death of Jane Doe. But till then, my friends, I am Tim Figueroa and this has been *Figure it Out with Figgy*."

Veronica moved forward in her chair at the conclusion of the episode, grabbing the glass and swallowing the last swig of whiskey. The exit music was a verisimilitude of the opening theme, and the embedded player began loading another episode automatically. She clicked the player closed as she set the now empty whiskey glass on the desk. She used the mouse to open her email, finding a dozen new messages in her inbox. She weeded through the spam absentmindedly, whittling the email down to two new messages. The subject line for one said *Overlook case* and the other said *Figueroa*. She recognized both email addresses.

"Motherfucker," she whispered under her breath.

She clicked on the *Overlook case* message from <u>felix.acosta@nysp</u> <u>.ny.gov</u>. It read: *Roni, I know you're pissed, but you knew what I had to do. Just like the old days. You haven't forgotten. Let's get together and smooth this all out. Please. Investigator F. Acosta, NYSP.*

Veronica immediately closed that email, shaking her head and moving the message into the trash. She clicked the second email. It read: *Veronica, we need to talk. Ann.* She stared at the words and focused on the name, and then the email address: <u>charles_ellis_70@y</u> <u>ahoo.com</u>. Whispering another curse, she sat back in her chair slowly. There was a knock at the office door just before it opened.

"What did I say..." she began, an annoyed growl roiling from her chest.

Bradley stood in the doorway with his hands raised. "Whoa, Ma, take it easy on me. I'm just the messenger."

"What?" Veronica said. Her patience was frayed.

"That asshole kid is at the door. You know, the one who locked me up."

14

When she answered the door, despite what Bradley had told her, Veronica was still not expecting to see Mike Ellis. Her frown betrayed her disappointment. She crossed her arms and narrowed her eyes. Mike wore a contrite half smile, his eyes were large, and his hands were folded neatly at his waist. He wore a sweater vest over a white T-shirt and jeans, appearing very unofficial. Veronica crossed her arms and blocked the entryway as if she were concealing his presence.

"You're not very welcome here," she said. "My son wants to beat your ass, and my niece would probably like to slice off an appendage or two."

Mike nodded his head delicately. "I'm aware."

"But here you are anyway. Brave or stupid?"

"You can judge. I have some news if that helps."

Veronica's expression remained discouraging, but her arms uncrossed, falling straight to her sides. She allowed her eyes to soften into curious pebbles, lifting her eyebrows and cocking her head slightly.

"Acosta seems satisfied that Laura is in the clear. Whatever she told him has him pretty pissed off. He's lost some sort of traction, and he's started grasping at straws again."

Veronica nodded satisfactorily. "That is helpful. Are you saying that you're back on our side?"

"I'm not on anyone's side. But I do want to go over a theory that's been in my head. It may be just as crazy as Laura being a suspect."

She did not move or give away her thoughts. She examined Mike some more, trying to see any weakness. He looked back at her with the same innocence he had when the encounter had begun.

"I'm going to catch hell if I invite you in."

But then, Veronica moved aside and allowed her momentum to push the door open as she motioned for Mike to proceed inside her home. She followed him after he crossed the threshold, closing the door behind him. Mike stood in the entryway looking in the living room right where Bradley lay on the couch. Veronica moved around Mike, going further into the house. She turned part of the way across the living room and addressed Mike.

"Come on through the gauntlet."

Bradley caught sight of Mike, and his face soured. He sat up and placed his feet on the floor. Veronica looked between them and continued into the kitchen adjacent to the living room area. She heard no words exchanged, but Mike wound up on her heels a moment later. He glanced back over his shoulder, wide-eyed.

"Crossed the moat with the ferocious crocodile," she said. She laughed at her own joke. "Let's sit down here, and you can explain your theory."

Veronica chose her seat at the kitchen table, taking the view of the living room and the hallway that led down toward the bedrooms. That left only one other chair, one directly across from her. Mike sat, immediately peeking over each shoulder quickly. He settled, established eye contact with Veronica, and let out a shallow breath.

"Something has cropped up too many times now for me to ignore."

"That is?"

"This Jane Doe of the Overlook case. There's this guy with a podcast who has been coming around me and my mom asking questions. Then you come around to tell me that you used to work with my father. And I learn that Acosta has the case at the same time I find out that you worked on it with my father. Plus, Carolina was killed at the Overlook trailhead."

"Where are you going with this?"

"I think maybe the two cases are linked."

Veronica could not be sure how her face was set as the words came out. She was sure it was dumbfounded, but she hoped it was pleasantly skeptical. But she listened anyway, exuding whatever body language would beckon more information.

"I don't know how, or why, or most importantly who. But with the attention that's being shown now, it may be the right time to dive into the cold case in order to keep Carolina's case hot."

The kid was trying to sell her the idea, this theory. She shook her head finally.

"If Charlie Ellis couldn't make heads or tails of that case after thirty-five years, how do you expect to? Then to tie your non-existent evidence to Carolina and hope it draws someone out? It's the dumbest thing I've heard in a long time."

Mike's face remained resolute. Her words had no effect on his demeanor. In her limited exposure to Mike, she had never seen him so confident.

"What did Felix say?" she asked.

"I haven't told him. But I'm sure he'd agree with you."

"That's for sure. He'd also be worried that you were showing him up if you found a lead in the Jane Doe case. He's had that since before I retired four years ago. No headway."

"Isn't that a reason to help me then?"

Veronica now smiled. He had found something to latch onto. It was cute. At about that time, Laura crept up the hallway toward them. Veronica's face dropped as she awaited what would happen next.

"What the fuck are you doing here?" Laura said. Her voice seethed and spit anger.

Mike closed his eyes. He didn't move. His stillness was as if he were playing opossum. Veronica watched closely.

"Roni, why is he here?"

"He's come, hat in hand. He even has a new plan."

Laura moved across the kitchen, her approach widening so that she could fully see Mike and so that Mike could see her fully. Mike opened his eyes but kept his focus on Veronica.

"What do you want?" Laura said.

She moved totally into his sight line now. He finally looked up at her.

"What were you hiding from me?" he asked.

It was a counterpunch which made Veronica grimace. Laura's whole body exploded in emotion. Her arms swung wildly, her back arched as she was gathering some strength for her voice. Her face and neck reddened.

"None of your God damn business," Laura said. It was a growl, guttural and grotesque in its understatement.

"Seems to me whatever you kept from me didn't matter a whole lot. Acosta has lowered your priority. You deceived me for nothing."

Laura's rage smoldered in her tight, terse lips and her dagger-like eyes. "What do you mean?"

"Acosta is just as good at keeping a secret as you are. What are you hiding?"

Laura seemed suddenly disarmed. Veronica glanced between Laura and Mike. Then she noticed Bradley standing at the living room doorway, his large frame hovering above them all.

"She said it's none of your fucking business," Bradley said.

Mike turned in his chair to look at Bradley, the movement sharp and desperate. Veronica considered her next move.

"Bradley, we're good in here," she said. "Please let us talk."

She watched her son carefully, her eyes insistent. He shook his head, eyes tight on Mike. Then, with lethargy, he went back out of the room.

Veronica turned her attention toward Laura. "And you should come sit down. Despite the bullshit between you two, Mike still has the best intentions in finding out who killed Carolina. So, hold your nose like I have to with Felix."

Laura's body deflated, and she quietly came toward the table. There was no other chair, so Mike got up and offered his seat to her.

"Please," he said. "Hear me out."

Laura reluctantly accepted the gesture by sitting. She leaned forward, propping her head on her hands.

"All ears," she said.

Mike recounted his theory. Laura seemed unimpressed. Veronica watched helplessly as Mike then tried to reframe his thought process. Both women were silent, and Veronica could see in Laura's face that she independently derided the idea. Mike looked at the table, concentrating on whatever his next words would be.

"Without getting too preachy," Mike said, "do you ever see the way God puts someone in a

place to do something specific?

"You're on a mission from God now?" Laura said.

"I didn't say that. I said that God places people in situations with a purpose. It is an amazing coincidence that the parallels exist between my father and me. I think it's God telling me that it's all connected."

"Does God send emails?" Laura said. "Or texts? Can you show me what God really wants here?"

Mike went silent. His last-ditch effort had floundered. Veronica, still skeptical, felt like she needed to jump in. But she couldn't determine which side she wanted to come down on.

"There is the redeeming quality of getting Felix's goat," she said. "But I don't know if there's enough to even grab on to."

"Yeah, how do you even start tying it all together?" Laura asked. Her patience was eroded, and her attention on Mike waned. Then, without any preamble, she mumbled, "What are you going to do, dig up the old body?"

Mike looked at Laura first, then at Veronica.

"Exhume the body of Jane Doe?" Veronica asked. "And do what? DNA testing?"

Her tone sounded like it was the worst idea she'd ever heard, but there was something also clicking in her head.

"How do we do that?" Mike asked.

"Get a shovel?" Laura said.

Veronica racked her brain. She had an idea.

"You'd need an order from a judge."

"You want me to call Judge Judy?" Laura said. She didn't seem to understand that her suggestion was resonating.

"No," Veronica said. She waved Laura off dismissively. "What we need first is an attorney to write a motion. Specifically, the district attorney. But most directly, an assistant district attorney."

Veronica looked at Mike intently now. She felt herself getting behind the idea. Maybe she didn't believe in his theory, but it was out of the box. Maybe something that Charlie Ellis would've done. She didn't say that though.

"I have an old contact, an ADA that I used to work with. I forget who owes who the favor, but I'm sure I can try to cash something in. Let me make a few calls tomorrow," Veronica said.

"Are we going to do this behind Acosta's back?" Mike asked.

"He'd squash it because it wasn't his idea," Veronica said. She made sure she looked very serious.

"I don't know, Aunt Roni. Can we trust him?" Laura asked.

Mike drew his face tight and locked his eyes with Laura. "I didn't set you up."

"That's not how it played out. Felix told me it was your idea."

Mike shook his head, his expression becoming very contrite. "I'm sorry that you believe that. I had no ill intent."

Laura's face struggled to maintain its anger. She looked at Veronica.

"Felix isn't known for his upstanding principles, my dear. I guess we'll just have to extend a little faith in Mike." She moved her attention from Laura to Mike, and then back again.

"This still seems far-fetched," Laura said.

Mike knelt and looked at her with all the humility he had shown Veronica at the front door. He fixed his eyes on hers.

"I'm sorry about everything that happened the other night. I just wanted to get to know you."

Laura maintained eye contact, but her face hardened.

"You better find something," she said.

15

His full name was Roderick Edward Bell, III but he simply went by Roscoe. He stood, looking out the bow window of his eat-in kitchen. His long, lanky frame was drawn like a stick figure into a blue Hanes pocket T-shirt and what he would call dungarees. A pack of Marlboro reds poked out of the pocket, and a lit cigarette smoldered in his left hand between his index and middle fingers. Roscoe chewed the last bit of smoke in his mouth watching as his son's seafoam blue Chevy C-10 pickup backed into a place off the driveway. He rubbed his cratered, stubbled chin.

"What the fuck is he doing here?" he said aloud.

There was no one else in the house to hear him, and having met the man on multiple occasions, he probably didn't even hear himself. Roscoe's sights were set not on his son, Hugh, but on his son's companion, the plump and awkward boy, Mike Ellis. The kid exited the passenger side of the C-10 and came around to meet Hugh at the driver's door. They were speaking, and from their body language, one of them did not want to be here.

Hugh stood behind the door, his head and shoulders above the frame, listening to Mike talk. Hugh appeared to be using the door as a shield, refusing to leave its sanctuary. Mike was already moving toward the house, his words and hand motions beckoning. Hugh was able to express his thoughts, but Mike was undeterred. Roscoe focused on his son, took a drag on the cigarette, and narrowed his good eye, the one of emerald green as the nicotine vapor drained from his nostrils. The dead eye, cloudy and gray, stared out interminably.

Hugh finally gave ground, coming from around the door but not yet shutting it. Mike retreated a few steps with more silent words, his posture curling into a plea. Roscoe observed his son close his door, push it shut without a sound, and walk toward the house with his head shaking.

Roscoe crushed his cigarette into the ashtray on the kitchen table and moved the collection of cigarette butts onto a counter. He started the coffee maker that he had pre-loaded the previous night. Roscoe shuffled his long body out into the hallway of the split-level home so that he could see the stairs that switched back up from the garage entrance. He faintly heard the door open, and a voice call out.

"Pop?" Hugh said.

"Yeah," Roscoe said. He could always pick up his son's baritone.

Hugh lumbered up the stairs, his hulking big-boned body moving with reluctance. At the landing by the main door to the house, his eyes found his father. Roscoe scrunched his face up inquisitively. Hugh made a wide-eyed stare and shook his head.

"Hiya, Pop," Hugh said. "Sorry to barge in on you on a Saturday."

"You know," Roscoe said with a tight laugh. "I had plans all day. You just happened to catch me."

The smile on Hugh's face was genuine, and Roscoe could feel the creeping and knowing smile spread on his own face. Mike Ellis crested the steps, forcing Hugh to make his way up the turn on the flight.

"I think you remember Mike," Hugh said. "He's Chief Charlie's son. You've met him before."

"I'm sure."

Hugh got to the main landing of the house. He gave his dad a hug. It was a gentle gesture considering the body size difference between the older and younger Bell. Mike was close behind and offered his hand toward Roscoe.

"Good morning, Mr. Bell," the kid said.

Roscoe took the hand and gave it a squeeze, using the bony strength to make an impression upon the younger man. Roscoe found that the kid met the force equally, presenting a confident handshake.

"Come in here. Coffee's brewing, so you'll have to give it a few minutes."

Roscoe led the other two men into the kitchen. He offered them the two seats positioned at the kitchen table. Hugh chose the corner seat with the most tactical view. Mike sat in the chair across from Hugh. Roscoe yanked a third chair from a corner on the near wall, positioning it facing out the bow window, sandwiched between his son and his son's friend.

"An interrogation then?" Roscoe said. He was bemused and chuckled to himself. He tapped a unmetered beat on the homemade wooden table.

"No, not an interrogation, Mr. Bell. I just really need your help," Mike said.

Roscoe was pleased with the pace of Mike's words. His tone was calm, almost soothing; an invitation, not a demand. Still, it was a little hard to hear, so Roscoe turned his focus toward the young man. The good eye bore into Mike, establishing direct contact, while the dead eye sat unfocused and sullen. Mike's double take betrayed his ignorance of Roscoe's particular attribute, but he recovered his composure quickly.

"Help? How can a broken-down old feller like me help the detective?"

"Pop, he's not a detective," Hugh said.

Roscoe swung his attention toward the other side of the table. "Not what I read. He's investigating a murder. That's a detective."

"I'm assisting the investigation, Mr. Bell."

"Oh hell, call me Roscoe. Mr. Bell was my father," Roscoe said. He moved his head back to Mike in a series of nods, his sentence finishing as he completed the transition.

Hugh snorted behind him. Mike's face dropped as he looked past Roscoe.

"Roscoe," Mike said. "I am trying to understand more about the Jane Doe that my father found on the Overlook."

"He didn't find her. Those hikers did. Just so happened that Charlie was at the trailhead when two of them hiked out. It was a coincidence."

Roscoe enunciated the last word deliberately, then chuckled again. The coffee maker announced its readiness with a series of beeps. Roscoe moved to get up, sliding the chair across the tattered linoleum floor.

"I'll get it, Pop," Hugh said. He put his substantial hand on Roscoe's sharp shoulder bone. The old man patted it and abandoned his movement.

"Roscoe, you were there. You're one of the last people that I can talk to about this. Can you tell me what happened? Firsthand?"

"Well, I spoke to the Figueroa fella. He had a lot of the same questions."

"Tell me what you told him."

"I'll tell you a little more. That weasel had some ulterior intentions."

"Okay, sure."

"So, your father, Charlie, was at the trailhead doing God knows what. It was a cold motherfucking day, I remember, and there he sat in his truck. These hikers rapped on the window. Charlie told me it scared the shit out of him. They told him the news that would change his whole career. There was a body up on the Overlook. I was working that morning too. Charlie radioed what he was told and said he was going up to check it out. I, of course, started toward the trailhead. The same one you're familiar with, I expect. I was the detective back then, but we also worked the road. So I rolled out there and found no one at the trailhead. I decided to close the area while I waited for more news."

Hugh returned with a coffee for Roscoe and for himself. He set the mug in front of his father, using the porcelain cup to push the ashtray away from him.

"What? He doesn't take caffeine?" Roscoe said, motioning to the two cups.

"It'll keep him up at night," Hugh said. "And stunt his growth."

Roscoe snorted. He took a pull from the mug and as he set it back on the table, he instinctively reached for the cigarette pack with one hand as the other reached for the Cinzano labeled ashtray. His good eye, however made contact with Hugh and he made a choice to forgo the nicotine.

"What happened later?" Mike asked. He leaned in, forcing Roscoe's interest back to the conversation at hand.

Roscoe picked the coffee up again and before taking a drink he said, "Well, everyone showed up and the day went on. Troopers, park rangers, firemen, the whole kit and kaboodle. I took the hike up once another uniform from the town showed up. I got to the crime scene, and Charlie looked like he'd seen a goddamn ghost. I didn't tell that Figgy guy this, but Charlie was not alright. I figured it was because it was his first body, so jitters from that. And it was sad. The girl was so young and very pretty. Dead, unfortunately, but in life, she would've been a real sweet-looking young lady. So, we did what we do—interviewed the hikers, protected what evidence was there, which there wasn't much."

"What was there?"

Roscoe took a gulp of the coffee, its scalding temperature not effecting him. "Footprints, but hard to tell which was the most recent. Drag marks that led to the body, something smooth, probably a sled. We took a lot of pictures. After a while, we bagged her up and took her away."

"In Figueroa's podcast, he said it had snowed," Mike said.

"Not that much. The movement was still obvious, but some of the detail was covered over."

"What happened next?"

"Nothing. The state police took over. They did their testing. No prints, a few fibers, but nothing remarkable. Tried to ID her, but they couldn't find anything. No missing persons. Nothing on her prints. It was amazing to me that no one was looking for her. More amazing still that no one in town knew her at all. She had a face that stuck with you. Certainly haunted Charlie."

"How?" Mike asked, his voice becoming insistent.

"You didn't really know your dad that well, did you?" Roscoe said. His face became gloomy. He took a long drink from the coffee mug, then absentmindedly slid the cigarette pack from his pocket. Looking down, he selected a sleeve of tobacco with his lips, finally pulling his face back up. His left hand already had fire on his lighter. The smoke curled above him as he waited for Mike's response.

"No," Mike said, the word was tentative.

"Charlie never let go of that face. Her ghost stuck with him from that day till his last."

"But why?" Mike pulled back all of his previous intensity. He asked the question in a flat, brooding tone.

"He never told me. Probably never told anyone. Charlie was a private man. Hell of a cop, though. He took whatever energy he got from the Overlook girl and poured it into every day on patrol, every day once he was the detective, and every day when he became a boss."

"Why did he get assigned to the investigation and you didn't?"

Roscoe chuckled through a drag of smoke. "Bothered me back then too. I was a decent detective, but Charlie got assigned. Heard that he made a speech to the boss that he needed to be involved. Might have pulled some strings too."

"What strings?"

"Some people always have strings. That was your dad. He had some friends in high places."

Mike shook his head. He looked over at Hugh sitting tight-lipped, politely listening.

"What are your thoughts about Jane Doe?" Mike asked.

Roscoe considered the question for a moment, staring at the ember of his cigarette. He made a curious sound to broadcast that he was mulling it over.

"Well, I think she was an unfortunate drifter. Last vestige of some hippie culture passing through. Someone in town probably had a run-in with her. It ended poorly, and that feller dumped her far away from where he could be tied to her."

"You think it was someone from here?" Mike said.

"Seems a little much to climb a mountain to get rid of a body," Hugh said.

Roscoe cocked his head toward his son, pulling smoke again from the cigarette. "You'd think so. But I'm probably wrong. We thought maybe a serial killer and tried to connect it to any other bodies in the entire northeast. No dice there."

"Why no news sources on her?" Mike asked.

"It was a little hubbub when it first happened, but interest died off quickly. Really there was no one to keep it going. Charlie stuck with it, and he worked with some state police investigators, but even before he started moving up, she'd already been tucked away in the freezer."

"Until now," Mike said.

"That's right. This Figgy feller comes around asking questions. Another girl dies. You come around asking questions. I bet Charlie would be intrigued, to say the least."

Roscoe finished off his coffee and then his cigarette. He stubbed the butt into the ashtray, looking sideways again at Hugh. His son took the cue, getting up to give Roscoe a refill on coffee.

"What's your thought on Carolina Velez?" Mike asked.

"Don't really know enough about it. Hispanic girl? Maybe drug dealers? Could again just be some asshole who got too handsy."

"And was less inclined to climb a mountain?" Hugh asked. He presented the fresh, hot coffee-filled mug.

Roscoe murmured some ascent to the question but did not verbalize his thought. He took a reckless sip of the steaming liquid, finding it an agreeable temperature and taking a deep slug.

"I have a theory," Mike said.

"Yeah, that's the issue," Hugh said. He had settled back in his seat, leaning into the conversation.

"What's your theory?" Roscoe asked.

"Carolina Velez and Jane Doe are linked."

Roscoe made a grunt, mixed with curiosity and surprise. "How do you prove that?"

"Here we go," Hugh said.

Roscoe held up a stiff hand.

"DNA. I want to exhume Jane Doe."

"What evidence do you have to back up your theory?"

"Nothing. It's based on nothing," Hugh said.

"What are you so worried about, Hugh?" Roscoe asked.

"I'm looking out for the kid, Pop. He has a great chance to get ahead in the job, and so far, he's done everything to fuck it up. He protects suspects and comes up with dumbass theories. Chief Bernie is probably going to pull him off the case—if this Acosta guy doesn't kick him off first."

"I'm guessing the state police are not on the same page?" Roscoe asked. His attention had switched to Mike.

"They don't know about it at all," Mike said. He lowered his gaze.

"That's a plus," Hugh said.

"And you want me to drop some sort of bombshell that I've been holding onto for forty years?" Roscoe asked. He set the mug down, his hand again going for the cigarette pack in his pocket. Hugh's meaty hand stopped Roscoe this time. The dead eye glared out emotionless, but the old man retracted his skeletal arm.

Mike continued as if this was not playing out. "I just want some fresh perspective on Jane Doe. See if there was something to grab onto. You knew my father."

Roscoe collected himself and refocused the good eye on the younger man. "Maybe there's someone else you should be talking to then?"

Mike looked back at Roscoe quizzically, screwing up into a tight grimace

"If you want to know about your father, you should talk to Ann. Your mother knew him better than anyone."

"I'm interested in Jane Doe, not him," Mike said.

"No one knew her better than him."

"I've tried talking to my mom. She won't give me anything."

"Try again," Roscoe said.

16

Ann sat alone in her kitchen, a cup of tea in her hand, mindlessly staring out into the nondescript noon. Balled-up tissues lay in a pile near her right elbow and the box they had started from sat just beyond, well within reach. The tea was no longer steaming as Ann looked down into the cup. She tried to remember how long ago she had made it. She took a sip, feeling the icy sting against her palette. She set the cup down. That was when she heard the front door close and footsteps coming toward the kitchen.

"Ma?" Mike's voice said.

She fumbled to collect the tissues and brush away any moisture from her face, clearing her throat as she stood. Ann heard Mike enter the kitchen behind her. She crossed the room to the garbage can. She deposited the tissues and turned to face him.

"Hi, Michael," she said. "How are you?"

"What are you doing?"

"Just having some tea." She smiled forcefully.

Mike's face offered some incredulity, his eyes narrowing into small slits, his lips compressed. He looked at the table to see the box of tissues and the teacup, nearly at the top of the rim. Set out just beyond her on the table was a pile of newspaper clippings. Mike did not investigate further. He just looked at Ann, his boyish face straining.

"I haven't been totally honest with you lately," he said.

"What do you mean?"

"I'm not working patrol right now. I'm also helping with a murder."

"A murder? Jesus."

Mike's eyebrows lowered and his head cocked to the side. "You don't really seem surprised."

Ann now washed away her apprehension. "I read the paper, Michael. I saw your picture."

"You let me lie to you?"

"You lied to me. I didn't let you do anything. I just didn't question you."

"What else do you know?"

"My burdens are mine alone."

Ann crossed back to the table to pick up her teacup. She retreated to the sink and emptied its contents. She turned to look back at Mike, who remained planted at the threshold of the kitchen.

"Mom, can you tell me about my father? Can you tell me about my father and Jane Doe of the Overlook?"

Ann felt the fear rise through her stomach, churning into some sort of rage before spilling out of her mouth. "I told you to leave that all alone."

Mike was shaken by her words and the way Ann said them. He backed up a step, shuddering. He did not say anything.

"I watched that tear your dad apart for more than thirty years. When we met, it was an interesting tidbit. He was brooding and serious. But it was cancer that sat like a dormant lump between us."

"I thought you were already together. You always said that he had you before he had the job."

"Wishful thinking."

"Maybe I've been coming at this all wrong. I'm making too many assumptions."

Ann pulled her shoulders down and crossed her arms. "I don't want to do this."

"Mom, please?"

Ann shook her whole body in the negative. "I can't do this."

"I think this new murder is tied to the old one. And Dad is the key."

Ann glanced up, staring back across the room. "You called him Dad."

"My father. Whatever. I need to understand him."

"You've always made assumptions about him. You turned him into the monster of your childhood."

"He was never there for me. In fact, he sent me away."

"He wanted to protect you."

"I remember it vividly. He wanted me far away from him."

"He didn't want you to get hurt. He was protecting you."

"From what?"

"From what was eating away at him."

"What was eating away at him?"

"I don't know."

"You have no idea what it was? What could it have been?"

"No, of course not."

Mike stopped himself mid-sentence. Their voices had been rising in volume and intensity.

"Don't give me nothing. You saw through my deception. You had to have seen through his."

"Maybe at first, but he stopped bringing it home."

Mike yanked a chair from the table and sat with his head in his hands. Ann turned away, fighting the urge to go over to him.

His voice came out now, stifled. "Can we start over again?" he asked.

Ann did not answer but turned around to meet his eyes.

"When did you meet Charlie Ellis?" he asked.

Ann took a breath and recounted for Mike the first time she had ever seen Charlie in his uniform. He had been directing traffic in a snowstorm, and she was in her parent's car coming through on their way to the ski mountain. Later that same weekend, she saw him in regular clothing out at a bar. She developed an instant crush on the young, handsome Charlie.

"You both lived up here, didn't you? You didn't grow up together?"

"That was before we moved up here," she said. "Gram and Gramps retired early to buy a bed and breakfast. I sort of tagged along."

Within a year of moving to the mountains, Ann recalled reading about the unknown woman found at the Overlook. But it was not a big deal as she remembered. Shortly after, she formally met Charlie when he stopped her for a traffic violation.

"He was so dapper in that uniform., so mature. His haircut, his shave, and his clothes were all so precise. He had a soft voice but strong words. But I could tell I had his attention, though," Ann said. A glow came to her eyes. "He just gave me a warning. He tripped over his words and said it was his lucky day."

She explained how things progressed between them from chance encounters out socially to a full-blown conversation when she ran into him at the market.

"He lived alone then. Just in his father's old hunting cabin. He had left Albany behind for serenity, he told me."

"He isn't from here either?" Mike asked.

"Oh no, you thought he was a local? Not by half. He came up to the mountains as a child, hunting with his father. I think that was his true love—the mountains. Your dad came from the inner city of Albany. Went to a rough public school there."

Ann reminisced as she described her courtship. They had dates around Charlie's work schedule. Ann found work in the school district as a teacher's aide. Almost a year to the day, Charlie had proposed. Ann described it as if it were inevitable.

"A year it was for him. We were going to get married or break up. No in-between. I was barely twenty-two. He was just twenty-four, but things were different back then. You got married younger, for better or worse."

"Was it romantic?" Mike asked.

"For your dad? Yes, it was. He left the ring box on the desk in my bedroom when he went up the hall to take a shower. I found it and opened it." She reached for her left ring finger with a phantom touch. "He came back and asked me, 'So what do you think?'"

"So, not romantic at all?"

Ann smiled at the memory. She described early married life—how happy and content she felt with Charlie. He worked a lot, but she never wanted for anything. They found a starter home, and Ann was a brilliant homemaker. Charlie never held her back on anything. He encouraged her to go to school and become a teacher. He facilitated her need to garden. He read all her poetry. Together, they never smoked, rarely drank, and never argued.

"And I mean never," Ann said. "We truly had some sort of kismet where we anticipated and complemented one another implicitly. We had disappointments, but not with each other."

"I don't remember any of that," Mike said. His voice was heavy.

"You wouldn't. We were married for seventeen years before you came into our lives."

"Why did you wait?"

Ann crossed the kitchen and pulled the second chair out from the table. She sat with a delicate motion, placing her hands on the table folded as if in prayer. Her eyes became teary, and she tried to blink it away, looking lovingly at Mike.

"We didn't wait. We were patient."

Ann softly explained, without intimate detail, the road she and Charlie had traveled with conception. First, they enjoyed being together and that lasted a few years. Then police work consumed Charlie as he started moving his way up, causing long periods of separation. Finally, Ann put her foot down, gently as she recalled, giving the ultimatum that she wanted to expand the family. Charlie, ever foreseeing his wife's intentions, agreed that it was time.

"But it was not God's time," she said. "After ten years of delay, He gave us seven years of testing our faith and our patience."

"You never gave up though?"

"Obviously not. You're here."

"How was Dad?"

She smiled. "Dad was frustrated. I could see it. He would say often that it was his curse. I didn't know what that meant. Still don't."

Then, one day, success. Ann explained the joy she felt when she finally conceived. Charlie became protective as if this opportunity would slip through his hands at any moment. But, without issue, Mike came into their lives healthy and thriving. That was when Charlie retreated inward.

"At about that time, he was offered the chief's position. It was a culmination of all the hard work he had put in. But he also felt like there was a microscope placed over his life. He supported me at home, but he'd go to work for eighteen-hour days. He hired a local woman to come help with basic nanny duties."

"This is more of what I remember. I feel like he would be home for a day but then disappear for three. He'd come for a Little League game and go off for a week."

"That's when the battles started. I couldn't get into his head. He couldn't anticipate me any longer. The more I wanted him home, the more he'd back away."

"You told me he was at work, protecting everyone."

"That's what I thought for a long time."

"He wasn't?"

"Most of the time, he probably was. But I found out that he was still going up to his father's old hunting cabin. He'd sit up there for days. I followed him there once. He stopped through the Stewarts to get supplied, and he beelined straight out of town."

Ann illustrated the twists and turns of the mountains she traversed in her pursuit. It took an hour, but she finally recognized the gravel roadway that snaked up to the property. She had backed off as she would stand out going that far. But sure enough, after giving Charlie a little space, she pulled up to the small building. There was smoke rising from the chimney and a couple small light bulbs illuminating the space. Through a window she observed Charlie at a roll top writing desk, pouring over stacks of paper. She also saw the bottle of Jack Daniels, the full one as well as the empty ones strewn about.

"My heart fell," Ann said. "The man I had married had changed and not for the better. He was fighting something, and he was keeping it from me."

"How old was I when this happened?"

"You were thirteen. It was such a slow burn of time and a descent that I couldn't see. But he had gotten away from me."

"Did you confront him?"

"Yes. He came home two days later. I could still smell the booze on him. He hadn't shaved and generally looked like a mess. He was the exact opposite of who I thought he was. I asked him why he stank so badly. He didn't expect that. His typically sharp intuition was dulled. It was like he didn't know me anymore. And I didn't know him. He sulked. He cried. Then he left again, not to be seen for three days."

"How did I miss all this?" Mike asked. It was not a question for Ann but for himself.

"When he returned, no alcohol smell, clean shaven. He tried to be a new man, like the one I used to know. We made the decision to send you away to St. Jude's after that. We figured it was the best way for your dad to recover fully."

"Did he?" Mike asked.

"No," Ann confessed. "He wasn't ever going to a ten step program or anything. He wouldn't admit to his guys that his life was messed up. He disappeared a little less and returned a lot quicker. But it never left him. And it was just a couple years after that he left me for good."

Ann's head dropped. She could no longer hold it in. It was a good five minutes before she collected herself. She raised her head to have her eyes meet Mike's. He wore the surprise on his face where he typically carried his resentment. Ann saw the transformation occur in Mike—the maturation from a little boy who longed for a father to a man who realized that there are ghosts that haunted even the most capable people. The ghosts had gotten his father, and profound sadness darkened Mike's face.

17

I was at the library with my good friend George Hunter. The summer nightfall was closing in amongst the dusky outside; we were saying our goodbyes. I had been back in town for a couple days as the positive results from my podcast episode, "Jane Doe of the Overlook" poured in over social media. There was little in the way of local attention, but with George's assistance, I was able to locate a few contacts.

"Well, George, you've been the greatest ally for my show."

"You never acknowledged me," he said. He raised an eyebrow. "I got lumped in at the end."

"Didn't want you to be crushed by the crazies, George. Do you know what kind of people listen to true crime podcasts? People who think murder is entertainment, people who believe killing might be a fun hobby, and people who take my research and build conspiracy theories."

"You built your own conspiracy theories," George said.

I grinned. "Perhaps, but I know how to sell a podcast. I'm still working on part two. Might even spin it off into something a little more."

"The constant self-promoter."

"George, I am my own product. Content production is the way of the future. It's a commodity that fluctuates in the value you hold for yourself."

"The old saying goes: 'If you're good at something, never do it for free,' and you're quite good at talking about yourself."

"You flatter me," I said, bowing low. It was a genuine sentiment.

I collected my belongings just as the front doors of the library shook. George had locked them about fifteen minutes before, so he could clean up and we could banter in peace. He looked past me at the silhouette in the door frame, encompassed by the growing darkness.

"That's Mike Ellis," he said.

I grew more intrigued. Other than my covert eavesdropping at bowling a few nights before, I hadn't spoken to him since before I finished the podcast. I set down my attaché case and leaned against the counter of the check-out desk. George slipped from behind the desk, crossing to the door and unlocking the three locks that held it secure.

"I'm sorry. I know you're closing," Mike said, sliding into the building.

He was dressed simply in jeans and a T-shirt, but he looked haggard. The faintest bit of stubble roughed his face, the tight haircut had an odd length shag, and his expression was one of desperation and excitement. He failed to notice me.

George spoke to him. "It's okay. I was hoping you would come back. I was just talking with someone regarding the same topic." He led Mike toward the check-out desk where I stood.

Mike's face dropped, but he kept making his way toward me, following behind George.

"Mike," I said.

"Mr. Figueroa."

"Call me Tim, please."

"Call me Officer Ellis."

The curtness was sharp and snappy like it was rehearsed. George had a look like he had stumbled into a television show mid-episode. I acquiesced.

"Officer Ellis, I'm glad to see you."

Mike did not say anything further to me. His attention drew onto George.

"You said that there were articles written about my father when he was on the Overlook case?"

"Yes. There are several articles about Charles Ellis over the years. When you came here the first time, you asked about the Overlook and the murder. You didn't ask about him."

"Can you show me?"

"I can show you," I said. I lifted my attaché case, pointing my head at it. "I printed everything about your father."

Mike adjusted his attention to me.

"You never seemed interested," I said.

"I wasn't."

"And now you are. Very nice."

Mike's youthful face showed strain in how tight he made it with his glaring eyes and twisted sneer. I could feel George tense up as he began tapping his hands gracelessly on the countertop.

"Come, gentlemen, let's take a table and sit down," he said. George ushered Mike and me toward the study tables.

"We can put all of our cards down," I said.

I followed George automatically. Mike stood flat-footed.

"Come on, Mike," George said. "You came here with questions. Let's try to find some answers."

Mike pivoted and marched over to the table, pulling a chair out. He sat facing toward the entrance, on the long side away from me.

"Looks like you might need to play intermediary, George," I said.

"No problem," the old man said.

I emptied the contents of the attaché case, pulling handfuls of paper out. I used binder clips instead of folders with a simple Post-it to label the packets. I found what I was looking for: *Charlie Ellis Newspaper*. I removed the binder clip and flipped through. The stack was as thick as a standard novel, which included grainy Xerox photographs as well as text articles.

"So, the first article regarding Charlie," I said. "I can call him Charlie, can't I?"

Mike said nothing, and I took the silence as an invitation to continue.

"The first article was written in February of 1982. It describes Charlie as a young patrolman working with the Overlook murder investigation. I quote 'Patrolman Ellis was one of the first officers on scene and has been a liaison with state police investigators since the discovery.' Sounds familiar, I bet."

"That's what I was telling him," George said. "I happened to read the recent article about Mike."

"I know all this already," Mike said.

I didn't react. "'Patrolman Ellis has been with the police department for two years, according to Chief Hunter."

"Oh, there I am," George said.

Mike's hard expression melted away. He looked up at George and then back at me.

"You really must turn over some rocks if you're going to investigate," I said.

I observed Mike's surfacing firsthand. He pulled himself from the depths of his ignorance, and I saw the genuine interest in his eyes, the true curiosity floated into his head. It was subtle but deliberate.

"Mike, I knew your old man probably better than anyone, including your mother," George said. "I gave him the job so that he could escape the city life. I did it as a favor to his father as kind of a dying wish. Charlie was always in town anyway, so I gave him a chance."

"What was he really like?" Mike asked. Emotion welled up in his voice.

"Charlie was a natural for police work. He stood out from day one and he never cared what the other guys thought. He'd run circles around them. That's why I assigned him to the Overlook task force they put together."

I picked up where I had left off. "Chief Hunter also said that he believes that persistent investigative work will lead to a swift resolution in this case."

"I believed that to my very bones," George said.

"My father let you down?"

"No, I let him down. My tenure was up, I was tired, and I left the department about four years later. The new guy was less supportive of the investigation, although he made Charlie the detective. Charlie was limited on the official time he could spend with the case, so he started doing things on his own. He came to see me to get advice."

"What would he ask about?" Mike asked.

"Procedural things at first, and then more and more, moral things."

Mike remained riveted. I shuffled through the clippings, coming to my favorite.

"'Local cop can't let go of his first case. New Chief of Police Charles Ellis moved into his new office this week, tacking an old clipping to the wall outlining the now seventeen-year-old cold case involving an unidentified woman found slain off a hiking trail. Chief Ellis told me that not a day goes by that he does not think of that poor woman. He said at this point, he just wanted to have her name published to allow some closure to come to any who mourns her loss.'"

"I assume, Mike, that you're the spitting image of your dad?" George asked.

Mike hesitated. "No, Mr. Hunter, I'm not. I've tried to be the best I could, but I'm not a natural."

"You wanted to be like your dad?" George asked.

Mike shook his head as he leveled his eyes at George.

"Anything but," I said. It was really a whisper, and neither of the other two men reacted.

"But here you are, stepping onto the same path," George said. "And you have one thing he no longer has."

"A chance?"

"If you turn over enough rocks, I believe you just might."

I looked at Mike as he mulled something over in his head. He looked at me sideways. His face told me that he was trying to gauge whether he should say anything further.

"We're looking to do something," he said. "But you can't let it out."

"Who am I going to tell?" I replied.

"The rest of the world. Can you keep a secret? At least for a little while?"

"Do you want to make some sort of deal, Mike?"

"No, I just want you to keep what I'm about to say to yourself."

I hesitated. Whatever the development was would be worth my temporary silence. The idea of getting a scoop like this was too enticing.

"Okay, okay. I will keep it under my hat," I said.

Mike nodded, choosing to believe me. "We are looking to exhume Jane Doe."

"Fantastic," I said. The exclamation was quick. "I had the same thought. But I didn't have the juice for it. Do you have something to convince a judge?"

"Not yet," Mike said. He hung his head. "I'm trying to find something before tomorrow. Veronica Salazar has a friend at the DA's office making a motion in County Court. We don't really have a leg to stand on. Unfortunately, your podcast hasn't had the local appeal you wanted. No one cares about her."

"I thought you were working on the Velez girl?" George asked.

"I am," Mike said as he brought his head back up.

"Then why the interest in Jane Doe?" I asked.

"I think the cases are related," Mike said.

"Absolutely," I said. "Why didn't I think of that? Wow. Can you imagine what that'll mean?"

Mike rested his elbows on the table and interlocked his hands, leaning his mouth into the knot of fingers. "That's why I didn't want to tell you."

"Listen, Mike, my goal is to do whatever I can to bring attention to Jane Doe. That's why I did the podcast in the first place. That's why I'm working on a second episode. This may be the basis for a third."

"You're looking out for your career. Your bottom line. I want to find some justice for Carolina."

"And for Jane?" I asked.

"How about your father?" George added.

Mike did not respond. The cards were on the table now.

18

I know it's late in the game to start introducing new people to the story, but I've nearly forgotten the last member of the team, the plucky and plump Ms. Amanda Domino, Esquire. She hurried along Main Street, her legs pumping hard in her skirt, her left arm pulling her shoulder briefcase against gravity, and her right hand clutching to a paper cup filled with coffee. Her hair was pulled back efficiently into a ponytail, the end of which flopped from the top of her head and moved very little in her haste. Reaching her destination, she stopped outside the door of the district attorney's office to collect herself and retrieve her identification badge from the briefcase's front pocket.

Amanda got a nod from the private security guard as she marched into the building, showing the small piece of rectangular plastic. She passed under a large digital clock reading 11:15 a.m. Her whispered curses began as she again picked up her pace and climbed the stairs. Breathing heavily, she burst through the back-office door. The two young men in shirts and ties reacted as she made her entrance, deciding to flatten themselves against the wall as Amanda came through. She continued up the hallway till she found her office.

The coffee cup was set down first, carefully, upon a small table just inside the doorway. The briefcase was second, slammed onto the top of the desk along with the frantic opening clasps and zippers. Amanda yanked out several legal-size manila folders hastily secured with a half dozen rubber bands each. The folders were arranged on the desk before the briefcase was picked up and tossed across the room to the waiting wooden framed plush chair against the wall.

"Ms. Domino?" a sweet voice said from the doorway.

Amanda looked up. The small elderly receptionist poked her head in, smiling innocently.

"What do you want, Doris?" Amanda asked.

"You've had two officers waiting for you since ten-thirty, dear."

"I know, I know."

Doris stood by, waiting for more direction, and Amanda gruffly looked at her. Amanda felt the sweat in her hair, sliding uncomfortably down her back. She knew she must look frightful, but Doris remained steadfast in the doorway.

"You can show them in," Amanda said. "Please." The pause between the two statements was interminable, like the pleasantry was pulled from some great depth.

"Certainly, my dear," Doris said. Her voice was sweet and stilted.

The older woman disappeared from the doorway. Amanda sighed. She adjusted herself, pulling the skirt around properly from where it had moved during her rush to the office. The ponytail was removed and replaced with its twin. She turned on the miniature desk fan and moved her face close to the tiny whirling blades, savoring the relief. Then she heard a knock on the doorframe.

"Hey, Amanda," Veronica Salazar said.

Amanda shot up at the sight of Veronica, her neck craning up toward the other woman. Veronica stood tall in a tailored blue-gray pantsuit, her straight black hair falling around her shoulders, and a compact messenger bag slung nonchalantly over her right arm. Amanda smoothed her clothing, wiping dry her sweaty palms as she crossed the office to greet Veronica.

"Investigator Salazar, it's been such a long time," Amanda said. She pillowed the agitation and dulled the sandpaper texture of her voice.

Reaching Veronica, Amanda held her hand out, and Veronica shook it firmly. Peeking from the hallway, Amanda caught sight of the young man dressed in a fine blue suit.

"Amanda, this is Mike Ellis. He's a police officer from Hunter."

Mike ducked around Veronica and offered his hand. Amanda looked into his soft eyes and felt a gentle blush as he smiled, and his round cheeks filled with life.

"Pleasure to meet you," Amanda said. She shook his hand as well.

"Looking forward to talking," Mike said.

Amanda invited Veronica and Mike into the office and closed the door behind them. She moved quickly to adjust one of the wooden framed plush chairs, casting aside her briefcase from the second chair while pulling it closer to the desk. Her guests settled in as Amanda took her seat.

"So, as I said over the phone, I am asking to have an exhumation completed on a Jane Doe buried in Hunter," Veronica said.

"Yes, and with your follow-up email, I drew up an order."

"That's excellent. Just need a judge to sign it?"

"After I get my boss to okay it. So far, he's a no."

Veronica was unfazed. Mike glanced over at her before looking back to Amanda.

"Well, I've brought a local officer to provide an affidavit."

"I'll tell you, Investigator Salazar, it did not go over that well when I brought the motion up. No one above me wants to get involved in any of this stuff. It's not the DA's black eye; it's the police. No offense."

Mike shook his head.

"I understand," Veronica said. "But what if we have some new evidence? What if we believe that this will bring justice not only for Jane Doe but as our theory posits, for Carolina Velez?"

"I had all of that outlined in the first motion," Amanda said. "I pretty much took everything you sent to me and transcribed it. You know I owe you, Investigator Salazar. I tried everything I could."

"First, you can call me Veronica. Or Roni. I've been retired for three years now. I'm not an investigator any longer. Second, if you owe me, why are you giving up after one try? Didn't I teach you anything?"

Amanda exhaled, sputtering her lips as she did. "Honestly, I don't have the best reputation around here, Veronica. I'm holding onto my county court assignment by a thread. After they dismissed me the first time, I thought I was screwed. Your recommendation is what saved me. I don't know if I can jump in the shark tank again."

Veronica leaned forward, placed her elbows on her knees, and rested her head on her hands. Amanda sat back, allowing Veronica time to process. She stole a glance at the young cop. He had a serious look on his face with his attention fixed on Veronica. But then his awareness shifted, catching Amanda's stare from the corner of his eye. She looked away, a flush flowing over her.

"Mike, if you provide an affidavit attesting to the investigative theory, we may have a better chance," said Veronica.

"We really have to articulate all the points," Amanda said. "In a different way than I have already."

"We need something direct," Mike said. "You're saying you may have one more chance at this?"

The question was directed to Amanda. She nodded.

"I have hearsay from my mom and two long-retired cops on memories from more than thirty years ago."

Veronica groaned. Amanda tapped her fingers on the desktop.

"But no direct evidence," Veronica said. "You said you've torn your house apart?"

Mike paused before he spoke. "I have a long shot."

Amanda perked up. Mike's passive demeanor was inflected with a measure of animation. Veronica lifted herself from her pensive position and listened closely.

"I've learned that my father had some secrets."

"Okay?" Amanda said.

"He was one of the initial responding officers to Jane's murder," Veronica explained.

"Okay."

"This case really ate him up. For decades it seems. As time passed, he took to keeping secrets from everyone he knew. Maybe my father knew something that he didn't want to tell anyone."

"Like what?" Veronica asked. "When I worked with him, we had no secrets."

"It's not a secret if he tells everyone," Amanda said.

"My mom said she followed my father out to an old hunting cabin. Maybe he has some sort of records out there."

"Why would he want to hide it out there?" Amanda asked.

"I don't know. But he was going out there to drown his sorrows, so maybe he left something behind."

"What? Like a sealed envelope with Jane's real name in it?" Veronica said.

"And the killer's name beneath that?" Amanda asked.

Despite the cyclical flow of air, Amanda felt herself flush as she looked at Mike. Small globules of sweat trickled down her neck as she waited for his answer. She instinctively rolled her head trying to dampen the moisture.

"I guess not," Mike said, he worked his mouth around as if he were trying to pull moisture from each duct individually, but finding nothing.

Amanda felt a chill skitter from her head to the bottom of her spine. She jerked herself upright. Her eyes flinched toward Veronica first, finding that the older woman was staring straight at her with wide eyes. Amanda then retreated toward Mike, staring off with a blank expression.

"It's definitely a long shot," Amanda said. "But we've got nothing else right now."

"Do you think we need a warrant?" Veronica asked.

Amanda pulled herself together with a quick, sharp breath before redirecting her attention back to Veronica, meeting a look of genuine interest and not the vexed skepticism.

"Not if the property belongs to his family," Amanda said. "Do you know where this magical cabin is?"

Mike spoke in a flat, even voice. "The cabin belongs to my family, I think. I have to figure out where it is."

"Well, find it," Veronica said. "I don't want to wait around on this. It's a new week, and I want a judge's signature by the middle of it."

"That's really ambitious," Amanda said.

"It's necessary. We're out of leads on my niece's murder, and if this theory has no legs, I want to be rid of it. I'm afraid that Carolina's murder will become cold."

"It's a long shot," Amanda said.

Mike added, "But it just might work."

19

Sitting three across in the cab of the Chevy C-10, Hugh, Paul, and Mike bounced along the scarcely paved, narrow roads above Prattsville. Hugh swung the wheel of the truck like a boat captain looking out into the dark roads only slightly illuminated by the headlights. Mike sat in the middle. His cell phone was opened to a map with turn-by-turn directions to the spot in the middle of nowhere. Paul grasped onto the passenger side door with his right arm and swung his left arm behind the headrest in a bracing maneuver.

"Hugh, we don't have to be in such a hurry," Paul said.

"You never did like my driving. Just be quiet over there. Where are we, Mike?"

Mike kept an eye on the phone's screen and the other out into the deep nothing beyond the reach of the light.

"It says we're about half a mile away."

"You're sure this is Chief Charlie's?" Hugh asked.

"No, it was his father's cabin. My grandfather. But neither of them owned the land, some guy named McKenna owns it."

"We're trespassing?" Paul said.

"How do we know this guy isn't up there?"

Hugh looked sideways toward Mike, trying to steady the truck.

"Listen, I'm a big-time detective now. I called the guy. He says my father and my grandfather had a hundred-year lease at a hundred dollars a month."

"And Charlie's still sending checks from beyond the grave?" Hugh asked.

"No. Apparently, he set up a direct deposit from an account my mom never knew about. Has a couple grand in it. Mr. McKenna said that as far as he was concerned, the lease was still good."

"So much for probate," Paul said. He took some deep breaths as the road swung sharply to the right, and Hugh never slowed.

"This is it," Mike said.

Hugh gracelessly touched the brakes, and the truck came to an abrupt stop on the road. Hugh looked at the GPS screen in Mike's hand and made an assuring face. He rolled the window down for a better view. In the dark, he could make out a driveway, somewhat overgrown, but carved out enough to make out despite the lack of light.

"Let's give it a whirl," Hugh said. He spun the wheel hard to the left and gave the accelerator the entire force of his foot.

The C-10 left the proper roadway to begin its climb of the ghost driveway, occasionally hitting holes along the way, jarring Paul into Mike, then Mike into Hugh. The path became steep, and Hugh dug something else out of the old pickup to crest the hill onto a flat area. In the near distance, hiding at the edge of the beams provided by the truck's lamps, was the shape of a small, broken-down shack.

"I'm a little disappointed," Hugh said.

As the truck inched closer, what was to be seen became fully illumi-nated. It was a stick-built construction with a tin roof. Set dead center was a single door made from solid wood with one small inset window to the right of the door. There was a stack of firewood half covered by a tarp beneath the window. The small pipe from the wood stove stuck out from the left side of the metal roof.

"We're shitting outdoors," Hugh said.

He gestured behind the cabin to the left, where there was a small wood frame privy, complete with the half-moon on the door.

"Let's get going," Paul said. He pulled out a flashlight and opened the door.

"You guys are packing, right?" Hugh asked.

He swung his door open, pulling his Glock pistol from the small of his back. On the opposite side of the truck, the sound of a retention break snapped. Hugh looked at Mike still in the center of the truck.

"What are you waiting for?"

Mike ambled across the seat, exiting the passenger side behind Paul. Hugh took the point position, reaching the door first. He tried the knob. It did not turn.

"Breacher up front," Hugh said.

Paul put his weapon away as he returned to the truck. Hugh glanced inside the window. He looked back at Mike silhouetted in the head-lamps, shaking his head.

"Can't see shit."

Paul returned with a sledgehammer and handed it to Mike. He then reached to his waist and retrieved his pistol.

"Smack it," Paul said.

Mike hefted the giant hammer and held the anvil close in his right hand and the handle in his left. He lifted it even with his head and coming down, slid his right hand to meet his left, nailing the door-knob. It fell to the ground. Inside the cabin, the other half of the knob clanked onto the floor, and the door began to swing open inch by inch.

Hugh was through the door first, turning to the deep corner as Paul took the remainder of the space. It was devoid of life.

"That was probably a little excessive," Mike said. He followed the others in holding a couple of keys. "These were under the flowerpot."

"Never hurts to train," Hugh said, securing his Glock.

Paul smiled, holstering his gun. "That was probably a little excessive," he agreed.

Mike took stock of the space as Hugh looked around, shining his flashlight at the walls and ceiling. He moved the beam toward the floor and discovered an old recliner with thick dust encrusting it. Hugh's light went past where Paul stood, landing on a roll top writing desk with a faux leather office chair angled from the last time someone got out of it. Paul turned, following the light, and using his own glow to locate a light switch. All three men looked up to see a fan and a light precariously hung from the ceiling.

"Give it a shot," Hugh said.

Paul flicked the switch. Miraculously, one of the three bulbs in the fan shined a dull luminescence through a layer of grime. It was plentiful for the small space. The flashlights all clicked off.

"Doesn't seem to be much here," Paul said. He searched around with his eyes.

"I'll look at the desk," Mike said.

Hugh moved toward the wood stove along the back wall. He could hear the roll top slide open, followed by the rustling of some paper behind him.

"There's a lot of stuff here. Mostly looks like copies of reports we have at the station," Mike said. "Not much else."

"Let me take a look with you," Paul said. His footsteps retreated toward Mike.

Hugh examined the stove, seeing that there was still ash in the firebox. He switched his flashlight back on, kneeling down to the creosote-stained glass of the door. Hugh inspected the pile of ash more closely, noticing the outline of a notebook.

"Guys, you gotta check this out."

Paul and Mike scurried across the wooden floor, flanking behind Hugh to try to see what the hulking frame was hiding. Hugh leaned back, allowing his partners an unobstructed view, and traced the outline of the notebook with his flashlight.

"Let me take a photo," Paul said. He held up his cell phone to capture an image. "Go ahead."

Hugh turned the handle, opening the glass door of the stove. He reached into the firebox tentatively, like he was expecting heat. He dusted the corner of the notebook, taking hold of it between his thumb and index finger. Delicately, he removed the rectangular book from the stove.

"Easy," Mike said.

"It's not hot," Hugh said.

Mike gave him a confused stare.

"I thought it was gonna be hot ash for some reason. I thought you were looking out for me."

"No, Hugh," Paul said. "He's worried about the half-burned notebook that's been lying in ash for a decade. It could disintegrate in your bear claw of a hand."

Hugh gave both Mike and Paul a hurt look. He provided special attention to the notebook, which after the ash had come off, was more specifically a black and white composition book. He placed his left hand beneath the backside cardboard cover and carried it over the roll top desk. Paul arrived ahead of him, clearing space for Hugh to slide the composition book onto the wood of the desk.

Mike came over to Hugh's left shoulder. The three of them stared down at the filthy and battered cardboard cover which protected singed pages containing the unknown.

"Thanks, Hugh," Mike said. "I guess I'll open it."

Paul interceded so he could snap a few digital images with his phone before allowing Mike to use the tip of his index finger to grip the discolored cardboard and lift it. The first third of the pages clung to the cover and to one another as they stiffly opened. The first visible pages were still sharp white, with the faint blue lines traversing the width and the double red line running the left margin like a line of longitude. These pages were blank, and a quick thumb through from Mike showed that whatever the book contained, it was in the collection of pages incorporated together. The edges of these sheets were crisp, the dehydration caused by the fire merging them into a block.

"Try taking the sheets off from the rear," Paul said.

"Here, use my knife," Hugh said. He produced a small flip-out blade.

Mike took the tool, using it as precisely as if it were a scalpel. He made blade space between the last set of sheets, running the knife slowly amid the paper, separating the toasted carbon at the edge. Over the next fifteen minutes, Mike painstakingly detached each sheet of paper, until he had freed the first third of the composition book. They all looked down at the partially faded ink on the first page.

Hugh poured his eyes over the letters, which were imprecise block shapes. He recognized them instantly.

"This is Chief Charlie's handwriting," he said. He looked to Mike for concurrence.

Mike grimaced. "I'm sad to say that I wouldn't know his handwriting."

"Well, then take my word. It's him."

"Okay," Mike said. "I believe you."

"Let's take this slowly," Paul said. He held up his phone.

The thirty-plus pages containing writing were handled with scrupulous concern. Mike turned each page slowly, so Paul could take an image. Hugh scanned the words for content without verbalizing what he read. When the process was completed, Mike exhaled deeply. Paul shook his hand to loosen a cramp in his wrist. Hugh stood quietly, his expression betraying the electricity running up the back of his neck.

"We need to go back over all of that," he said. "I think this is what you're looking for."

20

Felix Acosta pulled his company car, the Dodge Charger, into the municipal parking lot near the district attorney's office in the busy downtown of Catskill. He drove around for a moment before selecting a spot, deftly backing the vehicle between the lines. He scanned the parking lot from behind his Ray-Ban sunglasses. Felix glanced at the digital clock on the car's display, and it read 11:15 a.m. He retrieved his phone from the center console, looking for a message but not finding any new alerts.

From his vantage, he was able to observe all cars entering the parking lot. He kept a keen eye, being rewarded when he saw the large red Escalade roll in like a tank. Tracing its movements, he watched it go around the lot looking for a proper-sized space. Part of the way down the first aisle it pulled into a spot, lumbering in like an elephant. Felix couldn't see anyone get out of the Escalade, but he knew who to expect. He smiled when Veronica Salazar and Mike Ellis came into sight. She was smartly dressed in a tan pantsuit with an olive-green blouse. He wore a black suit, obviously new, with a white shirt and a gold tie.

Nonchalantly, Felix opened his door and got out of the car. He stood outside, keeping his eyes on Veronica and Mike as he opened the rear door to retrieve the suit jacket to match his silvery slacks and vest ensemble. He was unnoticed by the pair as they walked out of the lot. With his jacket slung over his left shoulder, hooked to his middle and ring fingers, he pursued them. He moved fast despite his short legs, reaching the street before his quarry had arrived at the end of the first block. Felix shadowed them. He slid the jacket on as he moved to cover his weapon and shield, thinking he would stand out less.

He silently closed the distance, coming within twenty feet before settling into a suitable spacing. The foot traffic was light, making his covert attempt to tail them difficult, but he was successful. Veronica and Mike slowed, slipping into a small cafe midway up the third block. Felix stopped in his tracks, considering his next move. He approached the large plate glass window, quickly identifying them sitting at a table with a third person who sat with her back to Felix. She was heavyset in a flowing cream-colored blouse. Her dark hair sat like a mop on her head, falling and snaking into multiple portions over her shoulder and down her back. Felix knew her well; it was Amanda Domino.

Felix kept a steady, sluggish pace, hoping that Veronica's sharp eyes wouldn't catch sight of him. Once he was out of view from the window, he moved toward the outside wall of the building and leaned back while grabbing his chin and ducking his head. After a moment, he began to nod his head. Abruptly, he went back to the cafe, swung the glass door open, and stood before the table where Veronica and Mike sat with Amanda.

Amanda Domino's chubby face lost all its color and as she gasped she said in the same breath, "Oh shit."

Veronica coolly took in his form as she raised an eyebrow and gave a thin, wry smile.

"About time you caught up," she said.

"You didn't know I was here," Felix said. He frowned and furrowed his brow, making deep wrinkles along the sides of his bald head.

Mike did not make eye contact. He looked at Amanda, straining to keep his attention there. Sweat dampened his features.

"Where have you been, partner?" Felix asked.

Mike did not answer.

"Come and sit down, Felix. We'll explain all the work we've been doing while you were out getting new suits," Veronica said.

Felix pursed his lips and clucked. He pulled the fourth chair out, the one between Amanda and Mike, and slid into it casually. He looked at Mike.

"How've you been, partner?" he asked again.

Mike finally broke his fixed view on Amanda, looking back at Felix. "You really screwed me over," he said. "That move cost me all of my integrity."

"With that Velez girl? You didn't have a chance anyway." Felix looked at Veronica. "No offense."

"You really are the biggest bastard, Felix," Veronica said.

"You don't think I have the right to be? You both were hiding the girl from me, forcing me to be the asshole. Lord knows what the three of you are sneaking around for now."

"Hi, I'm Amanda Domino. I'm with the district attorney's office," Amanda said.

"I know who you are. You obviously don't remember me. Felix Acosta, State Police Investigator."

"Oh shit," Amanda said again.

"That's what I think, anyway. 'Oh shit.' Do you want to take a guess on why I'm here?"

Mike looked at Veronica and then at Amanda. It appeared to Felix that the information he had received had been true after all. His face beamed in a look of smug satisfaction.

"Felix," Veronica said. "We've been following a slightly different path. I didn't think you'd be on board, so yeah, we went around you."

"Must've been a hell of a weekend, eh, partner?" Felix said to Mike.

"Yeah, I just got the judge to sign the order of exhumation," Amanda said.

Felix cut short his next sentence to Mike, slowly turning his head to Amanda.

"Exhumation? Of whom? Carolina Velez? She hasn't been in the ground a week yet. Why would we do that?"

Veronica sniffled. "Not Carolina."

Felix's face twisted with a puzzled grimace. He cast about between all three faces. He hoped to hide the desperation in his eyes because the information he had gotten was wrong.

"We're exhuming Jane Doe," Mike said.

Felix made a hoarse coughing sound. His whole face opened in surprise, mouth agape, eyes wide, ears forward. This was better than what he had expected. So much better.

"I'm guessing you didn't know about any of that?" Amanda said.

Felix straightened his gaze on the pinched, reddening of her face staring back across the table. He squeezed his features to match hers, and he doubled the focused emotion toward Veronica and Mike.

"I've got a theory that Carolina's murder is linked to Jane Doe. There are too many coincidences between them. We have been working with ADA Domino on it."

Felix turned his attention to Amanda again. "You know I hold the cold case file on that, too? First I'm hearing of this. What judge took some rookie cop's idiotic theory and ordered an exhumation?"

"The idiot rookie found something that persuaded the judge," Veronica said.

"What was that?"

"A written admission that one of the original investigators knew Jane Doe's identity," Amanda said.

Felix scanned the three of them, ending with his attention on Mike. The kid breathed heavily, his hands fumbled together, and his eyes looked a hundred yards past Felix. Felix shook his head.

"Who, pray-tell, made such an admission?"

Mike swallowed hard. "My father."

Felix was caught between shock and amusement. He tried to think of something to say, but words escaped him. Instead, his lips pursed but the cluck came out as more of a smack.

"He had a hunting cabin. He wrote it in a notebook that he tried to destroy," Mike said. He still refused eye contact with Felix.

"Can I see the affidavit? What did he say? Exactly?"

Mike forced another swallow. From apparent memory, he recited, "'You were the love of my life, and you were taken away. I'll never forget seeing you on the Overlook that day. My whole world was shattered along with my dreams. No one can ever know how my heart screams.'"

Felix coughed again. "Bad poetry? I don't hear a name in that."

"It's heartfelt," Veronica said. "He doesn't give her name, but it's clear that Charlie had a connection to that girl."

"From what I've learned, my father could never let this thing go. It almost cost him his marriage and his family. To the point where it was going to cost him his career. And now I found this very personal, very descriptive poem where my father pines after a dead woman. It's kind of all coming together for me."

Mike lounged back, his body vibrating uncomfortably. There was moisture in his eyes, but they refused to shed tears. The croak in his throat ached with the words, but his voice did not break. Felix leaned into the table.

"Still seems kind of like bullshit to me."

"Bullshit or not, we have the order, and we're digging her up tomorrow. Once we get a tissue sample for DNA, we'll put it out in the databases and see if there is a familial match. Kind of amazing we've never thought of this before," Amanda said.

Felix shot her a look. "We've never had such amazing, convenient evidence before. You know, 'Roses are red, violets are blue, hey there dead chick, I once knew you.'"

"If you're not with us, why don't you just go the fuck away," Veronica said.

Felix shook his head. "I could do that and leave you guys in the lurch. Mike's geographical area of employment is rather small compared to mine."

"Not when I got this," Veronica said. She produced a round mound of leather which surrounded a circular gold shield. It was embossed *Investigator* and *Greene County District Attorney.*

"You've got some juice. That's nice. But I'm not going to let you make me look like a fool. I'm in for a penny at least. You still haven't said how this finds your niece's killer."

Veronica stared back at him. The hard look on her face relaxed and receded into sadness.

"I don't know," she said. "If Mike's right, this might be a link that gets us rolling. It's a Hail Mary, but we haven't anything else right now. Unless there's something you're not telling us?"Felix felt the scowl on his face relax. A wash of guilt dumped from his head to his feet. He nodded as he maintained eye contact with Veronica.

"Okay, Roni. As long as we're both skeptical. This isn't going to hurt anything."

"Well, I'm glad you're on board, and it's all settled," Amanda said.

Felix peered over at her. She had a quizzical smile devoid of the emotion that was going around the rest of the table.

"I mean, it's going to happen, so we might as well prepare. Let's go serve the order to the caretaker and set up to dig a hole."

They each began to collect themselves and stand. Amanda peeled off first and exited the cafe before everyone else. Veronica went out after her, hurrying to catch up. Felix was alone with Mike.

"You broke my trust," Felix said.

"So, we're even. I didn't know you were following me to the restaurant."

"You played it well. I thought we were dancing."

"It was better for her to trust you than to trust me. I was hoping you would get something in the end." Mike stared down at the table with his eyes turned up. His shoulders hunched over with his hands around his back, not visible

Felix's face was piqued with cold interest. "She didn't tell you?"

Mike shook his head.

"You are probably better off, kid, if she never speaks to you again. Take it from me. She has a long history with drugs. Drug taking. Drug dealing. With the way this state 'punishes' people, she's done rehab a bunch of times. It appears to all be behind her. But her family has disowned her, so I couldn't be too sure. It was convenient that she showed up in town about twelve hours before her sister's death."Yo u've eliminated her as a suspect?"

"For now. I guess it's a little too convenient. But she's still got some secrets. I guess we can see who can pump her for the answers more quickly."

Felix gave Mike a toothy grin, lifting an eyebrow. Mike did not respond. He walked around Felix and out of the cafe. Felix turned, pulling his cell phone from his pocket. He watched Mike meet up with Veronica, and they started back toward the municipal lot. Once they were out of sight, Felix pulled up his recent calls, selecting the number at the top of the list. He held the device to his ear as it began to ring.

"Yeah, Bernie, you were way off. But you won't believe what we're doing now."

21

Bradley Salazar pulled his truck into a parking spot at the bowling alley, yanked the console shifter into Park, and looked over at his cousin, Laura. She was wearing a V-neck sweater and a nice pair of jeans and was actively checking her makeup in the visor's mirror. Bradley frowned heavily, sighing loudly, which drew Laura's attention.

"What are you scowling about?" she asked.

"You're here to see that stupid cop, right?"

"I'm here to see the officer who is investigating my sister's murder."

"Hence the cute getup. I thought you were pissed off at him?"

"I am. I was. Dammit, Brad, it's more complicated than that. It's been a month and a half. It's a whole new season. He's the only link I have to the investigation. I'm kind of forced to trust him."

Bradley leaned hard into his seat as he slapped the steering wheel. He watched as people made their way into the building.

"Never understood this game," he said. "You just do the same thing every time. Yeah, you gotta learn how to do it right, but once you get it, it should be simple."

Bradley looked on as Laura completed the inspection of her face. She closed the flip cover of the mirror and adjusted the visor up to the ceiling of the truck.

"I don't know. I've never bowled."

"Are you sure you can trust this asshole?" Bradley asked. He kept his eyes straight ahead.

"I have no choice. Are you going to behave?"

Bradley looked at her sidelong. His eyes pled innocence. She scrunched her face, giving him a look of maternal concern. In a smooth transition, she turned away, opening the door of the truck and hopped down to the ground. Bradley sighed again with even more depth. He opened his door to get out of the truck. Joining Laura, they crossed the parking lot to the main entrance.

"It's a lot all at once," Laura said as the cousins came into the bowling alley. They were greeted with the full sound of cheers and whoops, pins and balls, and the hum of chatter.

Bradley nodded. He looked around, searching for a familiar face, while also shielding himself with his hand up to his brow. Laura pulled him along with her momentum. He saw the bar and tried to suggest they go that way, but Laura continued toward the rear of the building. Soon, Bradley saw what was drawing her.

Mike Ellis was at a series of lanes along with a bunch of other guys. There was a big, tall older man and a fit younger guy. Two soft, dull-looking men about the age of the Jolly Green Giant were standing near one another, pointing and laughing at the others. It dawned on Bradley that they were all cops. As he and Laura got closer, he began to feel warm.

"Hey there," Laura said.

The whole group turned when she spoke. They were silent for a moment, then continued with business as usual. Mike stepped up from the lane to see her.

"I'm glad you came out," he said.

Mike looked sideways toward Bradley. He offered a hand. Bradley gave it a long stare of consideration before he made his rebuke. After giving his full attention, he acted as if the gesture had not been extended. He turned and looked elsewhere.

"Oh shit," one of the dull guys said.

"You gonna let him do that?" the other dull guy said.

Bradley stood proudly, his shoulders back and eyes on anything but the group of off-duty cops. He felt a hand on his chest, a soft touch.

"Why don't you go take a seat over there?" Laura said. "I'm going to talk to Mike for a couple minutes. Then, I promise, we can go."

Bradley looked down at her, catching a glimpse of Mike who stood with his outstretched hand. After a couple of beats, Mike retracted the hand. Bradley cracked his neck before nodding in agreement. He retreated to the bar, ordering a beer, and leaned back with his eyes trained on his cousin and the cop. He loosely held his beer bottle in his left hand, sucking at it occasionally to pass the time.

Without being able to hear their words, Bradley had to rely on body language and facial expressions. Mike sat straight, his hands gesturing to emphasize a point or to draw an imaginary picture in the air. He made Bradley uneasy. The apprehension was based on the way Mike paid Bradley no mind. Yes, Mike had offered peace through the handshake—and Bradley had rebuffed him—but Bradley wanted the fight. Mike was always on defense with Bradley, which made Bradley the aggressor. It made Bradley the asshole. Mike made Bradley the asshole.

Laura leaned into Mike, her eyes wide and her lips parted with genuine interest. She smiled with energy as she listened to his words.

Bradley thought about the bitterness she had expressed back in the summer, feeling that Mike had sold her out. Where had that negative energy gone? He thought about how Laura had checked herself in the visor mirror before coming in. Was she interested in this shithead? Bradley took a long swallow of his beer as he felt the seething anger welling beneath his skin.

Unexpectedly, Laura got up. She was excusing herself and heading toward the restroom, leaving Mike alone at the table. He looked truly alone, and a blind rage pushed Bradley to confront the young cop. Bradley crossed the bowling alley with a direct course. Mike's back was to him, leaving Bradley with an advantage of ambush. The noise resonating through the building offered Bradley additional cover as he beelined toward his prey. It was about that time, out of the corner of his eye, that Bradley saw Laura exit the bathroom, drying her hands with a paper towel. Distracted, he never saw the tall guy step up to him and get in his face, obstructing his goal of moving toward Mike. The big guy's massive frame bumped into Bradley's sturdy, muscular frame. Bradley could smell the beer on the big guy's breath, and while he said some words, those words were less important than his actions. Bradley anticipated the blows.

First, Bradley wound his right arm up for a jab just as Mike and the smaller, fit guy moved in to pull the big guy away. Their efforts dulled the force of Bradley's fist connecting with the big guy's chin. The big guy shook off his friends and delivered a haymaker with his right arm toward Bradley's head. Lighter and quicker than the big guy, Bradley was able to duck the punch. While in a squat, Bradley delivered two rapid blows to the big guy's solar plexus. The bigger, older man went down to a knee, gasping for breath. The fit guy moved in behind Bradley, applying a constricting bear hug, while Mike moved between the combatants.

The two dull looking guys also wedged themselves next to Mike, expanding the distance between Bradley and the big guy. Bradley struggled against the fit guy's grip, noticing Laura running toward the scrum. The mortified look on her face pierced through the fog of war that had settled in his eyes. She tripped over an unseen chair and fell hard to the ground. Her scream sliced through the din of the entire building, drawing the attention of everyone in the bowling alley.

Bradley finally muscled himself out of the fit guy's hold, but when he turned to face this foe, he realized that there was a greater challenge with the fit guy. Bradley held his hands up, and the fit guy de-escalated. Slowly, Bradley turned back to see the big guy still heaving breaths from the ground, holding his hand up as if to indicate that he was regaining his composure. Mike left the buffer zone to tend to Laura along with a few other bystanders. She held a hand to the side of her head.

"Alright, all of you out before I call the cops," a voice said, rising above the din. Bradley looked to the source of the voice as a large woman in a triple extra-large sized baseball jersey.

"The cops are here," another voice said.

Bradley looked over his shoulder, catching sight of his mother standing alongside Felix Acosta. His body spun around to greet them. Felix was dressed for the occasion in slacks and a polo shirt with some sort of electric sheen to it. His stop sign-shaped shield and a Glock 27 were exposed at his right hip. His mom, Veronica, was dressed similarly only with a differently shaped shield.

"I want these fuckers out of here if they're gonna fight," the gargantuan woman said.

"I think the problems are going to be over," Veronica said. "Right?"

She looked among the participants of the brawl. Her focused scowl landed on Bradley. Felix looked dismissively toward the local cops before downright spitting hatred toward Bradley. Everyone muttered and sputtered their agreement.

"Is she okay?" Veronica asked Mike.

"I'm okay," Laura said. She rose to her feet. Mike pulled a chair up for her to sit.

"I expected you all to be here, but I didn't know it was going to be fight night," Felix said.

"So you tracked us down?" one of the dull guys said.

"Not you, Haverthy," Felix said. "Them." He gestured toward Mike and Laura.

"Can we stay anyway?" the second dull guy asked.

"Fine, Jonesy," Veronica said.

"What's going on?" Mike asked. He moved over to help the fit guy get the big guy into the chair.

Bradley backed away from the group, finding a bar stool to lean up against. He looked to make sure there was enough space between himself and the others. Feeling more comfortable, he turned his attention toward his mother.

"Six weeks ago," Veronica said, "we collected tissue samples from the body of Jane Doe and extracted a DNA profile. We shared that profile with a few commercial companies who do familial testing."

"A lot of these companies are friendly with law enforcement and will share any profile matches or familial markers that they link," Felix said.

"You got a match?" the fit guy asked.

Felix took the lead. "Yes, I received a hit request this afternoon from one of these companies. They have a probable match to a woman living in Orange County, California."

"She is forty years old, and from what we're being told is that she shares fifty percent DNA with Jane Doe," Veronica said.

It took a silent moment for anyone to connect the dots.

"She's Jane's daughter?" Mike said.

"That's what we have to confirm," Felix said.

"It looks that way," Veronica said.

A confused Bradley looked from face to face. Even the dull looking guys had awed expressions. The wave of realization passed over them, and the demure celebration began.

Felix approached Mike, grabbing him by the shoulder. "Congratulations, kid, I knew you had it in you."

Mike gave him a sideways look with a warning in his eyes. "Thank you, Felix."

Mike turned to the fit guy and the big guy offering high fives. The fit guy reciprocated with a powerful slap. The big guy, still sore, returned the gesture gently.

"Glad I looked at that stove," the big guy said.

Laura stood unsteadily and approached Bradley.

"Does this mean anything for Carolina?" Bradley asked.

"Not yet. But for them, it's a big win. I hope Mike's theory is right."

Bradley felt a tap on his shoulder. He turned to face the angry countenance of his mother.

"What the hell are you doing?"

"I was giving Laura a ride here and that punk cop tried to show me up," Bradley said.

"So you fought a bunch of cops?"

"No, I just tagged the old guy."

"Doesn't make it any better. You're damn lucky I know all these guys and it's all gonna be forgotten. I'm tired of bailing you out, Bradley. You don't ever face up to the consequences of your actions. One of these days, I won't be able to help you."

Bradley hung his head. He was hiding his anger, not shame. He accepted the berating from his mother, then turned to leave. Before he got the chance, someone moved past him, approaching Veronica.

"Mrs. Salazar, I don't think we've met," I said. "I'm Tim Figueroa."

"Yeah, I know who you are. You're the whole reason we're chasing this lead. You've got Mike all twisted up."

"I understand he thinks that Carolina Velez is related to Jane Doe?"

"I guess we'll see. At least you got a follow-up for your podcast."

I smiled. She was right.

22

Felix guided the rental car along with the congestion of the freeway, coolly hanging back in the seat, the window down. He surveyed the bright world around him through his Ray-Bans, breathing in the salty air. His right hand, perched on the steering wheel, tapped along to the beat of a pop song playing on the radio. Comparatively, he was dressed down from his normal state of dress: light linen slacks with a blue dress shirt, no tie, and his sleeves rolled up to the elbow. He looked, in a relaxed way, over toward Veronica, sitting in the passenger seat.

She was at the height of her professional wardrobe, in a precisely tailored light blue pantsuit with a silky white dress shirt adorned with a gold broach near her throat. Veronica sat perfectly upright, pensive in her face and looking pessimistically out the windshield.

"So much traffic," she said.

"No one's in a hurry out here. Kind of like the mountains, only there's a lot more people."

"We're going to be late."

"Everyone out here is late. Don't worry."

"We have someone waiting on us."

"She'll be patient."

Veronica kept her gaze out the front of the car, her eyes stealing a look at the car's internal clock. She shook her head.

"I've been out here plenty of times," Felix said. "You gotta just go with the flow."

"When have you been out here 'plenty of times?'" Veronica asked. Her narrowed eyes reached over toward Felix.

Felix flashed a smile. He pursed his lips and clucked, settling himself more into the warm, salty air and the four-lane traffic. Veronica averted her stare back forward.

"The flow is too much for me. I've never liked it any of the times I've visited."

Felix looked into the rear-view mirror at Mike, sitting behind Veronica in the back seat of the rental car. He was dressed in his best suit—the blue one with the white shirt and red tie. He was wistfully staring out the window at the cars.

"What about you, kid? You ever been to California?"

"No, never been," Mike said. "Family vacations weren't a big thing growing up." He looked back at Felix's reflection in the rearview.

"Maybe you'll fall in love with the sunshine? And the beautiful women."

Mike shook his head, then his eyes drifted back out the window. Felix frowned and let the silence permeate the car as it traveled sluggishly down the freeway. The GPS indicated when to get off, followed by a couple zigzags till finally they reached the Hall of Justice, also known as a police department. Felix located a parking spot, slid the car into Park, and looked around the interior of the vehicle.

"This looks like the place."

"Okay, so let's go over our strategy again," Veronica said.

Felix sighed and lounged back in his seat. Mike moved in closer, nodding along.

"I'll handle the talking first. I'm hoping to build a rapport, woman to woman. Felix, I want you to back up any facts. But we aren't here to grill her. We're hoping she can help. You got that?"

Felix held up his hands. "No grill master today. Got it."

"What do you want me to do?" Mike asked.

Felix held in a laugh, poorly. "Nothing. You keep your mouth shut."

Veronica gave Felix a harsh look. She turned toward Mike. "You observe. Take some notes. It's an important job because we might miss something that you will catch."

Mike nodded again, his smile reluctant.

"What do we know about his lady?" Felix asked.

"Her name is Margaret Willow Farley. She's forty years old. She's married with four kids. Adopted in New York as an infant but raised almost entirely in California. Her husband is heir to a construction magnate. No criminal record, no discernible work history, and pretty much just a run-of-the-mill everyday American mom," Mike reported from a legal pad scribbled with information.

"So, actually pretty boring," Felix said.

"And we're about to throw a pile of dirt on her entire life," Veronica said.

"She took her own steps toward this, too," Felix said.

Veronica shook her head and a grave smile. "Here goes nothing."

The three of them exited the car. Felix rolled his sleeves down before fastening the buttons on the cuffs. He opened the rear door to retrieve his sports jacket from the garment hook. He rolled his neck, feeling the crack of cartilage. He led Veronica and Mike toward the front entrance of the police station. He climbed the small stone staircase, noticing the palm trees planted out front. Approaching the glass doors, Felix observed a man in a suit instinctively reacting by coming to the door.

"Investigator Acosta?" the suit asked, holding the door open with an extended arm.

"Yes," Felix said. He stopped to allow Veronica to enter first, then cut Mike off.

"Detective Alan Bullock. We spoke on the phone."

He was a tall, blond man. Tall as in taller than Felix, a little taller than Mike, and about the same height as Veronica. Bullock also had silver shocks in his hair, which gave the impression of being nearly white. He was sun-tanned a rich bronze color with broad shoulders. His suit was pricey, as Felix always noticed expense in menswear.

"Yes, good morning. Let me introduce my colleagues," Felix said.

He presented Veronica and Mike. Everyone shook hands and made pleasantries. Detective Bullock gestured through a door he opened with an electronic key swipe.

"Mrs. Farley is in an interview room with one of our detectives," he said.

They followed him through the door and into a long, brightly lit hallway.

"What's her demeanor?" Veronica asked.

"Nervous, I'd say. She drove herself here alone. Maybe a little embarrassed. We've done everything to make her comfortable. I don't think she appreciates all the fuss."

"Her life's about to change," Mike said.

Felix glanced back over his shoulder with a sharp eye on the kid. Mike caught the look and offered a culpable grimace.

"What's the deal with all this? We are sure glad to help, but I must admit, we've got a little bit of a pool going on why it is you guys want to talk with this lady. She's about the most normal person you'd ever want to meet."

Felix gave Detective Bullock the Cliffs Notes version. Dead woman, cold case, no identity, new homicide, old secrets, DNA match. He managed to get it all out just as Bullock slowed outside of a closed door with a large plate glass window.

"Isn't that some shit," Bullock said.

"Anyone have that in your pool?" Veronica asked.

Felix looked in casually through the window and identified the woman known as Margaret Willow Farley, sitting with another woman at a table. She had a long, slender neck that curved down to her feminine shoulders, which were wrapped in a knit sweater. Atop the long neck was a head full of shoulder length, silky midnight black hair combed straight down. The hair framed an oval face with chubby cheeks and wide curious-looking eyes. Her skin was the most delicate shade of coconut brown. She astutely saw Felix through the window. Their eyes met.

"You guys ready?" Felix asked. He rubbed his palms together.

An air of agreement filled the hallway. Felix pushed the door handle down and entered the room. Margaret Willow Farley pushed her chair out to stand up, mirroring the detective in the room.

"Please, Mrs. Farley, you don't have to stand," Veronica said. Her hand was up in a soothing gesture.

The woman stood anyway, extending her hand. Veronica introduced herself, then Felix, and finally Mike. She offered Margaret a chance to sit again, and the woman settled back into her chair. Veronica took the seat across from her. Felix sat on Veronica's left. The other detective excused herself, and Bullock replaced her seat. Felix stole a peek behind himself to see Mike locate an extra chair in a corner. He was in the process of placing himself there along with his legal pad.

"So, how do you all want to start?" the woman said. She looked among each of the faces at the table.

"Well, we have a lot of information. You have a lot of information. We'll have to see where it all intersects. We can each play cards." Veronica smiled.

"Sure, that seems balanced. You can go first."

Felix began, talking over Veronica. "We used the DNA sample you submitted, and it was matched to DNA that we have from an active criminal investigation."

"That's cryptic. Am I a suspect?"

Veronica shook her head. "No, not a suspect."

"Okay, that's good. I was worried that I was coming to a police station and not going to leave. So, my turn? Well, I am adopted, so that's why I did the DNA test. I was hoping to find some new relatives and broaden my family tree."

"Why now?" Veronica asked.

"I believe it's your turn to lay down a card."

Veronica's look soured a little. She glanced at Felix. He pursed his lips and clucked. Nodding, he fixed his eyes back on Maggie.

"Mrs. Farley..."

"You guys can call me Maggie. I don't have any pretense here. I took a DNA test a few months ago. Two days ago, I was contacted by Detective Bullock here. He asked me if I'd like to come in because some police officers were flying in to talk to me. I was so scared I didn't even tell anyone where I was going. I didn't want them to worry. Listen, I'm a very simple woman. Can we just cut to the chase and stop playing these games?"

Felix stole another look at Veronica, a desperate plea for control. Veronica held fast, stone-faced. She offered sympathetic half-smile, soft and warm but with cold eyes that were vigilant toward the woman before her.

"Maggie," she said. "We're here to understand the life you've led. It is our hope that something you can offer will trigger a reaction in our case. If we give you too much, I'm afraid it may poison your memory."

"I offered my card. I want it reciprocated." Maggie's voice had some new power behind it.

Veronica swallowed hard. Felix moved in his chair. Maggie folded her hands before them, digging in against their questions.

"We matched the DNA to your mother," Mike said from the corner of the room.

Everyone turned to face him. Felix and Veronica shot daggers at him with their eyes. Maggie's face softened, and she nodded, a peaceful acceptance in a warm smile.

"I was born in New York and raised briefly in a Catholic orphanage near Albany, wherever that is. I moved to California before I turned a year old, and I've never left."

Felix and Veronica looked back at Maggie.

"We don't know your mother's name," Mike said.

"And neither do I, unfortunately, if that's what you're hoping for."

"We didn't think you did," Felix said.

"But we were hopeful," Veronica added.

"She died, didn't she?" Maggie asked.

Veronica nodded, and Felix bowed his head.

"Yes. Most likely she was killed just weeks after you were born," Mike said.

"Killed?" Maggie said. Her exclamation was in genuine shock.

Felix made a slow, angry turn of his head at Mike. Mike didn't seem to acknowledge him. The kid was transfixed on Maggie, and you couldn't tell him that they weren't the only ones in the room.

"I don't know who my father was either," Maggie said. "If that's your next question."

Emotion had begun to swell up inside her, evident in her face, her posture, and her demeanor.

"Who raised you?" Veronica asked.

"Ron and Dorothy Willow."

"Good people?" Felix asked.

"The best I could have hoped for."

"Your mother was murdered and left on an overlook in the Catskill Mountains," Mike said.

Maggie heaved a sobbing sigh. "I don't even know what those are. Sounds picturesque."

"My father was the first police officer at the crime scene," Mike said.

Maggie now looked beyond the three people at the table, and Felix could tell she entered the same dimension with Mike.

"We think he knew your mother," Mike said.

"Did you ask him then?"

"He died seven years ago," Mike said.

"Kind of hard to ask now," Felix said.

"I guess you guys just figured that part out?"

"It's how we were able to get to this point," Veronica said.

"I feel like there's something else," Maggie said.

Felix looked at Veronica again, his dissatisfaction wearing plainly on his face. Maggie shook her head, bringing her focus wider than just on Mike. Felix adjusted his gaze to see what Mike would say next.

"There's been another murder, and I personally think your mother's death is related. Can you help us?"

Veronica considered the pictures on the entertainment stand in Maggie's living room. It was a massive piece of furniture with a row of shelves above the television and a column of shelves on either side of it. There was a youthful Maggie along with a young man, presumably her husband. Then one of Maggie, a little older, with the same man. Finally, a facsimile of Maggie now, again with the same guy. The top row was dedicated to baby portraits, four of them in all. A boy, with some age to the exposure; a girl, seeming a little more recently produced; and two identical boys that were obviously a digital image. The lowest frame of each column contained a professional photograph of an older couple. Veronica pointed at these specific pictures.

"Your parents?" she asked.

Maggie, leaning up against the opening between the living room and the kitchen, startled herself to attention.

"What?"

Veronica grabbed the picture and held it up. "Are these your parents?"

"No, those are Bill's," Maggie said.

Veronica set the picture back and retrieved the other photo. She examined the couple for a moment before replacing it where it had sat. Her attention turned to the children's portraits.

"What are their names?" she asked.

"Tommy's the oldest, all the way to the left. Then Patricia next. Finally, Aidan and Aaron are the twins. In that order."

"Where is everyone?" Felix asked. He stood in a corner opposite Maggie.

"My friend is watching the younger children. Bill and Tommy should be home soon."

"Do they have any idea this is happening?" Mike asked. He stood, arms crossed, along the wall near Maggie.

Maggie looked at him and shook her head. "Bill doesn't even know I did the DNA test."

"You should call Detective Bullock and have a patrol unit on stand-by," Felix said.

"I assume he's not going to take this well?" Veronica asked.

Maggie's face pinched itself with desperation. She nodded as she choked down a lump in her throat. But no tears fell. Veronica saw something new in Maggie's face as the wave of what she felt washed away. Something almost peaceful. A door behind Maggie opened.

"Hi Mom," a young male voice said.

Veronica watched a boy come up to Maggie as she turned and looked up at him. She embraced him and squeezed him around his waist. He was taller than Maggie but would not be considered partic-ularly big. He was built squarely but had a skinny-fat body.

"Hi, Tommy," she said.

At that point, Tommy noticed the guests in the house. He shot a quizzical look around at each person before returning to his mother's gaze. Tommy's face was mottled with melanin, with high, fat cheeks, and a weak chin.

"Tommy, these are police investigators. Acosta, Salazar, and Ellis." She pointed each of them out as she introduced them.

"Is everything okay?" Tommy asked. He moved himself in front of his mother.

"It's just fine," Maggie said. "Why don't you put your school stuff away? Where's Dad?"

"He's coming right behind me. He had to grab the garbage can."

Tommy moved through the living room on his way toward the hallway that led to the bedrooms. He nodded at Veronica as he passed.

"Big kid," Felix said. "Tall, I mean."

"Don't know where he gets the height, but the skin and bones are all from his father."

"So, what's the plan with your husband?" Veronica asked. Her tone was very serious.

"His name is Bill. And there is no plan. Can't put the vase back together now. Might as well come clean and suffer the consequences."

"I would have liked a plan," Veronica said. She was looking at Felix.

"This is all the kid's idea," Felix said, nodding his head toward Mike.

Veronica switched her attention over to Mike. He smiled sheepishly.

"She's going to need the support of her family if she's going to help us," Mike said.

"If this doesn't destroy it," Felix said.

The words were barely perceptible, but Veronica heard them, shooting her eyes over to Maggie. She was looking at Felix, the desperate look starting to take shape again.

"We're here with you, Margaret," Veronica said.

"Thank you," Maggie said.

The door opened again. There was a loud clomping of boots on the floor along with a boisterous whine of a voice.

"Honey, I'm home."

Bill Farley entered the room, his dusty pocket T-shirt draped loosely on his slight body, his jeans cinched with a belt, making his waist almost invisible. He saw Veronica as he approached his wife. The big grin on his face dissolved, and he looked at Maggie. He deciphered something in her eyes, and he slumped his shoulders. The sign he made was tinged with irritation. Then, as he noticed the two men flanking either side of the living room, his body language began to resemble that of a cornered animal.

"Hello," he said. His high-pitched tone wavered.

No one else spoke. Veronica looked at Felix, who glared across at Mike, who focused on Maggie. Bill broke the silence.

"I'm hoping we won something?" he said with a sardonic hope in his voice.

Maggie's face strained as she touched Bill's shoulder. He turned to face her. She searched again for the words, her head tilting down first before rising to meet his eyes.

"I went behind your back," Maggie said. Her confessional tone was sweet and even. "I did the DNA test."

"Was there an inheritance?" Bill asked. Veronica could hear that he was really trying to sound hopeful beneath his uneasy chuckle.

Maggie shook her head. "Unfortunately, no."

Bill ran his hands through his hair as frustration built up. Veronica kept an eye on him as she used her periphery to signal to Felix. He was not paying attention to her.

"I'm going to sit if that's alright?" Bill said. "Why don't you all join me and we can pull the lid off this can of worms."

There was a couch, a loveseat, and an easy chair in the room. Bill fell back into the single seat, rocking back in the recliner. Mike guided Maggie toward the couch, allowing her to choose her seat before he settled down. Felix moved behind the loveseat, placing his hands along the back as Veronica sat on the edge of one of the cushions.

"Why don't we start with who you all are?" Bill said.

"Mr. Farley, I'm Veronica Salazar. I'm an investigator with the Greene County District Attorney in New York."

"Felix Acosta, New York State Police Investigator."

Bill waited for Mike to speak. His eyes bore through the young man, who stared back with a dull expression.

"This is Mike," Maggie said.

"He can't speak?" Bill said. He leaned forward, trying to grab the kid's attention. "What's your name?"

Mike cleared his throat. "Mike Ellis, Town of Hunter Police. Also in New York."

"So, three cops from New York? What? Is Maggie some sort of criminal?"

Tommy entered the room and stood at an angle behind his father. He had his focus on Veronica.

"Holy shit, no way," he said.

"Thomas, language," Maggie said in a scolding manner.

"Sorry, Mom. But there's no way."

Bill turned himself in his easy chair. "What are you talking about?" he asked.

Tommy moved into the center of the room as he spoke. "Jane Doe of the Overlook? That was the Town of Hunter in New York. It was on 'Figure It Out With Figgy.'"

"What the hell is that?"

"William," Maggie snapped.

"Dad, it's a true crime podcast. Mom's the long-lost daughter of Jane Doe of the Overlook. That's so insane."

Veronica observed Bill's demeanor continuing to sour as he became more confused. Tommy's enthusiasm also appeared to wear on him.

"Mom's real mom was a murder victim forty years ago," Tommy said.

"Why don't you go do some homework, Tommy?" Maggie said. She was evidently picking up the same waves as Veronica.

"Oh man, I really want to hear this," Tommy said.

"Do as your mother says, please," Bill said. He spoke in short, tight phrases, emphasizing the denial of any further protest.

Tommy made a defiant, reluctant huff as he retreated from the room. Bill seemed to relax a bit as he began to rock steadily in the chair.

"Well, I know I didn't kill anyone, so why are you waiting here for me?"

No one said anything. Again, glances went around the room.

"You all don't seem to have your shit together," Bill said. He brought his attention to Maggie. "I don't know why we have to have an audience for me to find out you betrayed my trust."

Maggie cleared her throat before she spoke. The words began measured but unwound into something more desperate by the end. "Because you told me that something like this would happen. You said I should leave well enough alone. And here we are, you saying, 'I told you so' and me looking like a fool. I just wanted to understand where I came from. I never thought it was going to be like this."

Bill softened as he heard the emotion in his wife's voice. "But what do they all want?" He motioned toward Mike, Felix, and Veronica.

"Mr. Farley," Veronica said. "We're looking for Maggie's help back in New York."

"Oh," Bill said. "No."

"Mr. Farley..."

"I'm not going to see this blow up into something, okay? We know now that your mother is dead. I'm guessing no idea about the father. There's no way that this gets easier. Let's not, and say we did."

Bill's tone meant that his words stood firm. Veronica turned toward Felix, eyes pleading for help. Felix shook his head stoically.

The silence was broken again by Mike. "Bill," he said, "there's more at stake than you realize."

"I don't think you realize what's at stake for me. Is this personal for anyone else here? Or is it just me?" Bill asked.

"My father was a police officer who may have known who Maggie's mother really was. This could destroy his legacy."

"Maggie's identity could help us solve the murder of my niece," Veronica said.

Bill rocked in his chair, his eyes on Maggie.

"This could wind up being the worst thing to happen to us. The worst if you know what I mean. You do realize that?" he said directly to his wife.

Maggie's face held firm against its tears. She nodded.

"You want my support? You want a blessing? I can't do that. But I also can't stop you, Maggie. You're a grown-up. Just don't forget about the family you do have. The children, the husband, and his family who have accepted you as you are for twenty years, despite everything else. Have you talked to your dad about this?"

Maggie shook her head, finally losing control of her sobs.

"It might just break his heart. Turn over his whole existence. You really want to do that?"

Maggie took in a deep breath and settled herself by closing her eyes. She opened them, looking back at Bill.

"No," she whispered, "I guess I don't."

23

F elix woke with the first light coming through the gap in the blackout curtain in the hotel room. There was a racket of noise throughout the space—the sound of traffic on the street outside, the flow of water coursing through pipes in the wall, and a distant alarm clock electrically pulsing. He was wide awake in an instant, and that was when he noticed the sleeping form next to him. Her breathing was subtle but steady. Her exposed back was toward him, hair falling in a cascade onto the sheets. Felix shook his head, pursed his lips, and clucked. He slid out of bed and went to the bathroom.

He turned the light on, causing the fan to start up and drown out the other sounds invading his brain. He relieved himself without flushing, then looked at himself in the vanity mirror as he ran hot water. Whiskers were starting to build up into a faint beard, which he scratched before applying a hot washcloth and scrubbing the stubble. He turned off the water and the light, cutting the white noise of the fan before returning to the main space of the hotel room. There he saw that Veronica was awake.

She was sitting up with the covers pulled around her. She had a sad look on her face as her eyes followed Felix crossing the room. He sat on the small couch along the outside wall. They stared at each other for a long time. The sounds of the traffic and the flow of the water and electric pulsing resonated.

"I think that this whole thing has been just a waste of time," she said. Her statement cracking the air between them.

"I've been saying that for a long time."

"Yet here we are."

"Yeah," he said. "Here we are. Again."

"I'm not talking about that."

"Okay. We're following this lead and Bill Farley's probably right. There are no more answers at the end of the road. Just more questions."

"And not the questions I'm particularly interested in."

"The only lead I had was the girl's sister. I think that ship has sailed."

"I told you that from the beginning."

"I know. But here we are."

"Yeah. Again."

Felix chuckled. Veronica was curled up, her modesty all caught up in the blankets and sheets. He lifted his legs and placed his feet on the small coffee table, crossing them over each other. He looked down at his own nakedness.

"If we were going to bring her back to New York, it'd probably swing some attention our way. We can obviously piggyback Carolina's murder off the publicity," Felix said.

"It's like she's an afterthought."

"But it just might bring us some answers. I think the kid is wrong in his theory, but I never thought this was a terrible idea. Just not very fruitful."

"He's chasing the ghost of his dad. I'm chasing the ghost of my family."

"Is that what this is?" Felix asked, gesturing between them. "Ghosts?"

"No, this is stress and poor decisions. Jesus, I can't even blame alcohol."

"So just recreation?"

"You want something more? You never did before."

"We were younger then."

"You still broke my heart. After Ray, I was vulnerable."

"I thought you just wanted a daddy for your kid."

"He had a daddy before you and I got involved with each other," Veronica said. Her voice was wistful.

"Always felt like you wanted it more than I ever did. Ray seemed like he was always the second option."

Veronica made a harsh scoffing sound. She moved to get out of bed, keeping her train of blankets and sheets as she made her way to the bathroom. She collected her clothes from the ottoman in the hallway. The white noise of the fan kicked in with the light.

"We can't complicate this," she said. Her voice forced itself above the din of the fan. "It didn't happen. Like it never happened before. We certainly can't let Mike know. Who knows who he might tell. Don't need everyone back home thinking anything improper."

She came out of the bathroom, fully dressed. The fan kept droning on behind her. Felix maintained his pose, and she gave him a derisive look as he sat with a smug face.

"Put your clothes on," she said. "We've got to get our shit together."

Felix uncrossed his legs and rose to his feet. He searched around to locate his clothing. A messy pile formed at one side of the bed where he'd dropped everything in the passion of the previous evening. Once he was put back together, he looked at Veronica.

"So, this changes nothing?" he asked.

"I won't let it." She snorted. "You should go."

Felix nodded as he slid his shoes on. He kept his head high as he passed Veronica, clucking a few times as he made his way to the hotel room's door. He never looked back as he exited, letting the door close with a loud bang. He did not expect Mike Ellis to be in the hallway.

"Oh, hey Felix," Mike said.

The kid was dressed in jeans and a T-shirt, coming toward Veronica's room. Felix saw the inquisitive look in Mike's wide eyes. His mouth agape into a wordless question.

"Might want to give her a few minutes."

"Okay. Do you want to grab a coffee and speak then?"

Felix thought for a moment. The door behind him opened.

"Let's just get this over with," she said. "Both of you come in here."

Felix allowed Mike in first. Mike crossed the room and sat on the small couch, lounging back. Veronica settled into the plush chair to the right of the couch, leaving the desk chair for Felix. He tried not to smile as he sat.

"Mike, let me ask you a question," Veronica said. "How much time did your job give you to come out here on this?"

"They didn't give me time."

"You mean you're not here officially?" Felix asked.

"No, I've been using sick time."

"That's not going to jam you up?" Felix said.

"I'm in too deep on this now to quit."

Felix looked between Mike and Veronica. Her exasperated expression betrayed some motherly instinct. She slapped her hand on her thigh, breathing out a long, hollow breath.

"I think we've followed through this far enough, for now," Veronica said.

"We just got here."

Mike's protest was firm. He sat up now, toward the edge of the couch, his arms wide and animated. His face contorted into a snarl at Veronica. His immaturity was fully displayed in his childlike noises of disbelief.

"Kid, we've got a fresh murder investigation, which you're supposed to be helping me with. This little side quest has been fun, and I got to bask in the sunshine a little, see some pretty girls, etcetera etcetera..." Felix said, his head shaking in connection with the bad news.

"But Maggie has no connection to New York. No connection to Carolina. This is something we can pursue but only after we figure out who killed my niece," Veronica said.

She looked at Felix with wide eyes. Her nostrils flared and her lips were drawn into a pinpoint pucker. Her words were firm.

"But wait," Felix said. "You're three thousand miles from home on sick time?"

"Yeah, I just called out sick again before I came over here."

"You're gonna lose your damn job, kid."

Mike's eyes burned at Felix. He stood up. He huffed a voluminous amount of air and walked to the hotel room's door. Mike did not look back, he opened the door and left, letting the heavy portal slam shut.

"He doesn't see the problem," Felix said.

"He's lost."

Felix felt his cell phone vibrating in his pocket. He reached for it, seeing a number he did not recognize. He made a bewildered face at Veronica as he accepted the call.

"Hello, this is Investigator Acosta."

Felix listened to Maggie Farley. She was wild and emotional, speaking so rapidly that Felix could only make out the gist of what she was saying. He understood that she was in trouble but could not understand how serious.

"Okay, take a breath. Collect your thoughts. What's happening?"

Felix looked at Veronica with incomprehension. He listened to Maggie again, who slowed her pace, controlled her flow of words, and said very plainly, "My house is being invaded by the press."

"Hold on," Felix said. He manipulated the phone in his hand and turned on the speaker option. He motioned for Veronica to move closer. "Say that again, Veronica is listening now."

"Hey Veronica," Maggie said in a rushed breath. "So, I was telling Felix that I had a reporter knock on my door this morning. After I sent him away, two more came. Now I have three news vans and about twenty people set up in front of my house. Bill's at work and the kids are at school, but they're going to be home soon. I don't know what to do."

24

aggie sat at the island in her kitchen, her hands surrounding a cup of hot coffee. Her eyes darted back and forth around the room, glancing at the digital clock on the stove, at the window over the sink, and finally at the sliding glass door opposite the galley of the kitchen. She rocked almost imperceptibly on the stool, forward then back, forward then back. Absent-mindedly, Maggie took a sip of her coffee. It was after two o'clock.

There was a frantic knocking on the glass of the slider just as Maggie took her eyes from it. The suddenness of the noise startled her, and some of the coffee spilled with her start. When she looked over, she saw her friend, Diane. She wore sunglasses and a bandana over her head as she rapped on the glass, looking around frantically.

Maggie stood and wiped the liquid from her hands onto her jeans. She crossed the kitchen to the slider. Diane was still looking over her shoulder and upon turning she came face to face with Maggie. She screamed for a moment before she recognized her friend. Maggie unlocked the door and slid it open.

"Oh Jesus, Margaret, do you know how many people are at the end of your driveway?" Diane said. She gasped and held her hand to her head.

"A dozen or so?" Maggie asked.

"At least that."

Diane made her way into the house. She was dressed in a flowing black top equipped with sheer sleeves and extra material that acted like a cape. The top spilled below her waist, and she wore black leggings beneath that. She removed the bandana from her head as she came into the relative safety of the kitchen, revealing the long, bushy red hair that had been contained underneath.

"What is it all about?" Diane asked. She moved herself into the galley of the kitchen, searching the countertop.

"Would you like coffee?"

"Of course, I would. Where is it?"

"I'll have to make some more. I've had an IV of the stuff hooked up all day."

Maggie slid past Diane. She took to manufacturing a pot of coffee with her old drip machine. She could hear moving behind her, going around to sit at the counter, scraping a stool across the tile, and creaking into the seat with her weight. Maggie could not help but smile.

"I mean Jesus, Margaret, they're taking over the neighborhood. What is it all about? The cops you spoke to?"

Maggie hit the button on the coffee maker before turning to face Diane. She tried to portray some nonchalance with her eyes wide and a genial smile.

"Yeah, I mean it must be."

"Have you talked to any of these wackos? They damn near chased me up the driveway yelling about some nonsense. I tried to wave them off, but there I was, up against the microphones and the lenses."

"What did you say to them, Diane?" Maggie asked. Her voice matched the concern that creased her face.

"Oh, nothing," Diane said. She held her hands up innocently but averted the eye contact that Maggie was seeking. "I confirmed that you were who they thought you were. I told them I was just a concerned neighbor coming to check things out. Might have mentioned that you were an orphan and did a DNA test not too long ago."

"Why did you tell them that?" Maggie asked. Her exasperation sucked all the energy from the room.

Diane sat quietly, waiting for Maggie to calm down. "Well," she said. "First of all, they asked. It was just at the tip of my tongue. You know, in the front of my mind. I couldn't help myself."

Maggie held a hand to her head. "I guess it doesn't really matter."

"What are you going to do when Bill gets home?"

Maggie straightened, looking Diane in the eyes. "I'm hoping to get rid of them by then."

"Fat chance of that."

The coffee maker spit and sputtered its juice behind Maggie as she looked at Diane with a desperate frown. Diane gave her a sorrowful stare back. The machine began to beep its positive beacon that it had completed brewing. Maggie turned slowly and with deliberate motion pulled a coffee mug from the cupboard. She poured the dark hot liquid from the pot.

"Here you are," Maggie said. She presented the mug to Diane.

"Thank you, dear. What is your plan, then?"

"I have the police officers from New York coming here. I hope they're here soon."

At about that time, Maggie heard a car pulling up the driveway. It stopped, and she could hear three doors close. She moved toward the front door of the house, cutting through the living room and allowing

Felix, Veronica, and Mike inside. They all made welcome gestures, and Maggie led them back into the kitchen.

"Investigators Acosta, Salazar, and Ellis, this is my friend and neighbor, Diane," Maggie said.

"You've got your own squad, eh?" Diane said. She waved in a confident outside-to-inside arc of her hand. "You guys make it through the gauntlet, okay?"

"There's a whole lot of people down there," Mike said.

"I don't know what they want," Maggie said.

Felix made a derisive snort, which grabbed everyone's attention.

"They want to talk to you, Maggie," Veronica said.

"Why?"

Felix said, "Well, it seems that somehow the news of your DNA match got leaked."

"It leaked with some rocket fuel," Diane said. "There are four networks plus online journalists down there."

"How?" Maggie asked.

Felix turned his attention to Mike before he then glanced over at Veronica. He shrugged and scrunched his face to show his confusion.

"There's only one person who could have made this happen," Mike said.

"Who?" Maggie asked.

"That idiot Figueroa," Veronica said.

"Who is that?"

Maggie looked intently at Veronica, who looked like she was about to speak. But her attention switched when she heard a voice on the other side.

"Tell her, kid," Felix said.

Mike lifted his chin, his eyes seeing past Maggie. She could see his lips struggle, looking for the right way to say what he knew. Maggie brought her hands to her mouth as she waited.

"Tim Figueroa is the reason we're all here, I guess. He's got a podcast that he produced and released a couple months ago all about Jane Doe of the Overlook."

"Who's that?" Diane asked.

"My mother," Maggie said.

"And how did Figueroa know about all this?" Felix asked, his eyes squarely on Mike.

Mike hung his head but said nothing. Maggie didn't think he looked guilty, but he was assuming responsibility. He felt that this was all his fault.

"What's he have to do with the swarm at the bottom of the driveway?" Diane asked. She ping-ponged her eyes back and forth between everyone within the space of the kitchen.

"He's a dirtbag journalist," Veronica said. "He may have kicked this all off, but he's also very interested in being the center of attention. He knows we identified someone as a familial relative. Apparently, he figured out who you are and where you live."

"He descended with an army of reporters?" Maggie said.

"I wouldn't expect to know what his plan is, but I certainly wouldn't put it past him," Felix said. He crossed his arms as he shook his head.

"Can we call this asshole and get these people moved before Billy comes home?" Diane asked no one in particular.

"I don't have his number," Veronica said.

Felix shook his head.

Maggie turned her head, along with the others, toward Mike. He gave a sheepish grin and pulled out his cell phone.

"Anyone else want to talk to him?" he asked.

"He's your best buddy, kid."

Mike sighed as he tapped a button on the screen of the phone. There was a far ringing that became louder once Mike switched the audio to speaker mode. There was a second and third ring. Finally, a fourth ring. There was no answer. Then, a voice cut through the speaker, boisterous and proud.

"Hey there Mike," my voice came through. "Saw you guys pulling up the driveway. I was wondering when I was getting this call."

"Hi, Tim, listen, can we do something about all the reporters?" Mike asked.

There was hesitation on the other end of the phone. "Well, Mike, I've got a nice little contingent here all interested in my story. I called in a lot of favors to drag all these folks out here. Wouldn't look good if I sent them all away."

Mike looked at Felix and then Veronica. His eyes were wide and searching for any assistance. That was when Diane spoke up.

"Hey, asshole," she said. "You've got my friend cooped up in here like she's under siege. Her husband's gonna be home soon, and he is not going to like seeing your contingent parked in front of his house. If you want anything out of this, send your troops away."

Diane looked at Maggie. Maggie narrowed her stare while she thought about Diane's words.

"Who is this?" my voice came across the speaker.

Diane introduced herself in no uncertain terms. "My name's Diane. I'm the one you're dealing with now."

"What you're saying is," I said, "if I get all of the reporters out of here, Mrs. Farley will agree to talk to me?"

Maggie felt all eyes on her. I let the silence hang, not wanting to overplay my hand. She considered it for a solid minute or two. Then she said: "Yes, you have a deal."

I want to take this opportunity to dispel the rumors that I had television trucks and cameras parked in front of the Farley house. I recounted this opinion in the previous chapter, but I had about a dozen local newspaper reporters, independent journalists, and podcast producers on hand to demonstrate for Maggie the interest the case had garnered. It was not an attempt to intimidate anyone. Additionally, I was hoping that the buzz created by these grassroots writers would spin up to the big leagues. And I was right.

After I successfully defused the situation with my colleagues and promised them the scoop once I had completed my interview, I came up the driveway. The Farley's house was a pleasant home—single story with a clay shingle roof, white stucco exterior appointed with plenty of windows. I could see the crowd gathered in the kitchen, and they could see me. I decided to forgo the front door after I saw the porch on the side of the house with the sliding glass door.

I approached the door, making eye contact with Veronica Salazar first. She rolled her eyes as a greeting. Felix Acosta pointed my presence out to Maggie, who came over to the door with a half-smile. She slid the door open. I was hit by the cool air conditioning and the warm nutty odor of coffee.

"Why, aren't you the most beautiful woman," I said. "And with all you're going through, I just want to say how much I appreciate your time. I'm sure my friends helped prepare you. We've grown into such a family in the last few months. They are the best. If it weren't for them, you and I might never have met. But still, we have so much more work to do."

Maggie stood wide-eyed with her right hand extended and her mouth open as if she was going to say something.

"You don't mind if I come in, do you?" I asked.

Maggie moved, swinging her right arm in a welcoming gesture, and I entered her home.

"Hey, Mike," I said. "Good to see you. Investigator Acosta, good to see you. Ms. Salazar, you're as lovely as ever."

The three cops were in an adjoining living room, standing near each other, but their body language saying they were very far apart. They each faced different directions, Veronica's eyes on the ceiling, Mike's on floor, and Felix gazed through the kitchen and out a far window.

I stopped mid-stride. "And you, I don't believe I know."

The big woman on the stool looked me up and down with a taste of something sour in her mouth. She made a derisive noise that may have been words, but I couldn't tell. I raised my eyebrows and turned my head inquisitively. "Excuse me?"

"Diane," she said. "You're disrupting our neighborhood."

"Oh geez, I'm so sorry. I had a few of my professional friends and colleagues come with me. I certainly did not intend to cause a stir."

"Well, you're a little late on the apology," Diane said.

"What are you looking for Figueroa?" Felix said. His eyes drooped under a heavy brow; his mouth curled at the corners into an overall sad expression.

"Well, Investigator, I'm not here to step on any toes. Are you all done with your investigation? I'm still in the middle of mine, and I've not yet had the chance to speak with the woman of the hour." I turned back toward Maggie. "Mrs. Farley, I am here because I want to tell your story. The tragedy of your mother's death, the sadness that you never knew her, and the compelling bravery of your search for truth and hopefully some measure of justice. These fine officers will dig into the facts and the law, but I can bring you before the masses."

Maggie looked sideways toward me as I stopped talking, allowing the silence to breathe. No one else in the room had an inkling to say anything either. We all waited for Maggie to say something.

"Mr. Figueroa..." she began.

"Please, call me Tim."

"Let her talk, asshole," Diane said.

I held up my hands. My one hand slipped into my pocket for my recorder but came up empty. I kept forgetting that I lost it somewhere. The assembly watched me carefully, so using my other hand, I pulled an imaginary zipper across my lips.

"Tim," Maggie said. "I don't know what I want out of all of this. I never thought in a million years that my DNA test was going to come back to a murdered woman. I was hoping for some distant cousin or a half-brother that I could add to my life. The best laid plans had me finding my birth parents and discovering they were some teenagers who weren't ready for a child and gave me up to a better life. I wanted to thank them for letting me come into the world and be at peace with a past I'd never known."

"I totally get ... " I said

"Shut the hell up."

Maggie looked back at Diane. The bigger woman leaned on her hand, squishing the flesh of her face up. When Maggie came back to look at me, she dropped her eyes to the ground.

"Tim, I don't know if I want to go the rest of the way down this path. I feel like I'm at the beginning of the trail looking up at a mountain, not sure if I want to make the climb. I have a terrific family and a comfortable life here. I don't have any more information about Jane Doe than you all know already. My adoptive parents never met her. They got me from an orphanage where I'd been abandoned. I feel like this is going to be too hard for me."

I listened, trying to soften my gaze and look empathetic. I nodded along with her words. But I was thinking of my response the whole time.

"I can only imagine the fear you must have," I said.

"It's not fear."

"Then the apprehension. The uncertainty of the results. This is painful enough without having to share it with the whole world."

"Yeah," Maggie said. Her voice caught for a second, and she swallowed a lump in her throat. "And I don't want to let the family that I do have down."

I decided to change my approach.

"Mike, did you tell Mrs. Farley about your father?"

Veronica and Mike spoke at the same time, "He did" and "Yeah."

"Don't you see the depth of all of this? Your mother knew his father. She's dead. He's dead. No one left to tell the tale. Except if you two... Yeah, you two can join forces to bring justice to Jane Doe."

Lightning jumped across Mike's face, and I could see it broadly in his eyes. He fidgeted a little where he stood, his lips curling.

"What do you think of that, Mike?" I asked.

"I think it will be the hardest thing I'd ever have to do."

"You're not alone, Maggie," I said.

She looked past me now out the window behind me toward some far-off point. The room became still again. The air became burdensome. There was strain on Felix Acosta's face and disgust on Veronica Salazar's. Mike appeared to be searching the same distant landmark as Maggie. I was sure that his intrigued mind was spinning. Diane looked just plain fed up.

"Listen, asshole," she said. It had become her pet name for me. "You've done enough manipulating here today. Maggie does not need all this pressure. And neither does this guy. Bill's gonna be home soon, and he's gonna shit a brick with all these people here."

"You know, dear, you're one hundred percent correct. I need to give it some space. Let it lay out there a little, seep into your minds. I'm all high-pressure sales right now. I overdid it."

I began to back away with my hands up.

"Tim," Maggie said softly. "I appreciate what you said."

"Nope, nope. Give it some time. Mike has my number. He can give it to you if you want it. I'm gonna go. Thank you, thank you, thank you."

Reaching behind me, I found the sliding glass door handle and dragged it open in a fluid motion, continuing my reverse steps onto the porch. Once through the portal, I smoothly shut it, then I descended the steps. As I started across the driveway, a large Ford F350 pickup truck came toward me. The driver stopped where I stood, exited the vehicle, and stood before me. This was Bill Farley.

"Who the hell are you?" he asked.

"Mr. Farley? I'm Tim Figueroa, host of the podcast 'Figure It Out With Figgy.' I was just in briefly to speak with Mrs. Farley regarding a cold case murder that I profiled."

"I thought this whole thing was over?"

"No, sir. Well, not yet."

"I guess you can't put the shit back in the cow?"

I smiled and nodded.

"Are those cops back too?" he asked. He was looking around me at the rental car parked in the drive.

"Yes, the investigators are all here."

He began to shake his head. His expression was not anger, more of an exasperation. If I had known him better at the time, I'd say he was afraid.

"Well, Mr. Figgy, or whatever, I'm going in to speak with my wife."

"It was nice to meet you, Mr. Farley. You can call me Tim."

"Yeah, sure."

He climbed back up into the F350. I stood out of the way as he continued up toward the garage. I turned to admire the house once again. Everyone remained in the kitchen with their eyes on me. I waved. Then, turning around, I went down the driveway.

25

Laura sat on the hood of her car outside the police station. She wrapped herself in a thick sweatshirt as an insulation to the cooling fall air. A breeze cut through and that made her curl up, crossing her arms. She rocked ever so slightly. The sudden shine of headlights darted across her eyes. She looked to see the marked Durango pulling into the parking lot. It stopped perpendicular to Laura's car. Through the passenger side window, she could see Mike. He exited the vehicle and came around the front of the Durango.

"Hey," he said. "I didn't expect you to be here."

"I guess I didn't expect you either. This is the third night in a row I've waited out here."

"Why didn't you call?"

"Thought you were busy."

"I was. I was in California."

"I know. You told me before you left."

"Oh, that's right."

"How come you didn't call me?" she asked. She uncrossed her arms and slid from the hood. She stood near Mike.

"I just got back. This is my first shift."

"I've never seen you like this."

Mike looked down at his uniform. He touched items on his belt intermittently. He looked up into her eyes.

"You look different like this," Laura said. She gave him a coy smile. "Girls tend to like a guy in uniform."

Mike swallowed hard. "I'm sorry I didn't call you."

"You're forgiven. Did you get any more leads?"

Mike curled his face sheepishly, shaking his head slightly. "No, I didn't."

"What did you do in California?"

"We talked to the woman who matched Jane Doe's DNA. But she has no connection to Carolina."

"I thought you said this little side quest was going to help you?"

"I still think the two murders are related. I just don't know how."

Laura hung her head, crossing her arms again across her chest. She sagged onto the bumper of her car.

"She came back to New York with us," Mike said. "Maybe there's something she can help us with."

"How?" Laura asked. She raised her face to Mike.

Mike just shook his head again. "I don't know."

Laura looked into Mike's eyes through the light of the headlamps. There was sincerity in his conviction.

"I'll be honest with you about something," Laura said.

Mike's face perked up. "What's that?"

"I was looking forward to seeing you again."

"I thought you hated me?"

"I know you had no control over what Acosta did. Not many people have good things to say about me. You're one of the few people I have in my corner."

"Of course," Mike said.

"You want to go somewhere?" she asked.

"Sure. I'm off duty in ten minutes. If you can wait, I'll be back in twenty."

"Sure."

Mike retreated to the Durango and drove it over into a parking spot. After reversing into a space, Laura watched Mike go inside the building with an armload of equipment. She turned back toward her car, faced the police station again, and hopped her rear end onto the hood.

The night was soundless. The breeze alighted her shoulders. She shivered and pulled herself close again. She used her hands to warm the upper portion of her arms through friction. Her focus was far away, and she was not conscious of time passing.

"Hey there," a voice said.

She felt the startle in her heart as her whole body tensed and released. Laura's focus cleared, and she saw someone crossing the parking lot on foot. The silhouette was too short to be Mike. As the person came closer, she saw it was an older man. He was dressed in a uniform, but his shirt was white and his hat had a yellow rope around the crown. He wore a fleece jacket embroidered with a name, *JUSTIN,* on his right breast and a police badge on the left. The epaulets on his shoulders were adorned with stars.

"Hi," Laura answered. She narrowed her eyes to get a full picture of the man.

"I'm Police Chief Justin. I've noticed you sitting in our lot the last couple of nights. Thought I'd come out and speak with you."

Chief Justin arrived at Laura's car. She could see him clearly now. His silver-tinged hair escaped from the bottom of the hat, and fine creases were set into his face. He had sharp little eyes and a small mouth that seemed perpetually pursed. He extended his right hand.

Laura looked at the hand before she unfolded herself and returned the gesture.

"And you are?" he asked.

"Laura Velez," she said.

His expression brightened with a realization. "Oh, I am so sorry for your loss. How is your family?"

Laura sunk her eyes. "Thank you."

"Is there something I can help you with?" the chief asked.

"I was waiting for Mike."

"Oh, Ellis? Yes, he's still working on your sister's case part-time. Have you spoken to the state police investigator?"

"I've met him."

"I bet Ellis is a little easier on you, right? He's been sick the last couple of days."

Laura raised her head, cocking it slightly in bemusement. "I thought he was in California?"

"Why was he there?"

Laura took her time to answer the question. She was sure the confusion wore plainly on her face. "He was following up the DNA lead."

"Oh, that silly Jane Doe nonsense again? Wow, that's a dead-end. I spoke with Investigator Acosta about that. He was telling me that he no longer believes it is a viable option. And neither does the district attorney's office. Their investigator, your aunt, is also backing off from that line of follow-up. I guess Ellis is the only one who still believes in it."

Laura did not speak. She felt the hot rage curling up inside of her.

"I think he's grasping at straws. I personally have no great investigative mind, but Felix Acosta does. He's been doing this for a very long time. And so has your aunt. I know Veronica well. You should think about who you trust when it comes to the murder of your sister."

Chief Justin nodded in an expression of excusing himself. He turned, disappearing back into the darkness he had come from. Laura was left alone, still on the hood of her car. She watched in the direction the chief had gone in, losing herself again in thought.

"Hey," Mike's voice said. Laura was not startled. She coolly turned her head to face him.

"Got lost in some thoughts," she said.

"I didn't mean to scare you."

Laura shook her head as she slid from the hood of the car. She arched her back, pushing her chest out slightly. She bent almost imperceptibly, rising to flip her hair over her head. Mike was smiling.

"Convince me, Mike," she said.

Mike looked at her with a long stare. Her hands were on her hips, her shoulders squared, and she leaned toward him.

"Felix and Aunt Veronica aren't on board with your theory anymore."

"Maybe they aren't. But I haven't changed my mind."

"Convince me, then," she said.

"There's a lot of circumstantial belief. I'll admit that. But the parallels between the two cases are interesting. Single women, similar age. Strangulation as the method. Little or no physical evidence. The Overlook and the Overlook trailhead. Like bookends almost. The positioning of the bodies. And a cop named Ellis."

Laura shook her head. She raised it high into the sky as she felt the swelling of emotion in her chest. "That's not good enough," she said. "You don't have a suspect. Your theory has nothing to it."

"Well, Felix and Veronica don't have anything better. I still don't even know why you were a suspect."

Laura's eyes dropped to the ground. She kicked at the gravel beneath her feet.

"I'm surprised Acosta hasn't told you."

Mike didn't say anything.

"I want to tell you, Mike, but I don't want it to affect how you think of me."

"Why do you care?" He took a few steps toward her.

"Because I want you to have a good opinion of me. You seem to, and I don't want to ruin that."

Mike sighed. "Well, now that we're back home, I'm going to be spreading the word about the Jane Doe case. That'll keep the light on Carolina as well."

"How are you going to do that?"

"I told you Jane Doe's daughter came back with us. She and I are going to do some interviews with this podcast host Tim Figueroa. He did a whole episode dedicated to Jane Doe, and he's trying to take our lead and blow the whole story up."

"What's she like?" Laura asked. She felt a release of pressure in her chest.

"Who? Maggie? She's amazing. She's got four kids and manages them all while she still works. She's got her head up in this whole whirlwind of activity. She's confident and optimistic."

"And I'm the opposite."

"I wasn't trying to compare you to her."

"Maybe I should meet her?"

Mike took a beat as if he were judging the statement. "It's a good idea. She really is the ultimate mom. Maybe you could use someone like that?"

"Thank you," Laura said.

"For what?" Mike asked.

"You really are one of the only people on my side."

"What about your aunt and your cousin?"

"Aunt Roni knows I had nothing to do with Carolina's death. She welcomed me into her home. But that doesn't mean that she approves of me. Bradley is a different story altogether. He certainly doesn't trust me."

"This has to do with your past?" Mike asked.

"I'll tell you about it sometime. Just not right now."

"Okay, I get it," Mike said.

"Tell me something about yourself. That way I have a reason to give you something back."

Mike clenched his eyes, tilting his head skyward. A faint gurgle emitted from his throat as he thought.

"Okay, okay. Before I came back here to be a cop, I was actually in the seminary. I was working toward taking my vows."

"Oh, shit, really? You're a priest?"

"Just not long enough."

"No vows taken then?"

"No."

"Why?"

"Maybe I'll tell you when you tell me something."

"You pick up on games quickly."

"I do?"

Laura laughed in a short burst of sound. "I'm gonna keep trusting you, Mike Ellis."

"I won't let you down," he said.

###

I sat in the makeup chair as the young artist applied foundation to my face, the glow of artificial light illuminating each flaw in my skin. Between applications, I glanced over to see Maggie Farley sitting in the adjacent chair, another makeup artist busy with her. We were in the banquet room at one of the big ski hotels in Hunter, which awaited the first snowflakes of the season.

"I think, my dear, that this was the right decision," I said. I felt the correct amount of confidence and reassurance was inflected.

Maggie could not look over at me as the woman working with her was applying eye shadow. But she managed to say, "I hope so." A lengthy sigh exhaled from her chest.

"Okay," a voice said from behind me. "So, Mr. Figueroa and Mrs. Farley, I'm glad to see you both are almost ready. This is going to be a remote, so the anchor in New York City will be asking the questions. Do we know where Mr. Ellis is?"

I could hear the producer, a middle-aged man named Ivan, waving a clipboard as the attached papers fluttered around. One of the production assistants chirped some answers, and then I heard the heel-toe footsteps of someone running.

"Have you ever been on TV before?" Ivan asked.

"Sure," I said. "Of course."

"No," Maggie said.

"Okay, so quick run-down. You're going to be mic'd up with a little fella just like this." Ivan held up a small clip-on microphone. "I'm going to have you all sit together on one camera. Save the control booth some cuts."

"What are the questions going to be?" Maggie asked.

"Oh, honey, nothing you need to worry about. Just asking for some background. Nothing too heavy. You guys just want to get people talking," Ivan said.

"Yeah, I guess," Maggie said.

"This is an appetizer," I said. "Stories like this must be built. My podcast was a wonderful foundation, and my audience is there. But we want to reach out further. There may be some retired nun in Ohio that knows all about you. She's not listening to true crime podcasts. Unfortunately. But she's watching cable news in the day room. I promise you that."

"What he said," Ivan agreed. "Oh, there you are Mr. Ellis."

I was free to turn at that point to see Mike coming into the makeup area. He was sweating and had a fresh razor burn along his neck and part of his cheek. Good thing he was coming in here before going on camera. He wore a navy blue polo shirt with khakis, matching my white golf shirt with green stripes and gray slacks.

"Sorry I'm late," Mike said.

"Better late than never," Ivan said. "Let's get him made up quickly. We've got less than ten."

Ivan left the room in a hurry. I got out of my chair, allowing Mike to replace me.

"Are you nervous?" I asked him.

"Yeah, I think I'm nervous."

"You don't seem sure."

"I'm nervous, too," Maggie said. She was finished in the makeup chair, turning toward us for the conversation.

"You will be fine, both of you. Just be honest and forthright and sympathetic."

"How do I do that?" Mike asked.

"Let the audience know how you feel. Make them feel it too."

Mike relaxed a bit to allow the makeup artist to do her work. He stared at me from the side of his view.

"Where's Bill?" I asked Maggie.

"In the room. He's trying to be supportive, but he has his limits."

"He's brave, just like you."

"I don't know about 'brave.' I think it's possibly foolish for me to be here, calling all this attention to myself."

"Calling attention to your mother," I said.

She nodded and closed her eyes. "I just want this all to work out somehow."

"It will."

The hustle began again once Ivan returned with two more production assistants who ushered us from the makeup room onto the "set" that was put together in another function room at the hotel. There were three chairs made of sturdy, decorative wood formed into an arch shape with a camera aimed at the center. There were three stand-ins sitting in the chairs when we arrived, more production assistants, and possibly a van driver. Ivan shooed them away, looking at the camera operator to ensure the blocking was mapped out.

"Okay, okay. Mrs. Farley, you will be center. Mr. Ellis to her right. Mr. Figueroa on her left."

We each took our assigned seat. Maggie smoothed her floral-patterned dress as she crossed her legs at the ankle. Mike twitched in his chair, rolling his shoulders as far back as he could, sitting up with an overcorrected posture. I eased back in the seat. I put my hands on my lap and looked at the monitor before us.

We were fitted for the microphones and each of us received an earpiece.

"Hello?" a voice came across. "Raise a hand if you can hear me."

I raised my hand, looking over at Maggie and Mike who slowly brought their arms up.

"Excellent. Okay, Miranda, they're all yours."

The anchor in New York City, Miranda, came across the earpieces explaining that she was going to ask questions. She said she would attempt to direct questions at individuals, but in case she didn't, we should try not to talk over one another. She asked one more time if we were ready. Then it started.

The segment was scheduled for three minutes. Miranda began with me, and I explained my interest and my research.

"I saw a grave injustice for this young woman. I wanted to tell her story," I said in summary.

Next, Miranda focused on Maggie. Maggie briefly explained her life story, beginning with the orphanage and ending with the DNA testing.

"And of course, I had no idea that I was running headlong into this whole thing," she said.

Then Miranda came to Mike. I could sense his whole body tense as she began asking him questions. He recapped his father's involvement and how Mike had helped push for the exhumation of Jane Doe's body.

"What was it that finally got the judge to go along with it?" Miranda asked.

"I uncovered evidence that suggested that my father knew who Jane Doe really was," he said.

On the monitor, I could read the thoughts crossing over Miranda's mind. It was an unexpected statement. She scrambled for some notes on her desk.

"But we still don't know her identity to this day?"

Mike looked over at me. I crooked my neck to see him. We both straightened and looked back into the camera.

"No," I said.

Miranda's time was up, but again on the monitor, I saw that she wanted to ask something further. But she let it go. For now, I assumed. The segment ended. We unclipped our microphones, pulled the earpieces out, and stood up together. Mike released a long breath of air.

"That was intense," he said.

"Yes, it was," Maggie agreed.

I looked at my watch. "We have another one in about twenty minutes."

"What do you mean?" Mike asked.

"You don't just go on one channel, Mike. We've got to spread this out. Equal opportunity for all comers. I've got a couple podcast friends that want to have us on after that."

"I'm gonna go check on Bill and call home, then," Maggie said.

As she walked off, I clasped Mike's shoulder.

"That woman is going to bring us fame and fortune, young man. She is the key to this mystery. I just know it. Listen, I had an idea. Let me know what you think before I bring it up to her. They still haven't returned Jane Doe to the ground yet, have they?"

Mike shook his head. "I don't think so. After we got the leads, they wanted to keep her until more testing could be done."

"Outstanding. We'll have Maggie go to the cemetery when they bury her again. Let her pay her respects with an actual funeral."

"That may help her," Mike said. "A little closure at least."

"And think of the ratings. It'll be the image to close the book."

"Book?"

"Cover all the media, Mike: audio, video, print. I'm trying to saturate the market. It's a news cycle. Gotta keep feeding them quarters. This was a good start. You're doing great. That bombshell was perfect."

"Bombshell?" he asked.

"Yeah, about your dad. He knew her. He's the only one who knew her. Maybe he's the only one to..." I said.

Both Mike and I let the statement hang. Mike's eyes curled in their sockets as he looked at me. He moved away with a slow turn. Ivan, the producer, came walking across the set clapping his hands.

"Gentlemen, that was wonderful. We're watching our socials right now, and I do believe you're trending. So happy for you. I know you've got other spots, but we'd love to get all of you back on again."

"Give me a call later," I told him.

Mike did not say anything before he walked away, leaving me alone with Ivan. I watched his back as he disappeared around the other people.

26

Felix Acosta lounged loosely behind the wheel of the Charger. The seat reclined at a ridiculous angle, and his compact frame stretched out fully. From behind his Ray-Ban sunglasses, he gazed up at his right hand holding a sideways cell phone as a video played on the screen. Maggie Farley, Mike Ellis, and I sat in a row of chairs. An in-person interviewer was bantering with us, asking questions and restating answers.

"Why do you think your father kept Jane Doe's identity a secret for so long?" the interviewer asked.

A camera shot brought a close-up of Mike's face. His look was unhurried, and his expression was one of false modesty. His eyebrows rose, pulling his eyelids up. His nostrils flared with his sightline moving up and to the right. A demure smile shot across his lips before fading away. Felix reached up with his free hand to pull the Ray-Bans down. He waited for the answer to come from the young man's mouth.

"Well, Jake, I think whatever his connection was to her, he thought that it'd hurt him."

"That's obvious. But what do you think that is?"

Mike hardly reacted. Felix pulled the glasses from his face.

"That's impossible to tell with the information that I have. As we continue to investigate, we're hoping to uncover more answers."

"Do you think it's possible that he was involved in her death?" Jake the interviewer asked.

Mike looked up again. His face drew, his eyes narrowed. He looked down the line toward Tim and Maggie. Felix sat up in his seat.

"I don't think we can rule that out," Mike said.

Felix reached down to manipulate the chair's mechanical adjustment button. The back of the seat rose slowly, lifting Felix up to a seated position. The video on the phone continued as the interviewer switched his focus to Maggie and her background. Felix hit the button on the side of the phone, causing the screen to go blank before tossing it onto the passenger seat. He looked out of the windshield toward the rear of the Hunter Police Department. He observed the rear door of the building open and two uniformed officers come out. He recognized the two men, but then the door swung out again and Felix recognized Paul Hunter. Felix reached for the handle on the door to let himself out. He crossed the parking lot directly toward Paul. He began waving his hand to get the cop's attention. Paul stopped at one of the patrol vehicles, his attention on Felix.

"Officer Hunter," Felix said. "Can I talk to you?"

Paul set his patrol bag on the hood of his car and glanced at the other two officers. Felix approached, slowing his pace and controlling his breath so that he could speak.

"Investigator Acosta?" Paul asked.

"Yes, I know I've met you before. But maybe not so formally."

"I've heard some things about you. What's up?"

Felix took a moment before he spoke. His face might have betrayed an inkling of new suspicion. He consciously tried to install his poker face, setting his jaw, steeling his eyes, and smoothing the lines of emotion. He pursed his lips, but the cluck he liked to make was too dry. Paul's shoulders dropped with impatience.

"Sorry, yeah, I know. I have some questions about Ellis."

"Charlie or Mike?" one of the other officers asked. He approached the pair.

Felix looked at his nametape and read, *HAVERTHY*.

"Maybe both?" Felix said.

"I worked about half my career for Charlie," Haverthy said. "Almost twelve years."

"And Mike?"

"I've known the kid for probably less than six months. Odd little shit."

"What's your question?" Paul asked.

Felix paused again. The other officer came up to the group and Felix saw his nametape read, *JONES*.

"What's going on?" Jones asked.

"This guy has questions about Charlie Ellis."

Felix shook his head while holding up his hand.

"Gentlemen, please," he said. "I am here to ask a couple questions about Mike Ellis. Not Charlie."

"Aren't you working on that thing about the Jane Doe case? You know, with Mike?" Haverthy asked.

"No, I'm not. I am here because I'm investigating the murder of Carolina Velez. Mike was working with me on that."

"But not anymore?" Paul said.

"It doesn't seem that way, does it?" Felix said. "He's a little busy on TV. My first question to you is: did Mike know Carolina Velez?"

Paul's face changed first. Then, his head dropped, his eyes on his boots. "Yeah, he'd met her at the diner."

"And don't forget the bowling alley," Haverthy said.

"Yeah, Mike was definitely into her," Jones added.

"How could you tell?" Felix asked.

"He's a young kid. She was a hot, young piece of ass. I assume you were young once. You'd have to have taken vows not to pursue her," Haverthy answered.

"So, he was interested? Did he make any moves?"

Jones said, "He tried. He's just so fucking awkward."

"Man, we all tried with her in one way or another," Haverthy said. "Pickings are slim outside of tourists. She was new and exotic. And did I mention how hot she was?"

Paul looked at Haverthy and Jones.

"Okay, all of us were looking at her except the family man here."

Felix eyed Paul. He gave him a speedy once over, noticing his precise clothing, shiny boots, and the black rubber ring around his left ring finger. Felix changed tactics.

"Did Mike ever talk about her?"

"Not that I ever heard. But shit, he lit up around her," Haverthy said.

"Yeah, she worked the bar at the bowling alley. He'd volunteer to get us drinks so he could go up there," Jones said.

"And he and Bell timed dinner just so they had her as their waitress," Haverthy added.

"He'd seen her outside of those few times," Paul said.

Felix looked at him, but Paul's head was pointed toward the ground. "What do you mean?"

"After he first heard about the Overlook case, Mike went up there. He told me and Hugh that he had followed Carolina the entire way up. He told us that he kept his distance so that she didn't know he was there."

"He said it was a coincidence?"

"That's how it seemed. Mike had no intention of talking to her, but she approached him."

"What about the night she was killed?" Felix asked.

"What about it?" Haverthy said.

"Obviously Mike was working because he was the first one there. Were any of you on duty?"

Paul nodded as Haverthy and Jones shook their heads.

"You didn't respond?" Felix asked Paul.

"No, I was directed to remain free for calls. Hugh went to back Mike up."

"What was his post that night?"

"Post 2. The west side of town."

"Yet, he was the first on scene at the east end?"

"I guess so."

Felix nodded. He could sense his swagger returning as the thoughts flowed from his mind to his lips unencumbered. Paul was still not looking at him, but the answers he provided seemed sincere. Felix could read in his body language that his point was coming across.

"Now, about Charlie," Felix said. His attention turned toward Haverthy. "What do you know about him?"

"He was a good guy to work for. Always had our back."

"Did he ever do anything suspicious?" "What do you mean?"

Felix did not respond. He felt a twinge in his brain that told him to stop. He looked at his watch.

"I don't want to keep you fellas any longer. Why don't you guys go out and get after it? Be safe out there." He winked at the three cops.

He turned on his heel. As he walked away, he could hear some mumbling from Jones and Haverthy. His smile spread like an open wound showing all his teeth. Reaching his car, he swung into the driver's seat. Looking back across the parking lot through the windshield, he saw Paul Hunter still standing in front of his patrol car, his head now up and staring back at Felix. Blindly, Felix reached for his cell phone on the passenger seat. He glanced at it momentarily to find the contact he wanted: Veronica Salazar. He selected her name. The phone began to ring.

Veronica's voice came across in a harsh tone. "What do you want, Felix?"

Felix chewed the air for a second, feeling his mouth lubricate. "Nice to hear your voice, too."

"I haven't time for this, again. I told you what happened in California..."

"I know, I know. It stays there. That's not why I'm calling. Although it seems to be on the top of your mind."

"It's not. Trust me."

Felix chuckled. His eyes stayed trained on the solo figure of Paul Hunter in front of his car. The other two guys were pulling out as Felix looked on, but Paul remained in place. Felix got lost in the moment.

"What do you want, Felix?" Veronica's voice solicited, more forcefully.

"I've got a new angle on Carolina's murder. I'd like to talk to you in person. Also, I'd like to talk to your niece again."

"About what?"

"Mike Ellis."

###

Laura came into the diner by throwing open the door, the sleigh bells clanging a siren of warning. The trailing vapor of cigarette smoke escaped her mouth, and she looked like a rage-filled bull. She searched around, ignoring the waitress speaking to her until she located her target. She found him. Mike sat in the rear of the restaurant facing toward the door. He raised his hand to draw her attention until he saw the look on her face, and he lowered it. Laura turned precisely and allowed the click-clack of her heels to sync up to the thumps of her elevated heart rate. As she drew nearer to Mike, the shadow of terror seemed to crawl over him.

"Hi Laura," he said. The words dribbled from his lips.

The slap was probably over the top, and it grabbed the attention of everyone in the diner. Laura could feel all the eyes on her. Her breathing came out as seethes as her glaring eyes ripped into Mike's.

He did not bring his hand to his cheek. Seemingly, he turned the other toward her, staring back with confused eyes. Mike gently gestured with his head and a hand to the seat across from him. Laura looked to where he was pointing. She scowled at him, locking her eyes.

"Laura, please sit down," he said. His tone was high, sweet—warbling even.

She broke her eye contact. Mechanically, she moved toward the seat, finding herself falling into it. Her arms crossed; her eyes looked askance. Without any thought, she pulled a pack of cigarettes from her jacket pocket. Fumbling to open the cardboard box with her shaking hands, she selected a slender stick of nicotine. She looked around, reminding herself where she was, and held the cigarette in her closed fist.

"What is the matter?" Mike asked.

She did not answer. Her body vibrated arrhythmically. Her hands and face tingled, and her eyes stung as she stole glances at Mike's stupid, fat face.

"Please talk to me. I'm here for you."

Laura felt his arms reach out. She gave the outstretched hands a disgusted glance before she averted looking at him again altogether.

"Listen, you sat down. You obviously want to say something to me. Just say it."

The tension in her chest cascaded and finally, she unleashed. "You know what? You stupid motherfucker, I got played by you for the second time. I trusted you. Twice, I trusted you. Not only did you sell me out to the cop who was running me down, then you used my aunt to get what you wanted. Now you're all over the TV talking about your daddy issues with that bitch from California. You know who hasn't been on TV in the last few days? Do you?"

Mike did not respond. He pulled his arms back, defensively. The color drained from his whole face, and Laura could see the onset of cotton mouth as Mike began moving his mouth in a way to create saliva.

"Yeah, my sister. You know, Carolina? No one has a care in the world about her. You seemed to have forgotten your promise. Or were you just using her to get the attention on you and your issues? Sure is convenient that your daddy knew this dead lady and knew my sister. Oh boy, you got me creating conspiracy theories now. Shit, maybe I can get on one of these shows. Then at least my sister's name will come out of somebody's mouth."

Laura was not quiet, the strain in her vocal cords hurt as she pushed out the emotion. She felt the pressure in her eyes, the moisture welling up from the ducts. Something in her sucked those back though. She fought to keep herself together. With her mind emptied, she felt a release of tension in her chest and clarity washed over her. She watched for Mike's reaction.

He just sat there, the color in his face now turning red with his eyes wide and his mouth agape. He avoided eye contact now, while hers sought out the connection. His silence was as stark as her shouting had been. The whole diner seemed to be waiting for the next barrage, and Laura was very aware of it.

"What do you have to say now?" Laura asked.

Mike drew in a breath. "I haven't forgotten about Carolina. Jesus, I can't get her out of my head."

"That's not what I've been hearing any time I put on the TV."

"I still believe that following Jane Doe will tell us who killed Carolina."

"There's no link. Nothing at all."

"So far."

"It's been more than two months, Mike. Almost like three, really. The only suspect they brought in was me. I've been clear for two months. And you guys have shit."

"You still haven't told me why he brought you in."

"You expect me to tell you? You've lost my trust. Why don't you go talk to Acosta?"

"I don't want to hear it from him. I want to hear it from you."

"From me, huh?"

"You told me two nights ago that I was the only one in your corner."

"Yeah, I thought that was true. You told me you were going to put Carolina's name out there. Two solid days of interviews and I haven't heard my sister's name once. I don't believe you anymore."

Mike nodded. His hands crept slowly back across the table. Laura's arms unfolded, falling to her sides. Laura felt the adrenaline dump begin to fade. She saw Mike differently now. His boyish face was shattered with the realization of what he had done.

"You don't know me, Mike. You never will." Her volume was controlled, low, and calm now. She felt a pang to reach out to him.

"I know you can't go home to see your family. I know that you had to sit in the rear of the church during Carolina's funeral. I know you don't belong here. I just don't know why."

"And you won't."

"Okay."

"What about tying my sister to your TV appearances? Why did you lie to me?"

"We're building to that."

"What? After you finish tearing down your father's memory? Do you have loyalty to anyone?"

"Of course I do. I'm loyal to you and to your sister."

"It feels like you're just out for yourself. I've seen you on screen, telling your sad story about your daddy. You're making it look like he was the murderer. Do you know what's happening right now?"

Mike shook his head. His face was blank, completely oblivious.

"Felix came sniffing around my aunt a few hours ago. Did you know about that and didn't tell me? He sits at her kitchen table, and he tells her that he has a new theory. It's not about the victim's estranged sister or links to a long-dead cold case. No, it's about you."

Mike retracted his arms, placing his hands over his chest. His eyes widened and he mouthed the word, *Me?*

"Yes, you. Felix's new theory is that you killed my sister."

The information struck Mike hard. His short-circuited stammering of innocence was altogether unconvincing. Laura glared back at him in disbelief. She searched his whole face, which was contorted in a mix of fear, shock, and desperation. His arms moved to the top of the table, palms up. He sputtered some more denials.

"You can't believe that?" Mike said in conclusion.

Laura had an answer sitting in the front of her brain. But she let it sit there, some sort of filter blocking out the plain truth as she wanted to see it at this very moment. But her silence said it all for her.

"Laura, you have to listen to me," Mike said. It was a pathetic plea. He had no alibi, no argument against the suspicion. He simply wanted her trust.

Laura felt the tension rise again inside her. The swelling of her eyes caused her to blink uncontrollably.

"Don't you have to get back on TV?" she asked. She collected herself and began to get up. She opened the cardboard pack of cigarettes and moved to slide the loose cigarette back in. She stopped, reconsidered, and put the cigarette between her lips.

"Wait, what else did Felix say?"

"I don't know. But don't worry, I didn't lead him here or anything. I'm not like you."

She stood up fully, the pack of cigarettes going into her jacket pocket. Mike made a half-hearted lunge toward her, begging her to sit down. Now he wanted more information. Now he cared about Carolina. She removed the cigarette from her mouth.

"I don't want to see you again. Don't call me. Don't text. Go and figure it all out. I'm done with the Overlook. I'm done with this town. Maybe I just need to get out of here for a while. There's no justice for me. There's no justice for my sister."

She felt Mike's hand on her arm. She wouldn't let herself look down at his hand. She knew that she would see his face, and then maybe be powerless.

"I will find her killer. It wasn't me," he said. "You don't have to trust me. But I promise you there will be justice."

Laura shook his hand from her. She walked away and did not look back.

\#\#\#

Paul sat in the driveway in front of the Ellis house staring at the door. The Durango was still running, and the traffic on the radio murmured in his ear. He looked at the clock on the dashboard, calculating the minutes that he had been there. The night was fully installed, and the moon was rising over the distant mountains. He mumbled to himself as he exited the vehicle, hoping that it wasn't too late. He counted his steps as he walked up to the front door and rapt precisely three times.

The door opened. Paul greeted Ann Ellis with a big smile. She was such a sweet, older lady, covered from neck to toe in a pink housecoat that was moth eaten and stretched loosely.

"Can I help you?" she asked. She looked him up and down, inspecting his uniform. "Are you a friend of Michael's?"

"Yes, ma'am."

"What a surprise. On the clock?"

"Yes, Mrs. Ellis. But this isn't business."

"Well, thank the Lord. I thought you were here about the grapes I sampled in the supermarket. What's your name, son?"

"Paul Hunter, ma'am."

"Oh, Helen's boy? How's your mother?"

Paul laughed. "She's fine, Mrs. Ellis. She keeps busy."

"I saw her at church this past week. Was that your family then?"

"Yes, my wife and my boys: Jessica, Ryan, and Nicholas."

"But I didn't see you?"

"Work."

"Ah, yes, the old ball and chain. Charles missed a lot of church, too. It was like I was the mistress."

Paul's smile faded to something a little more uneasy, but he managed to control his overall pleasant look.

"I don't like to miss it, but I'm glad Jessica is bringing the boys."

"Yes, Jessica, and Ryan and Nicholas."

Ann's grin grew, and her eyes were glassy and wistful. Paul noticed that she keyed in on the name of his wife and his sons like she was trying to remember them for future use.

"Is Mike around?" Paul asked.

"Well, of course. You want a cup of coffee or something, Paul? You can come into the kitchen."

Paul followed Ann into the house, trailing behind her by three or four steps. She called for Mike as she went down the hallway before turning into the open passageway into the kitchen. Paul came into the unfamiliar room, placing his Stetson on the counter before positioning himself by the sink. Ann had turned the corner to the other opening that led to the bedroom, her voice calling after her son. After making some contact, she came back kneading her hands together.

"Now, for that coffee," she said.

"You don't have to..."

"I know I don't have to. But you didn't say you didn't want it. Just let me get to the water."

Paul moved so Ann could fill up the coffee pot, his attention on her as the water ran. She finished, and when they both turned, Mike was in the doorway coming from his room. He had pillow creases on his face, and his now longer hair was matted across the top. With heavy eyes and a weak head nod, Mike greeted Paul.

"Hey," he said. "What's up?"

Paul glanced to his right to see Ann busy at the coffee maker before looking back at Mike and saying, "What happened at the diner?" His voice was a whisper.

Mike sighed and came through the remainder of the doorway. Ann looked up from scooping coffee, her eyes fixed on Paul. Mike had a disgusted, embarrassed look on his face as he came across the kitchen.

"I don't know. What have you heard?" Mike said. He looked at Paul sullenly.

"I got a personal call that you and Laura Velez had some sort of heated discussion."

"That's a strange way to put it."

Paul straightened himself. He looked at Ann, seeing her slide the coffee grounds and filter under the percolator before hitting the switch for the machine to do its processing. She turned around to face her son. Paul switched his focus back to Mike.

"That's what I heard. A heated conversation. What was it about?"

Mike dropped his shoulders. His sad, sullen face became defeated and vulnerable. It looked as though he scarcely knew what to say."S he's frustrated. There hasn't been any progress on her sister's case in a few weeks, and she's pissed off."

"At you?"

"Me?"

"Yeah, you. She's in a heated discussion with you. About her sister. Is she mad at you?"

"I guess so," Mike admitted.

Ann held up a hand, drawing the attention of both young men. "Paul, do you want cream and sugar? And Michael, do you want coffee?"

Paul could see Mike roll his eyes. Paul stole a glance to see if Ann had caught the disrespectful look, but if she had, she ignored it.

"No thanks, Ma. It's nearly ten o'clock. And I was asleep before you woke me up."

Ann turned her head toward Paul, cocking it in an inquisitive direction. Paul, feeling himself on the spot again, nodded his head.

"Sure," he said.

Ann again busied herself with collecting coffee mugs, sugar bowls, and a trip to the fridge for the carton of half and half.

"Why is she mad at you?" Paul asked.

Mike's attention was redirected back. "Because I haven't been as involved with her sister's case as much. She wants information, and I've been giving her what I could."

"That's all?"

Mike threw up his hands and made a grumbling sigh. Ann turned to look at her son briefly before returning to her task of assembling coffee materials. Paul watched Mike closely, reading his body language devolve into a cranky, childlike tantrum.

"I've been a little busy, Paul. I remember you being there when I found out that my father had been holding on to the secret of a murdered woman's identity for the last forty years. It's been a bit of a roller coaster since then. No, I haven't had time for Carolina. Or Laura. Is that a sin?'

Paul was taken aback as Mike's tone and volume began to increase as he spoke. Ann finished her toddling around, returning to her position near the coffee maker. The machine made small steamy puffs and gurgles which dominated the room in the silence after Mike's outburst. Paul noticed Ann made no reaction.

"I saw you on TV today, Michael," Ann said. Her back was to both men.

"We all did," Paul agreed.

Mike backed out of the center of the room. He yanked a chair from the table, sitting down in a heap with an accompanying sound of frustration ejaculating from his throat.

"Everyone is so worried about what I've been doing when it comes to Jane Doe. I broke the case wide open. I've changed the lives of so many people in the last few weeks. I found her daughter. Why am I being penalized for that?"

Paul answered first. "Because you've neglected everything else in the meantime. You have no time left to take off. I know Acosta is about to kick you off the Velez investigation."

"And, Michael, you've turned against your father," Ann said.

"All I said was that it's suspicious that he kept it to himself for so long. And as for work, I have been back all week without missing any time."

"Mike, we're all worried about you," Paul said.

Ann nodded along. "Yes, Son."

She walked up even with Paul, and he felt her almost shoulder to shoulder with him. Mike fell back in the chair, his arms crossing high up on his chest.

"I'm still convinced that the attention on Jane Doe will bring out Carolina's killer."

"I'm afraid you may be right," Paul said. He was solemn and serious.

"Why is that? Why are you afraid?"

"Because if Laura hasn't told you already, I'm the one that's going to have to."

"Tell me what?"

Paul swallowed hard. The coffee maker began to chime its single-note indication of a completed brew. Ann did not move, despite her assembled accoutrement.

"Mike, you're a suspect now. Acosta was at the station when I started my tour this afternoon. He suspects you."

Mike sat silently. Ann released a small gasp. Paul sensed her backing away toward the sink now, away from him.

"Get out of here, Paul," she said. She was not angry, but whatever instinct to protect her son had bubbled to the surface.

Paul looked at her but did not move. "Mrs. Ellis, I'm here as a friend."

"Apparently," Mike said, "you're not. She's right. You should get out of here."

Paul held up his hands. "You know Acosta better than me. But he's put his sights on you. You're gonna need help. And the last time I looked, you don't have a ton of friends."

"You're my friend?" Mike said. "Not the way you're acting right now. I think you should be going. Now."

"I'm here for you, Mike. And so is Hugh. Let us help you."

Mike stood up, his arms falling helplessly to his side. He trailed off slowly down the hall. Paul looked at Ann, her face aghast with the horrific realization. She held her hands to her mouth, soft sobs coming from her throat.

"He should make himself scarce until we can figure out what to do," Paul said.

27

While he waited at the bar, Bradley had a double shot of whiskey nestled in his big hand. The electronic jukebox sat silently in the corner. No one else was in the bowling alley to select a song. Not that Bradley would have noticed. His focused gaze was straight ahead. He sipped the whiskey without thought, as if a muscle memory. His face was flat, blank, and aloof. A television was on the wall opposite of him, also mute. The screen carried images of that cop Ellis, that asshole Figueroa, as well as some middle-aged broad Bradley did not know. The bartender walked past.

"Can't go anywhere without seeing the guys on the news," the bartender said. "You know that one guy is a local cop?"

Bradley's concentration was broken, and he blinked a few times. He looked up at the guy. It took Bradley a moment to think of the bartender's name, but it surfaced.

"Yeah, I know, Steve."

"And the other dude is some famous journalist or something."

"I've met him."

"And the woman is something important, too. I haven't really watched a whole segment to get the story down."

Bradley nodded, absentmindedly finishing his whiskey. He automatically spun the glass from his hand toward Steve. Steve returned a nod at Bradley's gesture for a refill.

"Been a wild couple of months. Didn't you know Carolina? The girl that used to work here. She got killed."

Steve produced a fresh whiskey glass, clanking two ice cubes in it before filling it with a long pour of fluid, flourishing at the end. He gently brought the glass to Bradley, sliding it to him on a wooden coaster.

"She was my cousin," Bradley said. His hand enclosed around the fresh glass of amber liquid before him.

"Oh shit. I'm so sorry, man," Steve said.

Bradley held up a hand.

Steve leaned into the bar from his side, closing the gap between them a little. "She was a good egg, you know? Beautiful girl, beautiful soul, just awesome."

"Yeah, I know." Bradley lost himself in his drink. He took in the aroma and swished the whiskey over the small ice cubes. He hardened his face as he thought about Carolina. Then, along the same line, he thought about Laura.

"I hope they figure out who did that. I mean, who does something like that, you know?" Steve said.

Bradley only caught the last part of what he was saying. He grunted a response and sipped some of the whiskey, allowing the smooth burn to envelop him. Steve leaned into the bar, his eyes begging the last question he had asked. Bradley softened his stare, setting the glass down on the coaster.

"I don't know, man," he said.

Something grabbed Steve's attention further down the bar. Bradley was not interested in looking, so he kept his eyes forward as Steve made his way down the length of the wooden furniture. Bradley could hear some chatter from Steve as he spoke to some other customer that had come up. Bradley didn't look. Then Steve's voice caught his ear again.

"I was just talking to this guy down here about it," Steve said from a distance. "Yeah, you're the local cop, right? Oh man, you should talk to this guy here. His cousin was the one that got killed."

Bradley lifted his glass and swallowed a pull of whiskey. From his periphery, he saw Steve approach. Bradley let a sigh seep from his throat as he set the glass back down. He gave Steve a cross-eyed look of disdain. The bartender ignored it.

"No shit, talk of the devil, right? The local guy we were just talking about is here."

Bradley turned his entire torso, and his hardened vision cut into the embodiment of Mike Ellis sitting twenty feet away. Bradley smiled with a wry expression, then extended a hand. He looked down at his gesture deliberately.

"Glad you could make it," Bradley said. His tone was the opposite of the friendliness of the expression.

Mike gave the hand due consideration before he slid off the stool and approached. He got within four feet or so and gave the extended gesture a second look. Bradley flexed his fingers, maintaining the elevation of his arm and hand.

"Can I get you something?" Steve asked.

Without looking at him, Mike said, "I'll have a cider."

Steve turned away, leaving Bradley and Mike alone briefly before returning with a pint of hard cider. Mike kept his eyes on Bradley's hand. He brought his arm up and grabbed the pint from the bar, taking a long swallow. After he set the glass back, Mike swung his grip into Bradley's. Bradley squeezed, and the veins in his forearm surfaced along his skin.

"Why did you call me?" Mike asked. He kept his face steady, although Bradley could see the discomfort in his brow.

Bradley released Mike's hand, turning his torso back to the bar to retrieve his whiskey glass. After a short sip, he looked up at the television again, observing the highlights of another interview featuring Mike, Tim, and the woman he didn't know.

"I want you to leave my family alone. My mom, my living cousin, my dead cousin. Just forget that any of us exist."

"But I made a promise…"

"I'm letting you off the hook. Stop looking into it. Go do local cop shit. You're not meant for anything else."

"But I've been working with…"

"Let Acosta take care of it on his own. He's trying to solve a crime that matters right now."

"You know that Laura thinks…"

"That you killed Carolina? That's bullshit. She doesn't believe that at all. But she doesn't trust you all the same. You're never gonna get that back."

"Why are you giving me this message?"

"Because you need to hear it. I don't want to see anyone cry anymore."

"I'm not the cause…"

"You broke Laura's heart, you shit," Bradley said. He took another pull of the whiskey, this one longer than the previous. "And my mom thinks you sold her out."

"What does Felix think?"

"I don't care about that asshole. He thinks you killed Carolina. But I know you didn't."

"How can you be so sure?"

Bradley set the glass on the bar. He turned his whole body now toward Mike. His face betrayed something in the deepest part of his memory. He heaved a sigh with his entire body.

"Do you know what those girls were caught up in?" Bradley asked.

"No, she won't tell…"

"Of course, she won't. What did Acosta tell you?"

"Drugs?"

Bradley slid off the stool and stretched his long frame to its full height. He put a hand on Mike's shoulder. A gentle offering.

"Laura used to run around with some bad dudes back in the day. They got her to run their product all over the tri-state. She got locked up because she sucked at it. But her auntie is a state trooper. A deal was made. No time. But it's there in her past. Two years go by and then her sister is killed. The sister who looks very much like her. What are the odds?"

Mike looked at the paw on his shoulder, then back at the face of the paw's owner.

"Why are you telling me this?"

"So you understand. You got everyone running around thinking about your old man's deep dark secrets and making them believe that the past is the present. It ain't that way. No one's focusing on what's going on right now. My mom knows it. Laura knows it. Shit. Felix Acosta knows it. And now, you know it."

Bradley retracted his arm and swung his upper body back toward the bar. He scooped up the whiskey glass and finished the remaining liquid in one swallow. Steve, the bartender, lifted his head at the clink of the glass meeting the wooden bar. Bradley waved him off.

"With this knowledge, you have a few choices to make," Bradley said. "The one I hope you go with is to leave my family alone. Go do your interviews. But as for my dead cousin, keep her name out of your mouth. Let the real cops do the work."

"So it's drugs? It's what? Cartel shit?"

"No, man. Just some local assholes making a little cash. Amateurs. But maybe some serious amateurs. Stupid, but serious amateurs."

"You seem to know a lot."

"I don't know anything. And neither do you. Right?"

Bradley shot down a look full of daggers. He reached for his wallet, retrieving it from his right rear pocket. He selected a couple of bills and placed them on the bar.

"I got his," Bradley said. His eyes never moved from Mike's face.

Steve came scurrying over to collect the cash, and Bradley glanced slightly toward him.

"We good?" he asked.

Mike did not answer.

28

Sergeant Grant rested his eyes behind his desk. He could pick up the regular sound of the office in his ears. The buzz of the analog timepiece on the wall. The snap of the time clock in the corner. The murmur of voices from the tube TV on the rolling cart centered in the office. He reached up to rub his temples with both hands. He removed his glasses after a long moment. He had not heard Chief Justin come into the room.

"Hey Jimmy," the Chief said. "You got a full shift tonight?"

Sergeant Grant shifted in his chair before he opened his eyes. They fell upon Bernie Justin dressed in his uniform, complete equipment belt and keepers, his Stetson with the gold rope around the crown in his right hand just above his gun. The Sergeant looked past the white-shirted man. The hands on the electric clock on the wall pointed to just before three and a little after eleven. Sergeant Grant lifted his clipboard. He reached and placed the glasses back on his face to consider the duty roster before him.

"Well?" the Chief asked. The tone was hurried, sharp, and high-pitched.

Grant did not even look up yet. He found an inquisitive hum in his throat, pitching it till he found just the right note. Then he looked up at Chief Justin.

"Short a man. Rolling out with two tonight, plus me."

Chief Justin put his left hand on his hip, his head tilting the opposite way. His face was wide-eyed impatience.

"Who?"

"I got Bell and Jones tonight."

"Who's out?"

Sergeant Grant lowered his eyes, his entire face following them. He built the hum back up, searching again for the same note. After a full minute, he tossed the clipboard on the desk. The glasses were again pulled from his face. He looked up.

"Ellis is out."

Chief Justin's face slanted into a menacing glare. "Sick?"

"No, sir," Grant responded. "Took a floating holiday."

"Who approved that?"

Sergeant Grant feigned a look over each of his shoulders. He set his stare back at the chief. "I did, sir."

"The damn kid is out running over all the TV screens in the world. He can't be bothered to come to work?"

Bernie Justin's left arm pulled away from his hip, and his left hand took custody of the hat with the rope around the crown. His right hand came up with a vengeful index finger.

"You order him in," Chief Justin said. "He's to report within the hour. I don't care where he is. I don't care who he's being interviewed by. Order him in and be here in an hour."

The shrill volume amplified the emotion behind the chief's words. Sergeant Grant listened with a stoic face toward the animation of the white-shirted, gold-starred Bernie Justin waving his pointer finger around. His wide-brimmed hat with the gold rope around the crown was curled behind his back. Grant's placid expression, a conscious choice, seemed to rile the boss up even more. The Chief hopped up and down in place.

"Tell him to bring his gun, shield, and ID, too. Prepare a receipt for all items. Within the hour, Sergeant Grant."

The last words came out as a soprano-tinged echo as the chief decided mid-sentence that he was going to leave the office. The final order trailed him down the hallway toward his office. Sergeant Grant raised his eyebrows and blinked a few times rapidly. Hugh Bell walked into the office as the door slammed in the distance.

"Hey boss, what's going on?"

Grant rocked himself from his chair, grabbing the clipboard in the same motion. He lifted his gaze to Hugh's face. The large man looked down back at him, an innocent expression of curiosity in his big eyes. Sergeant Grant chewed his lip and blew a lungful of air through his nose.

"Chief was just here."

"Oh boy. What's he want?"

"Just letting me know how great things are going."

Hugh made a small laugh that could have been mistaken as a sigh. "You still hate him?"

"It's not hatred," Grant said. "I just know the man for who he really is. He stepped on my neck to get to where he got."

"If only Chief Charlie had known."

"You think he didn't? Bernie was so caught up in politics that Charlie had no choice but to promote him. Remember, I was a sergeant longer than him."

"It's like 'Who did I piss off?'"

"Everyone, lad. I pissed them all off. That's what Charlie liked best about me."

Dennis Jones shot into the office, still adjusting his Sam Browne belt and placing his keepers. He stole glances at both Hugh and Sergeant Grant, his complexion the shade of burgundy.

"Sorry I'm late, boss," Dennis said. He completed his adjustments, then snapped himself to attention.

"Easy, lad," Sergeant Grant said. "We're talking a little before we get down to business."

Dennis became like a marionette on strings, loose and relaxed. "What are we talking about?"

"Police chiefs," Hugh said.

"Oh, shit, I miss the hell out of Chief Ellis. How long's it been?"

"Seven years," Sergeant Grant said.

"Seems like forever," Hugh said.

"But also, just like yesterday," Grant replied.

The nostalgia hung in the air for a moment. Sergeant Grant could pick up the subtle sound again of clocks and televisions. He cleared his throat.

"Hugh, have you talked to Mike recently?" he asked.

Hugh shook his head. Grant looked at Dennis who made a surprised shrug before shaking his head in the negative.

"Well," he said. "Lad's in for a world of shit."

He looked down at his clipboard and provided each of his two cops with their assignments for the tour. Dennis nodded and left the office without hesitation. Hugh turned to leave but stood in the doorway.

"Is there anything we can do for Mike, Sarge?"

Sergeant Grant looked at Hugh's back. "I don't think so. You know how the chief can be. He's already got his mind made up."

"It's about the sick call outs?"

"I guess. I'm sure he doesn't like having Mike all over the TV either."

"I'll call him for you. Tell him to come in."

Sergeant Grant thought about the offer for a second. "No, Hugh, you should stay out of it. I'll do what I have to do."

Hugh did not say anything further, simply picked up his stride and left the office. His footsteps reverberated in the hallway. Sergeant Grant sat back in his seat. He pulled a Rolodex from the corner of the desk, fishing through the cards for one labeled *ELLIS, MICHAEL PO*. There was still one in front of it that read *ELLIS, CHARLES CHIEF*. Sergeant Grant did not even languish on it. He held the place for Mike's information as he pulled the receiver from the phone, which he wedged between his ear and his shoulder. The digits were dialed, and Sergeant Grant waited for the ringing to begin.

"Hello?" A female voice said in the earpiece.

"Ann?"

"Yes, who's this?"

"Jimmy Grant."

"Oh, hello Jimmy," Ann Ellis said. "How are you?"

"Just fine, dear. Is Michael home?"

"No, Jimmy. I'm afraid he's not. I thought he was at work. It's after three, isn't it?"

"It is. He's off today, but I need to ask him about something."

"You could try his cell phone," Ann said. "Do you have that number?"

"Oh yes, it's right here. Old habits die hard, always trying to call people at home. But I guess no one's ever home anymore. Always out and about."

"That's the case," she said. After a breathless pause, she added, "You don't come around much anymore."

"Tough memories, Ann. It's hard being in your home without Charlie around."

"You're telling me."

Sergeant Grant smiled. "We all miss him."

"Tell me, Jimmy, how's Michael doing there?"

His face dropped to a frown as did his tone of voice. "He's a good lad, Ann. Smart, ambitious."

She was silent on the other end, implying the other side of the disclaimer.

"But he is caught up in this outside mess. This whole Jane Doe thing. It's taking him away from his real work."

"So, despite what he wanted, he's become like his father?"

"Maybe just the opposite. Instead of holding it in and sneaking around, Mike's left it all out there for everyone to see."

"Hope it doesn't have the same consequences."

Sergeant Grant did not answer that. Movement in his periphery caught his attention, and he looked at the doorway. Mike stood there in his street clothes—a pair of jeans and a blue T-shirt. He had his hands in his pockets, leaning against the frame of the door jamb.

"I'll have to get back with you, Ann," Sergeant Grant said. "We can talk again soon. Maybe I will drop by."

"That'd be lovely, Jimmy. Tell Michael I'll see him later."

She hung up first, and the dial tone sounded in Grant's ear as he kept his eye on Mike. Slowly, he moved the phone away from his head and set it on the hook.

"Hey, Sarge," Mike said.

"Ellis, how are you?"

Sergeant Grant stood up, coming around to the front of his desk and resting his buttocks against it.

"I heard you're looking for me?"

"Not me," Grant said. "The Chief wants to see you."

"I'm not going to give him the satisfaction, sir."

Sergeant Grant nodded. "Are you just resigning then? 'Cause he wants to fire you?"

Mike straightened and reached behind his back to produce his Glock 22. He leaned over, putting it on the corner of the desk. Next, he retrieved his wallet. He pulled out a card, leaving it next to the gun. The wallet was replaced, and he stood before Sergeant Grant with deference. Mike reached around the back of his neck and pulled on a chain. From beneath his blue T-shirt, Mike fished out his shiny silver shield surrounded by a leather holder. Without looking at it, Mike put the shield on the desk and let the chain fall indiscriminately.

"Will that be all, sir?" Mike asked.

"That'll be all," Sergeant Grant said.

###

Hugh pulled his Durango into the parking lot of the diner, swinging the vehicle around to the side of the building near the dumpsters. He killed the lights but left the car running as he exited, ensuring the doors were locked with the fob attached to his belt. Hugh's steps were tentative as he moved through the parking lot. There were a lot of cars in the lot, filling it almost to capacity. Some of the vehicles were vans with four-letter call stations printed along the sides with words like "Late Breaking" and "Action" emblazoned on them. Others were large, dark SUVs with out-of-state plates.

"This place," Hugh said.

He finished his trek across the parking lot and mounted steps into the diner. He came through the door, meeting the rush of people inside. One of the waitresses hurried up to Hugh.

"Officer Bell, good evening. I tried holding onto your table as long as I could. But I had to seat someone there."

Hugh looked forlornly at the rear corner booth occupied by a couple of long-haired and bearded men in flannel and vests.

"I do have a counter seat. With some space."

Hugh looked at the long, white marble counter. There were a few vacant red stool seats, and Hugh eyed one at the far end.

"I'll take it. Thank you," he said.

He excused himself through the crowd and installed himself on the stool. Another waitress, also well-known to Hugh, brought him coffee. After preparing it with his cream and sugar, he sipped the warm liquid in long gulps. After setting the mug back down, he wiped caffeinated dew from his mustache.

Surveying the packed diner for a familiar face, he finally found one. It was remarkable how much Laura Velez resembled her deceased sister, and Hugh looked sympathetically at her from where she sat on the furthest side of the restaurant. Hugh found himself lost in his thoughts when he was pulled from the depths by yet another waitress talking to him.

"What'll it be, Officer?" she said.

Hugh shook himself out of his stupor, his dreamy eyes falling upon a fat, unfamiliar face. He did a double-take before taking up the menu that was laid out before him. He did not open it.

"Meatloaf dinner," he said.

The waitress did not bother to write down the request, merely retrieved the menu before ambling off toward the kitchen. Hugh scooped up his coffee mug again and took a long swallow of the drink, nearly draining the contents of the mug. He glanced around again, finding only strangers among him. Some of the faces were young, beautiful, or handsome, ready for the camera. Others were obviously behind-the-scene types. Hugh wiggled uncomfortably on his stool, keeping his hands shoulder width apart on top of the counter.

Then he caught sight of me moving across the diner on my way to the restroom.

"Hey," he said to me. "Is this all because of you?"

I feigned a blush and held my hand up modestly. "No, no, Officer Bell. They are not here for me. They are here for Jane Doe. Jane and her daughter, Margaret. And the young man who brought them together, Mike Ellis. It's truly a wonderful story of perseverance, don't you think?"

"I think you brought a bunch of sharks into my town looking for lunch," Hugh said.

I laughed. "This is temporary, Officer Bell. However, this is only the initial response to the story. As the cycle goes around, we'll have to change mediums. The television will go away, the interviews will dry up. I'll have to write a book, of course. And I'm talking to both Netflix and Amazon about a documentary. The attention will build up again. The next cycle."

"Sounds like a vicious cycle. But you haven't solved anything. You still don't know her real name or who killed her."

"That'd be the next step, my friend. But we don't want to move too quickly, do we?"

"And who's going to turn that over to you?"

"I'm hoping Mike will."

"I wouldn't be so sure about that."

I was vexed. "Whatever do you mean?"

"I mean, Mike Ellis is no longer a cop. He can't investigate any-thing."

"Well, that's a shame. But it doesn't leave us totally in the lurch."

"You think he's going to want to continue following this down when it's cost him so much?"

"Without another source of income? I'd bet he's more invested now."

Hugh paused. The fat waitress brought his meal out. I excused myself to use the restroom as I had planned. Hugh dug into his meat-loaf. He was about halfway through the generous helping when the commotion began. I had just exited the restroom, drying my hands with a soft brown paper towel.

"I need to talk to you," the excited and amplified voice of Mike Ellis said.

Hugh looked above the other patrons, turning their attention toward the loud voice.

"I don't want anything to fucking do with you," the serious voice of Laura Velez came back louder.

Their argument went back and forth. Laura got up from the table, trying to move away as Mike followed. Other people began to get up, enthralled in the action. Laura's firm denial was met with angry pleading from Mike. Hugh slid off the stool. Laura passed him on her way to the back of the diner. As Mike came around the counter, Hugh held his arm out to stop him.

"Move, Hugh," Mike said. It was a firm tone.

Hugh moved his entire frame in front of Mike. No words were needed.

"I need to talk to her. Please, let me through."

Hugh remained there to block, but Mike made no effort to get around him.

"Hugh, I'm desperate. Please let me see her."

"She doesn't want to see you," I said from my vantage point behind Hugh.

Mike ducked to Hugh's right side to see me standing there. Hugh moved to block him if he tried to make a run for it. Mike's better judgment won out, and he remained standing there before his friend.

"Just get him out of here," someone said.

Hugh did not bother to learn the origin of the request. He lifted his right arm and pointed toward the door. He hardened his face, a stern pout chiseled into the bone. The pitch of Mike's voice went up. His arms flailed as he saw his options waning. He changed the audience of his pleading.

"Laura, just hear me out," he said. "Give me a chance to talk to you."

I stepped up beside Hugh. The large man caught sight of me from the side of his left eye. His left arm shot out toward me.

I spoke in a frantic voice, "Mike, listen to your friend. Listen to me. You need to get out of here. Right now. This is going to take a whole lot of cleaning up, but you need to cut your losses now and get out of this diner."

Mike backed away from Hugh, moving slowly into a group of people who had gathered around to get a better look. Hugh took a long step, and then a second his right arm still extended, his face still an emotionless slate.

"Okay, okay," Mike said. "I'm going."

Hugh followed as Mike cut through the crowd. The people murmured in his ears as he passed, but he could not hear anything specific. He was focused on Mike and keeping up with Mike's pace. The bells jangled as the front door opened, and Mike turned down the concrete stairs with Hugh hot on his heels.

"You can stop following me now," Mike said.

Hugh did not acknowledge Mike. The kid kept walking out toward the large part of the parking lot. Hugh slowed his pace, giving Mike some breathing room now that he was outside.

"What the hell are you doing?" Hugh said finally.

"I have to talk to Laura, Hugh. She won't listen to me. I think I messed up really bad. Everything's getting away from me. They took my shield. I gave it up. Acosta is looking at me like I'm a suspect. And Laura won't hear me out. She's starting to believe all this shit. Can you help me? Can you help me, Hugh?"

Hugh was taken aback by the strain of emotion in Mike's voice. The kid was bent over like he had taken a punch to the gut. His words were vomited out in a hoarse gulp of air. Hugh approached Mike with his right arm up to comfort the young man.

"Just go," Laura called out.

Hugh turned around just as Mike straightened to see where the voice had originated. There was a silhouette of a woman on the rear emergency exit ramp, the exit sign illuminating her shape if not her features.

"Laura," Mike called out. He lunged to get past Hugh. Hugh caught him in a bear hug. Mike scrambled in Hugh's grasp, throwing his elbows and heels. Hugh threw the kid away from the building.

"Get the fuck out of here," Hugh said.

Mike was still within a few feet of Hugh, who was bent over from the struggle. Mike reared back and laid his right fist across Hugh's nose. Hugh turned away, wincing from the shock of pain in his face. His hands reflexively went to the source of the agony. He could first feel the trickle, then the oozing flow of blood in his hands. Unaware of the time it took to react, Hugh desperately looked to gain his bearings. His eyes were drawn to the lights from the diner and the shadows of the people observing inside behind the glass. His wits returned more fully, and he moved his right hand down toward his weapon. Finally, he looked toward where the blow came from. But the kid was gone. In the distance, he could hear an engine turn over. There was a squeal of rubber on the pavement before the sound of the car grew distant.

Hugh stood erect. The blood from his nose mixed into his facial hair. He felt a hand on his back as I came to his aid, a wet wash rag from the diner staff held out to him. Hugh accepted the relief, first wiping the tears welled in his eyes before applying the rag to his nose.

"What the hell happened?" I asked.

"I think we're losing the kid," he said.

29

Sitting at her kitchen table, a cup of tea in her hand, Ann stared off beyond where Mike stood on the opposite side of the kitchen. The quiet between them permeated into the passage of each arduous second. Ann had been counting the beat of time in her head with drips of water from the sink behind Mike. She had watched the dusk settle in and the sun go down. It was night again.

"We've been in this standoff for an hour," she said. Her hushed tone was severe.

Mike's head hung, eyes to the ground, shoulders slumped. Ann sipped her tea with care, the steam from the cup rising to fog her glasses. Satisfied with the warmth, she set the cup on a saucer and placed her hands together on the table.

"You and I are not honest with one another," Ann said.

The full volume of her voice grabbed Mike's attention. He raised his head. His sallow complexion with his sad eyes pulled at her heart.

"What do you mean?" he asked.

"Michael, I was lied to for years by your father. He kept secrets. He hid things about himself. He never shared his true feelings or intentions about anything. But he took care of me. I, in turn, kept a blind eye toward him. I accepted his treatment and supported his view of the world. I enabled him. I treat you the same way."

"I'm not like him."

"Oh, Michael, you are more like him than you would ever want to believe. He would try to protect me from the reality of his mind. He'd make up stories and give me good feelings about the work he was doing. It was like he had a playbook that he'd turn to every night when he came home."

"What do you mean?"

"The night you found that dead body, you told me that you'd arrested a drunk man. The off hours you've been keeping, you said you were covering open shifts when you were investigating a murder. And when you went to California, you told me you were going on training to Albany. I only found out the truth about the last thing when you started telling me from the television set."

"I didn't want you to worry."

"That's something your father would say. Like I was some sort of glass figurine that was going to shatter if I fell. Are you going to tell me that you got fired?"

Mike's face screwed up into a tight ball. His lips mashed into a cynical line. "I knew you already knew."

"That's honesty. So you know, Michael, I know a lot of things. I know all about your father's obsession with the woman you call Jane Doe. I know how you've taken up the cause. I know you're neglecting your duty. And that's why they let you go."

"I wasn't showing up for work."

"It's kind of hard when you're getting interviewed five times a day. But not just the police department. Your friends let you go, too. You let them all down."

Mike hung his head. "How do you know?"

"Veronica Salazar was a close friend of ours in the years before you were born. Roni and your father worked the best years of the Overlook case together. That was before she took a bigger job, and your dad was promoted. He never trusted anyone with the case again. Maybe not even himself."

"Did he know her?"

"Probably."

"How could you stay with him if you knew he was lying?" Mike asked.

"How could I not? He wasn't just lying to me; he was lying to himself. He had himself convinced that he was the only one with the answers. Whatever he found out, whatever he knew, he became the protector of the secrets. I loved him for his dedication. I loved him for the passion he had for her. Because I knew he had that same passion for me, and for that matter, you."

"I guess I never noticed it."

"You were a boy. In many ways, you still are a boy. Your father made his peace with me and with God before he died."

Ann took up the teacup again. She took a full swallow. She closed her eyes as she let the warmth spread through her. When she opened them again, Mike had crossed the room and was pulling the chair out from the table.

As he sat, he said, "Maybe it's time we reset our relationship?"

Ann smiled and set the cup back in the saucer. "How do we begin?"

"I left the seminary because they wouldn't let me move on."

Ann's face became serious. "Why not?"

"Because I was being honest with myself and honest with them. I couldn't forgive Dad for the life that he'd given me. I couldn't be at peace with the lack of love. I haven't been able to shake the fact that I don't belong. It was a crisis of conscience, and I told the Bishop that. That's why I left."

"I didn't know that," Ann said.

"I know I was adamant about the priesthood. I thought I had a true vocation. But maybe I misread the signs? The Bishop was actually pleased. He thought I hadn't enough life experience to make such a choice."

"It's a tough thing to devote yourself to something so serious, especially without knowing anything else about the world."

Mike smiled. He nodded in a serious manner, looking at his mother with something else at the tip of his tongue. He blushed a little before speaking.

"I also fell in love back in college. I carried on a relationship with a girl without telling a soul. It made it hard to take any vows."

"You were intimate?"

Mike blushed and sank his face. "Yes. We were dating for almost two years. It sort of happens these days."

"It always happens, my dear. That's what love's all about. Where is she now?"

"When I moved on to seminary, I broke it off. I tried to choose the harder path. I didn't realize how hard that would be."

"Why are you here now?"

"I think I wanted to walk a mile in Dad's footsteps. I could never understand why he was the way he was. I thought that maybe wearing a shield would allow me to come to peace with him."

"However?"

"It didn't. It was an even more difficult path. I can't escape his shadow here in this town. Both the bad and the good. So many of the guys that worked with him revere him. But then there are still others who found him an intense rival. I was just caught in between them and could never be myself."

"Who are you?"

"I don't know."

"Who do you want to be?"

"I don't know."

Ann smiled and reached her hands across the table. Mike instinctively lifted his hands, allowing his mother to close her hands over his.

"Let's think about what is important right now," Ann said.

"What is that?"

"You made a pledge to find who killed that girl. Veronica's niece. Why have you stopped that?"

"Well, I'm no longer a cop. The guy I was working with thinks that I did it. I burned bridges with the victim's sister and her aunt. I turned my back on both of my friends."

"Those are consequences of you failing to live up to your promise. You've been distracted with chasing your father's ghost. You forgot that something was haunting you."

"I wanted to connect the cases so badly. I thought that if I could solve Jane Doe, I could solve Carolina."

"Well, you made progress with that. Did it pan out for you?"

"No, it didn't. Maggie Farley may be related to Jane Doe, but she's not related to the Velez's. I'm the only connection between them."

"And why is that important?"

Mike shook his head. Ann pulled her hands back to herself.

"Michael, you have to accept the fact that you are your father's son. You've been placed in a parallel with his life. You both knew a girl who got killed. You both discovered the bodies. You should stop fighting your father's memory and embrace it."

"How?"

"You'll have to discover that for yourself."

Mike sat back in his chair and closed his eyes. "What would Dad think of me?"

Ann lifted her tea. She took a gulp of the lukewarm liquid. She did not answer the question.

"Dad always had a lot of thoughts about different people. I've heard them all. His opinion was the gold standard for a lot of his men. Good or bad, he'd tell them what he thought. So, what would Dad have thought of me?"

Ann kept her gaze upon her son. His eyes were still closed, and his head bounced slightly against the wall. He repeated the question again. Then he said it to himself again. And again, and again. Suddenly, he sat up straight, his eyes opened now. He turned to Ann.

"I have to go find out."

"Veronica," Amanda Domino called from some distance.

Closing the rear door to her car with her leg, Veronica hefted a box with both of her hands. She was dressed in business attire, sharp black slacks and a matching jacket, a purple blouse, and ivory-colored heels. Veronica turned around toward where she thought the voice was originating but did not see Amanda. She heard her name again, turned herself to the right, and finally caught sight of the short, plump attorney.

Amanda was dressed in a frumpy tan blazer with a darker brown knee-length skirt. Her blouse was a tight-fitting olive color, highlighted with a faux emerald necklace drooping below her breasts. She crossed the parking lot waving her hand over her head.

Veronica got her body beneath the box she carried and walked toward Amanda. She kept her eyes on the lawyer, who stopped in her tracks waiting. Veronica sighed as she approached.

"Good morning," Amanda said. "You look great."

"Thank you," Veronica said. "You, too." She tried to hide the inflection in her voice.

"I look like shit. I don't know why I'm hanging out with you."

"Are you ready for this?"

"I think so."

The women walked in earnest up the sidewalk. Veronica felt herself pulling in front of Amanda and slowed herself. She looked over her shoulder. Amanda marched at her own pace, not worrying about the gap that had developed between them.

"Sorry, my legs don't know how to be as long as yours," Amanda said.

"I'm just a bit anxious. I don't mean to run away from you."

"What do you think Felix has?"

"I hope something that is actionable."

Veronica stopped in front of the glass doors emblazoned with: *GREENE COUNTY DISTRICT ATTORNEY.* Amanda reached around her to open the door. Veronica moved into the vestibule, setting the box down before wringing her arms and hands.

"That was getting heavy."

Amanda pushed the call button for the elevator. As they waited, Amanda looked down at the box. Veronica followed her eyes to the open top file box filled with various items.

"What's that?"

"My things. Figured that if I'm going to do this job, I might as well make it comfortable."

Amanda smiled brightly. She took stock of some of the items in the box. Veronica watched her analyze some of the plaques and photographs lined up together.

"So, you're going to stay on?" Amanda asked. There was hope in her voice.

Veronica breathed out, crinkling her face in a modest smile. "I've been away long enough. Still have my certification, so I might as well put it to some good use. It's not like I'm going to work part-time somewhere chasing speeders and going to domestics."

"And it keeps you tapped in."

"And it keeps me tapped in. You're right."

The elevator arrived with a sharp ding. The doors opened as Veronica bent to grab her box from the floor.

"Mike," Amanda said. The surprise in her voice was tinged with a lilting excitement.

Veronica straightened immediately. The box remained in place at her feet. She glared into the elevator car. Mike Ellis stood in a state of shock. His eyes were wide as he stood mid-step to come out into the vestibule. Veronica crossed her arms at her waist. Her heeled left foot cocked sideways and began tapping.

"It's so great to see you," Amanda said. She reached out her hand.

Mike appeared as if he did not know what his next move could be. The doors of the elevator began to close. He scrambled to hit a button in the car, and the doors stopped and reopened. Without a pause, he stepped into the vestibule. He accepted Amanda's hand, giving it a delicate pump. He smiled at her as he held her hand. Her face exploded in an open smile.

"Hi, Ms. Domino," Mike said. His eyes darted toward Veronica.

"We were about to go up to see Investigator Acosta," Amanda said. Mike nodded with his focus still on Veronica. "I know."

"Well, you should come up, too. He's got something on the Velez case."

Mike let Amanda's hand go. He looked back at her. Veronica looked him over in that moment. He wore dirty khaki pants and an over-sized flannel shirt. His boyish stubble crept tentatively from his face, noticeable in the light. His once close-cropped hair was grown out and uneven with his cowlick half pasted to his head and half sticking straight up.

"Mr. Ellis is no longer a police officer," Veronica said. "He's not privy to this sort of information. Do you want to tell her why?"

Mike swallowed. He again looked at Veronica. "No, I don't."

"What happened?" Amanda asked.

"He was relieved of duty for multiple violations of policy, including failing to report to work, insubordination, and…"

"It's a load of horseshit. And I resigned, officially," Mike said.

"And I bet there's a reason he's coming back down here now. After he saw Felix."

Amanda turned toward Veronica. "Why?"

"Felix has that effect on people. Especially if he gets the idea in his head that someone is a suspect."

"You think Felix suspects Mike?"

"That's probably what he wants to see us about. Pretty big news to suspect the cop of doing the deed."

"You can't believe that," Mike said.

Veronica huffed in a derisive chuckle. "Oh, I believe that he suspects you. You're capitalizing on all of this attention. Plenty of it to go around for the Jane Doe case. I bet you're gonna write a book with that slimy podcast host."

"I'm not going to do anything," Mike said.

"Why are you here?" Amanda asked, looking at Mike.

Mike turned to her.

"He was trying to get ahead of it," Veronica said. "Who told you? I'm guessing Felix hasn't pulled you in yet."

Mike's whole body slumped. "I got a tip-off from a friend."

"Is that why Laura won't even speak your name?" Veronica asked.

"I don't know what she thinks."

"Does Felix have any evidence?" Amanda asked.

"I didn't do anything."

"Felix is in his emotional state right now. I'll say that he has a hunch and a strong desire to share it with someone else. Probably most definitely me. I would guess that there is no evidence. Yet."

"Of course, there isn't," Mike said. "I found Carolina. I didn't do anything to her."

Veronica looked Mike over. There was strain behind his eyes. He looked between the two women. Desperation pulled at his cheekbones. Veronica dropped her arms.

"I know," she said.

Amanda looked over to Veronica again. "You seem pretty sure?"

"I may be mad at him, but he's not a killer. Any more than his father was."

Mike smiled with a glum look of dread in it.

"So, what do we do?" Amanda asked.

"You and I are going to have our meeting with Felix. Mike's going to make himself scarce."

"Where?" Mike asked. "I've got to clear myself. I've got to figure out who actually did this."

"Glad your motivation is back," Veronica said. "But, like I've said, you're no longer a cop. And once Felix has a chance to put his theory out, he's going to hunt you down. Find a place to hide for now. I'll get back in touch with you."

Mike sighed deeply. "Can you talk any sense into him?"

"I can try," Veronica said. She thought for a moment. "But you have enough experience with him to know that he never rests."

Mike nodded. The elevator behind him began to make sounds of movement.

"Get out of here," Veronica said.

Mike said his farewells through quick glances as he disappeared out the door. The elevator made its sharp ding again before the doors opened. Felix Acosta, dressed elegantly in a three-piece royal blue suit with a crisp white shirt and red tie, stood in the car. His brow was furrowed.

"Where have you been?" he said. The tone of his voice was sharp and accusatory in its brusqueness.

"Traffic," Amanda said. "Plus, she's lugging this box of free weights or something."

Felix considered Amanda for a moment. Then he shifted his skeptical look to Veronica.

"She's got cramps and had to peel herself from behind the wheel," Veronica said.

Felix shuddered. Amanda let out a taught laugh.

"Now, are you ready to get this going?" Veronica said.

Felix looked at each of them again. "Did you run into Ellis?"

Amanda began to shake her head as she looked at Veronica. The taller woman crooked an eyebrow.

"Why would we have seen him?"

"Because he was here. I saw him get off the elevator and come down the hall before he caught a glimpse of me. He didn't see the hallway mirrors. I did."

Veronica held firm for a heartbeat. "Nope, we must've just missed him."

"Why would he avoid you?" Amanda asked. The words were forced, but Felix did not seem to notice.

Felix shook his head as he reached back to hit the elevator call button.

30

The Camry needed a little something more to scale the hill to Charlie Ellis' cabin. Paul turned the wheel sharply to the left and laid onto the gas pedal. The gravel and dirt kicked from beneath the Camry's tires like a snake spitting a warning. Paul leaned into the wheel with the vain hope it would force the small sedan up the driveway. He reached over to lower the volume on the car's radio, cutting the noise of guitars and high-pitched glam rock vocals from his ears. Mercifully, the Camry finally reached the crest of the hill. Paul laid his eyes on the cabin.

It was smaller in the light of day. It hunched itself on a small plateau, surrounded by trees. Its exterior color was mud, red from clay, brown from dirt, and black from decay. There was a Jeep Cherokee sitting almost behind the structure, but the building could not quite obscure the vehicle. As Paul sat, patting the wheel of the Camry, the door of the cabin opened, and Mike Ellis stood on the threshold. In his hands was a towel, which he worked along each finger individually. His clothes were worn with stitched patches on elbows and knees. They hung off him like he could fit a second person in the same outfit. Even from a distance, Paul could see a wet, scraggly beard forming on the once-virgin face. Droplets of water fell intermittently from Mike's face and finally he brought the towel up and scrubbed the moisture away. As he took a step further out the door, Paul caught sight of the rifle leaning next to the door.

Paul looked at Mike for a long moment, then held his hands up. He tried to smile in jest, but Mike did not seem agreeable. Mike looked behind him at the weapon as it appeared that he finally recognized the visitor. Paul opened the door and stuck his head out.

"Mike?" he called.

"Paul?" Mike said.

The exchange made Paul laugh a little. He came out of the car with his right hand extended toward Mike and his index finger pointed at the rifle.

"Expecting someone else?"

Mike looked down at the gun again, then back at Paul.

"Nope. Found it here. Only have like six rounds."

"So, your standoff won't be prolonged?" Paul tried to laugh, but it came back dry.

"Come on in," Mike said. He gestured with a friendly wave as he put the rifle inside the door of the cabin and stepped away from the entryway. "Thanks for coming out."

Paul closed the driver's door and looked down at the moist dirt and pockets of mud. He considered his clean boots. He sighed and followed behind Mike. The smell of the cabin hit him again—sour milk and fruity sweetness mixed with cold dirt. Stepping inside, he found the small square footage to be brightly lit and warm. He glanced around to see that the floors had been swept up. The dust balls that had been mounded in corners were gone. The layer of dust had been excavated from the surfaces of shelves and furniture. A candle flickered on the desk, emitting a pleasant cinnamon odor that transformed the inside into a cozy retreat. Along the back wall, near the desk was a weathered, moth eaten burlap cot of a color between Army OD green and black mold. The material stretched between an oxidized metal frame.

"You've been busy the last week or so," Paul said.

"Trying to keep myself sane. Gotta get organized, I guess."

Paul observed the recliner and the small table next to it. A large teacup rested nearby. Then Paul adjusted his gaze toward the writing desk. Across it in a line were multiple piles of organized papers. A box of .22 caliber shells was the nearest thing on the desk. The chair was askew. Mike crossed in front of Paul to rest the rifle near its rounds.

"I'm not gonna lie," Paul said. "The gun kind of scares me."

"My dad apparently used it for small game back in the day from what I see in some of the photo albums."

"Why'd you bring it to the door? I'm the only person you're expecting, right?"

"Guess I'm a little paranoid."

"You need to be a little smarter than that."

Mike accepted the chide. Paul came around toward the desk. He lifted the rifle, opened the action, and looked into it. It was empty. He looked up at Mike.

"How's everything back in town?" Mike asked.

"Nothing in the chamber?"

"Not that dumb."

"I brought you some supplies like you asked," Paul said. "Water, bread, some peanut butter and jelly."

"No one else knows where I am?"

Paul shook his head. "No one's asked. Even Hugh."

Mike shrugged. "I owe you."

Paul moved the rifle behind the desk, scooping the rounds into his hand. He put them in his pocket, jingling them audibly. Mike collapsed into the chair by the desk. He eyed the papers adjacent to him before looking back up at Paul. His face betrayed some defeat in his heart.

"I've been over every single word, and I still don't get anything," Mike said.

Paul turned toward the desk, tentatively eyeing the piles of paper, avoiding reaching out to touch them. The top sheets were all type-written. The depth of the letters on the paper was clearly from an actual typewriter. On top of the first pile was a narrative about the discovery of Jane Doe. It was descriptive down to the temperature and the wind speed. The next pile was topped with a list of names under the heading of *Interviewed Witnesses 1981*. As Paul's eyes scanned the list, nothing sparked recognition. The third pile was another list of names without a heading. However, each name was prefixed with a title of detective, officer, investigator, or sergeant. The fourth pile was difficult for Paul to see, but the first few words typeset at the top of the sheet were: *I am just so sorry...* Paul leaned in to look at this pile, but Mike spun around and interfered.

"Not time for that yet," Mike said.

"What are you looking for?"

"Thanks to me, people now think that my dad killed her. Felix Acosta and some other people think that I killed Carolina Velez. I know that I'm innocent, so maybe my dad was too. I think that if we're both innocent men, maybe there's a secret we share. I think I'm just trying to get into his head."

"You spent so long trying to push him out of your life."

"Yeah. Ironic, huh?"

Paul nodded. He backed away, moving away from where Mike sat, stewing over the papers on the desk. Paul took further stock of the interior, his hand still jingling the rifle shells in his pocket. Mike had a backpack in a corner with clothes spilling out onto the floor. On top of the bag was a Bible, which Paul picked up and held in his hand.

"So, what's your next move?" he asked.

"Besides clearing my name?"

Paul considered the Bible in his hands and looked between the black bound book and Mike. Lines formed in his forehead as he forced his eyebrows up, focused completely on the Bible now.

"Yeah. That'd be a start. Maybe getting your career back? I'm sure they will take you back."

"I don't think Bernie is going to do that," said Mike.

Paul caught Mike's stare. He lowered the book to his side and looked back at Mike.

"Well, we can see what happens."

Mike shook his head as he said, "No, first things, first. I need to get inside my father's head."

"How about the people who knew him?" Paul said. He turned, taking steps back toward the recliner.

"Like who?" Mike asked.

"My grandfather for one. He was the police chief for years. Your father had to have worked for him."

"Is he the old man that works at the library?"

"Yeah, he's at the desk there most days. He volunteers his time."

"I've met him. He's offered to help me out before. But he's also friendly with Tim Figueroa. I'd have to be careful."

Paul continued toward the wood stove sitting cold in the corner. He set the Bible on the top of the cast iron before he rotated his hips back toward Mike, who watched Paul with inquisitive eyes.

"And Hugh's father is still kicking around, isn't he?"

"I've talked to him. He wanted to push me in a certain direction," Mike said and began shaking his head back and forth again.

Paul rolled his shoulders back and released a sigh. Grabbing the Bible, he moved back to the center of the cabin.

"And of course, you've got the Sarge," he said.

"Sergeant Grant?"

"Yeah, he had to have worked his whole career with your dad."

"He's never talked to me about him," Mike said. He thought for a moment. "Well at least I didn't want to hear what he had to say."

"You asked?"

Mike lowered his head as he shook it. "He offered but I didn't bite."

"And lastly, there's Hugh."

Paul watched Mike raise his head, his eyes heavy, his cheeks pulled in as he tried to suck air through his nose. His movement ceased and the room became still. Paul put his hands up, palms out as he tried to come up with some more words to add.

"I don't think he'll want to talk to me," Mike said. His voice cracked as started speaking, the volume lowering as he continued, ending in a whisper.

Mike hung his head. Paul lowered his in hands and made a chagrined face. He allowed for Mike to feel sorry for himself briefly.

"Have you tried?" Paul asked.

Mike's head sunk lower into his chest, shaking back and forth for a minute before rising. He put his eyes on Paul. Mike shook his head again.

"Maybe you should talk to all of these guys. Listen to what they all have to say."

"I've never asked anyone about my father. Anything anyone's ever tried to tell me, I've always turned them away. I don't know if I can change that."

Mike stood, burying his hands in his pockets. He turned toward the desk, looking down at the piles of paper. His shoulders and arms twitched as if he wanted to pull his hands out. Paul couldn't decide what Mike wanted to do with those hands. He could obliterate the stacks, scattering them into the expanse of the cabin; or he could take from the top and begin to sort out his father's memories.

"You've got to come to terms with your dad's ghost."

"I've been asking myself a question for the last week or so."

"What's that?"

Mike slid his hands from his pockets, one hand picking up the top sheet of paper. He held it up so Paul could see the balanced handwriting. "What would my dad have thought of me?"

"There's no way you can know."

"If I understand him better, maybe I can figure that out."

"I know a way you can start."

Mike lifted his chin, cocking his head to the side inquisitively.

"Call Hugh," Paul said. Then he tossed the Bible at Mike. "And crack this open."

###

There were still faint sounds of bowling balls hurtling down the greased lanes in the distance as Hugh bent over to tie his Converse All Stars, moving aside the red, green, and blue motley configuration on the alley shoes he had just removed. But mostly the vast building was silent. He fumbled with the laces but managed to cinch a knot in each sneaker before rolling his large frame up into a seated position. And there was Mike.

Hugh made an audible and exaggerated harumph in his chest. He sat still briefly before deciding to ignore the kid standing before him. The alley shoes were collected from the floor and placed firmly beneath his left armpit. He stood up, allowed himself a moment to steady, and leaned over to grab the leather handles of his bowling bag. Hugh walked right past Mike.

At the main counter, Hugh offered the shoes to the old lady who stood behind the counter like a nun on Sunday. Her thick frame glasses in a butterfly shape were pressed up against her eyeballs. Hugh made a wisecrack that sank as it left his mouth. Humorlessly, the woman sprayed deodorizer into each of the shoes before replacing them on the shelf beneath the counter. When Hugh turned, there was Mike again.

The kid didn't say anything. Mike was casually attired in jeans, and his hands were deep into the center pocket of a pullover hoodie sweatshirt. An uneven and disheveled beard littered his face, and his hair was beginning to stick out from the trucker hat he was wearing. Hugh broke eye contact the second he felt it lock into place. He looked toward the exit door and glanced sidelong at the bar. A few people still adorned the stools, and a young lady was still serving drinks. Hugh thought for a moment, then walked over to the bar.

Upon arriving, he set his bowling ball on a stool and dragged a second up to set himself onto. The bartender saw him and made her way to him with a knowing swagger.

"What can I get you, Hughie," the woman said. Her coy demeanor seduced Hugh.

"I'll have a whiskey," Hugh said.

The bartender looked past Hugh, her eyes glinting at the question in her mind. He folded his hands on top of the bar and let out a deep sigh.

"You want anything?" he asked without looking behind him.

Mike approached from behind him. "I'll have the same."

Hugh flashed two fingers at the bartender who nodded her acknowledgement before setting to work retrieving glasses and pouring the booze. Hugh could feel Mike on his left shoulder. Looking toward that direction, he saw that there was no place for the kid to sit. He looked to the right to see his bowling bag lounging on the stool. Hugh hummed an inquisitive note before reaching over to pull the bag from its resting place and set it on the floor.

"I heard you were holed up in the cabin. What's it like shitting outdoors?"

Mike came around Hugh, sliding himself onto the now unoccupied stool. The liquor arrived. Hugh slid a twenty-dollar bill across the bar. Then he pulled the whiskey glass to his lips. After a discerning sniff, he sipped the alcohol before replacing the glass on the bar.

"It's a little cold right now."

"Paul told me you might come trying to find me."

Hugh glanced over at Mike, who held the glass near his mouth. Mike's eyes looked back at him regretfully. Mike took a sip of the amber liquid. His face screwed up at the burn.

Hugh shook his head. "I've really gotta teach you how to drink." Then after another long minute of silence, he added, "What do you want, Mike?"

Mike cleared his throat and took a haphazard swallow of the whisky, this time not scrunching up. "Hugh, I really messed up."

Hugh nodded, turning his head back toward the bar and consuming another generous portion from his glass.

"That's a real good start," Hugh said. "But have you gotten any splinters in your ass yet?" he said with a hearty laugh.

Hugh stole a glance at Mike, who had his eyebrows lifted impatiently as Hugh chortled. Then he waited a couple of extra beats after the laughter ceased.

"I got wrapped up in so many things that I thought mattered. I should've sought out help, from anyone. From you, probably," he said, his words ebbing out in a calm, unmeasured sincerity.

Hugh set his glass on the bar. He looked straight ahead, waiting to hear the words he wanted to hear, allowing the kid to keep guessing.

"I know you're always trying to protect me. You've always had my back. You're looking out for my best interest, aand I really messed that up."

"You fucked it up. Say it with me now: I. Fucked. Up."

Mike did not repeat the words. Hugh looked over at him.

"I didn't listen to you. You and Paul were my only friends, and I left you guys out. Now, I'm paying the price."

"You did what you thought you had to do. They gave you an impossible job." Hugh retrieved the glass from the bar but did not drink.

"I shut you guys out."

"You leaned into that trooper and to the podcast asshole. Both are just out for themselves. They could give a shit about you. That girl was depending on you. You really fucked that up."

"I see that now."

Hugh put the glass back down with an audible smack of glass against wood. He pushed himself away from the bar, turning toward Mike.

"What do you want? You've lost pretty much everything. Sounds like you might even lose your freedom."

Mike kept his posture straight, his face set in a soft honesty. He looked Hugh directly in the eye.

"You know I didn't kill Carolina. You were there. You know me."

"Are you depending on me to be a witness at your trial?"

Mike smiled, causing Hugh to smile.

"What I need to do is learn some things about my dad. All I've ever been told is how great of a cop he was. I want to get inside his head."

"Well, you kinda did there, briefly. Now every asshole in the true crime world thinks that he killed that lady."

"I'm sorry, Hugh," Mike said. He reached a hand out, placing it on the big man's shoulder.

"You know, I feel like I'm more upset about your dad than you are."

"I don't know what to think. You were there when we found that notebook. What do you think?"

"I have no idea. But I guess I'd rather believe in Chief Charlie than go against him."

Mike lowered his hand at the same time he lowered his eyes. Hugh watched him chew over the last statement. Mike raised his face back up at Hugh, tension melting out of it like candle wax, leaving an expression of tired acceptance.

"I guess I don't look at him like you do. I'm trying to figure him out," Mike said.

"How are you going to do that?"

"I'm gonna talk to the guys that knew him best. Paul's grandfather, your old man, Sergeant Grant, and hopefully, you."

"Building a team, eh?"

"I need help. I've got to clear my name. But more importantly, I must figure out who actually killed Carolina."

"What about Jane Doe? I thought that was your meal ticket?"

"That's the next adventure. I have my priorities straight now."

"Are you trying to win the girl back?" Hugh asked.

"No, Hugh. I'm trying to bring the killer to justice," Mike said, some of the serious returning to his voice.

Hugh swiveled back to the bar. He put his hand around the whisky glass but did not lift it. In his periphery, he saw Mike turn too. The kid pulled his glass into the air.

"Do you think we can try to clear Chief Charlie's name too?" Hugh asked with a hopeful lilt.

Mike cocked his head, considering the request. After a moment, he said, "I guess. I mean if I understand him better, maybe I can figure out why he kept the secret."

An uneasy feeling sat in Hugh's chest. He mulled it over, a serious look on his face. All of his strength fought the urge to face Mike. The glass in his hand felt suddenly heavy like he couldn't even fathom being able to lift it.

"What do you say?" Mike asked.

Hugh moved only his head, looking at the kid sideways. He hummed his inquisitive notes, looking at the kid with renewed skepticism. Mike gestured his glass toward Hugh. He looked like he meant every word he had said. Hugh allowed a beat to pass before he lifted his glass, clinking it against Mike's. Hugh took the remaining liquor into his mouth, swished it, and swallowed. Mike took a long sip, snorted, but then forced the rest of the liquid into his mouth. He swallowed painfully with a grimace engraved into his face.

"I've gotta teach you how to drink."

31

"I feel like we need something more," George said.

He had pulled chairs around the largest of the tables in the lower part of the library. It was a mix-and-match affair, with old hand-me-down dining room chairs coupled with a couple of metal folding seats and even a couple of beat-up rockers. There was a bowl with tortilla chips in the center of the table. George looked at the bowl for a long time.

"Like what?" Paul asked.

George turned his torso toward the stairway where his grandson was still descending. Paul carried a package of water bottles shrink-wrapped together. He reached the bottom of the flight of stairs and brought the bundle of liquid to the table.

"I don't know. Popcorn maybe?"

"How about a case of beer? Maybe some pork rinds?"

"I haven't seen or talked to some of these men in almost twenty years," George said.

"Whose fault is that?"

"Well..." George considered.

"We've got some water and some chips. No one's expecting a catered affair."

"You're so much like your father, Paul. Uncomplicated."

"I know. And he's so much like you. Family curse."

George let out a cheeky laugh and swatted a limp fist at his grandson's well-defined bicep. Paul glanced down at the older man, releasing a hearty laugh. He wrapped his arm around George, hugging him into his side firmly.

"I know there's a mission behind all this, but I am also looking forward to sitting down with Roscoe and Jimmy. One was my mentor and the other my protege."

"What about Chief Ellis?"

"He was different. He didn't want or need any help. Charlie just shined out his own sheer will."

There was a muffled ding somewhere behind them. Paul unwrapped his arm and turned toward the sound.

"Elevator," George said. "Roscoe must be here. That crippled old fool couldn't take the steps."

George shuffled around the table, looking up the short hallway. He saw Roscoe Bell stumbling down the hall half leaning on a cane, half skipping. His son, Hugh, was a careful distance away.

"Hello, Roderick," George said.

Roscoe stopped in his tracks, forcing Hugh to come up short before he trampled his dad. The older Bell looked George over discriminately. He chewed his cheek a little and moistened his lips with his tongue.

"Georgie Porgie puddin' pop," Roscoe recited. "Shorter, older, with nothing on top."

George closed the distance between himself and Roscoe, patting his friend on his own bald head.

"Seems like you've got some aerodynamics yourself, Roderick."

The two men traded a few more genial insults before George led Roscoe to the table. He offered Roscoe the most stable and most comfortable chair. George turned back toward Hugh and extended his hand.

"Nice to see you again, young man," George said.

Hugh's hand gobbled up George's, giving it a firm pump. "Likewise."

Sergeant Jimmy Grant appeared out of nowhere, standing at the head of the table just behind where Paul stood. George was taken aback, looking from Grant to the stairs.

"You just snuck right in here, didn't you Jimmy?" George said.

Grant nodded. He shook Paul's hand and then George's. He looked at Roscoe and Hugh, giving them considerate nods.

"So, where's our host?" Sergeant Grant asked.

George looked at his watch. He shrugged and looked at Paul.

"I'll text him," Paul said. He pulled a smartphone from his pocket.

"Well, let's all sit down. I have some chips and some water," George said.

"Next time we do this, let's have some beer," Roscoe said.

"Like the last time we did this?" Sergeant Grant asked. He pulled a scratched and tattered dining room chair out to sit in.

"This might be the only time," Hugh said.

"And that's the real shame," George said. He settled himself into a rocker.

"Yeah, there's no beer," Roscoe said.

Paul looked up from his phone. "He's here."

As the words left his mouth, an echo from the stairwell of steps on the soft treads came down toward the group. Mike finally appeared, his disheveled appearance serving as a shock to the men who hadn't seen him in a while.

"About time," Roscoe said. He looked over his shoulder at Mike crossing the room. "What? Did you take an extra-long shower?"

"Sorry, sorry," Mike said. He had a package beneath his arm that was noticeable as he came into the light. "I had to make a stop."

He produced a paper bag which he set on the table. He reached inside, pulling out two six-packs of Coors original.

"I didn't know what everyone liked, so I went middle of the road."

"It's my favorite brand," Hugh said. "Free."

"And cold," George added. He grabbed one of the cartons and passed a glass bottle to each of the men.

Mike found the last available seat to ease himself into. He yanked the cap off of a bottle and took a belt. He looked around as the side conversations began to die down.

"So, I bet you're all wondering why I called you here?"

"You're going to reveal the identity of the killer," Roscoe said. His coarse laugh went unaccompanied.

"No, not yet. But I want to try to figure out who killed Carolina Velez."

"I thought you wanted to figure out who Jane Doe was?" Sergeant Grant said. "Wasn't that what you were going after in California?"

"Yes and no, Sarge. My whole point all along was that the two cases were connected."

"But you haven't put anything together?" George asked. "I've changed my mind. It was just a coincidence."

"Perhaps," Mike said. "But there is one thing both have in common. A policeman named Ellis. You each have tried to impart to me the type of man my father was. All I have done is bring suspicion on him and on myself. I brought you all together because I want to hear it all. I want to understand who my dad really was."

"Where do you want to start?" Paul asked.

"Wherever you guys think we should."

Mike scanned around the table.

Hugh spoke first. "I've known your dad since I was a little boy. He was always very nice to me. He'd give me baseball cards or Matchbox cars whenever he came over. And he was over a lot. He and my dad spent a lot of time together."

Roscoe nodded. "Well he was always in my back pocket. Couldn't get rid of him. He'd follow me home sometimes, especially before he got married. Felt like he was my adult ward at times. Thing about Charlie was that he always asked good questions."

"Oh, did he ask questions? He'd grill me every day I came back after a tour. Where I was, who'd I seen," Hugh said.

"And what did you learn," Sergeant Grant said. "He believed that when you stopped learning, it was time to go. If you didn't have an answer, he'd sit you in the station the next day until you had something. Then you'd have to go find something for that day."

George chuckled sharply, cutting into the conversation. "He got that from his old man. Mike, you never met your grandfather, but he was a good friend of mine. Discipline was the name of the game. 'Early is on time. On time is late. Late is ...'"

"Not acceptable," said the chorus of Hugh, Grant, and Mike.

"You learned that one at least," George said.

"Well, it wasn't that my dad instilled nothing in me," Mike said. "I knew his brand of discipline, but I also knew it from a distance. My dad kept me at arm's length my whole life."

"The Charlie that worked for me was seriously dedicated," George said. "He was trying to remake himself up here in the mountains. He was trying to leave behind the city life that he'd known. The city relationships that he'd had. Your grandfather called in a few favors to get Charlie his job."

"And he'd be at my table most nights after work chewing my ear," Roscoe said.

"I remember that," Hugh agreed. "Chief Charlie was at the house for dinner all the time when I was really small."

"Were you ever small?" Paul asked.

Mike looked up at Hugh, smiling. "Okay, that's a very different picture than the one I have of him. But what made him so successful?"

"Work ethic," George said.

"Relentless dedication," Roscoe added.

"How about his judgment of character?" Sergeant Grant asked. "Charlie was my sergeant when I started. Yes, he'd grill you about learning things, but he tried to understand you. He knew your wife's name and all your kids. Knew your anniversary or if you had a death in the family. He'd push you in the right direction."

"Did he ever not like someone?" Mike asked.

"Yeah," Hugh said. "Most people. If he liked you, you knew it. If he didn't like you, you knew it all too well. Case in point: Bernie Justin."

"What about him?

George snorted. "Bernie was the last guy I hired before I left. In the short time that he worked for me, I saw him try to single-handedly step on the necks of everyone in the agency."

"He field-trained me," Grant said. "Tried to fail me."

"Why?"

"'Cause Jimmy was smarter than him, and he knew it," Roscoe said. "Luckily, George had already promoted Charlie to sergeant, and he looked after Jimmy."

"How'd he get to the position he's in now?"

"Crawled over everyone to get ahead, including your dad," Grant said. "Your dad became chief when you were born, Mike. Bernie Justin coveted that position, waiting in the wings for years. He got impatient.

Whatever he had, it was fortunate that your old man had a heart attack before ever having the chance to take him down."

Mike looked at Sergeant Grant as the words were spoken, his face betraying his confusion.

"He made it sound like my dad helped him to get ahead," Mike said.

"Not in the way you'd have thought," Hugh said. "I should've warned you about him."

"Mike, you were set up for failure as soon as you got hired," Sergeant Grant said. "Everything with that man is personal."

"Has any of this helped you?" Roscoe said. "'Cause it sure as hell has me confused."

"Pop," Hugh said. "He's trying to learn some truths."

"You want the truth?" Roscoe said. He looked at Mike intently, a wrinkled finger pointed at him. "Truth is that your father had a lot of redeeming qualities *and* a lot of secrets he was trying to hide. You need to get past those secrets. Find out who has the most to gain from the death of the girl, and you'll find who killed her. No emotions. No secrets. Just plain, God's honest truth."

"Understand the people," Sergeant Grant said. "The investigators, the family, and everyone else on the sidelines."

George had the final word. "And go right after them. Don't let them see you coming."

32

Walking through the portal from the church into the morning light, Bernie Justin shoved his hands into the deepest wells of the pockets of his Carhartt jacket. He held in his desire to shiver as the wind kicked up. He took a deep breath of the cool autumn air. Other parishioners scattered around him as he stood still on the small veranda. That was when he felt the hand on his shoulder. Bernie whipped around like a cyclone. His wide eyes fell upon Mike Ellis.

"Mister Ellis," he said. The words hissed from behind his teeth.

"Hello, Bernie," Mike said.

It was a cavalier smugness that immediately rubbed Bernie Justin the wrong way. A warm prickle shot up his neck, settling in the back of his brain. He studied the young man's face. Beneath the growth in stubble, a maturity had developed where it had previously lacked. It was in Ellis' complexion, mottled with patches of hair, yet uncharacteristically clean and clear. It was in his eyes, hardened and sharp. It was Mike's expression, a sly, confident grin that spelled out an intention beyond Bernie's knowledge.

"I'm not sure what you're looking for," he said. "I don't think I have any further business with you."

"Well, I wanted to talk to you. I feel like you owe my father the courtesy."

Bernie lifted an eyebrow. He weighed the statement. A part of him became interested in what the young Ellis might have to say. The other part of him felt that he owed neither Charlie nor Mike Ellis anything. Looking behind him, he saw that the church had fully emptied. The pastor had gone back in, but one of the large entry doors remained open. Bernie motioned for Mike to follow him inside.

"Do you feel comfortable coming in?" he asked. "You're not going to get struck down or anything?"

Mike did not answer. Bernie entered inside the nave of the church, turning back toward the entry door of the narthex. Mike paused there with his gaze fixed on the small pool of Holy water. After a long moment, he dipped his index and ring finger into the blessed liquid and crossed himself. Then, he fully entered the building, walking past Bernie and up a few aisles before selecting a pew. He sat down facing the sanctuary. He did not look back at Bernie which made the older man even more intrigued. With a lethargic stride, Bernie made his way up to where Mike sat. When he reached the pew Mike resided in, he found room enough for him to slide in to sit next to Mike. He settled, staring straight at the sanctuary also.

"I grew up in this church," Mike said.

"I remember you," Bernie said, "when you were a child anyway."

"My father's funeral was here. You weren't there."

"No, I was away. I passed my condolences to your mother."

"I wasn't here when he died. I was away at school. Sergeant Grant came to the funeral. He told me that he arrived for work one morning and saw my father's car in its spot. He said it wasn't strange to see it there most days, but this was a Sunday. He went in and knocked on his office door. There was no answer. He went in to find my father's body sitting in his chair."

"If that's what he told you," Bernie said. His voice was a whisper. "Then that's what happened."

"Did my father like you?"

The change in direction snapped Bernie out of his trance. He swallowed hard, an audible gulp sliding over a guilty lump in his throat. A flush of warmth, then a chill scampered up his back muscles, electrifying his brain. His eyes darted back and forth. The sound became mute in his ears. He steeled himself a bit before he answered.

"Your father didn't like many people. I don't think I was special."

"Did you like him?"

"I've told you I didn't. But we had a mutual respect—an understanding."

"Did you want his job?"

"Of course."

"Did he want you to succeed him?"

"He didn't have a choice in the matter, unfortunately. His death caused the necessity of a selection."

"Between you and Sergeant Grant?"

"Yes. We were both sergeants. We both had taken the exam and were reachable."

"And you took over."

Bernie let the inquiry go without the obvious answer. The silence permeated between them, Mike controlling the cadence as his question went without a response.

"What do you think of me?"

"You're young. You're talented. You worked hard, but you want to do your own thing. I can't have that. I have the whole agency to think of."

"What would my father have thought of me?"

Bernie didn't have an answer for that. The heat subsided in his chest and face. He let the question hang in the air for a long time.

"You know what I think?" Mike said.

Bernie turned his head toward Mike, finding the young man was already looking back at him. He tilted his head forward, inviting Mike's opinion wordlessly.

"I don't think you knew anything about my father. He came up with an opinion about you early on. You resented him for it. I also think that if he had had a choice, Sergeant Grant would've been promoted to chief instead of you."

Bernie responded immediately. "I guess we'll never know."

"You do. But maybe the rest of us will never know for certain."

Bernie laughed, then cut himself off. He cleared his throat and asked, "What is the purpose of this?"

"I'm trying to figure out what you had on my dad."

Bernie smiled broadly. "I didn't have a damn thing. You're the one who seems to have all the dirt on him. What is this about?"

"I'm trying to figure out who killed Carolina Velez."

"That's not your job anymore."

"Not my job, but my duty."

"Last I checked, you were the next suspect."

"You know I didn't kill her. That's why you didn't try to arrest me outside. But you're interested in what I have to say."

"Perhaps," Bernie conceded.

"I think you still hold a grudge against my father, and you set me up to fail."

"I didn't set you up for anything. You simply failed."

"No, I mean you set the whole thing up. A deep-seeded plan from your jealous heart to kill Carolina, leave her at the Overlook, have me find her, and then assign me to the case. Make it a repeat of my father's life. Could you be that sinister?"

Bernie felt a different warmth. It was a hot, boiling rage coursing through him now. He slid into the pew, closer to where Mike sat. He came face to face with the bedraggled young man.

"Are you accusing me of murder?" Bernie Justin said. The words came out and all sound dropped out.

Stone-faced, Mike stared back at Bernie, his eyes resting calmly on the crucifix in the sacristy. Finally, he made a sheepish grin, then turned away.

"I'm just positing that you could've orchestrated a murder to have the last word in a decade-long struggle with your deceased predecessor. I don't have any proof. There's no evidence."

"You're damned right there's no evidence."

Mike repositioned himself, bringing his focus down to his feet. Bernie scowled at him, finding his brain and body misaligned. Something in the primitive part of his thoughts told him to leave. But there he sat, face aghast, hunching into a secretive posture. Bernie imagined voices all around him with sneering remarks and wild allegations.

"The truth is," Mike said, not averting his downward gaze, "that you're a dirty politician who has no good motivation for the people you serve. The police department is a fiefdom you can lord over. You damaged my father's reputation. You were planning to get him pushed out, but he died before you had the chance. You hired me because you missed the satisfaction of destroying him. Carolina's death was a convenient vehicle." Then he said quietly, yet definitively, "I know you didn't kill her."

At that, Mike stood, looked over at Bernie, and gave him a full two minutes of time to speak. Bernie had nothing to say. He made no movement, and Mike seemed to grow impatient. He must've decided that Bernie was not going to move out of his way, so he turned, making his way to the far end of the pew. Bernie watched him closely as Mike walked down the far aisle to the narthex. Mike reached the door, turned to cross himself, and exited.

###

"I don't think that was a smart thing to do," Veronica said.

She paced around in Ann Ellis' kitchen, one hand upon her hip, the other pushed back the bangs on her forehead. Her eyes were fixed on the middle ground, at nobody in particular as her heels clacked against the linoleum. Words whispered under her breath she hoped were inaudible thoughts no one else in the room could hear.

"Roni, dear, please sit down. Your coffee is getting cold," Ann said.

Veronica stopped her sentence mid-mumble. She stared over at Ann, wrapped in an honest-to-God housecoat with a curler bag over her head. There was a cup and saucer set out, the coffee still steaming, right next to a small sugar bowl and matching creamer vessel. She took a long eye at her watch, trying hard to read the small hands without her cheater glasses.

"Jesus, it's already twelve-fifteen," she said. She picked up where her cadence had been interrupted. "Where is Mike?"

"He'll be here soon," Ann said. She patted the table but did not repeat the invitation verbally.

Veronica maintained her back-and-forth circuit, saying small personal incantations in her frazzled state. Then she stopped again, looking over to Ann again.

"He really said he was going to confront Bernie Justin. That's what he said?"

"When he left at eight-thirty this morning, yes," Ann said. "Come and sit now."

Ann sounded impatient and just a little aggravated now. The tone of her voice woke Veronica from her focus.

"I'm sorry," she said. "I have been a terrible guest. You called me and invited me over. I've been caught up in myself."

"And with Mike."

"And Mike," she agreed. "It's so fascinating to see how much that boy is like his father, you know?"

Veronica crossed the kitchen and pulled the chair out. She sat, preparing her coffee.

"It's refreshing that he finally is accepting that fact. I think the more he acts like his father, the better."

"He never saw what we did," Veronica said.

"Charlie honestly never gave him the chance. He was an old man by the time Mike came into our lives. You had already come and gone by then. Mike would never know the dumb youth of his father. I figure Charlie felt like he'd already made all his mistakes, learning from them. I think he was disappointed that Mike didn't come out all complete out of the box."

"It's the same way with Bradley. You remember my son, don't you?" Ann nodded.

"He never even knew his father, really. He was just a framed photo on the mantle and folded flag in a case."

"All Charlie wanted to do was keep Mike away. It happened to line up with the worst of his sneaking around. Charlie put me at arm's length too."

"I'm sorry I wasn't around in those days."

"It's alright, dear. We all had our lives happening."

"Are you aware of what's going on with Mike? Why he went to see Bernie Justin?"

"He told me that he had another theory about the murder of your poor niece."

"I hope he didn't lean into this too hard. He just won't give up."

"It's just like Charlie. He had one theory and chased it for all those years. Could never put it together though. I'm praying Mike will be able to."

"He's already cut himself off so much. You know he lost his shield, right?""Yes, poor dear. Maybe he'll go back to school then. Back to the seminary."

Veronica gave Ann an inquisitive look. The question was on the tip of her tongue when the front door slammed.

"Michael?" Ann called.

"Yeah, Ma."

Mike walked into the kitchen, observed Veronica at the table, and crossed the room to the coffeemaker, filling them in about his encounter with Bernie Justin. As he spoke, he pulled the carafe out and looked down into the inky liquid.

"So this new theory is wasted," he said. He replaced the carafe and turned to the refrigerator.

"What did you do?" Veronica said. She gripped the chair as the urge to get up and pace tugged at her muscles.

"Nothing," Mike said as he turned to face them, a carton of milk in his hand. "I had a talk with Bernie. I told him the things that I had figured out, and I was able to tell whether I was onto something."

"What things did you figure out, dear?" Ann asked.

Mike poured a glass of milk and explained what he learned about Bernie and his father's death, the political moves Bernie had made to set himself up, the missed satisfaction of seeing Charlie step down to turn the reins over to Bernie, or the next best thing, Charlie being fired and Bernie coming in to save the day.

"And he didn't deny any of that. I could feel that I was onto something. But then I took it too far."

"How?"

Mike delved into his train of thought about Bernie Justin's ultimate revenge. As Veronica listened, the nerves finally overtook her, and she stood up. She began to pace, hearing Mike's words.

"That is the dumbest thing I've ever heard," she said once he finished.

"You know," he said, "at least I've had some ideas. What have you and Felix brought to the table? He pursued Laura for about a week and hasn't had another lead."

"He's fixed on you now. And you're running around accusing the police chief of desperate plots to extract retribution. Shit, who's next on your list? Me? Your mom? Rip Van Winkle?"

Veronica felt her frustration pour out, her voice rising in pitch as she became more and more breathless.

"I was thinking about Bradley," Mike said.

It was such a matter-of-fact tone that it caught Veronica off guard at first. It was as if she did not catch the name, so she nodded along. Then it hit her.

"We're not doing this with my son," she said.

"We need to start eliminating people."

"Consider him eliminated."

"Well, I think that's pretty dumb," Mike said.

"She was his cousin. His family. I vouch for him."

Mike finally held his hands up. "I know it wasn't me," he said. "I know it wasn't you." He pointed at Veronica. "Or you." He glanced at Ann. "Not Hugh or Paul. Or Sergeant Grant or Bernie Justin."

"What about your buddy, Tim Figueroa?" Veronica asked.

"That's an idea. I doubt it, but there's also Jones and Haverthy. Maybe one of them? They knew Carolina."

"You have a knack for accusing a lot of cops, considering you used to be one," Veronica said. She felt herself calm.

"Yeah, that's a bad habit. I just still think somehow this will lead back to Jane Doe."

Veronica shook her head. "You still believe your dad had something to do with that?"

"I don't know. I'm trying to make peace with him and his memory, so it doesn't help to think of him as the murderer. But it's undeniable that he had more knowledge than he ever shared with you, my mom, or anyone else."

"That was his flaw," Ann interjected.

"Maybe."

"So, what's your next move?" Veronica asked.

"If you won't let me talk to Bradley, maybe I'll talk to Tim."

###

Bradley maneuvered up the winding mountain road, past the falls, digging deep into the accelerator around each switchback turn, shooting by smaller, slower vehicles when the passing lanes appeared in the infrequent straightaways. The audio from his stereo both thumped and bumped, aggressive melodies screeching in his ears, drowning out all his other cares as his tunneled vision focused on the next obstructing car or bend in the road. His truck crested the top of the mountain. In the distance, he caught sight of the low-hanging sun drooping below Hunter Mountain in the west, the direction that he was heading. That was when the emergency lights appeared in his rear-view mirror, grabbing his attention.

"Not this bullshit again," he said. It was a scream into the aggression of the music.

Bradley pulled his right foot from the gas pedal and mashed it on the brake, squealing the tires. He smiled, knowing that some of the rubber was now staining the roadway. He watched in the rear-view mirror as the police car stopped short, making an evasive move to avoid striking the rear of his truck. His smile widened, and he casually hit the right turn signal to indicate that he was pulling over. The truck glided over to the side of the road. Still observing in the mirror, Bradley watched the SUV with its lights still ablaze pull in behind him. He waited to see who got out of the car.

The officer seemed familiar, but not one that Bradley knew by name. His uniform looked precise, measured, and clean. The Stetson was already affixed when he exited the patrol car, the cop deliberately looked Bradley's truck over before he approached. This cop did a driver-side approach, Bradley picking him up in the side mirror as he pressed the button to lower the window.

"Good evening, sir," the cop said. "I'm Officer Hunter with the town police."

"Hunter? Like the town?" Bradley said. It was a snort that exited as much through his nose as his mouth.

"Yes, sir, just like the town. May I see your license and registration, please?" Paul said. He was unflappable in his response.

"What's the reason for the stop?" Bradley asked. He was turning up the smooth and sassy talk. This guy was young, maybe his age, and while not as green as Mike Ellis, he looked too friendly.

"Well, I observed your vehicle traveling at sixty-eight miles per hour, which I estimated and confirmed on my calibrated radar detection unit. The posted speed limit is forty miles per hour. You and your vehicle are in violation of the Vehicle and Traffic Law section 1180.

Now, may I see your license and registration as required by the Vehicle and Traffic Law section 507 subsection 2?"

Bradley sat with his mouth slightly agape, his eyes shifting across the face of Officer Hunter, looking for some sort of vulnerability. The cop's face still looked friendly, almost inviting, and his tone was calm, matter of fact, and non-threatening.

"I have to reach for my wallet," Bradley said.

"Certainly."

Bradley maintained his eye contact as he reached into his rear pocket for his wallet. He opened the brown billfold and blindly pulled out his license and the courtesy card. He passed them over to Officer Hunter. The cop considered them. He turned without saying anything, heading back toward his patrol vehicle. Bradley leaned out of the window, watching the officer walk away. The passenger door opened.

Twisting quickly, Bradley met the face of Mike Ellis, unshaven and unkempt. He had an odor that reached Bradley at the same time—musty and dirty. It took Bradley a moment to recognize Mike, he looked so different. The expression on his face, something underlying, had changed also. This was not the same kid he had met for the first time a few months before.

"Hi, Brad," Mike said. He pulled himself into the passenger seat, closing the door behind him.

Bradley raised an eyebrow, the shock having worn off. He glanced into the rear-view mirror at the cop, who was sitting in his car, looking back at Bradley. He fixed his stare back at Mike, who wore an open, patient face. He looked as if he were waiting for something.

"What the fuck are you doing?" Bradley said. He snarled as he turned back toward the windshield.

"That's all you want to ask?" Mike said.

There was a sound of movement from the passenger seat, but Bradley kept his attention forward. He brought his left hand to the steering wheel and began to tap his wrist in measured beats.

"You're not a cop anymore," he said.

The response came from a close proximity, in a whisper. "You're right. I'm not a cop. No more rules. I'm going right after people now."

Bradley swallowed a golf ball sized lump in his throat, forcing the movement with all that he had. But his eyes remained locked facing forward.

"Who are you going after?" Bradley asked. The words were tentative.

"You were the last person to see or talk to Carolina that night, right?" Mike asked.

Bradley scowled, his lips curling up like he had consumed sour milk. His chin crooked faintly and he looked at Mike with a predatory glower. He had been scared for no reason.

"What if I was? I spoke to Felix already," Bradley said. His voice rose in timbre.

Mike didn't flinch. "Who was she going to meet?"

Bradley swiveled his whole body toward the passenger seat and he leaned his face into Mike's. They came eye to eye.

"I have no idea. It was none of my business. She didn't tell me anything. You were the one who was hanging all over her. How do I know she wasn't going to see you?" He spoke tight lipped in an even tempo.

"You don't. But I was working," Mike said. His head retreated in short movements, his tone growing casual.

Bradley laughed. A vulturine smile swept across his entire face as his eyes narrowed.

"I guess you've never heard of cops banging girls on duty. Happens all the time."

"I don't know anything about that. What do you know, Brad?" Mike asked. Without indication, he lounged back against the passenger seat and looked out the windshield.

Bradley relaxed his muscles, pulling himself back into his own chair. He looked in the side mirror, looking to see if the cop was coming, but he was still sitting in the car. Bradley sighed hard, exhaling aggression along with the breath.

"Listen, I know that Felix suspects you. But I know you didn't do anything. Just like I didn't do anything. Right?" Bradley said. He tried to sound pacifying. He glanced back over at Mike.

Mike did not answer. He looked poised. His face betrayed nothing. Bradley sat up in his seat, his body collapsing on itself a little, guarding himself. He looked sideways at Mike.

"Who do you think killed Carolina?" Bradley asked.

Mike took a moment, then said, "I don't know, Brad. But I'd really like to know who you left her with."

Bradley shook his head. "She was at the diner. You should know, you had dinner there."

Mike remained silent, listening.

"I stopped in before closing. I was passing through. She always slipped me a dessert or something. We talked for maybe ten minutes, and I left."

"Which way were you coming from?" Mike asked.

"I was going down the mountain to my house."

Mike followed up with another question. "What time did you get home?"

"I don't know. I didn't go straight there."

Bradley closed himself in more, his head sank to the steering wheel. He bounced his forehead in small taps.

"But you were headed that way?"

"Yeah."

Bradley rotated his neck to look at Mike. He stared straight ahead, his face blank, his eyes unblinking.

"She didn't say she had any plans?"

"I told you she wouldn't tell me things like that. Not my business."

Mike's face showed a flash of satisfaction. Bradley thought the look told him that he said something expected.

"Who do you think killed Carolina, Bradley?"

"I wish I knew, man. I really wish I did. It was really fucked up. They didn't have to do her like that."

Mike sat back a little, his face dropping with some realization that Bradley could not guess. Mike's look melted into a quizzical expression. His eyes sharply aimed up to the right with his nose flaring and his mouth in a bent line leaning to the left.

"I-I mean... I mean," Bradley said. No one should die like that."

"Like what?" Mike asked.

Bradley threw his hands up. "Strangled and left out in the woods."

Mike had no discernible reaction. Bradley tried to read what was kicking around in his head, but Mike's new blank expression did not disclose anything.

"I didn't do anything," Bradley said.

"Okay," Mike said. "I really believe that I guess. I mean you had no reason, right? But you had no idea who she was going to see after work?" Mike's words increased in rhythm.

"As far as I know, she was going home."

"But she didn't. She went to the Overlook. Well, the trailhead. She lives in the opposite direction."

Bradley kept his stare fixed as Mike's mind seemed to work something around in it. It looked like he was chewing bubble gum. It was quick, deliberate. Bradley glanced over at the digital clock on the dash. He watched a minute tick away. He investigated his rearview at the cop still sitting in his car. Bradley realized that there had been many minutes that had passed since he had been stopped. Was this all a ruse? A ploy to give Mike this chance to make accusations?

"Wait a minute..." Bradley began to say.

"No, my minute's up." Mike reached behind himself and pulled the latch on the door. He looked at Bradley before he climbed out. It was a look that revealed something horrifying. Bradley opened his mouth to finish his sentence, but Mike slid out and closed the door. Bradley's eyes remained fixed on the passenger side door.

"Here's your paperwork," Officer Hunter said.

Startled, Bradley spun around in his seat. He looked out at the cop. Officer Hunter held out Bradley's license and courtesy card.

"Sorry, I had a little computer trouble," Hunter said. "Have a nice night. Drive safely."

Bradley accepted the extended plastic cards. Hunter turned sharply on his heel and walked back toward his patrol car. Bradley watched him in the side mirror until he climbed into the vehicle and turned the emergency lights off. As the marked SUV pulled past him, Bradley thumbed the voice control button on his steering wheel.

"Call Felix," he said.

33

My rental car nearly died on its way up the hill to the cabin, but it miraculously reached the top. I had passed the "driveway" two times. The GPS in the borrowed sedan couldn't pinpoint the exact address of Charlie Ellis' cabin. Mike greeted me with a small .22 rifle but vetted me with my little wave of truce. He allowed me inside the depths of his isolation to see the darkness within. There were piles of documents lined up on the desk, appearing to have been sorted through, but I never got close enough to read the pages. Not this time at least. We made small talk regarding the next set of interviews that I had lined up. Which reminded me of the most important thing I had to tell him.

"I've decided to have a funeral."

"You seem a little young, still. In good health and all."

It wasn't a joke, but I did laugh.

"For Maggie's mother."

"We still don't have a name," Mike said.

"We can add that once we figure that out. But Maggie wants to go back to her life at some point, right? She's been here for a couple of weeks already. Her husband has the bags packed and an Uber on speed dial."

"We don't have Uber up here."

"Well, the Rocky Mountain equivalent then."

I fell into the recliner, comfortably rocking back and forth to a rhythm in my head, watching Mike as closely as he watched me.

"So," he said, "when's the service?"

"We were able to get the local priest to perform a graveside service. He wasn't keen on the whole in-church thing, especially when he asked about cameras and the news types being there. He was a little uncertain considering we don't know the state of poor Jane's soul. But for the graveside in the non-denominational section of the cemetery, he said he could accommodate us. Plus, the donation I made seemed to help."

"You bribed a priest?"

"I've done worse," I admitted. "But yeah, we're looking to do the burial in two days."

"Maggie looking forward to it?"

"Don't think so. She won't be there."

Mike's voice dropped lower. "Why?"

"Doesn't want to be there. Doesn't want to be here anymore, I suspect."

"Where do we go from there?"

"You tell me. I have more podcast episodes to record. I have a book to write. I have my own interviews. You have no job. You have no one to answer to. You have to clear your name."

"What do you know about that?"

"What? Your name? From what I understand, it's as good as mud around here. Good thing you still have a few friends on the force. But the state police are looking for you. And their jurisdiction goes beyond the town limits. Fortunately, your friends haven't sold you out yet."

"Will you?"

"Mikey, Mikey, Mikey," I said. It was an attempt to soothe. "I am your best friend. I have been with you this whole time. I couldn't sell you out. Not to a bonehead like Felix Acosta or a curmudgeon like Bernie Justin. No matter that your wild accusations make you seem completely desperate. I know that you have a plan."

Mike looked at me with a hangdog expression. "I don't have a plan. That was my plan, Tim. I thought I could get someone to break."

"I don't think you have the knack for that," I said. "I'm just being honest here, Mike. You just aren't intimidating. You're not very clever. And you don't have the most important thing."

"What's that?"

"Evidence. Or the truth. You have nothing to trap anyone into. It's a puddle, not a pit full of punjis."

I saw hurt in Mike's face. The honest syrup I was serving up must have been too bitter. But I was in a mood to let him know exactly where he stood. In all reality, Felix Acosta would probably get the address for the cabin in the next couple of days. That was a shot of truth that I was sitting on. But with his reckless nature of late, Mike was bound to be scooped up in town the next time he ventured out.

"You're right," he said.

I nodded in satisfaction. Of course, I was.

"I'm still playing the game my way."

I was puzzled over the statement for a moment. "Your game?"

"I'm trying to get at people by asking myself what I think of them. Really going with my gut. I, of course, can't stand Chief Justin, and Bradley Salazar has been the bane of my existence for months. But just because I don't like someone, doesn't mean that they killed Carolina. Or had her killed. Or had some crazy conspiracy theory."

"That's your plan?" I asked. My head shook back and forth, my eyes blinking wildly.

"It's how my father operated. He'd trust his instincts and aggressively pursue his target."

"Seems that's how Felix Acosta operates."

"He feeds on his emotion and his bias. He doesn't know when to stop listening to his gut."

"But that's just what you described as your approach."

"Exactly," Mike said. He made an agreeable huff with the statement, but then he paused. I waited for something more to come, but he rested on those three syllables.

"Exactly what?" I asked finally.

"My approach was wrong."

I waited impatiently for him to continue, but he again left me hanging. I asked, "So what now?"

Mike shook his head. I felt like pressing, so I did.

"It's simple to clear your name, you know," I continued. "I imagine there is no direct evidence against you. That is saying you didn't do anything."

That caught Mike's attention and he looked right at me. "I didn't."

I furnished the conversation a curt laugh. "You need to learn to take a joke. I know you didn't do anything. You were the unfortunate police officer in the right place at the wrong time. If you had been in a different spot, maybe you could have prevented the whole thing. Who knows?"

Mike was degrading in his emotions as I spoke. I was pushing some buttons, and the narrowed eyes and the burning flush of his skin gave away his thoughts. I eyed the rifle, which seemed out of reach, but might have been placed ever so precisely as to provide the perfect retrieval.

Mike spoke very deliberately. "I had no power or agency over what happened to Carolina. It is a tragedy, and there's part of me that is glad that I was the one who found her."

"Hey, man, you gotta tell yourself whatever you can, right? I mean, if I had been seen with a beautiful young woman multiple times in the few days leading up to her grisly murder, I'd be nervous. If I happened to be in a position of authority and unsupervised in the hundred square miles or so of a town but managed to be the first at the scene of the crime, I'd be uneasy."

I smiled a wicked smile. I felt that I had pushed enough to this point. He looked close to the edge, and I didn't want to nudge him off. I wanted him to fall. I sprang up from the recliner and clapped my hands, causing Mike's head to jerk up at me.

He did not say anything. There were wheels turning in his head. Those sprockets were speeding up, too. I kept an eye on the rifle. Mike saw me. There was a moment of indecision before he grabbed it. He stood as he did. His eyes trained on me in a sympathetic way, not menacing.

"Do you want this or something?" he asked. "You keep looking at it."

"No, no. It's just out there in an obvious way. What are you going to do with it?"

Mike gave the weapon careful consideration. He had pointed in a safe direction—down and toward the floorboards. His finger was maintained outside the trigger guard.

"I'm not going to do anything with it. It's an heirloom. It's a part of my family history that I know nothing about. Really, it's another secret that has been kept from me. I found it here. I feel like I need it to make this place feel whole."

There was sincerity in his voice. I tried to empathize.

"Must be tough not having a father."

He looked at me, setting the rifle back where it had been.

"I had a father. He was a good man. Now I aim to make him proud of me." Mike began to collect items from the nearby desk and table, his wallet, keys, and jacket. He looked back at me.

"What are you going to do?" I asked him.

"Going to take care of this uneasiness."

34

Staring at the phone on his desk, Bernie Justin's eyes burned with rage. The rest of his face was set as flint. He exhaled a long hot breath. His right hand moved toward the receiver. A twitch passed along the bridge of his nose. Breathing in now, Bernie lifted the receiver and dialed a number. Cradling the receiver between his shoulder and his left ear, he looked out in front of him. Felix Acosta stood leaning against the far wall of the office, observing the scene.

The phone began to ring in Bernie's ear. He glanced at the ornate gold-colored analog clock on his desk. The small hand was fighting from touching the Roman numeral two. The ringing continued. Bernie made a face of confusion and frustration at Felix. Mercifully, the ringing ended, and a voice took over. Bernie reached forward, tapping the speakerphone icon on the phone's console before replacing the handset.

The electronic voice echoed in the room indicating that the call was being sent to a voicemail box. A youthful, recognizable voice broke in between the automated directions, reporting the voicemail belonged to "Mike." Bernie kept his eyes on Felix, raising an eyebrow in question. Felix shook his head, then cut his left hand across his throat. Bernie ended the call with a flick of his finger.

The chief kept his stare across the room to where the investigator stood. Felix was finely dressed, as always, in a soft blue three-piece with a golden yellow shirt and a tie that added a show of electric blue to the ensemble. He stood still, his mouth moving around like he was rehearsing what he was going to say. Bernie remained pensively leaning over the desk, hand above the phone.

"Again," Felix said.

Bernie turned the speaker phone back on and hit the redial button. The ringing was the only sound in the room. It continued interminably until the electronic voice returned with now curt sounding "Mike" coming across. Bernie never took his eye off Felix. After the voice was finished, Felix again motioned to end the connection. Bernie tapped the button and remained like a statue.

"What's the next plan?" Bernie asked.

Felix took time answering. He fixed his jaw before pursing his lips and clucking. Then he took a breath and said, "Right now, this is what I have. No idea where the kid might be. I've heard that he might be holed up in some cabin, but I can't find any property records that will lead me to where I need to go."

"Maybe we leave a message then?"

"He'll see the call. He knows this number, I assume?"

"I guess. He didn't work here all that long."

Felix looked unimpressed. "Again."

The burgeoning ritual replayed, same voicemail, now the "Mike" sounded like it was mocking them. Bernie cut the connection.

"You know," Bernie said. "Your methods are a little strange."

"My methods?"

"You just latch onto an idea and chase it down. It was the same with the sister, if I recall. All that effort just to eliminate her."

"That's why it's so much easier if people cooperate. But I would say that no one in this town really wants to get to the bottom of this. Especially the Salazars and the Ellises."

"Maybe because they know they're walking into a trap."

"Just because it worked on you doesn't mean it's a trap."

Bernie shuddered. He took it on his own accord to call Mike this time. Same result. However, as he watched Felix closely and the investigator's focus waned for a moment, Bernie took some ownership. The electronic voice introduced the tone. It sounded. Bernie grabbed the handset.

"Mr. Ellis, this is Chief Bernard Justin. I'm looking for you to come into the station. I think that we have some things to discuss and go over. I'm thinking my decision to terminate your employment may have been a little rash. I know you have a union, but I think we can settle this like men. Call me back or stop in."

Bernie hung up the phone. Felix had shifted his weight forward but had little discerning reaction. His brown face remained emotionless and unchanged except for a perceptible twist of his lips. There was an unspoken protest there. Felix pursed his lips, then held the thought.

"I don't think that's going to work," Felix said. He vaguely frowned.

Bernie did not have a response. He returned the frown with a wry smile that held a hapless chuckle behind it. The two men went back to waiting. Silently waiting. Impotent.

"Can't call him again," Felix said.

Bernie raised his eyebrows. "Why?"

"You laid the cards down. Now you just look desperate. You gave him a couple pokes with the first calls. But now you've opened the dialogue. The first shot has been fired, so to speak."

"I just want to get this over with."

"You don't agree with me?"

"That Mike Ellis while on duty and in uniform murdered that girl. No, I don't."

"What evidence do you have to prove that?"

"What probable cause do you have to arrest?"

Felix grunted. "I'm not looking to arrest Mike. I want to interview him. I've been doing this for a long time, Chief. If there's something there, I will find it."

"I've been doing this a long time, too, Investigator. And I know my guys."

"He was one of your guys. Why did you hire him in the first place?"

"He was reachable. He passed a background. He had already put himself through the first phase of training on his own dime. And I owed it to his father."

"The Charlie Ellis I knew didn't think very highly of you. And correct me if I'm wrong, but you didn't like Charlie Ellis very much either."

"Of course not. He was the biggest asshole in the world."

"So, you hired his kid? No other motivation behind that?"

Bernie bit his tongue before he lost control. Heat bulged from behind his eyes, but he focused the anger into his stare. He kept his jaw set in an uncomfortable clench, wanting to display his compliance, but betraying the seething beneath the surface.

The well-dressed and compact investigator cracked a Cheshire smile, which floated into his eyes. An inaudible laugh bubbled up out of Felix's chest, escaping as a chortled breath. He took a step from the wall toward the desk Bernie sat behind.

"You see, Chief, when you have a crime and it's not blatantly obvious who the perpetrator is, you must develop theories. Take for instance, first, the cold-case murder that Ellis was pursuing, Jane Doe of the Overlook. Initial thought was what? Drifter, prostitute, serial killer. No one knew her, so no one had a motive. But now, a little crack in the shell, the theory abounds that the town's top cop knew the woman and may very well have killed her. Can we prove this? Will there be a trial? Do I have probable cause? No. And I don't need it."

There was an obvious dramatic pause. Felix had reached the desk during his monologue, placing his hands upon it and leaning in toward Bernie. Due to his stature, the desk came to just beneath his armpits, and there was no way that he could tower over the chief. But Felix was trying anyway.

"And then there's poor Carolina Velez. Theories abound. Some stranger? Her sister? Local cop who seems to be everywhere she was for days? Is it connected to the forty-year-old cold case? That was a fun little distraction. I've got to get to business because I don't want my name as the original investigator on a cold case. Your pathetic police department has lengthened my job. You give me a kid still on field training? Just so he can fail. But no motivation behind that?"

The heat in Bernie's head reached a searing temperature. It was bursting at the very edge of his lips, his eyes, his ears. But he remained collected, stoic on the exterior. With a cool stability, he rose from his chair, his height and the platform of his desk allowed him to look down on Felix.

"I think you should leave my office. Leave my station. You should never come back. I hope that you solve this, but I don't think you can. You look down your nose at me and at this agency, but you'll never understand this place the way that we do. I gave you my brightest light, a legacy of a policeman. He was someone to give you the lay of the land, and you squandered your chance. It's no wonder that the state police haven't solved the Overlook case for forty years."

Felix stood his ground. He puffed himself up. There was a sharp look in his eye as he glared up at Bernie. There were no more words between them.

The phone rang. The sound slid through the space like a scalpel. Felix did not flinch. Bernie would not budge. The phone rang again. Another tear in the tension. Bernie's shoulders rolled down. Felix's eyes fell toward the sound. A third ring reverberated. Bernie looked at the phone now. Felix glanced back up at Bernie. Bernie reached out and pressed the speakerphone button.

"Chief Justin."

The person on the opposite end of the line took a beat to respond. Bernie found that caught his breath while waiting. Felix had as well. Finally, the familiar voice came across, sending an electric shock up Bernie's back.

"It's Mike Ellis. I'm outside."

###

Felix sat in the interview room at the Hunter Police Department alone. A yellow legal pad lay before him. A Bic pen twirled in his left hand as he read down the notes he had made. The precise penmanship appeared as though it had been typed. Even mistakes were simply lined through once with initials. Felix read along, his lips silently sounding the words as he reviewed the line by line of the interview to this point.

In silence, he read: *Subject Ellis, Michael Robert date of birth 26 July 1999. Discovered body of decedent; Velez, Carolina date of birth 23 January 2000 at approximately 2235 hours 22 July 2023. Subject Ellis was an active, on-duty police officer and called to location for a check the welfare. Subject Ellis located Decedent Velez's vehicle, a 2014 Ford Focus four door. Driver side door was open, dome light on. Subject Ellis then noticed a 'glint' in the distance from his flashlight. Approximately 50 yards from the vehicle he discovered the body of Decedent Velez. Additional law enforcement arrives, Police Officer Hugh Bell. Scene secured and additional resources requested. Subject Ellis states that Decedent Velez was obviously deceased, and no disturbance was made to the corpse.*

Felix nodded before he continued. *Subject Ellis states that Decedent Velez' face was covered at the time of discovery. Subject Ellis reports that he identified Decedent Velez from a saint's medal on a chain around her neck. Again, states that no disturbance was made to the corpse. Additional law enforcement arrived at approximately 2300 hours, Sergeant James Grant and Police Officer Paul Hunter. Subject Ellis was relieved at this time. He was directed to return to the police department and remain there until he spoke to Sergeant Grant.*

Felix stopped as the door to the interview room opened. Mike came into the room with two cans of Coke. He set one down and slid it toward Felix. Felix watched Mike with his head down and his eyes rolled up. Mike yanked the chair from the table, sitting with a collapse of his legs. He cracked his can, swallowed a bit of the soda, then set the can on the table. He folded his hands in front of him.

"So, now that we rehashed what we already knew. Can we move on?"

Felix laughed in a short burst of air. "Sure, kid."

They spoke, turning over the first days after the murder. Mike described the leave he was offered and the pleasant county employee who did a critical incident debriefing with him.

"He was really into how I felt seeing the body. Like even more than you. But he encouraged me to find a few healthy ways of getting through the initial shock."

"You drink a lot?"

"Never was a drinker."

"Go hit on some cute girls maybe? Exercise away some of your stress?"

"No."

"What? Did you go to church or something?"

"That's more like it."

Felix held in a chortle, but he listened to Mike laugh out loud at his expense.

"So, did you want to fuck her?"

Mike straightened his face. "Who?"

"Carolina? I have information that says you were hitting on her. Someone else told me that you had followed her around a little bit, including up to the Overlook. Sounds a little stalker-ish to me."

"Those are true. But it has nothing to do with whether I was attracted to her."

"I didn't say 'attracted.' I said you wanted to fuck her."

"Now you're trying to get a rise out of me. No, I didn't feel like I wanted to have intercourse. I was just playing around with the notion of asking a girl out. She was someone familiar, and I thought she was pretty. The Overlook was mere coincidence. In all honesty, with all the rumors and conjecture that's out there, I still didn't know Carolina all that well."

"But maybe you were hoping to?"

"Yeah."

Felix set to writing some of this information on the pad. He finished the page he had begun, flipping to the next page and continuing.

"The next thing is of course that we began working together. How did that occur?"

"I was asked by Sergeant Grant if I wanted to be involved in the investigation. I turned him down."

"Is that a fact?"

"Yes."

Felix wrote hurriedly. He sat back in the chair and considered the next question in his head. Trying not to look flustered despite the churning in his stomach and the flush in his head, Felix picked up the pad to hide his face and then set it back down.

"Then why did you get involved?"

Mike described his interaction with Veronica Salazar and Laura Velez in the vestibule a couple days after the murder. He said that he was trying to help them.

"So you saw the way the sister looked, and you were in?"

"That had nothing to do with it. I felt bad for her. And Veronica told me all about you. I didn't ask anything further. I knew that I was going to have to be involved. That's when I joined you."

"So you're telling me that your dick had nothing to do with your decisions?"

Mike shook his head. His face remained calm.

"So let's come back around then. You protect the girl from me, but I ambush you both and finally, I get my interview. She must've been pretty pissed."

"Yes."

"And then we go on our little side quest. Everyone gets all hot and bothered with the Jane Doe case, and we go out to California. But that's a dead end."

"So far."

"Yeah, very far. So now you're famous."

Mike gave a smile that admitted something along with a shrug.

"Everyone's falling over themselves. When's your book coming out?"

Mike took a breath before answering. "I'm not writing a book."

"I heard a documentary. Netflix perhaps?"

Mike was quick to shake his head. "Not even mentioned to me."

Felix watched Mike coolly. He took the pause to memorialize the last exchange in his notes, glancing up irregularly to monitor Mike's reaction.

"You're telling me that you have spent the last week or so on every new program, YouTube talk show, and two-bit podcast in the world, but you know nothing about the next steps."

"I'm not looking to make money," Mike said. There was an easy sincerity to the statement. It was quick, but not rushed, reactive without thought, to the point without being directed. "I don't want notoriety. I wanted to get some answers."

"So why did you hide from me?"

"I've never been considered a suspect in a murder before."

"Makes you look guilty."

"To someone looking to place guilt, it may."

Felix laughed and gave the room a complete once-over before continuing. "So your altruistic attempt to get attention is to help solve what? Jane Doe? Carolina Velez?"

"My theory is that they're still connected."

"I thought we put that to bed back in California?"

"You and I haven't been working together since we got back. Have you added anything to your cold case file regarding Maggie Farley?"

"Don't try and tell me how to do my job, Rookie." Felix remained even in his delivery. His hands folded. He leaned his body forward.

"I wouldn't want to. I think that this might go better if we worked together," Mike said.

Felix snorted. "I don't think you were really bringing much to the table."

"We found Jane Doe's daughter."

"Not any closer to an answer."

"But not further away."

"I'm not going to help you, kid. All I'm going to say is that you appear to be the one most likely to benefit from the death of Carolina Velez. So you're my new number one suspect."

Mike moved in his chair, his face contorting uncomfortably. But he pulled himself together, sat up straight, and kept his eyes on Felix.

"But right now I have nothing to hold you."

35

Pulling a pack from the trunk of his car, Paul peered into the opening at the top, mentally checking off the contents. With a satisfied grunt, he zipped the bag closed and slung it over his shoulder. He fastened the pack's waist strap and pulled the chest strap together. Next, he retrieved the trekking poles and extended them to his desired length before testing them on the partially frozen earth. Finally, Paul pulled a bottle of water from the truck, took a big swing of liquid, and settled the bottle into a pocket of the pack. He shut the trunk. He could now see where Mike stood next to the hood of the car, examining his own pack. Similarly satisfied, Mike sealed his bag, preparing to go.

Paul watched as Mike ambled away from the car, looking off the escarpment into the vast horizon before him. Paul admired the shadows pointing east as the sun drooped behind him. Mike's elongated silhouette reached the edge of the cliff and disappeared. Paul checked his watch, his face screwing up as he calculated in his head.

"We have about two and a half hours," Paul said.

Mike lifted his left hand to acknowledge him.

"But I guess it's all downhill, right?" Paul asked.

Walking away, Mike turned mid-stride. His expression was optimistic.

"And we've got headlamps," Paul said. "You ready yet?"

Paul began moving toward Mike, who remained fixed near the edge of the escarpment. A sharp, cold breeze snapped through the trees, brushing some of the last leaves clinging to the branches in the air. Paul's steps were tentative, although if you asked him, he could not say why. Mike seemed to stay the same distance away until Paul finally reached him.

"Let's go," Mike said.

Mike led the way onto the white blazed trail. He moved with an easy exertion. His footfalls were determined. They reached the break in the trail relatively quickly, where the white blazes continued along the escarpment and a triangle of red blazes descended.

"This leads down to the Overlook?" Mike said. "I've never gone this way."

"I've done it before, but not in a long time," Paul said. "It gets steep at times."

Mike nodded and wordlessly turned down the trail marked with red blazes. The path rolled slightly into a sharp descent which went for almost a quarter mile before it turned into a series of equally sharp switchbacks. Paul maintained distance behind Mike, swishing his booted feet through the freshly fallen leaves that blanketed the ground. Mike, very determined, picked up his pace through each turn in the trail.

"Tell me again. What are you hoping to find?" Paul asked.

Mike said something that sounded like "I don't know." The wind caught his words, dampening them, but Paul got the gist. Finally, when the switchbacks ended, the trail leveled out into a vast flat area with stick trees dominating a sea of red, yellow, and orange leaves. The failing light from the sky cast a solemn pall over the scene, causing Paul to stop. Mike continued till he must have felt something, so he stopped and turned to look at Paul.

"What do you think this is like in the winter?" Mike asked.

"Frozen."

"Yeah," Mike said. He worked something out in his head, looking around at the entirety of the space.

"What are you thinking?"

"Nothing. Come on. Let's keep going."

Mike picked up his pace and Paul, still wary, trudged behind him. They followed the mostly even terrain of the trail for another half mile when they arrived at the next fork in the road. The red trail meandered ahead a few hundred feet before it climbed up to the main body of the Overlook trail. A small rock cairn sat next to a well-worn side path that led down to the actual Overlook. Mike took his own pause here.

"One of the last times I saw Carolina Velez was here," Mike said.

Paul did not answer. He gave Mike an intrigued look.

"It was the morning before she died. I'd come out here to check it out after listening to Tim Figueroa's story. Carolina used to come up here all the time. It was a workout plus a head clearing experience for her. She'd climb up to catch the sunrise, then go back down before she was due at the diner."

"What did you talk about?" Paul asked.

Mike looked at him with a quiet way of saying he did not remember. "Not really sure."

"Are we going down there?"

Mike kept his thoughts to himself. He looked down the path and then back up at the sky.

"What time is it?" he asked.

Paul checked his watch. "It's five forty-five."

Mike made a curious hum. He was calculating in his head again. "So, another twenty minutes until dark?"

Paul agreed. "Why do you ask?"

"What time was sunset at the end of July? When Carolina was killed."

"I have no idea."

Mike was thinking again. "What time does the diner close in the summer?"

"We work nearly across the street from it. I guess around nine."

Paul felt a gurgle in his stomach. Sweat formed along the back of his neck.

"I've been going off the idea that both Jane Doe and Carolina were left purposely so that my dad and then I would be the person to find them. I don't know why Jane Doe was left at the Overlook. But it's obvious that someone was trying to drive home a point by having it be Carolina and knowing she'd be here."

"You've eliminated Chief Justin, right? That theory?"

"Wrong motive. The chief has some issues, but he's not about to kill someone just to embarrass me or my father. That was just a stupid idea."

"But you're sticking to your theory about the two cases being connected?"

"It's the only tune I know."

The light dissolved from the woods. Paul felt like the sun was retreating faster.

"Why the Overlook?" Mike asked. It was directed toward Paul.

"Do you want to go down there?"

"I've been there."

"What are we doing now? It's going to be dark."

Mike looked at Paul, nodding in a single, tight motion.

"Let's climb down. Hugh's going to meet us down there," Mike said.

Paul agreed and took the lead following the red-blazed trail. The visibility was low, but as the rhodopsin took over, his night vision became enhanced. The second part of the trail wound down in a perpetual corkscrew, never changing the angle of descent, but an endless downward spiral. The low light made it more exciting than it would have been normally. In the daylight, it was a monotonous trek either up or down. The Overlook was worth it though. Paul vaguely began to hear mumbling from behind him.

Slowing a bit, Paul let Mike close the gap between them, but the whisper of Mike's voice was not any more clear. At one point, Mike passed by Paul, and Paul could not catch back up. They made the mile-long descent in about twenty minutes. When they arrived at the plateau above the parking lot, the last of the daylight slipped away. Paul could see a truck parked in the closing darkness. Mike walked right toward it.

###

From the cab of his truck, Hugh saw the shapes of two men approaching. He pulled the handle on the door and placed a leg on the ground. His head swung out, winding up above the door frame before he had even pulled his other leg out. Hugh could make Paul out with his compact stride, which made the lumbering shape Mike. The chilly air bristled along the back of Hugh's neck, so he reached back inside the truck to grab a windbreaker.

"How'd you do?" Hugh asked his approaching friends.

"Made it down in about twenty minutes from the top of the Overlook," Mike said.

Mike arrived at Hugh and the truck first with Paul just behind him.

"So now can you tell me what that was all about?" Paul asked.

"Theory number five, is it?" Hugh said.

"I've lost count."

"We all have."

"Let's go with four," Mike said. "Makes it seem less like I'm an idiot."

"Okay. Theory four is that someone targeted the poor Velez girl because of Mike," Paul said.

"But not the chief?" Hugh asked.

Mike shook his head. "No, definitely not the chief."

"Then who?"

"Slow down a little," Hugh said. Then after a moment. "Yeah, who?"

Mike did not answer. He examined the darkened plateau. Hugh's truck was parked almost exactly where Carolina's car had been located, just as Mike had asked him to do. The truck, however, faced toward the trail, whereas Carolina's car was pointed in the other direction. Hugh watched the younger man with interest. Mike was mumbling to himself.

"So if he came down here..."

Hugh caught Paul's wide eyes pinned to the sideways stare bouncing between Mike and Hugh. Hugh shrugged, making a deliberate, inquisitive gesture with his face and hands.

"What's this all mean?" Mike said under his breath.

"He thinks someone ambushed the poor girl here," Hugh said. "Someone who knew she'd be here at that specific time. At dusk. But he hasn't said who."

"Well, that'd still make him the best suspect, wouldn't it? I mean, he spent almost a full twenty-four hours before her death running into her like crazy," Paul said.

"Old news," Hugh said.

Mike squatted near the truck as if he were sitting in a car. He looked over his shoulder, then rolled his head back toward the front until he found a particular angle. Hugh stepped up near him, looking in the same direction.

"What do you see?"

Mike did not answer. He turned his attention forward. He swiveled his head back. Then front.

"Someone came from behind her," Mike said. The surprise in his voice sounded as if he had just come up with the idea.

"Okay, that's easy to believe," Hugh said.

"But who?" asked Paul.

Mike stood. He pivoted on his left foot. Carefully, he walked in a line from the truck to the brush alongside the trail about a hundred feet. Hugh watched him, leaning against the truck. Paul, however, walked behind Mike, keeping a small distance.

"Are you channeling her ghost or something?" Hugh asked. "Are you a medium now?"

Mike completed his traverse to the tall grassy area. He knelt now. With delicate attention, he hollowed out spaces in the bed of leaves.

"Didn't they do a grid search for evidence?" Paul asked.

Hugh watched Mike continue his excavation from a distance. Paul looked back at him, causing Hugh to change his focus. Paul had his hands buried in his jacket and a nervous look on his face.

"Do we help him?" Paul asked.

"I don't know what he's doing."

"What are we doing here then?"

Hugh laughed. "I guess having enough direct observation to get him on a seventy-two-hour hold."

"You think he's crazy?"

"No, I think he's allowing Chief Charlie to take the wheel."

"What do you mean?"

"If we had something heavy or involved, Chief Charlie would shut the whole world out. Bad wreck with a dead kid in the backseat, he'd analyze the thing for hours. Even if it closed the highway coming up the mountain for hours. But he never said a word aloud. Mumbled a lot, but nothing in plain English."

"Mike mumbled the whole way down the second leg."

"He went inside himself. Found his old man."

"Do you think it's going to make a difference?"

"Your guess is as good as mine," Hugh said.

He started to cross the plateau. Darkness had settled in now. A steady, cold wind poured over the area. Hugh pulled the collars of his jacket closer as he moved. He passed by where Paul stood. As he approached, a light illuminated from where Mike was elbow-deep in leaves.

"Turn on the lights," Mike said. His pace of leaf moving grew more frantic.

A light came on behind Hugh as he reached into the cargo pocket of his tactical pants to retrieve his Scorpion flashlight. Paul came shoulder to shoulder with Hugh, increasing the brilliance of light further.

"Thanks," Mike said, not looking up.

Hugh and Paul maintained illumination as Mike settled himself. He meticulously cleared the area surrounding the brush of fallen dead leaves. Over the next ten minutes, Mike cleared a sixteen square foot area in and around the tall, weathered grass. After that labor was completed, Mike fell back on his haunches. In the artificial light, Hugh saw sweat coming down Mike's face. Mike's chest heaved in small beats as he looked about the cleared space. His face showed disappointment.

"Do you wanna ask?" Hugh said, looking over at Paul.

Paul glanced up at Hugh. The light from the headlamp caught Hugh's sight, forcing him to turn his whole upper body.

"Shit, dude, dowse the schnoz."

Paul turned the headlamp sideways.

"Wait," Mike said. His voice was quiet. "Do that again."

Hugh and Paul made eye contact and looked back down at Mike. Paul readjusted his headlamp, then shifted it in the same fashion.

"No. The other thing."

"What other thing?" Hugh asked.

"That way," Mike said, pointing to where Hugh's light had gone when he turned away from the light in his eyes. His voice continued its steady tone.

Hugh sighed and turned his torso in an abrupt motion.

"Slower," Mike said.

Hugh made a louder sigh as he returned to his original position. Then he very deliberately began to rotate his hips. He squinted his eyes into the light wash abyss.

"Stop."

Mike turned the adjustment knob on his headlamp, focusing the light into a sharp beam. He crawled on his hands and knees through the excavated area, reaching the far corner of the space. He repeated his attentive movement of the layers of leaves following the line of the tall grass. He stopped suddenly. Mike leaned in.

"Bring me the camera," he said.

"What camera?" Hugh asked.

Paul moved forward, slinging his backpack across his chest and opening the top. He pulled out a Canon camera and flipped it on. He arrived at Mike's location before handing the device down to him. Mike adjusted his headlamp again, broadening the beam out. He brought the camera up and squeezed off a few pictures. Then he moved closer, recording a few more photos. Mike handed the camera back up to Paul. He leaned in again, moving his hand into the tall grass. He removed a relatively small item.

"What is it?" Hugh asked. He had given up trying to squint.

Paul looked back at him, the headlamp's light catching Hugh in his eyes again. Hugh held up a hand to shade himself.

"You've gotta see this," Paul said.

36

Laura stood outside the diner, her arms wrapped around her shoulders as she shivered, a half-smoked cigarette in her mouth. Her eyes squinted in the early morning sunlight coming up over the High Peak. She sucked on the cigarette. She tentatively unwrapped the fist on her right hand and removed the butt from between her lips. She exhaled deliberately before replacing the cigarette and wrapping herself back up. A car pulled into the parking lot. A family of tourists piled out, the mother giving Laura a sideways glance as she ushered the school-aged children to the opposite entrance. The father's leering look melted over Laura's body before he realized he was taking too long. Laura shook her head and took the last drag. The butt went into the smokeless ashtray contraption at the door, the nicotine breath exhaling from her before she opened the door.

The interior of the diner was only slightly warmer. Laura rubbed her shoulders and arms as she made her way to the counter to retrieve her notepad. The other waitress raised her eyebrows at Laura from behind the counter, her eyes rolling toward the family.

"I'll take them," Laura said.

She walked down the aisle, approaching the table with the mother looking right at her. The mother was dressed in brand-new, designer outerwear. She all but held her nose when Laura began talking with them. Laura recorded their order with patience as the three children shouted back and forth. She could feel the husband's eyes on her again, but he cautiously averted his hungry stare when Laura turned her attention toward him. After a solid five minutes which both Laura and the mother could not handle a second more, food decisions had been finalized, and Laura made her way to the kitchen with the notepad. She could hear the mother breathe out as though she had been stifling herself. Laura could only smile.

As she turned between the halves of the counter into the kitchen, she heard the jingle of the bells on the front door. After she dropped the order, she came back through the swinging door to find no one waiting for her. She looked to the left. The other waitress was tending to an older couple at the far corner of the restaurant behind the family. She looked to the right, observing the back of a shaggy-haired man in a ball cap sitting in the first booth by the door. He wore a heavy fatigue jacket with scorched and burned fabric littered along the back. Through some of these gaps, she could see white flannel. Her head cocked sideways, and her eyes narrowed as she continued to look at him.

After a quick glance over her shoulder to see the other waitress still wrapped up on the other side of the diner, Laura approached the lone man.

"Good morning," she said. "Can I get you…"

Her voice trailed off as she finally saw Mike's face. Tufts of facial hair disconnected little islands lining his cheeks and neck. His hair spilled out of the ball cap, nearly falling across his eyes. The open jacket revealed the moth-eaten collar of the flannel shirt. Laura took in a hard breath and held it. Her eyes betrayed her disbelief.

"Hi, Laura," Mike said. "I'm sorry to ambush you like this. But I come in peace."

Laura felt the flush come from her chest to her face and head. She heard the sharp ring of the bell from the kitchen. Her attention split as she looked back toward the counter to see the other waitress settling behind it. She waited for a beat, and the ringing sounded again. Her foot turned with her hips ready to follow. But then she looked down at Mike. His mottled face transfixed her as his eyes begged sincerely.

"Rose, can you cover that?" Laura asked. The waitress looked up at her. Laura whispered, "That woman doesn't like me anyway."

Rose made a pacifying face with a shrug of her shoulders before she turned into the kitchen. Laura smiled half-heartedly, turning back toward Mike, where her face dropped into a serious straight line.

"What do you want?" she asked.

Mike motioned to the booth bench opposite him. Laura did not move.

"I'm here to tell you that I've cleared my name."

"That's good for you."

"And I think I have a new theory."

Laura felt her body begin to move away again. There was something in her head that told her to flee. But a different feeling held her in place.

"You all have your theories. Nothing has panned out. All you've done is waste time."

"I'm through wasting time. But I need your help."

"What?" Laura asked. Her hands fell to her hips as they turned back square toward Mike.

"Come with me to a funeral."

Laura's brow furrowed. Her arms crossed. "What?"

"We're burying Jane Doe's remains again tomorrow morning. Will you come?"

"I don't have any reason to be there. Why would I attend something like that?"

Mike's folded hands came apart, again offering the seat across from him. Laura looked over her shoulder again. The family was digging into their breakfast. Rose was keeping an eye on them and the couple on the far side. Laura sighed and slid into the booth.

"You look like shit," Mike said.

Laura laughed. "Have you seen a mirror lately?"

Mike smiled, rubbing his face. "Undercover. Makes me look too distinguished."

"I'll tell you, the rumors run around this town. It makes it very hard to believe you."

"Those who know, know."

"So why do you want me to go to this funeral?"

"Talk to Maggie Farley."

"Her mother is the cold case murder victim? The one you've been all over the news with?"

"Yes, exactly."

"What do I have to say to her?"

"Maybe she has something to say to you."

"I doubt that."

"Could I ask you to come for me?" Mike asked. He didn't plead or beg. He said it seriously, sincerely.

"For you? Why?"

"I want you to see why I believe in this so much. Even if I didn't go about it in the right way."

"I really don't care," Laura said. She began to slide back out of the booth.

"Do it for Carolina."

Laura stopped. The heat in her body that had cooled began again to swirl up. Her eyes stung with salinization. She pulled back a sniffle from her nose. There was an urge to look at Mike, though her brain fought it. There was a distant ring from the kitchen. She caught her breath and wiped her eyes. Finally, she turned to Mike.

"How fucking dare you?" she said in a controlled hiss. It should have been a scream.

"I dare to trust that this is all coming to an end."

She felt the twisting in her face, the damp makeup beneath her eyes, and the droplets of perspiration and snot forming along her upper lip from her nose. Mike's eyes were steady and empathetic, falling lightly into Laura's own. His lips were parted as if to speak, but holding something in. It froze her.

"I've believed you before. What's changed?" Laura asked. Her voice trembled at its low volume.

"Nothing. Just trust me."

Laura remained still. The ringing from the kitchen became insistent. Rose, the other waitress, was sitting two other tables full of tourists. Mike stared straight into Laura. She could feel it soothe the heat again. She let go. Mike passed a napkin to her.

"Okay," she said. She blew her nose after wiping her face. "I'll be there."

###

Maggie silently shut the door to the hotel room. She grimaced as the bolt clicked. Swiftly, she walked down the hallway toward the elevator, glancing over her shoulder as she moved toward the elevator doors. Maggie slipped in, pushing the button for the lobby followed by the door close button at the same time. She relaxed against the wall of the car.

Maggie retrieved her cell phone from the pouch on her pullover sweatshirt emblazoned with the words: *HUNTER MOUNTAIN.* Her last text message was still on the screen. She read it over, nodding to herself. She lifted her head when the elevator dinged and gasped. Bill stood in the open doors.

"Running off?" he asked.

Maggie sighed. "I just didn't want to disturb you."

"You make me feel like a jealous husband. I'm always having to catch you in something."

Maggie did not respond. Bill gave her a path so that she could walk off the elevator. She looked down at the phone still in her hand, then back up to Bill. He looked like a child who just dropped his ice cream cone.

"Where are you going?" he asked. His voice sounded like he was searching for sympathy.

"I'm going to see Mike. He texted me a little while ago."

"What does he want?" Bill asked. There was a tinge of jealousy souring his words now.

"I'm not sure. Maybe something about my mother's case?"

Bill crossed his arms, looking at her with skepticism. "Do you think he's broken something open? Really?"

"I don't know. He and Tim have been at my side throughout all of this. There may be something that he just found."

The phone buzzed in her hand and a sharp dinging sound reverberated between Maggie and Bill. She looked at the message.

"He's in the parking lot," Maggie said.

"Then, let's go together," Bill said. "Maybe I can be an ally too."

Maggie slumped her shoulders. She pouted at him. "Okay."

She led the way through the front door of the hotel where Mike walked across the lot. He balked at seeing Bill, coming up short in his stride and moving his hands into the pockets of the tattered jacket he wore. Maggie continued toward him, Bill in step, almost ahead of her.

"Hey there," Bill said. He waved his right hand in a big arc.

Mike did not react other than to start walking again. He physically sighed, his shoulders rising and falling with a puff of air rushing from his nose. The three met in the middle of the parking lot.

"Good morning," Mike said. He offered a hand to Bill.

Bill pumped Mike's arm three times. "What's going on?"

Mike looked at Maggie. "Sorry for the early texts."

Maggie smiled. "It's fine. What's up?"

Mike motioned toward an outdoor sitting area surrounding a propane fireplace. The three of them all moved to the spot, each taking seats. Bill pulled a chair close to Maggie, who sat across the fireplace from Mike.

"I'm looking for some advice," Mike said.

"About what?" Maggie asked.

"I've run out of fresh perspectives. Everyone I know already has an opinion and has made up their own minds."

"Okay," Maggie said. "I'm here to help."

"Me too," Bill said.

Mike looked at Bill with wide eyes. His lips pressed into a thin line for a moment, pausing as it was clear he was thinking about something.

"I told you back at your house that there was a recent murder. I told you at the time that I thought it was connected to your mother."

"It's what got us to come here," Bill said. He scoffed.

"Yes," Maggie said. "I remember. It hasn't really come up since we've been here."

"That's because things sort of fell out between me and Investigator Acosta and Investigator Salazar. They stopped believing in my theory.

And I have been focused on all the attention we've been getting along with Tim."

"Do you still have the same theory?"

"Yes. Put simply, I have this feeling that they're connected, but I just can't find the link. And now I'm on the outside of all of it."

"What do you mean?" Maggie asked.

"I'm not a cop anymore."

Bill chortled a laugh. "What happened? You get fired?"

"I'm sorry to hear that, Mike."

"It's worse. I'm also a murder suspect."

"Like father, like son?" Bill said.

Maggie turned her head slowly toward Bill. A sharpness in her eye seemed to grab his attention. He stopped laughing and cleared his throat.

"I don't think you killed anyone," Maggie said, her warm look returning to Mike. "And, for what it's worth, I don't think your father killed my mother."

"Thank you," Mike said. "There's nothing to tie me to the murder, so it's just Acosta's theory at this point."

"He's in the same position you are? All theory and no substance," Bill said.

Mike nodded.

"So, how can we help?" Maggie asked, her eyes moving toward her husband.

"You know they're laying your mother to rest again tomorrow?"

"Yes, Tim's making it a whole production. I think there's an exclusive from some network or other."

"And you don't want to be there?"

"Not particularly," Bill answered for her.

Maggie shook her head lightly. She dabbed a wrist into each eye.

"Wouldn't you want to close this whole thing up?" Mike said, looking at Bill.

Maggie stood up and spread her arms between the two men. "I think we'd all like some closure. But I don't see how the funeral will help if we don't even know her name."

"We have a family to get back to though. I think it's time for us to move on," Bill said.

"Tim Figueroa does not want any of us to move on. Have you heard about all his media deals?"

Maggie held her hand to her mouth and shot a look at Bill. "No."

"I didn't think so. He's been spreading a story that I've been seeking all of this attention. I think he's trying to shift focus off him. He doesn't want to be the story."

"But he wants to make money from it," Bill said.

"Holy shit," Maggie said. She surprised herself when she said it.

"Tim needs this to stay at the top of the news cycle. But what if the story was about him?" Mike said.

Maggie and Bill shared another look between themselves.

"What are you getting at?"

"Yeah, what are you saying?"

Mike curled his lips. "I'm going to shed some light on Tim Figueroa for once. Do you want to help?"

37

It was the ideal fall mountain afternoon. The sun sat above the cemetery warming the open plain of property. Its rays penetrated deep into the dark dresses and coats of all the gathered mourners. Those mourners were crossing the freshly mown grass with its hints of finely chopped leaves sprinkled within the blades, forming a hasty procession. The wind sliced through the space bringing the hint of a winter to follow, only to allow the warming radiance to predominate the affair. And we were all there.

The three suited law enforcement professionals circled near the casket. Amanda Domino stood near the front, as short as she was, in a respectful dark pantsuit. She gravitated around Veronica Salazar, who towered over Amanda as well as outshined her in professional finery in a flowing black skirt highlighted with pinstripes. Felix Acosta also maintained an orbit near Veronica, decked out in the finest mournful clothing available, a charcoal suit with a checkered black and white shirt and a bottomless black silk tie.

In uniform were four Town of Hunter police officers. Chief Bernard Justin wore his full-dress uniform with a blazer and real metal stars on his shoulder and collar. Sergeant James Grant was in a Class A type uniform with a tie and stripes running along his pant legs, topped with a shell jacket with his sleeves adorned with blue stripes. Officers Hugh Bell and Paul Hunter were attired in utility uniforms with embroidered decorations and cargo pants. All four of the officers were adorned with Stetsons, standing together in a line opposite the group of mourners.

Two older men, my friends George Hunter and Roderick Bell stood a great distance away, each in long black trench coats and slouch caps. Old Roscoe leaned on a cane, slanting into George who was talking into Roscoe's ear and animating the scene with arm movements.

Maggie and Bill Farley were the only ones sitting in the row of chairs nearest to the grave. I was surprised to see either of them that morning when I arrived. She wore a simple dark gray sweater and solid black slacks, a prominent gold crucifix protruding from beneath the folds of the sweater's neck. Bill wore a black suit, a white shirt, and a gray and black tie. He had an arm around Maggie, who leaned into him. Her face was red, and tear streaks were evident on her face. Bill looked coldly ahead, out into the distance with a wide-eyed stare looking for something out of his reach.

Off to the rear of Amanda, Veronica, and Felix stood a young woman who looked very familiar. I would come to know her as Laura Velez, but at this moment, we had not been acquainted. She ate up most of my attention. Laura stood out, not only for her youthful beauty but also wore a lavender peacoat. She was a splash of color in a drab collection of darkness. Laura caught me staring at her. She glared back at me till I eventually turned my attention away. When I turned, I caught sight of Mike Ellis.

He still looked as disheveled as I had last seen him at the cabin, his beard patches starting to link together. He had a suit on, but from twenty-five yards, I could tell that the jacket did not match the pants. Both were black, but each had their own independent sheen and texture. His tie was knotted like a noose and was yet another shade and pattern of black that stood out like a shock against the yellowish pearl of the shirt he wore. He topped the whole ensemble with an appropriately black baseball cap.

I locked eyes with Mike. He strolled toward me with nonchalance with his hands thrust into his trouser pockets and his shoulders hunched up to his ears.

"Who the hell is that?" A voice over my shoulder whispered in an abrasive tone. I glanced over my shoulder at the producer, Ivan, who had just finished assembling the three camera crews present to capture the event. Had I forgotten to mention all of them? Well, I meant to because the show was for them. Mixed in amongst the cameras were the other town residents who were curious about the whole affair and had made the pilgrimage to pay their respects. Ivan should have recognized Mike, having worked with him before, but I couldn't blame him for not seeing through the inadvertent disguise.

"That's Ellis," I told Ivan.

"He looks like shit. Are we interviewing him?"

"No need to. Focus on Maggie."

I watched things unfold. The pastor from the Immaculate Conception Church, Father Eustis, approached from his car. He gave me a wink as he passed. I waved and smiled. As he approached the grave, I shot a look at Ivan.

"You're rolling?"

Ivan nodded and held a finger to his lips. I returned to the little scene I had orchestrated. It was all going according to plan.

Father Eustis approached Maggie, offering his condolences. He shook Bill's hand. Then he turned to acknowledge the people gathered, offering a welcoming, open-armed gesture. He beckoned the crowd to move closer.

"Come, let us bring warmth to a cold, cold thing. Gather around," the priest said. He had a lilt and precision to his enunciation. "Please, let Margaret feel the love that this community and the love that God has for her mother."

Father Eustis opened a pocket hymnal to a Bible ribbon delineated page. He read the passage with practiced sincerity. The rhythm he gave the words settled poetically amongst the people. I tried to pick out faces from the people I had met in my research. No one stood out quite like Mike Ellis. His lips moved as if he were reading along with the priest. When the passage concluded, Mike dipped his head low.

"Friends, we are gathered here today to celebrate the life of Jane Doe. We are here to give thanks to our Lord that Jane has a family that cares for her. A daughter and grandchildren that carry on her light. Also, we pray that someday the answers will come. We hope that someday Jane Doe will have a name, a face, a history. And we pray for justice, a justice that only God can give."

I glanced back at the producer. I nodded at him and mouthed the repeated line "a justice that only God can give." He gave me a quizzical look, so I waved him off. It was something that could wait.

Father Eustis invited the mourners to place the white carnations on the casket. There were about a hundred people surrounding us now, and we were prepared. Everyone was issued a carnation. They were directed how to approach and leave their flower atop the brown walnut of the coffin. It was carefully choreographed. It looked amazing. I was so caught up in the moment that I missed Mike Ellis coming around the crowd to my shoulder. I think I smelled him before I saw him. It was a stench of dirt and smoke with dried sweat and hand soap. He also spoke.

"Hi, Tim."

I turned, taken aback with surprise. "Oh, hi, Mike. Looks pretty great, doesn't it? All of this would impress your dad, I think. A little slice of closure after all the years he spent on this case. Somehow, Maggie even came to her senses."

"He's no longer our number one suspect?" Mike asked.

"No more than you are," I said.

I caught a wry smile curl onto his lips. My attention returned to the people paying their respects. The last of the mourners approached the casket. Roscoe Bell, helped by George Hunter, left his carnation near the head of the casket. Roscoe shot a sad look at Maggie and ambled off, leaning into his cane. George leaned in to give Maggie a kiss on her cheek before giving Bill's arm a pump. The thought crossed my mind that I needed to get both of those men on camera.

The crowd thinned after paying their respects. Pockets of locals spread out through the cemetery, using the opportunity to visit a loved one while they were in the neighborhood. Those closest to the case formed a circle around the grave: Amanda Domino, Veronica Salazar, Felix Acosta, Bernie Justin, Paul and George Hunter, and Hugh and Rose Bell. Mike Ellis was at my side. Maggie approached me.

"Mr. Figueroa," she said. "I want to thank you for your dedication to this case."

I feigned humility by gesturing my hands up and breaking eye contact. Ivan, the producer, leaned to whisper something in my ear.

"You want us to keep rolling?"

I nodded toward the moment that I saw developing between Maggie and me. My eyes told a more urgent message that said, *Of course, you idiot.*

Maggie's eyes glistened, and I caught her looking from Ivan back to me. She had a sly half-smile that crept along her lips. She had seen the exchange.

"As I was saying," she said. "Without you, I personally would not have the level of closure I have now. And while I'm not wholly satisfied that all my questions have been answered, I sincerely feel grateful that at least I know I had a mother, and she didn't abandon me."

I felt myself puff up in my chest. There was a lump building in my throat and a sting in my eyes. The ear-to-ear smile almost hurt. I was, for the first time in my life, at a loss for words.

"Maggie," I choked out her name. I swallowed back the tightness in my larynx. "You are the hero of the story." I paused, nodding my head to my shoulder to dab a tear. "Your faith in me and your bravery in moving forward with making your story known are inspirational." I was warmed up now. "Because without you, I have no story to tell. I have a poor woman with no identity. You give that identity to poor Jane Doe. She lives again in the family you have made, the world that you belong to. None of us knew Jane, but I can believe that she is proud of the woman you are."

Maggie mopped at her face with a handkerchief, her eyes never breaking from mine. I could feel the camera on my left shoulder, Ivan the producer just behind my right. The circle of people remaining closed in: Amanda and Veronica, Roscoe and George, Hugh and Paul, Bernie, Felix and Mike.

I caught them in my periphery: Mike and Felix. The thought sparkled through my head that I was surprised that they seemed to be together. My eyes started to tug me away from Maggie's beautiful emotion.

"Mr. Figueroa," Maggie said.

I winced away from the distraction, refocusing on her. Bill, her husband, had drawn up close to her, his arm sliding around her shoulders.

"Yes?" I said.

"Mr. Figueroa, I don't know what the next steps are in all of this. But I want you to know that I'm going home. And I don't know when I'll be back. If ever."

Maggie's statement dropped on me like a load of sandbags. I searched her face. The sympathetic emotion was gone. She was stone-faced, resolute. I glanced at Bill, who had a mirrored emotion set in his appearance.

"But, I thought," I said. "I thought that we would continue. The next search is for your mother's identity. The game is afoot, to coin a phrase. We were going to track down her killer."

"Mr. Figueroa, I have a life to live. I am content with the closure that I have right now. I want to make my mother proud. Whoever she was, she has a place to rest. Do you really need me?"

"Of course, my dear. I may have promised your cooperation."

"With what?"

"All sorts of deals. Books, movies, documentaries. We have to strike while the iron is hot. The news cycle will fade quickly. It's wonderful that we buried the body, but we have to dig up the rest of her past."

Maggie, her eyes dead set, burning into mine said, "I don't want to."

I stammered some objections and reached out to her. Bill turned her away, and they began to walk off. I started after them when Felix Acosta got in my way.

"Listen, Tim," he said, "I wanted to ask you a few questions."

I looked down at him. His smooth brown face was fixed in a grim expression you would expect from a TV doctor about to say "We did all we could." I glanced back up to see the Farleys retreating and thought about following them still. But I looked back at Felix, and I surrendered.

"Sure, Detective," I said. My defeat emptied in a long exhale.

"Investigator," he corrected. "But when we spoke before, you said Mr. Ellis was pursuing these deals. The 'books, movies, and documentaries.'" He held his hands up for air quotes. "Why would you tell me that?"

"I believe it was 'we' as in the whole group of us." I gestured toward Mike and at the faraway thought of Maggie.

"No, distinctly, I recall, and I recorded in my note," he said and produced a yellow legal pad. "Figueroa says Ellis is in negotiations to produce a written account in the form of a book. He is exploring how to option the story to a film production company. Interest in a documentary with backing from Netflix."

I felt my face drop as a rock also tumbled in my stomach. Felix looked back with soft, welcoming eyes. His mouth was taught. He leaned in toward me, his ears pricked up. About that time, I felt the presence of Hugh Bell behind me, his shadow falling over both me and Felix. I did not look. I left it up to my assumptions and imagination. I knew I had to say something.

"I guess that's what I said, then."

"But you say something different today?"

"Colloquially. We're all in this together." I pointed with my chin at Mike, my hand rising and falling toward the invisible Maggie.

"Mrs. Farley did not seem to be in on it. Mr. Ellis also tells me that he had no knowledge of any such deals. Were you the only one having these conversations?"

"At this stage," I said, "yes, of course." My brain swam against the rising tide of allegations.

"Do you record your interviews?" Felix asked.

The shift of the interrogation caught me. I thought for a moment. Felix did not allow me to finish.

"Does this appear familiar?"

With subtlety, he produced a sealed plastic bag with a miniature audio recording device in it. Something clicked in my head, finally.

"I had something like it," I said.

"Use of the past tense?"

"I lost it." The tide of allegations was settling inside my mind. I began paddling with the current, allowing myself some hand in where it was taking me.

"What if I told you that I have heard your voice recorded into a file on this device?"

"Then I would be very happy, indeed," I said. "You have located my lost recorder."

Felix looked at me with wolfish eyes and a foolish grin.

"Do you know where I found this?"

"After so many months, I would have no idea."

Mike moved forward and turned. He stood shoulder to shoulder with Felix.

"Tim," Mike said. "Did you go to the Overlook on July 26?"

"I'd have to check my calendar."

"Were you in the Town of Hunter on or about that date?" Felix asked.

I drew a smile, but let it fade into a feigned shock. "I was still conducting my research. So yes, probably."

"We checked the metadata on the audio file," Mike said.

"I'll bet it said it was recorded on July 26th," I conceded.

Felix's serious smile curled a bit more, and his teeth began to show. Mike looked much more serious, however. His eyes almost pleaded with their glassy sheen.

"Do you want to guess a time?" Felix said.

"I wouldn't fathom a guess. But I'd say you'd never ask a question you didn't know the answer to. What time?"

"The file was created at 7:47 p.m. It is a sixty-five-minute file," Mike said.

"I listened to your horseshit for an hour, you know," Felix said.

I lifted my chin away from him, turning my attention fully to Mike.

"The contents of the recording describe the area around the Overlook. You indicate a lot of individual thoughts and beliefs. There is background noise suggesting you were outside. Were you at the Overlook when you recorded it?"

"No geotags?" I asked.

Mike shook his head. "Not on this device. But based on the time, it places you at the Overlook around 8:47 p.m. It takes about forty-five minutes to come down the trail. Which has you near the bottom around nine-thirty p.m."

The tide in my head was still with my mind floating along peacefully. I could see everything around me very clearly. There was going to be a decision that had to be made, but I was not yet ready to make it.

"Let me ask you this," Felix said. "Did you see anything at the bottom of the Overlook trail when you got there?"

I looked at Felix, then at Mike. I again felt the over-hulking presence of Hugh Bell. But I remembered, somehow, that cameras were trained on this exchange. Ivan was still recording because I had instructed him to with a look. Now was the time to make a choice.

"It looks like, gentlemen," I said, "that we ought to move this conversation elsewhere and I should involve a lawyer."

Felix pursed his lips, and the cluck resonated in my ear. The scene slowed down for me as I was officially taken into custody. Hugh cuffed me behind my back, and he and Paul led me away to Felix's unmarked car. I could feel the camera following me, and I tried to look surprised. I tried to look concerned. But all I could do was smile on the inside.

38

Bradley Salazar sat in the driver's seat of his truck. It hummed beneath him, trembling through his tight grip on the steering wheel. Behind the Ray-Bans, his eyes glared forward through the windshield. His jaw moved in chews of unspoken words. Through the glass in front of him, he watched his cousin, Laura talking to a man. Whoever this guy was had been going into the diner as she was coming out, and he stopped her in conversation. Bradley seethed as he watched them on the diner's nighttime flood lights.

Minutes ticked away from the digital clock on the radio. The scream of guitars and the howl of vocals rumbled in low tones from the speakers that surrounded the cab. The index finger on Bradley's right hand hovered below the volume control mounted to the steering wheel. He tapped it twice, and the music lowered to an inaudible level. His right hand moved to the center of the wheel, resting there as he contemplated pressing the horn.

Outside, on the small concrete staircase where Laura and the guy stood, Bradley saw Laura indicate toward the truck. The guy looked, his face resolving to the revelation that Bradley was nearby. When

Bradley saw the guy's face, he saw a younger man with a full scruffy beard. The facial hair encompassed the man's look, a rat's nest of hair, completely unkempt. At the same time, Bradley observed the guy's attire. It was a haphazard collection of flannel and denim and a baseball cap upon a greasy waterfall of hair that spilled out onto his shoulders. It was at that time that Bradley recognized Mike.

His left hand moved to the door handle; the right remained near the horn. Mike looked at him from about twenty feet away. Laura prattled on with her conversation. Bradley did not know what his move should be. As he sat in limbo, Bradley caught movement on the stairs as Laura touched Mike's shoulder before she ran back inside. Mike walked directly toward Bradley's truck.

Mike's gait was loose and comfortable. He swung his arms in big motions front and back as he stepped. His beard became more ferocious as he approached. Bradley remained frozen with one hand on the door latch and one hand hovering above the horn. His eyes moved back and forth between the door to the diner and Mike closing in on him.

"Shit," he muttered.

Mike reached the passenger side door and gently rapped on the window. Bradley robotically moved his left hand from the door handle to the power window button. He looked at the offending hand, sighing as he clicked the down arrow. Bradley lifted his head to his center, looking at the door of the diner. He did not hide any disappointment when he turned to face Mike.

"Hey there, Brad," he said. He was affable, light-hearted almost.

"Hi," Bradley replied.

"How's everything going? Haven't seen you in a while."

Bradley lifted an eyebrow. His eyes searched Mike's face for some sort of hidden intention. Mike seemed too sincere. Bradley squirmed uneasily in his seat.

"I've been alright, I guess."

"That's great. But you're here to get Laura?"

"Yeah."

"How's your mom?"

"She's good."

"Is she still seeing Felix?"

"Yeah, he's been around. A lot."

"Awesome."

Bradley shuddered. "Thanks, I guess, for catching that guy for killing Carolina," Bradley said. He felt something come off his chest with the words.

"Hate to say it, but it's not over. This has only just begun."

"But you think he did it, right?"

"Yeah. But justice has to balance, right? Innocent till proven guilty."

"What about that other thing?"

"What? The Jane Doe case?"

"Yeah. Don't they think you old man killed her?"

"No one really knows what to think. But I don't believe he did it."

"You gonna prove that too?"

Mike did not say anything. In the distance, the door to the diner rattled closed, catching the attention of both men. Laura walked down the stairs with care. Bradley watched her intently as she crossed the parking lot.

"How has she been?" Mike asked.

Without looking at him, Bradley replied, "It's been better for her. She has a little more peace now. But I think she knows what you said. It ain't over."

When Laura reached the truck, Mike opened the passenger door for her. She climbed up on her own and settled in the seat. Patting her belly, she sighed deeply. Mike closed the door but remained at the window.

"What's next for you?" Laura asked Mike.

"Don't know just yet. I've thought about going back to school if they'll have me."

"What about Maggie? What about Jane Doe?" Laura said.

"When it's time, she'll come back. I don't think she's ready right now. After everything that happened with Tim, I don't know if she can truly trust any of us East Coast elites," Mike answered quickly.

"Elite?" Bradley said. "Us?"

Mike scoffed. "Doesn't matter the coast. She's got a lot on her plate right now. I think it was a smart move to get out of here for a while."

"Do you want to stay around here? I mean, if school doesn't work out?" Laura asked.

"I don't know if I'm really going back to school."

Laura looked away from Mike, catching Bradley's eyes and smiling as she did. Her cheeks blushed, but she straightened her face before turning back toward Mike.

"You're going to have to testify in the trial, right? If there is a trial. Maybe he'll cut a deal."

"He's not going to cut a deal. Tim will milk this whole thing for all its worth."

"Why would he do that? Wouldn't he face life in prison?"

"For murder? Absolutely. But this just became the second season of the show he's running in his head. This trial will be the biggest thing this county has ever seen."

"I can't wait," Laura said. She forced herself back in the seat. Reaching up, she pulled the seatbelt across her body, tucking the lap belt beneath her stomach. "We should get going."

"I'll see you around," Mike said. He looked at both Laura and Bradley.

Bradley caught Mike's eyes, and the two men locked in a moment. A thought moved into the front of Bradley's head. He said the words before he really had a chance to think about it.

"So, you're done with being a cop?"

"Right now, I have nowhere to work."

"What would your old man think of that?"

Mike thought for a moment. He looked at Laura with a twinkling appreciation in his eyes. When he looked at Bradley, a different sort of glimmer touched his eye.

"I think that he'd like it very much."

ACKNOWLEDGEMENTS

I want to thank all the people I have met along this journey to completing my first novel:

Daniel J. Volpe, who was an invaluable resource for me in the self publishing process, offering answers to even the most inane questions.

JR Boles, my editor who made me believe in this book when I had the worst imposter syndrome.

Ray Braun, who's proofreading was the last bit of polish on the final product.

Danna Mathias Steele who put a cover on this project on the first try.

All of my friends and co-workers who have followed me through this process.

But most of all I want to thank my wife, Laura and my daughter, Fraley. They have supported me in immeasurable ways.